NETHERGEIST

BOOK 2

NICK STEVENSON

Text copyright © 2025 by Nick Bendall

Cover Illustration © Nuno Moreira

ISBN: 978-1-998076-94-9
Ebook: 978-1-998076-95-6

FIC009070 FICTION / Fantasy / Dark Fantasy
FIC009020 FICTION / Fantasy / Epic
FIC009140 FICTION / Fantasy / Military

#Nethergeist

Follow Rising Action on our socials!
Twitter: @RAPubCollective
Instagram: @risingactionpublishingco
Tiktok: @risingactionpublishingco

DRAMATIS PERSONAE

X Gemina Brotherhood

AYILIA, Regent, House of Kiya, the Lord General of the X Gemina Brotherhood of Knights

JARRAK, Ayilia's mentor in her youth

AARON, Captain

KEMET, Lieutenant and mentor

NESSAN, Second Lieutenant

SOREN, Private

KOFI, Private

The Lifeless Rebels of Etherwolde

VESPASIAN, ex-Pro Consul of The Pit

STILGEN, Captain

BREASAL

YOUSIFF, Commander

Asthen Magi Raiders of the Ascendancy

BARRACKUS, Commander

SHEYNA, Major

ADIRA, Captain

SKYRON, Captain

LARS, Captain

ANDROMEDUS, Dust Tracker

GORLAN, Private

DAYLA, Private

<u>Krayal</u>

SEFTUS, Chief

JARONG G'LAITH, Chief's Second

<u>Caulderwell</u>

Unnamed Shaitan demon, Praetor

AURELIAN, Legate

PROBOS, Tribune

Socii, allied Imperial citizenry

Peregrini, landed citizens living outside the capital

GALA, human wanderer

<u>Imperium Hierarchy</u>

THE GOAT (AKA: Abomination, God, Imperator, Undying One), Emperor of the universe

MYRIAN, Viceroy demon lord

YEREB SANGUI, Arch General

GOLUB-YAVEN, Arch General

PHARSALUS, Arch General

MABIUS

OTHO

VITALLIUS

<u>Military Units of Nethergeist (Present)</u>

LIFELESS, soldiers. Replaces beast soldiers from past (Imperial Magi, Centurions, legionnaires, ballista operators, archers, slingshots, optios (communications))

LUBBERKIN, giant, hairy creatures used to drag large weapons of war

Military Units of Nethergeist (Past)

IMPERIAL MAGI, sorcerers serving the Goat

WIRRAL, Imperial Carnivore Legion

WOLVERINE, Imperial Carnivore Legion

GOBLIN, Imperial Carnivore Legion

PROTO-GOBLINS, Imperial Carnivore Legion

VENSA, Imperial airborne demon

Others

First Gryphon Sceptre **AGELFI BIL'HAZEN**, a mage, an alleged Heretic of the Resistance and Ayilia's tutor

AL KIMIYA, alleged necromantic terrorist

CHRONICLER, storyteller

PROWLERS, Lifeless mounts—requires little nourishment if any

Points of Interest

THE UNCERTAINTY DOCTORATE, THE DISEQUILIBRI-UM PARADOX OF SPITE, vast organizations like the Imperium have too much weight and resource to support the moral bankruptcy, the eternal hoax of power and greed, and will consequently fall.

JI'NAA, the purest stage of being for any Magi, when soul, thought and mind combine to create the ultimate being.

Cruelty, like every other vice, requires no motive outside of itself; it only requires opportunity. –George Eliot

NETHERGEIST

BOOK 2

CHAPTER ONE

PROLOGUE

T he young girl was sprinting through the garden again, bleak statues flashing in the squall. They clawed at her soaked body as the night reached out to take her.

Ayilia came to with a start.

The portal's vortex was filling her skull with light and an impression of great distances travelled. Stilgen was sending them into an organisation so colossal, it appeared to her Kimiya-violated mind as an endless darkness. Like an obsidian blight, it rose from one corner of the visible cosmos and set on the other. It smothered the feral aspirations of all subject species, immolating their hopes, dreams and spite. Only one light burned: the desolated oasis of Resistance worlds. Their flickering aura alone stemmed the tide of a soulless meta-civilisation, and it was winking out.

Within the embrace of the portal, the view quietly atomised, and she merged into brilliance. Suns were burning like Roman candles within shoals of nebulae. Worlds as multitudinous as the atoms holding them together swirled in circles around a glassy nova—pinpricks within superclusters coalescing at the apex of the universe and the universes beyond. Even these were just DNA strands of fire, fingernails of matter within an empyrean existence.

Her senses, inserted uninvited by the Al Kimiya Arch Mage and terrorist, hit overload. Data pillaged a mind close to imploding. Everything Ayilia was and everything this winged desecrator had put into her head meshed, and it made no sense.

Ayilia opened her mouth, but nothing come out. Even if it had, it would've been lost in the eddies of the portal, which buffeted the mannequins that were her companions. Electrified code downloaded at light speed through the Kimiya parasite in her head. No one understood the scale of the intrusion by the neural interloper within. It sucked away her vitality, leaving nothing tangible. She was a facsimile, invaded by a force long since dead.

She felt the Emperor Goat's fiefdom. She felt the Imperium's massive heart beating, its arterial network of portals clogged with Imperial traffic, the coaled eyes of its rulers glazed and dead. An ancient, corpulent mind, woke and peeled back her consciousness like a marauder. It was eternal and all-seeing, both god and aberration.

The Kimiya's imprint responded immediately. In mutual self-defence, it blanked her thoughts with static. She was mummified within a sarcophagus of numbers, symbols and texts. The human-Kimiya combine became a part of the flux surrounding them, blinking out of sight.

The gelid intellect turned away, uninterested.

Ayilia had learned two things. The first, the most obvious, was to keep her mind to herself the next time they jumped. The second was the realisation that in such an unfettered space, where matter and energy were the same, not only could one enhanced consciousness observe, but in the process, be observed.

He wanted her.

This she already knew, but it was the extent that was chilling.

He wanted her more than anything.

Chapter Two

BEYOND ETERNITY

Andromedus, arguably the Asthen Ascendancy's best Dust Tracker, stared down in disbelief at the mechanical maze of the Imperial factory as it pumped refuse with clockwork punctuality from wealds of dirty chimneys. Assembly lines and cogged wheels thundered below like rusted teratoids. Changing shape as they climbed, billowing vapours passed the silent watchers on the ledges to join the smog-beast above. The air was poison, the slate roofs dark and toxic.

Another cloud roiled by in a sore of fumes.

Charge flickered within the fug carapace. The corrosive microclimate was spreading, yet the combustion machines puffed on within a canyon of pistons and hammers.

The group of Asthen Raiders, on command, drew staves designed for peace, now fine-tuned to kill, and aimed them at the industrial behemoth. In response, quicksilver Mage Fire flickered across the horizon of pipes and tubes.

The din was appalling. Nevertheless, Andromedus watched as their chief, Barrackus, weaved destruction with his mace. The commander was a sculptor, moulding and kneading power and discharging it with pinprick accuracy. Beneath, a glass dome imploded. Andromedus could see agonised forms flailing in the blaze within.

Andromedus looked up, alarmed. Imperial hooded Magi were filing into sight on an opposing ledge, taking an attack formation. He saw Barrackus hurriedly barking at his troop to aim. Before the neon figures had a chance to respond, Asthen flame, or Mage Fire, blitzed their positions. As they did, the Raider's defensive shield simultaneously kicked in. It was barely in time to hold off a volley of Imperial fire from a fresh batch of arrivals.

A series of detonations flowered across the edifice, as Asthen firepower tore gaps in the metallic matrixes below and the sorcerers above. Despite their numerical advantage, the foes were quickly depleted. Magi lay sprawled along the ridges or were seen falling in showers of flaming robes.

The Dust Tracker caught Barrackus muttering something and turned to face him.

"Boss?"

"Something ailing you, Andromedus?"

"Talking to yourself again, boss?"

Barrackus chuckled. "Just a one-way conversation."

Andromedus grimaced but said nothing. The bodies of the necromancers on the far ledge kept falling. It was almost soporific. Barrackus nodded towards them. "Feels good giving the Imperium a hiding again, after running for our lives the other day."

"I prefer the term withdrawal; sounds a lot more ... orderly." Andromedus scratched his fleshy arms and grunted. "What happens now—I mean, the mission? You know, the ambitious plan to take out Command Central and bring a stop to the Imperium's push?"

"Ah yes, the mission!"

The portly frame of the Tracker shifted uneasily. He rubbed his sweating head. He wasn't comfortable with words. It was another wedge between him and the fancy-talking officer class, who never seemed quite as egalitarian as the Ascendancy claimed it to be. "I worry about the tannan fluids in our Mage packs, Commander. We're too long in the field: it equals too much exposure! Erodes both the grey matter upstairs and our reserves."

Scratching his armpit at the same time as delivering his opinions had robbed them of some of the impact. Barrackus was barely listening, either way. There seemed something wrong about the commander. He used to be more conservative, reluctant to take overt risks, but something indefinable seemed to be inside him. It was likely just the paranoia of being endlessly at war, but Andromedus swore he could sense something there, growing.

"This destruction ..." Barrackus murmured. "All these years of fighting the Emperor, destroying His aberrations, yet so little changes. You forget who you are if you do it long enough; for most of us, it's a life sentence." He watched impassively as a knot of Magi were blown into parts. "But I'd spend my entire existence fighting if it means keeping His hams off the Asthen world. Even if I never go back and actually see it."

He brushed silver hair away from bleary eyes. "See the explosions, Andromedus, engulfing those assembly lines? See the colours ... for a few short moments, it felt like wading in a field of poppies the size of suns back on my birth moon. So much uncorrupted, free-ranging energy there ... you wouldn't believe it. The night seas were like wading through dappled scarlet, and you could see auroras over every crystal fall. The companion moons were the sharpest diamonds—they looked like gleaming necklaces, no matter which one you were standing on.

"You know, some say we didn't evolve on the home world, that we migrated from faraway places, rich in thaumaturgic splendour. That would explain a lot, if true." His face furrowed. "Look at our allies. They'll never surpass themselves and reach the heights required of a cosmic civilisation. They have no gift, and they imagine we're somehow going to pull them out of this hell." Barrackus blew a smoke ring from his stave towards the smog glowering above. "Now, allied resources are critically stretched, and there's nothing left in the pot."

The uncomfortable silence was populated only by the cries of the dying and the

explosions below.

Andromedus coughed. The smoke was in his lungs. "So that's why we're going so bloody deep, risking the best unit in the Ascendancy, with barely the time to destroy a critical factory on the way." He peered down—the damage was shocking. "Seriously, that's the biggest operation I've seen. Any other time, I'd say job done, let's get the holy crap out of here!"

"No one else has entered this uncharted micro-universe within a portal universe," Barrackus replied, almost in awe. "That means no one else is this deep right now, nor will be again." He wiped soot from his face. "The blood-filled road to the Core might have to get a little ... unorthodox."

The Dust Tracker whistled. "Now, why don't I like the sound of that?"

Barrackus slapped a reassuring hand on his shoulder. "This network may be enigmatic, but the portals are unbelievably powerful. They cover unheard-of distances, and lead inwards. We've just one shot before their army swamps it! You know what that means, don't you?"

"No?"

"It means only the mission counts. It means we are expendable, Andromedus!"

Andromedus let out a long, tortured sigh. The urge to retreat was irrepressible.

There was another line of detonations. The monstrous brume above was growing.

Andromedus gulped. The commander's features were a rictus mask in the red light. The Tracker grimly wiped his neck with his singlet and scrutinised the destruction.

"Are we freedom fighters or gods of death?"

The commander exhaled. "Sheyna believes the Imperium doesn't have the depth to maintain the interstellar war fronts and guard the portals of hundreds of thousands of moons, asteroids, and worlds in each Prefecture. Fortunately, portals can't be blocked. That thaumaturgic, high-class lock we encountered on the gate to this secret universe is, at best, astonishingly rare. And the super portal it protected was invisible on all charts. We wouldn't have known that rain world even existed had we not had that intel. We are *not* expected!"

Barrackus' irises gleamed like gems. The Tracker saw flashes refracting from the violence back at him. "|Our luck can't hold commander. Let's finish torching this place, then blaze a route home. No one was meant to skulk in this hidden purgatory."

Barrackus smiled. It came out the blue. "Our enemy expects retreat. He'll figure we'll bolt home, melt back into the ethers like we always do."

Andromedus was a compendium of savage shades. He was doing a bad job of disguising his anxiety. His throat was tightening like a garrotte;

it was becoming hard to breathe. "You have no intention of eradicating Command Central, do you?"

The commander's face clouded. That dread inside Andromedus' soul turned into an ache. He tried to keep calm, but he wasn't doing a good job of it. "Boss?"

"The Senate!"

Andromedus couldn't move. He could no longer hear the noise around him.

"Central Command is staffed by ineffective generals, chartists and soothsayers, Andromedus—the Senate has it all." Barrackus' imperious gaze was focused on the destruction below. "They've no serious protection, as no one has ever reached the Core. We take out the Senate, and this war grinds to a halt. The Goat can't direct such a vast organisation without them. We can turn the Abomination over, force Him to treat." He watched the fiery chaos. He seemed to see the elements, the particles that seethed within. "We can lay waste to everything He's created, maybe even slit His almighty throat down to the bone."

Something exploded below. Andromedus turned his gaze to shield his eyes and fleetingly caught their shadows streaking across the rock.

Barrackus didn't react. "The further we go, the greater the surprise. We mask our tracks, make them think we're trying another way home." He leaned forwards, his face devilish in the flickering light. "We go *all* the way to the centre, right to where it's all happening. If anyone has the skillset, we do!"

An odd sensation rose inside, but Andromedus realised it was just a part of his mind going insane. When his jowls seemed to be in sync with what was left of his wits, he finally spoke.

"Nethergeist? You mean to go to the capital world, the centre of all that's screwed, and eradicate the seat of the Imperial government? By all that's holy, that's seriously fu—"

"*Don't!*"

The commander held his finger to the Asthen's gobsmacked mouth. He looked around conspiratorially. "By all that's holy, my friend, keep a lid on it. The very mention of that world invites the damned."

"I ... I ..."

"You should've seen Sheyna's face!"

Andromedus had practically doubled up. Barrackus put his arm across his back and spoke in a grave voice. "I've felt this moment many times," he murmured, eyes grim. "Ever since we first crossed the threshold of this forbidden cosmos, I've had ... clarity. This place is rich in exotic sorceries that inflame the mind into possibilities I only dreamed of. Not since I was a student have I felt my consciousness soar like this. Then, I was ... controlled. For the shortest of whiles treated for ..." He looked away. "If it hadn't been for the war, I might never have gotten out. I've always had something undefinable within, but for the first time in a life immerged in theurgy, I can *relate*!"

Andromedus made no attempt to hide his dismay. His long-trusted superior was a madman. And not just any old madman, but a madman with unfathomable powers. Rank and seniority seemed irrelevant now. They'd screwed him up before, and now the senior class were doing it again, and there was nowhere to run. No longer were they individuals overlooking hell.

"There are stories about the world of the accursed!" Andromedus spat. "Seas flow like serpents, corpses and people walk in tandem, and the ground is so bedevilled that the very dust would tear the skin off the flesh. We can't go there!"

"We have to! The Core is too big to trace the military headquarters. It has to be there!" Barrackus' voice shut the Tracker down before he could interject. "Asthen Command themselves have informed me personally that the unthinkable has happened, that it's as good as over!"

"Bullshit!" Andromedus snarled, terrified. Before he knew it, his arm flashed at Barrackus' face, but the commander pinned it down with ease. That didn't stop the words from flying. "Screw you, and screw your type. Suicide is far from clever, and going Core-wards to find that bastard planet is the same as slitting our wrists here and now!"

"His Imperial Highness the Goat has switched the onus to our allies, old friend." Barrackus was calm as ice. He released the panting Tracker. "They shelter behind our leadership and our gift, and we use their numbers. We are not a populous people—that's the deal. But our enemy attacks them on exposed positions, grinding them down. At the same time, the Abomination keeps us occupied with legions of whatever vat-reared, armoured Carnivore legion He can lay His hands on. This is why we go in. Otherwise, Andromedus—we are done."

He had no response. They were surrounded by utter, utter silence.

The Raiders left the precipice and melted into the gloom, away from the melee. There was nothing left to see. Flames raged through the edifice. Despite giving the indecipherable shapes within the chance to run, they hadn't.

Sheyna wasn't happy. In fact, she was livid. She'd not only seen the commander's exchange with Andromedus, but he'd already given her enough pointers prior to the battle to work it out. Making her way to the front of the column, she hissed ferociously in the ear of their commander.

"Why? We don't need to go further in. The politicians can sort this shitty shit-crap out; they're responsible for strategy. We don't stand a chance."

Barrackus brushed battle grime from his body and lowered his voice. "The Asthen are finished."

"You said that already, and I told you already, our leaders are jacking with your mind! You are a good Raider, Barrackus, but you are politically naïve—they're playing games. Someone wants your position or maybe your reputation, or you! We can't just give up our families, our worlds, our homes. And what about the lesser civilisations ... which is all of them? They're lost without our leadership."

"Sheyna, we have to face the fact the Asthen Ascendancy don't have the numbers to win this war without doing something ... exceptional!"

"We have our goddamned gift—that evens it up!" Sheyna was almost shouting. She saw other people trying not to stare. Things were falling apart, and it was all coming from him, her once-venerated commander.

"It's not enough, *not* anymore!" He checked behind him that no one had gotten too close. "The Empire's entire organisation would haemorrhage on every front if their mind was eradicated. The Imperium is notoriously centralist, one big mother of a control freak. Otherwise, the best we can hope for is to tread water!"

"Tread water?" Sheyna was aghast. "That's the best they, our best boffins, can do —a stagnant stalemate?"

"Aren't all stalemates stagnant?" He smiled.

Sheyna gave no response.

His tone dropped to a whisper. "I've come to believe the authorities thought all along we couldn't win. I think they were hoping something would turn the war in our favour. Things are terrible and now I hear that renegade bastard Pharsalus is making gains against us. He's the best general the Imperium's has and the worst traitor we ever had. He's out there. I can feel him, waiting."

"No." She groaned as a red mist discoloured her vision. The explosion was as predictable as it was unpleasant. Barrackus had already steeled himself. "Why the bloody hell has this bloody war been going on for so bloody long, if they bloody knew the whole time we couldn't bloody win?"

The soldiers around them were staring again. Inquisitiveness, fear and terror combined into one on their faces. Barrackus' teeth shone in the light. "I don't have the answers, Sheyna, but they did reveal something ... interesting. Apparently, the Imperium would rather nail our hides to a large wheel than take down an entire allied army. They're terrified of us, of what *we* do."

She hocked in derision. "That's doesn't help, not even a bit. This mission is still the biggest pile of dung this side of the galaxy. We should go home, now. While we still can." Her brows knitted. "You scared Andromedus, and now you're doing the same to me. God's teeth, Barrackus, you're doing my frigging nut in!"

He indicated the alien landscape around them. "I don't know why, but there's so much radical sorcery here it's triggered something, some kind of ... I'm not sure."

Her gaze was wild. "We're going to that hell planet on a sense of 'I'm not sure?' I should have you removed on medical grounds!"

She turned to go, but he grabbed her shoulder. She whirled and whacked him in the mouth. Blood squirted from his lip. It flooded down his dirty armour and spattered over his feet. She struck him again with so much strength his head turned sideways, then again. When she'd stopped, panting hard, he took a hand glowing with soft power and healed the wound, leaving only the gore. The troop's mouths hung open.

"You'll be pleased to know ... you're a lot faster than Andromedus," Barrackus muttered as he wiped the mess away. It joined the war stains on his sleeve.

Sheyna stood, eyes closed, trying for a calm that always seemed to elude her. She opened her eyes and glowered at the Raiders who were still staring.

"Get a move on! Whatever you think you saw, you'll always be in the best hands here, more than anywhere else in this godforsaken cunt-hole of a universe!"

They hurried off, not once glancing back. She shook her head and faced the man with the burning eyes. Something inexplicable was happening. However, she was—used to be—his friend. Tentatively, she laid a hand on his arm. "Barrackus, I'm sorry. I ... can't seem to control my temper anymore. It's always been... problematic. Been out doing this so long, so many years, blood and violence seems to be the only thing I have control over."

He looked down, eyes dark with conflict. "No, I'm sorry. I'm sorry for taking you on the most tortured routes imaginable, meeting the most horrific filth conceivable."

She felt the flash again. "Don't patronise me, Commander. I'm a bitch out here, and I need to do something about it, but I stand by what I said." She caught her tongue. "Even so, I don't know anyone who's wasted more cutthroats and turned over more munition dumps in the entire Ascendancy than you!" She fought back something that never happened, not to her: an urge to weep. "If we do this, this is the last mission you and I should go on. You don't mean to, but you push us too far. I don't think I have the temperament to support you anymore."

Tears finally broke through her resolve and rolled down her cheeks. Translucent and bright, they seemed the only purity in that world. "I will fight and die with you, Barrackus; I will see the destruction of all my dreams of an ordinary life, doing ordinary things in an ordinary place." She brushed the wetness away impatiently. "This is on the Goat. If He happens to be there at the Senate when we kick down that door to the vipers within, it will be my blade that cuts His dirty, hate-filled head clean from His withered neck." She leaned close. She could feel the heat of his breath. "Promise me that. Promise me that."

His gaze shone like fire. "I promise!"

She closed her eyes, nodded and walked on. He stared at her back. She was so staunch, so loyal, yet filled with a turmoil she couldn't control. The pang that unexpectedly shook him was so potent he winced.

CHAPTER THREE

INSIDE THE IMPERIUM

S he was perching on the edge of a garden, looking at a faded, cream-coloured house. Rain pattered on her knuckles where they gripped the wooden fence. Trees rustled like dry silk beneath darkening clouds. Ayilia looked but couldn't sense anything inside. Nor could she remember the name of the man who'd arrived the moment she considered entering. She knew she didn't like him. She also knew she'd met him already.

Why was he always here?

Deep down, she sensed she'd called him and that was worse, but how was anyone's guess. Why call someone she loathed? And what was his name?

She came to.

She was lying face down in grit and water. Her hair was matted to the contours of her cheeks, her garb drenched. Gravel imprints ran across her skin. Turning over slowly, Ayilia looked up. Thunder rumbled across a sky so black, it threatened to collapse under its own weight. Waterfalls tipped down craggy ridges in the distance.

She squinted against a horizon flatlining into a blur. A host of blue suns were just visible through the clouds. Ayilia could make out a wilderness with barely adequate vitality for life. Rubbery fronds and spiny grasses dotted a vista of onyx rocks. Minute flowers formed ivory specks in the wet. Twisted rock skyscrapers and calderas were lit by the lightning that burst amid the winds and rain.

"Kemet? Soren? Anybody?"

The wind crooned a vacant reply. Ayilia dragged herself to her feet. Shrubs waved manically in the gale. She tried to ignore a surge of panic. Liquid blew sideways into her face whenever the wind changed directions. Despite being as damp as a wet sponge, the air was surprisingly temperate, and she didn't feel cold.

"Keeeemet!"

She fought back fear. It felt like she was that youth again, lost within cavernous hallways lined with alabaster figures, lifeless but watching.

She cursed. It made her feel better.

Had the others been shotblasted into other dimensions? Without a Lifeless ally with the requisite training in portal mechanics, there was no way of getting back. She was stranded. Her blood froze at the thought.

There was a sudden pressure on her shoulder. Ayilia swivelled round. Her left arm displaced the intruder's hold with a hard swipe, as her right slid out her blade. In less than a heartbeat, she'd thrust its tip at the figure's face. It was their turn to freeze. She glimpsed a silhouetted head bathed in a watery aura.

Ayilia wiped stinging rain from her eyes. "One move and you're headless!"

"Clumsy, but effective ... for a hume." He looked her up and down. "A bedraggled one at that."

She shook her head in disbelief. Seftus, the recalcitrant Krayal chief, was staring back.

Of all the people.

Despite the fact he was a pompous cold-blood, she felt a wave of relief.

"Believe me, Regent, I'd have chosen other company had fate been kinder, but that is a luxury I've been living without most my life." Seftus looked around. "Where're the others? They can't be far!"

"Stilgen screwed up!" She regretted the words as soon as she spoke them.

"Well, he is made from mud and crap. When it comes to the Lifeless, I always expect bad news." He regarded her sword. "Time to lose the cutter, hume, especially when there's no dead men present to bond us in battle with their questionable charisma."

Ayilia smiled grimly, then returned it to its very damp holster. "I could really do with some good news. Not only don't I know where the others are, I don't even know where we are. Maybe we left the Empire behind?"

"Oh, we're in Empire alright. You'd have to jump quite far to leave it, and you can't do that in one go. As to who lives here, try that."

She followed his gaze. On a mountaintop, swathed by mist and low-level clouds, a foreboding, ribbed fortress stood covered in buttresses arranged in pockmarked rows. There was no light shining from within.

"We didn't all jump as one, so therefore I assume we landed at different times. Fortunately, as I clearly jumped before them and you went after, the very fact we're both here implies those in between are ... somewhere."

"I'm reassured." She was, secretly. It was better than being dead or trapped in the portal forever.

"Don't be—we don't know who's up there." He looked around wearily. "I seem to have passed out during passage. I think everyone arrived at different times. It happens if you're in a hurry. A consequence of having no time to prep, itself being a consequence of having undead maniacs right up our spleens. As for the Pro Consul, I saw him flying into happy-happy land over our heads before I lost consciousness. A botch up for sure, but all-in-all we're lucky to still have our skins."

"I'll feel a bit luckier once we're out of this rain." Ayilia grunted. "Let's just find the others and a way to the Resistance."

"You mean back home?"

"There is no home, Seftus—not without them."

"That's something a hungry, angry, and very lost Krayal with a bad disposition doesn't want to hear. It's a good thing I'm civil, considering we're alone."

"What the hell does that mean?"

"Face it, hume leader, you've lost your dim-witted city and your even more dim-witted sidekicks. A less-inclined person might consider robbing you and leaving you to rot in the rain. Bare that in mind while you make schemes for us without due consultation." He grinned, an alarming sight amid the storm. "It's also fortuitous I don't eat meat, as I'm very, very hungry."

It was so outrageous that Ayilia found herself laughing. She rubbed at her face, desperately trying to dry it. Unsurprisingly, it was a futile gesture. "Good thing I'm civil too, or I might have severed your mouth from your arse when you jumped me from behind."

"Ummph."

"Wait a mo'—up there. They're there."

"Where?"

"Follow me, Seftus."

"Follow you, where?"

"Where I'm going, doofus!"

Far above them, faint figures were climbing the rise leading to the dark fortress. With palpable apprehension, Seftus and Ayilia trekked after them, carefully stepping over rocks and dark shale. Rain pelted every surface. There was just enough heat from the suns to warm the world. A cascade of steps had been chiselled directly into the rock face and around the walls, spiralling to the imposing castle.

"Deserted," she muttered. "Looks derelict."

"You don't know that there isn't someone up there, waiting to slit our throats."

She paused, then looked at him directly. "You're right, I don't."

The climb was tiring but not excessively arduous. The gradient remained manageable, and the view impressive, however Ayilia belatedly rediscovered a forgotten distrust of heights. The wind was stronger as they ascended, threatening to blow them off. Old iron grips kept them steady.

At the top, they faced a chasm separating them and the fortification. Weather-beaten stone pillars resembling a string of damaged teeth, stood on either side of a fragile looking walkway linking both sides. The entire thing wobbled alarmingly in the gale.

"Fuck that," Ayilia muttered.

"Scared of a small breeze, hume?"

"I'm scared of dropping a dozen leagues to our deaths, Seftus."

After scanning the scene intently, Ayilia approached the walkway. The rickety bridge swayed, but their weight stabilised it, a bit. Though the rain was a maelstrom in the crosswind, they struggled to the pillars opposite. From there, a rubble path led to an arched entrance, guarded by sinewy goblins and gargoyles carved from stone. After checking for a possible ambush, Ayilia led Seftus through the entrance into a courtyard beyond that softly sheened with rainwater.

Immensely relieved they were still alive, Seftus faced his companion and one-time adversary with a satisfied flourish. "We're here."

"I noticed," Ayilia replied softly.

"Well, where are they then?"

"I swear that was them ahead of us," she said.

Seftus walked between the marble pillars. Like the arches and vaulted roofs beyond, they were draped with creepers.

"Still nothing." He vanished through the nearest doors. She followed hurriedly, finding a large room on the other side.

"Umm, basic architecture," she heard him muttering as his back disappeared through a second doorway. Ayilia sped up, but he'd already slipped through a gateway between some tree-sized ferns to another courtyard within. Rain pattered gently through holes in the rafters. The ground was firm in some places and squishy in others. The Krayal was scouting among a set of classical, stark buildings in the distance. Ayilia quickened her pace, aware of the irony of preferring the company of an officious reptile, to being alone in the dimness.

An eclectic assortment of buildings awaited them, from outhouses to kitchens, bathhouses, symposiums, barracks, and even a possible brothel. The exotic bulk of a hybrid temple lurked beyond. The designs were alien, but there was a beauty in their bleakness. The antiquated styles screamed Imperium or a closely affiliated power.

Only the pitter-patter of water broke the serenity. It dribbled down foliage and brickwork to collect at a grating in the centre of a faded piazza.

It was an intoxicating mesh of geometric exposition and nature, timeless and surreal.

No sign of Seftus. Or the others.

She felt a sudden sense of doom. A blurred shape moved to her right—she began to turn, but something thunked her on the back of the head. The drum of rain was replaced with the roar of the sea.

The cavern was dark and hot. Seftus lay shackled on the floor opposite, his face a vivid red. Dislocated movements shuffled nearby, accompanied by a series of clicking noises.

Something was watching her.

Ayilia groaned and lurched upright. Pandemonium erupted. Colours and shapes vortexed together. She was groggy. Belatedly, she realised her weapon had been taken, and she reflexed into combat poise. A chirping cacophony struck her, a living wall of din. A distinctly inhospitable sight shimmied into view.

She was facing what looked like a super-hive.

Intricate webbing clung to stone etched with hieroglyphics and illuminated by torches. Effervescent light glowed from saffron orbs fastened to the ceilings like miniature stars. A bitter murmur came from all directions. Some kind of shape appeared to be communicating. Ayilia side-turned, minimising herself as a target. She winced at the smell of fungi and dead tissue, then winced again when she made out the thing facing her.

It was an anthropomorphic crossbreed, a hominid-arthropod hulk in the dark. Thickly coated by a resinous hide and chitinous, multijointed appendages, its upper torso had shoulders, arms, and a head. Hexagonal, compound eyes diffracted the light into mosaic pinpricks around concave bulbs. Its skull was an ebony riot of bristles. A milky-green abdomen the texture of mildew lay beneath a segmented thorax. A variety of organs moved visibly underneath the skin.

Despite a nausea that struck her, Ayilia felt somehow obliged to speak, as though it was expected of her.

"Back off... or get hurt." She rolled her eyes and sighed inside even as she was finishing the words. That could've been better.

Nothing moved.

Ayilia edged towards what looked like an exit, only to see another shape block her off. After a pregnant pause, the first creature spoke abruptly, in an obsolete Nethergestian dialect. For the first time she was grateful for those stultifying years learning redundant Imperial languages.

"The candidate is of sufficient calibre, notwithstanding the enigma of the genus. Prepare interstice upper level, adjunct thirty-three for insemination." It regarded the prone Krayal. "Howbeit, its cold-blood companion is of dubious quality—send it to the mines." It scrutinised her beadily. "I want to examine the oblation closely. Bring it."

Appendages grabbed her from nowhere, propelling her forwards. Closer proximity revealed leathery features and spiny hairs. The stench was indescribable.

"Adequate." It faced the others. "There is a declivity of productivity in the hive; supplementary drones required. The Imperial Intellect looks elsewhere, now that the Heretical Resistance is neutralised. The commune is no longer valued, and His supplies, consequently, are dangerously low. The creature can be used."

Ayilia flinched. She was stuck in an auxiliary Imperial fiefdom. And she was weaponless.

"Remove to Berth Chamber Three, cell 42. I will attend."

The pincers swept her away. Long corridors, hewn out of the rock, rushed past. Ayilia could see shapeless edifices in neon lighting in the distance. The glow from lanterns oscillated between dim and even dimmer. Water gurgled in hidden sumps under her feet and covered the corridors in dampness. It was like being in a nautical hellhole wedged under a slate-grey graveyard, once a city.

A globular, beige sac hung suspended from the ceiling like a cancerous polyp. Metal struts gripped it tightly, as though it were in the process of being cauterised. Around and beneath, honeycomb structures ran in regimented but inchoate lines. The smell was toxic, the din the same clicking chorus but louder. Several hundred creatures toiled on a central dais scaling walls, towers, and constructs as they swarmed across hexagonal cells. They streamed towards the sac at the centre, a neo-city of geometric patterns. Miasmic clouds, wind systems, and trickling streams weaved among sickly-looking shrubs hugging a meagre existence wherever they could. Cinnamon membranes stretched to the ground everywhere. The creatures swept effortlessly over them using the invisible hooks on their limbs.

"Hell," Ayilia muttered.

The ground became empty space as they leapt into darkness, then scaled down the webbing. Compact rooms and compartments without roofs filled the horizon. Cocoons were wedded fast to coffin-shaped spaces in the walls. Pentacles, depictions of triangular temples and night-mare forms, were carved into the walls of each room.

Someone shoved her forward, and she flopped across the floor of an empty chamber. A slab stood empty and uninviting. The guards retreated up the fronds with impressive alacrity.

After a deep breath, Ayilia rolled over and staggered to her feet.

"The one time I need Seftus, and he's fast asleep."

Dust devils weaved around the troop, depositing sand grains in spidery scrawls across their worn boots. Standing mutely on the brow of a ridge, Aaron took in the desiccated wastelands and a bridge wrought from the bones of human and Krayal thralls. Crafted centuries ago, the crossing had been "beautified" with heroic figures slaying cyclopean quadrupeds from Imperial history—undead purity etched into long-dead people. It was artistic, striking, disturbing. The crossing arced to a crumbled fortress of stone and wood on the far side of a gorge. Spears and banners fluttered languidly above legionnaires watching them with hollow eyes. Stunted trees closeted the edifice like tombstones, curled roots larger than the boughs themselves.

Aaron hocked venomously across the ground.

Old childhood nightmares resurfaced. Creatures, like the ones opposite, would erupt from the earth, clawing at the soil, dirt powdering off stringy tongues. The ground was rejecting an indigestible army, spewing up gaunt shapes until they had surrounded him in their thousands.

Then silence.

Complete, stony quiet as the things stared at him, the only organic in the centre of that horror.

It reminded him of his time protecting enslaved humans in the Occupied Lands, as an X Gemina soldier. After Abandonment, when the Imperium had deserted their world and left the toothless Pro Consul Vespasian to stupefy into his seat, things had settled. The killers had gone, leaving a runt force of drones and soldiers metamorphosing into unrepaired piss-merchants. Some even invited the Gemina into their taverns. Often, the Gemina joined them. Friendships weren't uncommon—an impossibility when the Pit was resolutely Imperial.

But there had been an occasion when a village thief was found half-eaten amid a row of bramble at the end of a disused field. The lifeless, liquor-addled commander of the prefecture could barely stand that day, and he'd simply rounded up some hapless but innocent Lifeless drones to bestow punishment. Fortunately, Aaron's people had traced a path to some delinquent soldiers with fresh bloodstains on their teeth and nails. Though they denied any wrongdoing, they helpfully added that the world would be a better place for everyone if thieves were eaten. The commander had shrugged, then given the order for them to be executed where they stood. When Aaron had insisted on a trial first, as stipulated by Treaty, in the highly unlikely case they were innocent, the commander just belched and ordered their execution anyway, citing a distaste for paperwork.

The motheaten soldiers present dispatched the shocked defendants on the spot with surprising speed, splitting their skulls with their blades.

Even as Aaron was recovering his wits, some thralls had arrived with a bloody sack. Inside were the heads of half a dozen missing people. The soldiers had gone renegade and consumed them, even though too much human meat might be lethal to the Lifeless. For some, it rotted their brains. For others, it could end in the cannibalism of their own kind, something that sent shivers up the spines of every Lifeless chief.

The commander then smiled and growled: "So they *were* guilty. And to think, you were going to force me to do all that paperwork!"

Aaron snorted at the memory and spat again for good effect, as though the act could exorcise the demons, before launching forwards. His troop immediately followed. He quickly reached the crossing spanning the gorge. The partially eroded planks were sturdy, but the rest of the bridge looked alarmingly rickety. The pylons that held the ropes were the calcified remains of antediluvian giants. Their old bones were no longer reliable.

An impossibly gaunt centurion, some two hands taller than the X Gemina soldier, regarded Aaron with disdain before walking imperiously across the crossing to meet him, leaving a small force on the other side.

Aaron spoke before it could, taking in the surroundings. "Nice place you've got here."

The Lifeless cut straight to the point. "Who do you speak for now, hume—now that your squatting rights on this world have been rescinded? There is no respite here. Your bitch queen has been lost to a reactivated Pit. Turn back before the Everlasting One slaps a hefty price on your scab-encased ass."

The bad dreams threatened to return. Despite himself, Aaron smiled. "Well, this ... 'scab-encased ass' wants her back and will do all he can to find her."

The Centurion's teeth shone dully under the three suns. Its parchment strip of paper-thin skin, a fabulous rarity and one often bought on the black market, furrowed before inadvertently splitting. The exaggeration had been comically overdone.

"Perhaps breeders are hard of hearing. This way lies death." It thumbed its bony hand in the direction of the ramshackle fort, "if you hide in the hills like the Krayal scale-skulls, the legend that is Mabius might take a little longer to hog-roast your watery sacs to crispy slag." It tried to look thoughtful. "Say, a few days. Count your blessings and vanish!"

Aaron glanced at the others, then pulled a thoughtful face of his own. "Actually, I offer some council of my own, Centurion." He leaned close. "Our path is ahead. Your garrison is in the way. It is also understaffed and underfunded. You're not nicely scrubbed off-world models, you're Pit—decrepit—and that hole you skulk in is just that, a hole!" Aaron's face slipped into mock puzzlement. "I never really understood it, you know. You guys hate anything with a pulse, then spend your best coin trying to look like us by slapping on a hide that looks like it spent its best years inside a rodent's anus." Muffled laugher sounded from behind him. "Let me be plain, Centurion ... the numbers don't work for you. You guard a dump made from mud, and we are murderously tired. No need for nastiness here, when no one knows what goes on in this sterile corner of nowhere!" He nodded conspiratorially. "I can see some half-decent, illegal liquor casks through those window bars. Why perish when you could forget all about this and just let us pass, perhaps sink a few while you're at it?"

The Centurion regarded him for a drawn-out moment, then spun around and strode towards his soldiers, knocking some aside in the process.

A line formed on the battlements, bows primed.

With a single nod from the Centurion, a volley of arrows arced towards the humans, twanging off their shields. Aaron cursed and shouted. Gemina sappers swiftly unveiled mobile artillery pieces from underneath dirty sackcloth and emptied their buckshot back, shredding most of the Lifeless where they stood. The upper walls of the bastion, mostly sand and dried manure, ruptured into terracotta plumes. As the walls blistered, a smaller donjon beyond was revealed. The resistance, from what little was left of the top walls, vanished as the rattle and thumps of the hand-operated artillery finished them off. Most ended up as a motley pile of broken limbs, weaponry, and loose mortar.

Aaron raised his sword. The troops emerged from their wall of shields and surged towards a fort dotted with unmoving mannequins. One or two defenders tried to rise, but they were effortlessly cut down. Spears, pennants, outstretched stumps, broken cuirasses, and prostrate Lifeless littered the fort in a macabre carpet, their mouths gaping at the wind.

Those few who surrendered were sent off unharmed, with nothing but their garments. Some Gemina wanted them executed—after all, they weren't "alive" in the first place—but Aaron reluctantly muttered something obscene about the Treaty and let them go.

Once within the fortress itself, the humans were greeted by a cacophony of chants and renditions of religious scripture from Nethergestian texts. But the dilapidated, highly delusional, and somewhat inebriated Pit soldiers hurriedly surrendered when they saw their comrades at the entry hacked to pieces in clumps of tendon. The humans let them go as well.

Aaron scouted the rubble-streaked barracks, the back office, the mess rooms, and the casket-filled cellars before exiting back to the open courtyard, absentmindedly stepping over mangled bodies without a second thought.

Nessan approached him, looking highly satisfied. "All clear, sir. We've swept the entire area. Nothing moving save the dregs you let go." She made little attempt to keep her disdain for the decision hidden. "We suffered no casualties except some scrapes. Geena got a bolt in her arse, but it's only a flesh impact as the armour took most of it. Medic is on it now, figuratively speaking." Aaron could tell she was trying not to smirk. "She'll be fine in a few days but try telling her that!"

He nodded briskly, still trying to supress the nightmares. "Pass my compliments to the troop and gunners. Make sure everyone's rested and fed. While you're at it, please reinforce the periphery with guards who can stay awake, unlike the other night." With a measure of disgust, he flicked a piece of sinew from his sword. "On the plus side, I doubt the Pit will realise this hole has been taken for some considerable time. I mean, would you?"

"Aye!" She paused. "Aaron ... one other thing." Something in her voice caught his attention. "We found something in the one and only dungeon they have down here."

"Something?"

She shrugged. "Some undead dreg from the Pit. He's a low-level acolyte class, one ruined by gambling. He has something to say that he believes you may want to hear. A soldier's fetching him now."

Aaron nodded pensively. Nessan flexed battle-stiff fingers and took a look around. "Do you still intend to storm the Pit?"

"Having second thoughts?"

"No, not really ..." She rubbed the back of her head uneasily. "Well, yes!"

"The stiffs have Ayilia and the others, and we want them back. We don't have a choice."

"Normally, I'd agree, but there are thousands of highly equipped off-world killers embedded there, and we don't even have a hundred here. Maybe there's another way?"

"There isn't. They're there, and we're here."

Aaron swatted away some nasty-looking bluebottles. They seemed to love his perma-red face, pumped up with blood. Must be sweet nirvana for them compared to the recent inhabitants. He glowered fiercely, his mood already going south. "As for the Heretics and their bloody Resistance, with whom we were meant to be liaising, it'll take months to find that mutt-eared portal up north, and even then, only if we had the Krayal to guide us. They're in the Pit too! Their scaly pals melted away the moment the regent was taken by that Sythian, fire-oath Mabius, so they're the only lizards we have left."

"Here he is," Nessan said with a grimace The soldier had appeared with a sullen-looking drone, his hands in restraints. He'd clearly been manufactured in the Pit—and not recently, either. His Lifeless advantages, such as they were, were ragged in attire and build.

"Phew." Aaron snorted. "You've seen better times."

"And smelled them," the soldier whistled through his teeth.

"Trust me, there're more to come," the drone muttered in a slightly whiny voice.

Aaron and Nessan exchanged a glance. "Okay, leave him with us. Nessan's going to sort it out, but give those guards over there a kick while you're at it? Looks like they're already kipping."

Aaron regarded the dirty creature. He was spindly, with a hoary smorgasbord of gnarled lumps dotted around his frame, especially on the shoulders. Though Pit were substandard compared to off-worlders, this one seemed more substandard than normal. The thing was studying him keenly, getting the measure of the man even though he was the captor. For some reason, it really annoyed him. Nessan shifted uneasily on her feet but stayed quiet.

"Okay, Mr ... dead man. What were you doing in that cell? Been at the liquor again, or have your debts been too burdensome to pay off?"

The response was short and icy but displayed unnerving hints of intelligence. "Unlike our compatriots, hume, I don't always care for fermented grains. Amusing, isn't it, that it wasn't the organic's sword that skewered my people, but their mead."

He shut his mouth with a firm plop.

Aaron scratched his scalp. It itched like crazy in this heat. Nevertheless, he'd always refused to cut his locks. As a child, he'd believed he'd lose his sword skills, and he found that hard to change, though he readily acknowledged he'd been a stupid kid.

"Fascinating." He rolled his eyes at Nessan. "What's your identity, and why are you here? Speak quickly, dead thing!"

"No need for the macho talk, hume, or the patronising species bigotry. I came seeking your little band of rebels personally, of my own free will. I'm Breasal. And I'm really pissed off!"

The humans' eyes widened.

"Pissed off at what?" Nessan spluttered.

"Whom! Pissed off at whom! To be here, talking to you. Can you understand that." It wasn't a question.

Aaron grunted. "Well, I'm really sorry to hear it, Breasal, I really am. Would you mind enlightening this bigot-head as to what the hell you're talking about?"

"Stilgen!"

"Stilgen?" Aaron repeated like a parrot.

"Yes, Stilgen." Breasal brushed at his sides.

Aaron sighed. "What has that mutt-head got to do with us or you?"

"What do you think? He sent me!"

"Why?" Nessan asked, clearly trying to stifle a grin. "Someone owes him money? We haven't got any, and I don't think the stiffs we found here are in any state to pay!"

"No sweat, hume—I robbed them anyway. It's probably why they arrested me in the first place, on reflection." He winked at Nessan, who looked astonished now. Somehow, the thing had wriggled free of his restraints. "I'm here to guide you to a portal!"

"Ah, of course you are," Aaron growled sarcastically. "Why didn't you just say so?"

"Why didn't you just ask?" Breasal seemed immune to irony.

Nessan cut in quickly, clearly concerned about Aaron's infamously short fuse. "Breasal, instead of turning our questions on us, explain why the Pro Consul's best mate—only mate—would send you? They hate human guts!"

Breasal drew closer. He stank inexplicably of sweaty boot leather. "Us! He sent us, not me."

"I give up already." Aaron clenched his hands, considering what part of the Lifeless' throat to squeeze first.

"Stilgen sent us ... a group of scouts, to find *you*," he explained, clearly vexed. "Vespasian, that washed-up Pit warlord, is a neuter Sythian dolt—part god, part deckchair. It was Stilgen who ran the Pit. Drones like me still owe him fealty—he brought us order and respect. The

Consul's aides couldn't even find their way out of the latrines once it got dark, though hell knows why they even needed them."

"You're making no sense, stitch-face!" Aaron snapped. He could feel his face going puce. "You're saying that Stilgen, the half-wit Pro Consul's right-hand carcass, sent a whole bunch of messengers looking for us because they love him so much? Meanwhile, the guards of this unimposing little shithole threw you in the slammer because you robbed them on the way?"

"A guy's gotta eat!" Breasal gave them a lopsided smile.

Aaron's hands were flexing frantically. "Why would he want to help us find a portal? Despite the arrival of Mabius, Stilgen and the Pro Consul are still our foe!"

"Not anymore. They've gone through ... they've gone through the portal in the Pit to somewhere far beyond. Just before, Stilgen hid a drone from Mabius' armed piglets so it could rustle up help." Breasal's mouth turned down. "And for free. No wonder I had to borrow a bit of coin while I was at it. It's only fair!"

"What?" Aaron exchanged a stupefied glance with Nessan. Breasal continued to study them with those lazy black dots he had for eyes. "Where have they gone, dead man? Why?"

"Why?" The undead looked amazed. "Either that or become the main dish on a Sythian barbecue! Stilgen went through with your regent, some other watery-sack hume, pals much like yourselves, Mr. Sapless the Pro Consul, and some Krayal scale-heads before they got diced!" His fist slammed into his palm theatrically. Nessan's eyes popped. "The messenger fella eventually slipped through to us in the Occupied Lands, those of us who still owe Stilgen and whom Mabius can't be assed to butcher. They were sent off in all directions." He bowed with a flourish. "And 'ere I am!"

When neither human replied, Breasal scratched his rump unhelpfully, gave a rasping cough, then spoke in a conspiratorial whisper: "All this intel's for a small charge, of course!"

"Wait! Just wait." Aaron breathed, for once forgetting the gnats that were feasting on his face. "They sent word ... via you, to us? I'm talking of the regent here!"

"Huh." He sniffed. "I ain't had nothing to do with regents or humes, hume!"

Aaron spluttered. "Is Ayilia—the regent I mean—a prisoner?"

"Yes ... except that's wrong, so no!"

Aaron leaned close. Very close. Breasal gulped. "Don't talk, dead man—listen. Then nod. If you don't nod and instead indulge in further twattle, I'll twattle your head clean off and you can watch it twatteling its way down the nearest sump." Aaron held his finger up to his lips. Breasal nodded, for once holding a respectful silence. "The very few of us who've met Stilgen say he was unusual for Pit. Highly aware, astute. I think maybe he saw such a day coming, when the Imperium might return. He covertly made plans?" He gave Breasal a hard look. "Am I right? Don't speak—just nod."

Breasal nodded.

"Good. I think he was prepared. They went together, your lot and mine—the regent, Kemet, Vespasian, Stilgen, Soren, Kofi, the scale heads Seftus and Jarong. I think they had no choice and probably no time. Right?"

He nodded once more, then opened his mouth, but Aaron's hand plugged it swiftly closed. "All I want to know is, did Stilgen actually send word to us, or are you flying by the seat of your britches—as in, talking baloney?"

Breasal's face squeezed with internal pressures. His mouth urged to move. The effort to stay quiet seemed to be nearly killing him.

Aaron released him. "Okay, you can talk."

"Yes! I have coordinates for a rendezvous off-world. Probably already out of date, but we have to hurry all the same. There's no knowing how long they can wait." He spat. It was infuriating. Nessan wanted to thump him but managed to hold off. "It explains why I'm so pissed off. I knew I'd be the one to find you! I knew I'd be the one saddled as your guide. Unlike my dishwashing compatriots who also went looking for you, I don't need or want this—I have skills, you know."

"Stilgen's got more grey stuff than I gave him credit for." Aaron stroked his bug-bothered head, deep in thought. He regarded Breasal again, his eyes glinting. "Despite your 'skills,' your flea-bitten rear end has clearly got no future under this new order, so you're forced to come with us anyway. Tell me about the regent. Is she alright? Tell me quickly, dead man, as I haven't decided about you yet!"

Breasal shot him a murky red stare. His eyes were rheumy, almost pink, nothing like the shock of scarlet of the off-world breed. "Not that I care, but I assume so, live man. She was, apparently, seen guffing out the portal. Considering there are many thousands of destinations in this part of the void alone, I can't rule out she ain't propping up the stomach lining of a giant mollusc right now." He cleared his throat, loudly. "And by the way, I ain't necessarily finished here. I got skills, you know!"

Nessan looked at the commander with disbelief. "Guffing?"

"Don't ask," Aaron growled.

"I would be only too pleased to help you, my new friends and your wonderful, watery tissue." Breasal grinned suddenly, changing tack. "But context first." He tried to look gravely serious. "This dump of a world is a forlorn backwater fit only for midges, but once it might've had mining potential or archaeological significances for the Ancients, who built these portals of whom we speak."

"Of which we speak," Nessan immediately corrected. "Portals aren't people!"

"That's exactly what I tell them, hume female." He leaned forward to whisper darkly, "Many, many other worlds have secondary and thirdary jump gates."

"It's not 'thirdary,' Breasal," Nessan muttered. She gave the impression she was beginning to feel like its personal assistant.

Breasal didn't respond, obliviously lost in his own diatribe. "The Pit was built much later, around the biggest and most reliable portal by far on this sewer of a desert world, hence its position in the middle of absolutely nowhere. You see"—he moved closer to Nessan, who leaned away— "millions of years ago, the area was probably fertile wetland, or a great gleaming, metropolis, or maybe even a fairly priced tavern!"

"Not sure that exists anywhere," Aaron said.

Breasal continued, "After the Ancients winked out, we had the vaguely libertarian Interregnum and its pointlessly benign dysenteries. It went teats-up against the nexus of crushed worlds, the Core, run by the Blighted Curse at ... Nethergeist." He hissed the name. "Of course, it's now the epicentre of the Imperium, the largest, meanest bag of crap-guts ever voided into existence. Not even the Arse-ten could stop them!"

"The Asthen," Nessan snapped. "And I think you meant dynasties before!"

Breasal attempted a hurt look. "It's my accent. Meat-sacks like your good selves don't understand my refined way of spoking!"

Aaron held his finger up. "Finish, now, or I'll show you what being dead really means!" Breasal tried to look indignant, but somehow triggered such a severe coughing fit that he covered Aaron's breastplate in green phlegm.

Nessan burst out laughing.

Breasal pulled a disgusting rag from his pocket and attempted to clean the mess, but that only made it worse.

"Stop that, for the love of God," Aaron protested.

Bresasl shrugged and pocketed the rag. Aaron furiously wiped the gunk away with water from his flask. The Lifeless straightened himself, immensely satisfied. "You meat bags don't know how lucky you are, having me around."

Nessan was giggling uncontrollably, but Aaron gave him a murderous look. Probably out a sense of self-preservation, the Lifeless decided to finish the story. "I was a soldier once, and before Abandonment I could have been a great physician!" Silence. "Okay, I was just a cog wiper and fixer. I was known for providing anything you needed for the right coin, but so you know ... I didn't do it."

Stunned silence.

"Alright, I did do it. It was an accident, mostly, and they successfully sewed his head back on."

Aaron felt his jaw slack to his belt.

"Listen, he wasn't that important, and he could still work the grinders. I was only a freshly stitched greenhorn then." Breasal smiled winsomely. "Now, you have to stop changing the subject, hume. The alternative portal we now seek is only known to a few, outside of the Krayal one up north. However, it's a real titch!"

"Where?" Aaron muttered, still covered in green. "*Where is it?*"

"Commander, understand your reputation is just as sullied to us as it is to everyone else! Give time for mistrust to bloom! Think of the glorious death-orchid that only opens when the blood from a hawk's kill patters as vermillion rain on its root. If I deceive, I perish. If I reveal the location too readily, I perish! We need time to ... bond." His toothy beam was as reassuring as a prehistoric ice wolf's. "Rest assured, dear living, breathing, haversacks of gut-gas, I talk of a sister portal, a tiny sibling of the one in the Pit. Stilgen and I discovered its possible location down south, somewhere not too far from here by happenchance going thru the secrets in the Pit's centuries-old book-stable."

"Library?" Nessan sighed.

"I said that, hume." He growled. "In all truth, sister portals are a phenomenon so uncommon I've never heard of one, not in all my learnings—but then again, I don't learn. The funnel has some reported targeting difficulties, but at least it's close to its bigger relative. Who knows why the Ancients—"

"Okay, for the love of God, I give in! We'll go as soon as we're rested." Aaron turned to Nessan. "Please keep an eye on this deadbeat. If he's lying at any point, you know what to do, and don't feel bad about having to do it. These things aren't alive and never have been—isn't that right, Breasal? Hardly a sin, killing a dipstick of wet mud and wonky bone!"

Breasal pretended to look upset, but his eyes were shining. "Fret not. Bigotry flourishes the greatest among the deliberately ignorant. I'd probably have already killed me if I was him, and if I were me, I'd certainly kill him."

Nessan looked disturbed. Aaron, as he grappled with his insect-marked, reddening head, managed a final mutter, "I have a feeling he does this all the time."

Chapter Four
Hive Mentality

A dark shape blotted out the light before landing effortlessly on the ground, directly opposite the altar. Ayilia backed away. She'd tried to escape, but the walls were too high. The simplistic space, a hexagonal bolt hole, was scarred with demonic images and bathed in a tangerine light. The atmosphere was stultifying, the altar enmeshed with barbed razors. It sounded like something gnawing its way through an adjacent cell.

The shape mumbled something, but she didn't understand. That typical Nethergestian dialect again, archaic as shit.

She nodded towards the exit. "Try the next hovel down the road!"

It uncurled from a crouching squat in the shadows. "Kneel on the pentacle, within the offering dais."

Ayilia shook her head. Her forehead was damp in the suffocating heat, her body caked with sweat. "Why don't you!"

It regarded her darkly. "The covey necessitates compliance."

"I'm still not going anywhere near that thing!"

It paused. Clearly, it wasn't used to resistance. "You are ... honoured incubator, an esteemed privilege in this colony."

Ayilia shook her head.

With impressive dexterity, the thing flipped close. Amid a wave of revulsion, Ayilia swung her foot and kicked it squarely on the twitching end before pivoting on the other to swing against the creature's head. It yammered in pain. Ayilia smacked her palm in the same spot, following that with another kick. The creature was both reassuringly sensitive and completely unprepared for prey to fight back. As it wavered uncertainly, she whammed her foot into its thorax with all the strength she had.

It buckled and scuttled back.

"Apostasy!"

"Satisfying." She beamed royally.

"Do you realise—"

"I realise I might've narrowly avoided one of those pupae being shoved in places it just doesn't belong!"

It breathed heavily, as if considering its options, but stayed where it was. Eventually, it spoke. "The covey requires acquiescence!"

"The covey can require whatever it likes." Ayilia snorted. "But, if you try something again, I'll pull your feelers out one by one."

It hissed from between the chitinous segments yet retracted the point of the abdomen. An intense silence followed before it spoke again, startlingly soft now. "Hear me, child," it murmured. "The parturient, those like you, are highly venerated during rarefaction. We are indeed ... benevolent. The Selected, the being that you were, is melded into the apiary but remains conscious, enhanced. It is the Transpiration. All hurt is banished, inside and out, once the Selected is commuted into the hive reticulation. Believe! The body transmutes, and you will be joyous!"

"Transpiration?"

"The degradation of a supercilious relic, you, the parturient, to elated servitude within the apiary mind. You will no longer be severed from consciousness. The Transpiration is the joining, the birthing into the colony." It's eyes gleamed. "It is species rapture."

"I see, but this 'relic' prefers to stay severed. It's a health thing."

The creature leaned menacingly close. "We once craved strain isolation, like you. The forced Transpiration by the Unholy One *enriched* our hive soul. Without Him, we nestled like individual fungi, germinating unaware among rock and shingle under a dark sky. Now, our will has stellar reach, significance once impossible for the mud-dwellers we were and defence from the avarice of the separated who violated our past!

"We cannot breed; the apiary is symbiotic but sterile. We are a race of neuter helots serving the Master Goat, the self-same god that delivered us. We feed only when necessary, as is the will of kismet. But your kind, your strain of existence, takes life for hate, not just for sustenance. You brutalise the soul out of every world you touch!"

It seemed to be desperately searching inwards for words. "We are fortunate. No Imperial garrisons reside here; no legions drive us, succour was plentiful. Our regulated autonomy is preferable to the baleful antipathy of yore. The price? Dependence on His munificence, His grace! But now His war is won, the future is precarious. The colony needs the parturient more than ever for procreation. We need you!"

Ayilia suddenly felt fearful. It wanted to alter her via sympathy into what appeared to be an arthropod-breeding machine. It was self-governing slavery, forced cooperation. The hive were super-slaves, top dogs of all the helots, free to kill whoever didn't sport Imperial insignia. It wanted the renegade human to consent to the ending of her own life, an elevated death into something else. So absorbed had it become in its act of individual genocide, it failed to notice her inching something down her grimy sleeve.

Her fingertips touched the metal of the dirk she kept under the arm of her tunic, easily missed during their rudimentary search. Its senses started screeching inside her head, like cerebral klaxons. It had become aware of its own peril. A "bug's sixth sense" had kicked in, picking out the killer in her "simplified" mammalian mind.

Ayilia felt the cool hilt slip into her palm. The creature's breath was rasping on her cheeks, sickly sweet.

"Accept," it stuttered. "There is only partial suffering. The host is devoured from within, but without fully realising. The higher functions of its encephalon must merge into the apiary."

"Stop using big words—it's far too hot!" She took a step forward. "And it doesn't change the fact you're still killers."

"Are your kind so different?"

She flicked the knife round and moved to slit its windpipe and gut it.

"You wish to leave?" it hissed. "To find the Phoenix? Are you the golden thief? Many seek it, but none will find it! The Sythian warlord Mabius will reach it first!"

She stopped, rooted to the spot. "You know?"

"We are culturally hermetic, but not fools. All know... everywhere! They say Al Kimiya is incarcerated in a golden oval on the edge of forever. Why do you think you are chosen when your kind are thaumaturgically sterile? They say you know the oval's location. The Goat thinks you sense its carapace. He thinks your insight will lead Him there, at the apex of the General's forces. Imagine, the value your memories would bring this hive. How many of us you would save. We *need* your compliance."

Momentarily, the slim, hot metal between her fingers was forgotten. It was the only protection within a surreal sea of compartments and fog. Lurking overhead, the transparent canopy of streamers formed a grotesque chandelier around the polyp in the centre. Creatures sped with ease along fronds, filament highways in the sky.

It was loathsome having to decide whether to kill it, but escape was paramount. "Listen! There's no map to some mythological psychoneurotic, wizard; I can use big words too! You've been conned. We all have."

It rose high. "Your gods are dead, and so is hope. When Al Kimiya lies slain, an Imperial scythe will suck the lifeblood of an entire universe. Some essence, a scrap of your mammalian mind, will be preserved by us in a hermetically sealed membrane, a receptacle for the unfettered Untermensch. With this priceless gift, we shall bargain for this hive while we have time."

She spat back, "What the hell does that even mean?"

But it leapt forwards, and the blade twisted awkwardly in her grasp. It had talked its way to survival. She'd been caught out far too easily, again. It hadn't always been that way. Agefi had seen something inside her from the start, but she'd always refused to accept it. The very thought of him, brought a slew of memories that fleetingly overwhelmed her.

"Everything's a preparation for what's to come, Ayilia." Agelfi smiled, looking at birds pirouetting over slate waters. The three suns had turned the skies silver, but a cloudbank was drawing near, small flickers of charge

already visible. It promised to be bad, *she thought,* but not a planet-wide one, not this time.

Ayilia was still young enough not to listen, yet he'd more than once revealed he thought she was different. Though he had sworn there wasn't a trace of theurgy inside her, his Magi senses picked up something indefinable, perhaps something dangerous. Of course, he'd never admitted the last part; she'd just knew he was feeling it. Yet, he'd insisted, such a thing was impossible for someone who belonged to a race of beings incapable of gift. Nevertheless, something was there and the Heretics, the Magi leaders of the Resistance, refused to believe it and that clearly infuriated him.

Yet, it was hardly surprising he'd eventually conceded. After all, he was past his prime. He, more often than not, got things wrong. He even confessed that one day, they'd actually retired him on medical grounds. Undiagnosed, thaumaturgic dementia slowly ate away at his mind and there was nothing anyone could do. The person he once was had already died; he was just good at hiding it. He could not be relied upon to deliver what the Resistance needed anymore. He was tolerated.

Even so, Agelfi had snorted openly in derision. Animated suddenly. he claimed the way things were going, the Resistance would likely die off quicker than he would. Already there were rumours that their forces were going the same way as the Asthen Ascendancy and the Interregnum and many others before. Once they were gone, there would be no one left to fight the Goat. The universe would be His. Ominously, Agelfi had finished his diatribe with a warning. Ayilia had to be prepared. He was the only one who could train her to meet the killers when they came for her, but it would be her wits, or her sword, that would likely have to do the work—once she had grown up of course.

However, inside, Ayilia didn't really care. Outside the fact it sounded like baloney, her highest and only priority was to survive her own people and their insular ways. Talk of far-off Imperial demons and the Goat, at such a young age, even then felt ridiculous.

Fortunately, there was a dragon-kyte to fly and seaside creamed-ice to eat, though no one in Ayilia's city knew how to make proper ice so it was mostly cream. Her one and only friend at the time, Ylana, was also with them, and she seemed particularly bored.

"Take our enemies," Agelfi winked, desperately trying to find his pipe as he shifted on the overly stony shingle.

"I don't have any enemies," Ayilia snapped, too proud to admit to her status of elevated loneliness.

"Of course, you don't," he muttered in a hurry. "I was, of course, talking figuratively. Ahh, there it is." He picked up the pipe from a wine-coloured pouch packed with phials, medicines, and feathered bundles. "However, what people don't realise is it is often a blessing to have the odd enemy, from time to time. "

"What do you mean?" her friend asked, appalled.

Jarrak grunted from a comfy wicker chair. He always had a knack for finding the most comfortable things to sprawl on. Ayilia smiled to herself. She could tell Agelfi was letting him think he was simply a clapped-out sorcerer, or at best, an enigmatic magus. As long as he remained beneficial for Ayilia's development, her safety even, Jarrak just about put up with him.

"Never ask a Magi anything directly, girls. You'll never get a direct answer!" Jarrak said, impressed at his own wisdom.

"I mean," Agelfi replied, clearly pleased that someone was actually showing an interest in his wittering. "I mean, life is about challenges as well

as joy. They define us. They make us into the people we are, leaving behind the people we were never meant to be. True joy has to be earned. We cannot be entitled enough to think these things are free, or that we would even appreciate them without the thorny road that takes us there. Personally, I find challenges and completing them far more satisfying than drifting along, having everything handed to me. There are lessons only a detractor can give. Some in my order, though I admit it's tough to comprehend, believe we should actually be grateful to them, thank them even!"

"Why?" they both asked, stupefied.

"Well, imagine" he mumbled gently, "what kind of life would that be … if you could eat creamed ice all day long and not get ill?"

"Fantastic!" they both yelled.

"Of course." He grinned, eyes twinkling. "But eventually, it'd get tiresome. Think how quickly you'd get bored if your birthday was every day, after all!"

"No chance!" Ayilia and Ylana shouted in perfect unison.

"I remember how you loved the horse bridle and the expensive dirk your father gave you, Ayilia." He winked. "And yet, it was always the little things you loved the most, not the expensive stuff." He shook his pipe. "Okay, silly examples perhaps, but if we were spoilt every day of our lives and had no need for endeavour, what then?"

Ylana and Ayilia exchanged perplexed glances.

"Think of all those achievements waiting for you, the skills learned, the amazing journeys taken with kin and kith … that is joy, not how we look or our perceived status."

"God's teeth man, do you always have to lecture them?" Jarrak groaned, sounding anxious to go back to sleep. "Let them have some fun."

"Why the bad things, though?" Ylana piped up. She'd been studying the seabirds skimming over the brine. "They happen all the time. My mum's best friend was killed by a horse and cart, the same day her husband died on that boat, the one I told you about before."

Jarrak flinched. "See what you did, wizard. She'll have nightmares for weeks now!"

Agelfi nodded sagely. The girls exchange knowing glances. "Well?" they said.

"Well, that is admittedly a tough one, and I'm afraid I don't know. Some challenges are tougher than others ... but it is rare in life we face something we're given that we're not resilient enough to handle. Sometimes, I think our souls are the ones that choose the journey to come, not fate."

They raised their brows quizzically. Ylana squealed, "That's no good, I thought you knew everything!"

"Who told you that?" he replied mockingly.

"You did." They giggled again in unison.

"Well..." He seemed to ponder his words. "Very bad things do happen, and if you live long enough, they will touch all lives. They are upsetting and not very nice at all, but life does have to go on. No one lives forever, so our existence is defined by the time we are given. It's all about community—and the more you give, without expecting anything, the more the universe gives. Some of the problems we face are from the choices we make and the thoughts we think. But such lessons can also make us rich!"

"We get rich by helping others? I don't get it."

"Not in money, Ayilia—rich in experiences and fellowship. You do not tread that path without unseen help on the way. Setbacks gives you the skills for things ahead. Without setbacks, there is no impetus for growth and there is no growth, period."

Ylana wasn't having it. "It sounds horrid."

Jarrak stood up suddenly, unable to conceal his vexation. "By the gods, Agelfi, you're doing our nuts in, especially as my head's been burnt by those cursed suns listening for so long to this claptrap. Let's get some more flavoured ice before it melts. That witless vendor's ice box got broken by his three-legged mule and let all the cold air out!"

"Excellent." Agelfi beamed happily. "Once we've loaded up on what hasn't completely melted, we'll head for the quayside for a quick stroll before that nasty-looking squall hits. Gather your stuff quickly, girls, or I'll get told off by assorted parents if we're late, again!"

And with that, they left.

Six months later, Ylana went to another school and Ayilia never saw her again, likely whisked away from her by the parents. It always happened. When they realised she had that "curse," the one that let her sense things. No matter what she did, the adults looked at her oddly and the kids her age huddled, mouthing that word only an adult could have taught them:

"Witch!"

She tried to treat loneliness as an opportunity. She forged sword skills, learned as much as she could, grew into her role. She joined the X Gemina, the regency guard, on missions to the bad lands, the Occupied Territories. Ayilia learned how to keep the sodden Pit guards, those mobile cadavers, from harming a world of enslaved humans. In reality it wasn't too bad. Some of the Pit were fun, surprisingly gentle. One or two even became friends after Abandonment, when the Imperium left their world as it was too pitiful to bother with and the outpost became a toothless ruin, no longer interested in power.

But even those ultimately melted away.

The creature's blood splattered its front, staining its shiny carapace. It collapsed immediately, its head lolling backwards, a gash in its throat. As it slumped across her boots and lay twitching among the spreading fluids, Ayilia tried not to retch.

Using the corpse as an impromptu stepladder, she sprung up the walls, managing to get a fingerhold at the top. Her boots squeaked against the surface, but there was no leverage, so she swung across the wall like a human pendulum and gained the momentum to pull up. Within moments, she was clambering across a catacomb maze overlooking rooms that contained opaque cocoons and wriggling shapes. As she fled, a murky shape leapt upwards from a cell. Without pausing, Ayilia slit its milky head open, immediately covering herself in gore. Glancing downwards as she ran, she caught a glimpse of a dying larva, her Kimiya senses seemed to think, created from the remains of people like her—a hybrid predator.

She inadvertently thought of the politicians back home.

Ayilia ran faster. After a sprint, she reached a winding path that ran throughout a subterranean metropolis without roofs or homes. It looked unused. The things seemed to prefer the fronds for travel.

The Al Kimiya interloper imprint perked up. She had a sense of an exit far off in the distance and sped towards it and what looked like a low-level frond, bloody knife in hand.

It worked. First time, too Barrackus thought.

The unused portal, nicked round the gloriously carved edges, irised open into infinity in front of them. Barrackus stepped forwards but was blocked by Sheyna.

"Oh no. This time, it's me!"

She turned and regarded the edifice. The portal stood on a grand plinth of the purest glass. It rose majestically above the crystalline canopy of a glassy forest, one that rippled in quartz sheens. Red flowers like poppies were scattered throughout and along the rustling branches.

"Hold it, Sheyna, I—"

"No, it's always you. I'm going in first, whatever you say."

"Ah." He smirked. "Nothing like respect for one's seniors."

"You're right, it's nothing like respect," she chided softly. "You are obsessed, Barrackus, with the rigidities of ritual."

"Umm, I quite like them."

Sheyna leaned forwards. "I don't—not when we're going to get killed on a kamikaze outing." She flashed him an unexpected smile. "Don't worry; I promise to behave ... whenever the others are listening."

She stepped through. Immediately, her form haloed into pinpricks, then vanished. Andromedus, kneeling beside the controls, watched darkly.

"She's one feisty Side Arm," Andromedus breathed a bit too loudly.

His tone grated. Barrackus faced him sharply. "You sure the settings are correct?"

"Aye, sir."

"You're *positive* they can't follow."

"I laid a false trail leading *well* away from the Core. Frankly, no one in their right mind would head towards that death zone if they didn't have to. Anyway, they can't Track us for long with my abilities—I'll bet my life on it." His tone was significantly surlier than before. A surge of uncharacteristic irritation rose in Barrackus. The man was becoming quietly disobedient in front of his eyes.

"Betting your life on it is exactly what we're all doing." He turned and faced the others. "Alright everyone, Xylon battle stance. Follow me." He entered the kaleidoscopic inferno as quickly as he could.

CHAPTER FIVE

GRAVEYARDS OF VERILLION

The jump ended in a heartbeat, though it felt longer. Barrackus was propelled uncontrollably forwards as he came out of the exit. The gate was virulent—for its size, it packed a shocking punch. He'd never experienced anything like it, but they were in a portal universe within a universe, and maybe even an eternally functioning funnel had difficulties. Barely able to balance, the Raider leader skidded into something hard and solid. The granite gravestone that broke his exit juddered but held. Clumps of moss pattered over him like a brown snowfall.

Something was odd, but his mind was a fug. His breathing was laboured, his movements sluggish. The atmosphere was damp, cloying. Cloudy puffs hung in hazes after each breath, dissipating slowly. Though residues of portal light still sparked across his sight, he realised that debris was drifting languidly in front of his face.

"What?"

"It's the atmosphere. It's heavy."

"Sheyna?"

"Here!"

He swung round. She was standing, weapon drawn, a few hands off. Beyond her shoulders flowed a sea of variously sized tombs, with broken stones and twisted ironwork. It hung suspended in the air, moving slowly but with purpose. It was a stream absent of water, headed towards a misty horizon. Trees hung over vaults grimly resplendent with fantastical shapes. Their chiselled impassiveness shone eerily among the supine figurines of unknown deities. Their empty faces, frozen mouths, and petrified curls watched the growing band of fighters spill out from the lichen-encrusted gate with apathetic splendour.

"We're in hell." She grimaced.

"The Graveyards of Verillion. As you ordered!"

They looked up. Andromedus was walking towards them. Somehow, his landing had been better. Had he guessed beforehand? Around him, troops branched out carefully, checking every cluster of ancient brickwork within the mausoleum surrounding them. Opaque worlds hung in the turquoise sky. Their light flicked along the sepulchres, pillars, archways, cracked urns, and cloaked statues as they drifted by.

"Not what I expected from the fables." Andromedus grinned, looking acutely pleased with himself. "It's run down, in all truth—no maintenance anymore, none at all." He rubbed rheumy eyes that were sinking deeper into receding sockets, supporting ever-more-hanging jowls. "We've jumped deep ... *unbelievably* deep. You can thank me for that; no one else could've done it and not been seen. Essentially, we piggybacked behind some Imperial traffic along their collective wake, like cosmic shit. All this in *one* go, a single jump that leaves less trace than if we had stopped and started over two dozen times, which is how far we've come."

He rubbed his hands in satisfaction. He had good reason to be proud, Barrackus admitted to himself. Andromedus, now in his element, continued. "A single, covert jump, if possible a long one, avoids excess tidal displacement. Ripples of disruption, if jumps are repeated often enough, they categorically blow our cover right out the waters. Only way around that—outside a long wait for the static to subside—is open travel on Imperial channels, but that'd blow our cover even quicker." He smiled, his grin widening when his eyes met Sheyna's something that made Barrackus cringe inside. "*Immeasurably* fine timing was required, I might add. One slip and we'd be Goblin meat. I doubt there's another Tracker alive today among us who could've managed that! Having said that, we were lucky to find this long-distance funnel. I've never seen anything like it in the open networks, only this hidden lair."

"You did well Andromedus, no doubt, but does it lead us to the Core group of worlds at the centre?" Barrackus said quietly, still finding it impossible to believe they had reached such a legendary place.

The Dust Tracker's eyes were gleaming. "Dramatically closer." His voice sank to a conspiratorial whisper. "We've already gone further than anyone. However," he growled, studying his shoes. "there's fewer inhabited worlds and moons in the Core, compared to the swarm in the central and outer zones. It's going to be much, much harder, to avoid detection. The number of liveable places that aren't guarded diminishes along with the quality of the inhabitable environments available to us. It's why we're here. Rough and ready for sure, but no military or strategic value and, in all likelihood, deserted."

Sheyna looked unconvinced. "I'd thought the Imperium would love a place like this?"

"There's nothing to love. Verillion is an exotic fable, but the place is dead. Always has been, always will be—well, as far as recent timelines go—don't be fooled by the undergrowth. It's bereft of any raw materials, has nothing to exploit, and has a poor oxygen count, which is vital for a thrall labour force and the beast troop warding them. The Imperium hates nonstrategic occupations that don't pay their way, especially ones that have no Indigenous population to co-opt or arable land to exploit!" His voice became a warning. "It's also *full* of dangerous, wild theurgy from the time of the Ancients, hence the floating real estate. The further in we go, the more sorcery-poisoned the Core becomes, though only the gods know what the hell happened here." He scratched his nostrils, which were sprouting ungainly, stubby black hairs, then sighed. "We're so far in, I doubt they'll believe we're here anyway."

Sheyna shot Barrackus a look. "This place is an Imperial wet dream!"

Andromedus seemed lost in a world of wonder still. "This cemetery is gigantic. From what I've read, it blankets this world from pole to pole, holding war dead from all sides, from battles so ancient they precede even the Emperor Goat. There're so many unused portals here, they're like petrified worm holes in putrefied rusks. Clearly, this place was critical once." He eyed them carefully. "To the Ancients, of course."

Sheyna inhaled deeply. Barrackus sensed underneath that grand exterior she was just as overwhelmed as he was. "Oxygen count really is appalling here," she grimaced.

"Stands to reason."

"Eh?"

Andromedus scanned the skies with a gold sextant he'd pulled from his pocket. He seemed almost oblivious. "I'm not surprised they let it go … the atmosphere I mean. This world's collapsed. Obviously, only their historians and such ever go here now. We're not just centuries out of date, but millennia!"

"Collapsed?"

"Bluntly speaking, if we stay too long, we'll perish. Only foliage, rodents, and insects have adapted." He scratched an armpit. "The soupy atmosphere will clog our lungs and double them over like pancakes. There's nothing we can do, except limit our stay to no more than two or three days."

"That'll do." Barrackus grunted, inwardly anxious to make camp. "A chance for some *real* rest, unlike that glass weald back there when we were on the run most the time. Andromedus, find the portals for the best routes to the Core and ... Nethergeist."

"Just a league or two over there."

"That close?"

"This place is riddled to the quick with gates for reasons we'll never know. It may even have been a capital world for the Ancients once."

Barrackus ignored the barely concealed testiness. The Tracker had, after all, done an astonishing job. "Sheyna, take us there when ready. If they did trace us, I don't want them to catch us with our proverbial britches down. Tell the scouts to utilise maximum psi for that extra warning."

Sheyna and Andromedus sprang to life. It was like olden times. Simple strategy, understandable command decisions, crystal-clear objectives. Of course, Barrackus was aware the troop secretly prayed for a change of plan. They'd already survived the impossible but how long would it take them to realise their leader would not double back this time, leaving furrows of ruin and slaughter across vast swathes of territory. How long would they remain loyal if they did?

Prowlers huffed, people bustled, and equipment clinked. The Dust Tracker repeatedly triggered the gate's mouth, inserting instruments into the vortex. Obscure pictorials and data spun between the prongs of a theurgy diviner. Mathematical images prismed into clarity as he scrolled through diagrams. The moment he was done hiding their empyreal tracks, they moved out along a series of overgrown pathways that wound through the Byzantine graveyard. Most objects remained fastened reassuringly to the ground, but those that weren't, could cause trouble for the seriously unwary. The growth was dense, but the older shrubs were rotting at the edges. When brushed, they released clouds of yellow vapour with a gut-wrenching stink.

Pieces of basilica floated by, occasionally interspersed with serene looking sacella. Fog rolled across the ground in writhing shapes. To Barrackus, it seemed someone had tipped a rusted chest and released a menagerie of achromatic hobgoblins towards their boots, only to fade into oblivion by the time they got close. Sheyna seemed to especially hate the towering willows. Their leaves draped against exposed faces, while their roots emerged from graves in a web of dank bark. The bone-white crocuses collecting in mournful gatherings over the shrines didn't help her either.

But Barrackus loved the monastic quiet. He closed his eyes and sucked in the richness, felt the unfettered maguey in the air. Asphodels massed in shoals over catacombs preferring the burial casings that were cracked, while floret clusters hugged stone walls. The further they trekked, the greater the concentration of wych elms and wolfsbane growing within creepers and bracken.

Nobody spoke. Eventually, they made camp.

Andromedus set to work immediately on a promising portal. Station guards were posted almost a quarter of a league round the epicentre. Despite everything, it was a rare moment of peace. As Barrackus watched, however, he felt unease. Andromedus was the only Tracker they had—standard procedure, of course. Trackers were in short supply, and each unit was restricted to just one—if any. Though every fighter was trained in gate dynamics, things like daemon locks, navigating unknown territory, and working exotic portals was another level of warfare altogether. Rescue by a compatriot unit was not uncommon, but not this far in.

Andromedus was their only hope.

Barrackus sighed.

Maybe it was the solitude, but he found himself recalling stories of Verillion he'd heard as a child from a weather-beaten chronicler. Bloody and tragic tales. Tales involving fabled spirits roaming ancient woods while lost eidolons crossed the divide between sleep and consciousness. All around, statues floated by in a placid but sinister manner. Nothing stirred. The stillness cloaked every plain, dip and hill. Embalmed by a past they never knew, the soldiers worked in hushed tones.

The Goat was as enigmatic as the race of Ancients who had preceded everyone. He was as inscrutable as the rumoured domain that the Ancients were alleged to have unearthed before they vanished.

Barrackus snorted.

Crap. The gossip mongers, the bitch-bladers, believed anything. They were right about one thing, however. The Asthen Ascendancy was running out of fighters. Despite their leadership, they had always been low in numbers. Centuries of unremitting warfare had left the thaumaturgically gifted species depleted. Absolutely no one was like them, and no one knew why. Before the arrival of the Asthen, the Empire had grown, swelling like the belly of a predator in a pen of oxen. The alliance with other races was strong like the Interregnum before them eons past, and like the Interregnum they pushed back the advance. But not for long.

Barrackus, was an unknown, with a gift no augur understood. He was turning into a legend. His raids went deeper than most, destroyed more than most. Most of the Raiders he took returned. Ruin lay in their footsteps. In public, his name was revered, in private feared, at least among the seniors. They called him a warrior-witch, an obsidian necromancer who lived between life and non-life.

The Asthen leaders tested his powers. They asked Barrackus questions. They asked him if he had the gift of prophecy. He said quite truthfully that he didn't, but the official soothsayer had called him terrible things. It was in their nature to believe the worst, especially the envious. He thought it best to let the detractors founder on the inconsistencies of their scorn, but the process took too long and the corrosive rumours persisted.

"So, you *are* a witch?" one of them had snarled slyly.

He'd bit his tongue, trying not to grow angry. "How I can be that which I so readily slay?"

The accuser had shut up, but the more frightened they grew, the more they'd look for scapegoats. His people were cultured, but the more pressured things got, the more paranoid they became. It was amazing what such things did to apparently sane, educated people. Paranoia could justify anything.

It wasn't all destruction and killing. They had amassed something else—knowledge. They had done what an age of alchemists, scientists, and astronomers could not. Yet, things had gone wrong almost immediately—after a few innocuous jumps, they'd been greeted in that pouring rain by Wirral. Wirral, of all things. Was it an accident? Possibly. They were in a wilderness sector of no use to anyone, but one still bigger than the Ascendancy three times over.

"I know what you're thinking. Stop it!" Sheyna regarded him coolly.

He looked up, eyes darting around in agitation. "The whole bloody universe depends on us, and they don't even know it."

"I said, *stop it*. It's in the hands of the gods. Maybe we can't kill the enemy, but we can deflate them enough for a radical rethink." She patted him on the arm, even though both of them knew full well that he didn't believe in gods. He knew she didn't either. "Didn't you tell me sometime that there'll be others if we fail? Not very reassuring, but it has a ring to it." *Not very reassuring at all*, he thought. "Actually Barrackus, I didn't come to talk to you about the Abomination. There's something over here you should see, beyond that tree line."

"Let me guess, you found Pharsalus' body." He smiled grimly. "And the Imperium's most dangerous general ever is eating worms in one of those graves we just passed."

"I would hope the worms would be eating *him*, Commander. No, this is just ... strange!" With a puzzled look, he followed the Side Arm through trees so petrified they looked more dead than alive. When the branches finally parted, he caught his breath.

"My God!"

"I asked Andromedus already. Unsurprisingly, he was *full* of answers."

"That man's head is filled with every fact going, but not always in the right order." Barrackus put his hand to his brow. "What the hell is this? What does he reckon?"

She didn't answer.

Veering into the sky, stretched a wall of water. It rose so high it became a liquid mountain, with a hazy summit of froth. Seabirds dived at the peak. The water was flowing gradually but purposefully upwards. He could see choppy waves in aquamarine and slate grey. Knotted weed meshed with the watery flux. Eddies formed and reformed within a current that defied gravity. He followed the progress of a twist of kelp as it progressed to the top of the titanic maelstrom in a journey that seemed to go on forever. When it reached the pinnacle, it was lost within the whitest of crests. Playing along the tip of the suspended tsunami, like a rainbow of wraiths, he could see an array of refracted prisms along the foam.

It was astonishingly beautiful.

The trees around them tapered off into white spits and crystal-sanded coves. They went as far as the eye could see. Before them, a dried seabed ran to the base of the wall. It sucked what was left of the sea towards it with tidal ferocity, forming a frozen breaker bigger than a thousand cities. It hung there, silent and unmoving. The lightest of sprays whiskered their faces, forming minute droplets in their hair.

A background hiss was barely audible. It would become a roar if they got close. The power it exuded overwhelmed Barrackus. By chance, the rarest of flukes, a Godlight event, split the sky at the wave's apex. A dozen mini-suns broke through the summit. A tiara of light fired along the rim surrounded by a simmer of magenta. The effect left them speechless. Sheyna's eyes misted as Barrackus forget to breathe. An ellipse of bright phosphorescence flared before vanishing into a soft hue.

They didn't move.

"How ... is ... this ... possible?" Barrackus breathed.

Sheyna sighed. "According to our erstwhile Tracker, it's rampant theurgy from the Ancients, like everything else around these necromantically polluted parts. Obsolete, leftover ... super-magick." She shrugged. Words weren't her thing. "Some say they fought battles so immense, that they necromantically ruined the ecology of everything in charted space, especially the Core itself. The tendrils went out into everything, everywhere. Andromedus claims this world is filling up ever so slowly with vapour. Eventually the atmosphere will condensate into a weak sea. It'll take time—a few million years or so. If we ever get to scalp the Abomination, someone can, apparently, put this right!"

Dizziness overtook Barrackus. Tiredness vied with wonder. He was smiling like an idiot.

Sheyna glanced over at him and broke into a grin. "What? Why's that thing funny?"

"I dunno." He wiped tears from his eyes. "Here we are, facing this frozen wave as high as the eye can see and as powerful as a sun, and our portly friend doesn't even come and look—as he has all the answers, already. All those endless theories! He knows it all, *everything*, before he's even looked at it, before he even knows it's there." He chuckled. "I mean, perhaps the sea likes it this way!"

Eyes watering, Sheyna put her hand over her mouth.

"I can see him officiously stating facts," she said, trying to keep a straight face. "While hordes of Goblins close in to rip us to bits with cavernous jaws and big, fat tongues, saying how they're bred to eat the living 'cos we smell so bad' and that it was 'obvious' this would happen. So, 'what's the big fuss'—it's just the natural order of things, and we should have known anyway!" Sheyna was making as little sense as he was, not helped by the low-grade quality of the air. "Yet he still wouldn't tell us in advance, despite his all-seeing knowledge, that they were there in the bloody first place!"

Barrackus let out a boom of laughter, and Sheyna joined in. In the end, death had been with them so long it had become funny.

Their laughter died immediately when they heard a mild cough. Horrified, they swung round to see Adira, Lars, Skyron and ... Andromedus.

Adira, clearly embarrassed, spoke first. "We thought we'd come and see the ... phenomenon."

Sheyna carefully stepped back, left hand futilely covering her mouth, which was still twitching at the corners. Shame gripped Barrackus. The Tracker's genuine puzzlement made it worse.

The commander stuttered. "Ah, just talking of you ... but only professionally."

Andromedus looked confused. "Portly?"

Barrackus was mortified. He'd never once given into personal cruelty.

Adira quickly stepped in. Sheyna's eyes seemed to narrow at her overly enthusiastic attempt to protect the commander. "Andromedus was telling us about how a massive battle between the Ancients and some unknown foe turned the laws of nature inside out and ... Blast, I can't remember!"

Andromedus attempted to answer, and he did it in the exact way Sheyna had mimicked, which made the whole thing torturous. The man's vaguely blotchy face had reddened, flushing like a drunk. He looked confused, but also like a man incapable of processing complex social situations. Barrackus realised he was infinitively more comfortable with necromancer locks and portal matrixes than the company of people. He mentally kicked himself for being so unprofessional, so personal. Fortunately, the longer the Tracker took to explain, the more the bruised hue vanished as he began to immerse himself within the artificial sanctuary of figures.

"Not massive—we're talking catastrophic," Andromedus corrected, getting into his groove. "The sorcery pollution runs through *all* charted space, it's just that the Core is the epicentre. What we'll see there will be on this scale—the rest of the universe is just a cosmic oil spill in comparison."

Barrackus found himself joining in. "You sure it'll get worse the further in we go?"

"My sextants don't just navigate; they give me timescales. This *staggering* excess of raw power has not deconstructed to chaotic, atomic fuzz, as per the laws of entropy, but remained volatile and highly stable—an impossible feat over such a timescale. Instead of subsiding to a low-energy state of existence over time, it has remained *intensely* caustic. Until it finally erodes, if it does, every physical object in its path will be literally turned upside down."

"So, we are in the maw of a permanent detonation of magick, in essence?"

"Yes, exactly. A frozen explosion of raw power that may only intensify as we go in. It's not uniform, but it *is* common and its effects are utterly unpredictable, considering we've never gone so deep before."

Sheyna edged off quietly, now desperately bored of the man. Barrackus, however, and his Tracker, were jabbering like kids. Adira and Lars gave each other alarmed glances, then quickly followed the Side Arm. Skyron, clearly exhausted, hesitated. He appeared undeniably curious, nevertheless he turned to follow the others. As he did, he announced wanly, "I think grub's up," but neither Barrackus nor Tracker registered, so he shrugged and left.

Each world varied; each had a different sunset and sunrise, sometimes multiple rises and settings in one day. The worst was permanent daylight on places continuously enveloped by suns. Usually, the world was habitable. The network builders, the Ancients, seemed to have had the same set of physical needs as everyone else. As Skyron disappeared back to camp, the two men chatted animatedly. It was rare they were this happy.

"... but who were the Ancients, Andromedus? I mean, you must've picked up *some* indication this deep?"

"Nothing! I doubt even the highest Imperial generals know, except maybe the Abomination and His jackal generals, Myrian and Golub-Yavan. The Ancients vanished ... *Pow*. Gone!"

"Maybe the answers lie ahead?" Barrackus inhaled.

"It gets worse ... or should I say more intriguing."

"Why?"

"When I was searching for Nethergeist itself—"

"You found it? Its exact location?"

"No, but I did find Armerhurst!"

Barrackus was staggered. The man was indeed insane—he had to be. "The old capital world of the Interregnum? God's eyes, they said that didn't exist anymore, that it was legend."

"Well, either the scrolls were wrong, or they were lying."

"Our best scientists, our electromagnetic graviton chartists, the historical telemetry specialists have found nothing, ever! How can you just find it?"

"Simple. I wasn't looking for it ... and it wasn't looking for me. But primarily because, as we've said, we just haven't been this far. All of our records are Imperial-based and, therefore, as valid as the fluff on a steer's ass."

"I'll bear that in mind," Barrackus said, smiling. "Hell, it would be the greatest discovery in modern times. By the gods, man, if we were at peace, you'd be hailed as the greatest scientist of the Fifth Age. Double hell, I'd have to call you sir."

"That'll be the day."

After several moments of contemplative silence, they automatically turned to go, aware, belatedly, of the call to dinner. They left the stricken water cathedral churning behind them.

Six drones pounded in pursuit, their chitinous armour clacking like dice teeth in a pot. Ayilia tore her tunic into a strip and flung it over a frond before tying the ends tightly around each wrist, making an impromptu sling. Something buzzed overhead as she thrust into open space, legs trailing. Before she knew it, she was flying through the dark with considerable speed. She glimpsed thousands of similar strands bunched like arteries across the ceilings, but they swiftly disappeared behind. The wind whisked through her hair, stinging the wounds on her skin.

Perhaps it was her first piece of luck—a series of exits opened ahead, leading away from the subterranean city. It appeared her frond was headed towards the middle. With a degree of relief, Ayilia noticed that the taut strand was levelling. The hurtling acceleration tapered off dramatically, as a light filtered through in a murky burst.

The relief was short lived.

The area was swarming with honeycombed, hexagonal cells. Larvae from every species, from every corner of the occupied universe chewed their way out of comatose shapes. Most appeared humanoid. The sightless eyes of the hosts stared blankly. Mandibles emerged from exposed ribbing, fluid clotted floors. Antennae bristled as creatures with segmented legs struggled from bloody forms.

Something skimmed her knee.

Glancing back, Ayilia saw a drone pursuing, aiming something in her direction. Without breaking momentum, she reached for her blade and swivelled abruptly to face her assailant, swinging both legs into the creature's thorax. As it recoiled, she slammed the knife into a gap between its leathery segments. The thing squealed so loudly she almost let go, yet she managed to slam the blooded weapon into the neck. The noise ceased as it plummeted into the dark.

Her wrists were throbbing. Though the angle was slighter, Ayilia picked up speed. Fronds all around twanged as pursuers joined the chase. She yanked her rope taut, squeezing every ounce of acceleration possible. The escaped "prey" hurtled at terrifying speeds over the chamber. An array of cords twanged loudly, reverberating round her fleeing form. She shifted her weight, balancing the strain across both arms, but it only helped a little.

Her ears were buzzing, and she was feeling faint.

Though she fought to stay awake, she started to black out. An aperture opened inside her mind's eye. She glimpsed a lone candle falling towards a lake of pitch and a vision of fire petals floating within an abyss. She was propelled towards a beach on a world that didn't exist—with water like glass. Ayilia looked up, covered in sand beneath a vast, revolving galaxy. The scene abruptly spun, then rearranged into a vista of hanging gardens with trailing orchids, among a peristyle court of urns and immaculate lawns. The gardens, with their geometric designs and long, gypsum terraces, were entirely surrounded by a desert.

A man was sitting at an old table.

Ayilia took a breath and laid a hand on his shoulder. Soft pink eyes blazed at her from Vespasian's ruined face, before he and the gardens immolated. The vision immediately reformed. She could sense the violator inside, the Phoenix lighting up her senses like a furnace. Now she was a six-year-old child holding her mother's hand on her birthday. Someone coughed, and she turned to see a younger Jarrak smiling. In his outstretched hand he held her present: a blunt, wooden dagger. The impression evaporated, replaced by a torrent of memories. Friends came and went in a revolving door of images, before something cold touched her consciousness. The Kimiya had burrowed deeply within, uninvited and unwanted. Its iris gleamed dully without emotion and focused directly on her, from directly inside.

Her eyes bolted open.

Ayilia thundered into something yielding, jettisoning unquantifiable debris in all directions. She scrambled up, fumbling for balance. A stench, pungent and bitter, nearly made her gag. Three predators thumped into the ground nearby. The nearest was the immediate recipient of a knife thrust that splintered its front as its momentum propelled it onto her blade. She withdrew it with a sucking wrench and kicked the creature over.

The others rose jerkily in pursuit. Ayilia clambered away, thighs deep in unseen muck. A pursuer leapt and grabbed her by the hair. Ayilia swept round and smashed her palm in its face in a timed blow so unexpectedly effective, that the creature flipped backwards. The other kicked her in the side with a limb as hard as a brickbat, while trying to degut her with a curved blade. The woman rolled through the blackness, scrabbling for a footing, the sound of her assailant's approach in her ears. Someone lit a torch. Everything flared up in sharp relief around her in a macabre maze of bone and tattered cloth. Her face inadvertently came to rest against a cluster of ribs and the forehead of a skull with horns and ridges. Ayilia released an undignified yelp as she kicked away femurs, bloody clothing, and rusted metals. Her lungs were squeezing the life out of each and every molecule, in the urgent search for oxygen in a room depleted of it.

A shadow flitted. A weapon glinted. She rolled again, grabbing a bludgeon of bone, and parried a blow more sensed that seen. The bone gave out a hollow *clock* and shattered into specks, yet she managed to slam her right leg into the assailant's abdomen. Caught unawares, it stumbled backwards. Energised, Ayilia reached for another heavy cudgel and slammed it against the thing's cranium as it lurched back to attack.

Finally, it fell.

Ayilia stood still, breathing heavily. Sweat ran off her in sheets, and her dagger hand was dark with filth. A deafening clicking rose from white pupae around her.

She was isolated.

A frond quivered, signalling fresh arrivals.

Ayilia slid down a hill of discarded bodies, part on her ass, part on all fours, over the remains of a vast, broken cog. The arthropod highway was a twanging tempest. A group was coming. Ayilia wrestled her knife out and severed the fibre. It parted with a loud thwack, whiplashing upwards along with a dozen creatures. Teeth clenched, she slashed all the overhead cords she could reach, then fled towards the floor.

She ran without pause. The area was poorly lit, but she made out squirming larvae as needle jaws tried to slice her calves. As she ran, she slit them open, leaving a gloop of blue-veined flesh. There was a dimly lit passage beyond, so Ayilia bolted over as many heads as possible, her outline pirouetting among a field of pupae. Her weapon flashed like a conductor's wand in the gloom, but there was no orchestra to follow.

The stink was overpowering. Nurseries passed in a blur. There were no strands above her, but the creatures were still following. Blood cloaked one half of her face. Scuttling sounds came from everywhere. They knew the place well and saw clearly in the dark.

The clicking grew. The things were probably swearing at her. If she had the energy, she'd have called them names back. The blood gushed through her head while her body flagged. Not only was she not picking up speed, she was slowing down. One came sprinting up, effortlessly gliding over the bobbing heads. The instinct to survive was overwhelming. Turning abruptly, she whacked the wet blade into the head of the leading pursuer. As it fell, Ayilia dropped to her haunches and held the weapon to its throat. The small group skidded to a halt. Prey didn't do such things, especially the female ones.

Ayilia spat out a clot of blood. Somehow, she'd bitten the skin on the inside of her mouth.

"Back off or he's bug meat," she hissed in the best Nethergestian she could manage.

"Concede!" the nearest replied unexpectedly.

"I concede I want to be out this crap hole." She smiled sardonically, taking heavy breaths. "However, if you don't back off, I'll turn him into cootie chow."

Others were coming. Ayilia was spent—she couldn't fight anymore. The wounded arthropod she'd refused to kill shifted uneasily.

"Listen, bug balls, I'm a merciful human—trust me, there aren't many left. Speak truthfully and you keep your antenna! Is there another way out of here other than the main atrium we just came from?"

It answered immediately in pure Nethergestian, though its accent and dialect made it hard to follow. "There are many exits in each demesne. All flow along the back walls."

"Where?"

"Not far off. Pray the fronds reach them." It leaned close. "For us this is ... sport."

"You don't get out much, do you? Last chance."

"They run to your grave."

Ayilia pressed the cutter so hard it flinched. Fluid spluttered over her hand.

"Overflow ducts below, down that hole, there ... prevents gridlock during storm flooding ... Ducts run to ... outside."

"Thanks. You've been *most* helpful."

She kicked it over and bolted in the direction it had indicated. As she went, she heard it cry, "It won't make a difference ... you're the meat now."

The others pursued without pause. In a surprisingly short time, she reached the hole, a gap in the floor by the wall. Grabbing a strand, she dropped so rapidly the wind sang in her ears. She felt it vibrate as the others leapt on the same frond. The level below was a plateau of foundries. Pipes enveloped in red scale arched away from a metallic leviathan decaying away at the seams. Ayilia dropped further, fully bypassing the next layer, one containing a smelting centre and hills of sulphur. The hive's extracted ores were being heated with noxious-smelling chemicals producing base metals likely bound for the Imperium. The acrid stink of bituminous, superheated coal hurt her lungs. She recognised the glowing by-product, a black carbon. It lay near a succession of blast furnaces at the back. Oxidised kiln machines fired up in sheets of flame. Her Kimiya senses downloaded impressions of metallurgical processes involving zinc, magnesium, and possibly lead.

She couldn't have cared less.

Rickety bridges crisscrossed fields of melted amber. Trains of humanoid thralls from dozens of species crawled like sorrel termites, appearing shockingly similar to humans. They worked as they fell, the dead being disposed of in a lake where they liquefied into feed for larvae. The slaves were making tools for the old and being fed to the young. Ayilia free-fell to the bottom, running the moment her feet touched ground, blade glinting in her hand. A dozen soldiers spun around.

Inside, her Phoenix annexed mind went into overdrive. Somewhere, something answered. She was an automaton. To stop was to fall. She was someone else.

Ayilia cut down the first guard without a thought and took its sabre. Sprinting, muscles filled with fire, she sprang airwards, legs scissoring midair at the nearest two, kicking them into an indigo tributary, where they burned. Slaves hunched down in terror or dived into holes.

She sheathed her weapon, preferring the agility of the sabre, which reminded her of a favoured blade. It buzzed like a hummingbird as it cut one, then another, then another, with sickening lightness. The guards fell in hollow thuds around her, like disjointed mannequins. They were unable to touch her, even in pairs. She was a thresher cutting a grisly harvest.

At one point, the sword was yanked from her grip as it stuck in the head of a tough-skinned unfortunate. Surrounded but energised, Ayilia kicked one over with her hard boots. The constricted pathway was restricting their ability to manoeuvre. She redrew her dagger to kill another where it stood. A few more collided and slipped in their scrabble to retreat, as another cowered on its knees, transfixed in terror. Ayilia gestured it away. The slave-killer bolted in disbelief.

Amidst a squall of negative emotions, Ayilia felt confident yet contemptuous—a Kimiya-enhanced god standing within a mausoleum of her own making. Before the coup in her home city of Agathon, she'd never killed. Now she was a serial destroyer, and it felt deranged. The bloodlust began to pass, replaced by weariness. Her blade banged against the exposed cartilage of her knee, unwittingly prompting a loud yell and an expletive.

She sagged against a rock, oblivious to the wide-eyed astonishment of a growing group of enslaved.

It was obvious that there was nothing that could be done for the captives. She was alone. Yet, she hesitated.

"Hume, over here!"

Swivelling round, she scanned a row of bobbing heads. Ahead of some gingerly advancing bugs, she saw a shape frantically waving.

"Seftus!"

The relief almost knocked her off her feet.

"By the gods, give me a weapon, hume," he called, "or I'll use one of these wretches here as a living battering ram!"

Grinning madly, Ayilia tossed him a discarded "bug blade." It spun haphazardly, but Seftus caught it deftly, grunting as he did. Only then did she see his bonded wrists. The Krayal bent down with the weapon in between his knees and severed the twine. Within a flash, he was wielding the sword mercilessly among a recently arrived arthropod attack force. He must have looked more frightening than she did, as a number began fleeing immediately, despite his desperate pleas for them to stay and die. A burly thing tried to gut him but, almost on an afterthought, Seftus severed its head so cleanly that the cranium bounced bloodily across the floor and clacked against the legs of four new arrivals, even as it was mouthing obscenities. Clearly, they'd never encountered prey like this either, and they split in all directions with impressive alacrity.

"We've got to move, hume!"

"That's *all* I've been doing!"

"Plenty more coming from the rest of the nest." He looked thoughtful. "By the gods, that rhymes!"

"Wait."

"Wait ... *what*?"

"Can't do this."

"Can't do what?" He was genuinely perplexed. "If you're getting the shakes dicing some aphids, leave that to me! It's what Krayal do best!" His brow puckered as he realised how dumb that sounded.

"Can't leave ... *them*!" Ayilia pointed at the thralls.

She hurried over and started hacking at their bonds. Whole rows were scrabbling out of the dips and ravines between the rises. She worked feverishly, grimacing with the effort. It was short work but not swift enough—Seftus looked up and, despite his bravado, appeared to be dismayed to see a disorganised pack of reinforcements filling the gangways. Standing fully upright, he turned to face them.

"Hell's teeth! Be quick, hume; they're really bugging me this time!"

"Hooooold!"

"Hold what?"

"Just a few more!"

The freed were helping their fellow thralls. Already, an army of slaves were being set lose. They scrambled to pick up the swords of the dead and continued to release others. Within less than a minute, there was a melee of running shapes. The arriving creatures darted in all directions, confused as to who to attack first. A number went for Ayilia directly, but two freed thralls came out the gloom to stand at either shoulder, grappling the weapons of the fallen, displaying reassuringly competent sword skills. Many of the arthropods, those that hadn't fled, followed their quarry into the dark corners of the cavern, where they were jumped by even more freed.

It was a short battle. The guard were overwhelmingly outnumbered and totally unprepared. Some captives were killed, but the liberated had grown to a horde. With all the guards dead, they bolted towards the exits with their captured weapons and, Ayilia presumed, the world's portals. A number opted to hang around her and Seftus.

A ragtag bunch of abused people had become a warrior unit.

Ayilia beamed grimly at the Krayal. "Never thought I'd be so happy to see your scaled, over-paranoid, unnecessarily suspicious mug again, Seftus!"

"Ditto," he gasped out, wiping insect flesh from his blade. "Though it has to be said, yours is so covered in louse guts it was completely unrecognisable. Fortunately"—he attempted a smile—"you still stink of hume."

"Well, thank you too," she said, laughing. "That, truthfully, is the nicest thing I've heard since I got here!"

"All the same, my ... thanks, Regent. Take it while you can—gratitude's not something I'm good at." He exhaled and checked his wrists. They were raw from the bonds. "We need to move. I can hear more armed roaches coming."

"Let's go, before my battered arms give up the ghost."

"Ghost?" Seftus frowned, studying the pursuit keenly. Alarmed, he realised he was talking to himself. Ayilia had already gone. He followed, swiftly.

With a series of grunts, Ayilia severed the cogs off a row of casks of viscous oils. They erupted one after the other, hissing like rudely woken fire gods. The edifice was a bone-dry tinderbox. As the liquid engulfed the wood, rubber, and plaster in a growing sarcophagus of flame, there was a violent flare. A storage zone filled with hundreds of crates of inflammables went up in a dirty cloud. Flames rivered along struts as a fire-tornado swept through the greased machines. As pandemonium broke, Seftus and the liberated slaves were forced to dive as blistering heat rolled over their heads in the direction of the guards. Like some of their predecessors, they decided valour was overrated and began to flee for their lives.

CHAPTER SIX

FAKE GUIDE, CUTTHROAT, THIEF ... OR ALL THREE?

The three suns burned. The dragoons limped forwards lethargically. A shifty-looking Breasal led the way. Nessan glowered after him, close behind. Aaron followed nearby. No one had spoken for days. The journey along the periphery of the Pit's hinterland, deep into deserts and mountains, had taken weeks. Food hadn't been a problem. Outside of supplies, the tundra supported a surprising amount of wildlife. Unlike the Krayal, some of humanity feasted on flesh. The bushmeat was partially edible, especially mixed with local herbs, roots, and vegetables in a soup they called cawl. But water supplies were rationed. Mix all that with the heat, and tempers frayed.

During the day, the land turned ochre; at night, it glowed neon. Breasal had finally confirmed they were in the Widow Maker, a place even the vultures never went.

* · ☠ · ☠ · ☠ · *

That evening, as the shadows lengthened and a mist thickened, Breasal began dusting himself down. Nessan said nothing.

Aaron eyed him suspiciously. "I still don't see anything, dead man."

"That's because you're a breeder, not a Seer!"

"But I am a see-*er*, and I see squat."

"My point is confirmed!"

"Where's the bloody gate, Breasal?" Aaron snarled, staring at a thin line of hills in a crescent formation ahead of them.

"It's by a dead lake on the other side of that hump of rocks. Don't fret if it doesn't work—there're plenty more nearby."

"You told us there was only *one* portal, a sister or cousin or grandma, or something equally dumb!"

"I told you there was only one portal *near* the main portal ... in the Pit. This forgotten desert where no one goes and no one has ever gone is full of 'em; no one knows why. No one's ever known why! In fact, no one knows they're even there except a few fellow ... operators like me." He looked thoughtful. "In fact, no one knows if they're even there at all, as no one's ever been, so there might only be the one."

"Kept that quiet didn't you, fungus brain!"

"Perhaps he didn't want to us to do the right thing and leave him in that flea-infested clink back there." Nessan sighed.

Breasal shrugged, as though it was nothing to do with him. "Sometimes, it helps to be ... economical with the facts. You are, after all, waterfilled sack-bags!"

"*Dangerous* water-filled sack-bags!" Aaron snapped. Uncontrollable irritation was a constant companion. Each day that passed, the regent drew further away. He was convinced that this road of suns and dust was a deception. "All you do is speak in tongues!"

"We *are* here, but not the here where you thought was here!" Breasal smiled, displaying an impressive range of cracked teeth.

Aaron resisted an impulse to skewer the Lifeless. "And where the hell *is* here? It's not on any of our charts."

"If it was obvious, everybody would know." Breasal arched his brow. "Really, Captain, you're the one speaking in tongues."Aaron leaned in close and whispered venomously, "I told you, corpse, I'm not the captain. You'd better spill the beans because I feel close to spilling something else, which is a shame as I'm not easily upset!"

Someone let out an ironic snigger, then choked it off. Aaron glanced around furiously to see who it was.

"Meatbags are so easily upset, as they have the temperament of micro-grubs." Breasal replied sagely. He suddenly looked up, eyes wide. "We've arrived—not quite at the portal, but at the, um ... rendezvous."

"*Rendezvous*? What rendezvous—who the *hell* are we rendezvousing with?"

"Them!" Breasal pointed. In the shade of the dark hills, a group of thirty riders were cantering forward. Mirage rivers flowed in their wake from the heavy-set hooves of their prowlers.

"By God! Lifeless! More of them. Nessan, get the shooters armed, crossbolts, the lot, and form a defensive ring." He turned on Breasal and spat. "You dead-skinned, toad-eating, amphibious frog, this is betrayal. I'll cut your—"

Breasal held up his hands. "Easy captain, they're my friends—or should that be fiends? I think 'associates' is probably better."

"I don't care, bone-sack—I'll make firewood out of them if they get too close. Undead stick together like deadwood, always, that's what we say."

Breasal's eyes were rolling. For a Lifeless, he appeared excessively agitated. "Listen to me, hume, I'm thinking they were sent to scout for you. That Sythian mutt-hog, Mabius, didn't slay *all* of Stilgen's men; plenty managed to skulk away. They'll still hate your squirmies like the rest of us, but after spending some time in that Sythian oik's company with all the executions, lashings, and enforced kitchen duties, they've certainly come to see the Imperium in a new light. I guess the ol' Pro Consul doesn't seem so bad now." He beamed a toothy grin, as though everything was alright now. "Sure, they would rather have your head spiked than talk to it, but don't let that put you off. They're default allies!"

Before Aaron could respond, the leading rider approached and addressed Breasal directly, completely ignoring the dumbfounded humans.

"*You*! I told you I'd make soup of your bowels and omelette from your brains if you showed that sneak face again."

"Youssif!" Breasal spluttered, looking to all the world like he'd just had the proverbial brains sucked out through his ears and any other orifice available. Unusually clammy, even by his startlingly clammy standards, he smiled weakly at the humans. "We're old friends—brothers, really."

Youssif leant forwards. "Yes, blood brothers ... and you'll be supplying the blood."

"So, you don't get on?" Aaron looked suddenly interested.

"He's a thief, a swindler, a mead smuggler, a failed cockalorum, a kitchen duty avoider, and a lying, cheating piece of leathery scum! He'd sell you to the highest bidder, then sell the bidder and the bidder's mother and her brothers and sisters and go looking for their grandmother while he's at it. And that's just the breeders! That skull of his is only useful as a busted night lantern in an empty morgue, and even then it wouldn't work, as it'd have sold off all the fuel!"

Aaron shot Nessan a bemused glance. "I think I like this guy!"

"I've been slandered." Breasal looked stricken. "Insinuating I avoid the cookhouse rota is the worst insult a Lifeless could ever receive!"

"You didn't just avoid the rota, Breasal, you avoided the whole cookhouse!" Youssif turned to Aaron. "He once stole my lucky talisman and sold it for scrap, then came back for the chain, having missed it the first time. I've had it since I was stitched together in the Pit's vats! It was given to me by a drone—she was the only girl who ever loved me. After she died in a machine accident, he stole her timepiece ... the one *I* gave her for her annual stitch-day!"

Breasal brushed sweaty palms against his garb. Aaron was impressed. He couldn't ever recall having seen a Lifeless perspire.

"I have personally brought the humes to you. If it wasn't for me, you would've missed them—Stilgen will be pleased. He especially requested them."

"You didn't even know we'd be here—you just saw us before they did. I bet you even told the water-sacks this was planned."

"I—"

"I'm going to cut the crap out of your gut, Breasal the Weasel." The sound of a blade sliding out from a battered sheath sent a bolt through their collective spines. Youssif was within a whisker of slaying the renegade.

"Wait."

All eyes swept to Aaron.

Youssif's brow creased. "You wish that this inverted intestine on a stick ... live?" He stared in complete incomprehension. "A hu-man protecting an undead from the hands of a fellow undead?"

"I've been doing nothing else but fantasise about braining Breasal rump-to-toe myself, but it just came to me ..." Aaron sighed uneasily and rubbed his eyes, which were turning in on themselves. "It pains me more than you could ever know, but we might need him."

An alarmed Nessan leant towards Aaron, making sure that Youssif could actually hear. "The Lifeless leader is right, Commander—kill the wretch now. He'll trade us to Mabius at the first sniff of a freshly minted coin and a glass of cat piss."

"Not now, Nessan," Aaron hissed. He was losing his grip of the situation. It always seemed to happen when chaos flourished. "Look, Youssif—if I can use first-name terms? You have to realise, this ... scullery scab might be the only thing that gets us to where we want to go. I can't risk murdering the runt until I know he deserves to be murdered, if you get my drift."

"You can't murder a turd!" Nessan glowered.

Breasal was red faced and still sweating. The Lifeless group leader faced him, features implacable.

Aaron took a depth breath, ignoring the incredulous expressions of everyone who knew him. "Let's give the gobby carrion a few more days!"

Youssif's demeanour could have been disdainful, or pleased, but there was something different about this Pit man. "Very well, it's no skin off my bone, but he so much as lets off, I'll grind his brain into krill feed and use his skull as a spittoon."

Aaron, still crimson with conflicting fidelities, took a step forward. Commander Youssif's enigmatic black-red orbs scrutinised him intensely.

"I'm Aaron ... I command this troop in our leader's absence. You met Nessan just now. We're after the human regent, Ayilia, who's apparently with your man, Stilgen."

Stilgen's name sparked an immediate reaction. The new arrival's demeanour softened somewhat, but only for a heartbeat. "To our dismay, they fled this world through the Pit's portal as unwitting allies." He spat across the terrain. "That our kind could formally unite with water-beings is an affront to Lifeless civilisation. It took many long nights to accept such a thing could happen, though by the undead god we hope Stilgen understands it must not last."

Aaron bristled but held his tongue.

"You are enemies of the Eternal One, are you not ... Aaron?"

"Word sure gets around."

"So, it now seems, are we!"

"Seems like we have the same problem Ayilia and Stilgen had." Intrigue and irritation battled within him. The cadavers had a habit of getting his goat at the best of times. "Why don't you just do a collective runner from this termite-infested hole before Mabius finds you?"

Youssif's features didn't flicker. "Think it through, Commander. We have nowhere to go. Soon, this world will be crawling with off-worlders. Our only hope is to flee the Imperium, a veritable impossibility without the help of what's left of the Resistance. Your regent is the missing piece of the puzzle. Unfathomably, the Goat wants her, which means the Resistance does too. We are willing to offer our guidance until she reaches them, providing she negotiates for a new homeland for us within the void, far from the Imperium. Despite our hatred of the Heretics, we recognise the Resistance's millennia of experience out there." He nodded at the skies.

"You still need me, Captain," Breasal suddenly chirped in. "I found yous and I got yous all here to the rendezvous, despite your filthy need to imbibe runny liquids all the time."

"We found you rotting in a Lifeless jail, after robbing said Lifeless of their dosh," Nessan growled.

Aaron ignored Breasal's pleas. "Do you know where these portals are, Commander?"

"No one does," Youssif replied drily. "Breasal found the information in the unused Pit archives and sold it to the smuggling rackets, but they were too pissed to go this far. We think the Ancients once had a long-lost capital somewhere around here, so this 'hole' may not have been quite so hole-like once." He inhaled. "The weasel was not lying about that."

"I spoke righteousness the entire time," Breasal spluttered. "Hell's teats, I've been laundered."

"Slandered," Nessan cut in.

"Seems we have a deal, Aaron." Youssif shot him a level but murderous glare. "But no flights of fancy, Commander. I respect the fact you are clearly honourable, but our kinds will always be foes. We were man-ufactured to hate your species and the Krayal geckos in the rises. Any sign of betrayal and we'll slit you gut-to-neck, like our people did the geckos back in the day when the Pit was first Imperium. I want you to understand that, so there can be no misunderstandings!"

Aaron allowed himself a thin smile. "Let me tell you something, Commander. I dreamt about you lot when I was a kid. Not good ones either. Ever since, I've wanted to ram my blade into those red sockets of almost every one of you." Aaron was practically nose to nose with the Lifeless. "So yes, we have a deal ... and I *will* honour it. But Breasal aside, as the talking bowel-movement can't help himself, any sign of treachery, then it's going to be a case of lights out all around."

Nessan, the X Gemina soldiers, and the Lifeless warriors tensed, hands itching for the hilts of their blades. The silence seemed to drag on forever.

"One being's heresy is another's realism!" Youssif replied quietly. "Mutual hate is one thing we both implicitly understand and which, paradoxically, unites us." He regarded Aaron thoughtfully. "But you know what troubles me the most?"

"I don't think I do?"

"I think I might even come to ... tolerate you!" His eyes narrowed. "I find that the most disquieting thing of all."

"Great, two charisma-congenitally-challenged fools sorted ... only half a universe left," Breasal blurted.

Out of tension or simply because she couldn't help herself, Nessan giggled.

Aaron swivelled on the bug-eyed guide and whispered forcefully in its ear. "You owe me, *Breasal the Weasal*. You will be my eyes and ears on this trip. You be my gate operator, and you will monitor our new friends and report anything, no matter how bland, to me and me alone. I, and only I, will tell you when your debt is relinquished. You will not cheat or fiddle anyone who is our ally or our friend, or I guarantee that is the last thing you will fiddle in your wheeler-dealer non-life. If at any time you transgress, I will let these charming fellows deal with you how they see fit and, if they don't, Nessan and I will do it instead, terminally!" He smiled coldly. "Is that clear?"Breasal nodded furiously. "Perfectly, Captain!"

For the first time since they'd met, Aaron had the feeling the Lifeless was telling the truth.

The portal had gone mad. Plasma was raging within the quantum flux. Somehow, he'd been taken down a different route from the others.

Typical.

Flames blazed through his head. He jerked and twisted violently. They roared out of his mouth, engulfing his torso, hands, feet, and fingers—a renegade crucified in glory or a hobo on fire, it depended on the point of view. Abducted by a blinding heat he couldn't feel, he was carried forwards on the crest of a wave. Tens of thousands of doors opened and closed around him leading to a hundred thousand interlinking corridors. Merchants, travellers, guards, platoons, even an army, entered and exited a confetto of gates within a labyrinth of lines above, below and around his stricken frame. He was a bottle on an atom sea within a neo-gated universe, knitting millions of spheres together. There could have been more, or half that number. He didn't know and wouldn't care if he did. All that mattered was the wonder of the place, how unimportant the politics of his and everyone's non-life were compared to this.

For the first time in my whole shit-filled existence, I am part of something. How ironic. So much wonder transporting the bitterest screwhead this side of the galactic centre.

He gasped at the realization that his destination was an onyx singularity. The hole elongated into a rectangle, then a door in the vacuum. He exited the portal like a bullet, a photonic birth that smashed through branches and bows, disappearing into a mound of roots and mulch. For a long time, the new arrival lay prostrate, exhausted with what might have been terror.

After a while, Vespasian opened his eyes and shook his head.

It really shouldn't have thrown me out like that!

Acrid smoke choked his unused lungs, forcing the Sythian to cough in hacking wheezes. He wanted to vomit but managed to control the urge. Maybe he hadn't been stitched together in some vat-filled lab, but he had been undead-converted, and God knew what he might end up throwing up with it.

He got to his feet shakily, using a tree nearby as leverage. Judging the sheer quantity of dust descending inside what was a small clearing, he got the feeling he'd come through a gate not frequently used. There was enough visibility to make out a wood covered with fern and bracken, intermixed with scatterings of boulders tinged with glassy quartz.

Vespasian started to hurry.

He was lost, disorientated, and enveloped in a brain fog. Burning flakes from the exit whirled after his fleeing form, while leaves and clumps of moss smouldered. The whole wood seemed about to ignite. Spotting a clearing, he made a beeline for it.

His non-beating heart lurched. Scrunching to a sudden stop, he made out his own feet perched precariously above a rocky precipice.

Nothing but sky faced him. A blue horizon framed a serrated series of peaks jutting from the far end of a crater so stunningly cavernous it was a world in its own right. The entire outer rim was a line of rocky sentinels parading in frozen majesty over the basin below. Thundering within a halo of rainbows, hundreds of vast waterfalls formed a semicircle at least twenty leagues long. The waters chundered in spires into a distant network of tributaries below. Sunlit rivers threaded through gorse, grasses, scree, and broken stone amid a scrim of steaming caldera. A spread of stars and planets were just visible above against the skies.

The vista triggered something deep within Vespasian's sick and sickened mind, combining with the trauma of the fight for survival only moments ago in the Pit on his home world. He blacked out. His eyes rolled, and he fell forwards into the spectacular abyss, a lifetime of punishment catching up with weariness. Immobile, resigned, he slipped into oblivion, doing what he should have done a long time ago. As he fell, a delicate flame spread like feathering down from his torso to his feet.

All he could feel was a deep sense of relief and, perhaps, even gratitude.

Blackness.

"Err ... got 'im."

Meat hooks leered out from the gloom. There was a feeling of impalement. Something, which was probably him, was being dragged from swamps pitted with tapering roots and bent trees of fuscous warts. He half heard rustling grass. Another sense: one of movement, but not of time. More blackness. In that void, sounds of scraping and pulling mixed with grunts and guttural talk. No feeling, no sensation, certainly no pain.

Vespasian was now sure it was him being dragged.Something shimmied into view, but from the bottom of a deep pool. Images blurred in and out of focus. After many long seconds, a scene filled his vision.

"I tell ya, it's a bloody drone. Musta been swept in from somewhere aways."

The speaking figure was clothed in basic cloths: heavy farming overalls and a smock. Others were standing around in similar garb.

Organics!

All looked and smelled the same. He couldn't tell them apart. He couldn't even tell which one he was meant to be. With a start, he realised they were talking of him. Their accent was pastoral.

"Dolt—there's no factories near round. He's from Caulderwell, he must be!"

The other shook his head vehemently. "Naw, the current flows *to* Caulderwell, not from it. He's from the ridges, back there some way off.""You can't be sure." A third had to have his say. "There's plenty of 'em all round."The second rounded on him impatiently. "I know that; I'm no fool. But there's none like that one, not from round 'ere anyways. He's different, I tell ya, and none like him ever go to Caulderwell. It's a city—and not just any city, but the *capital* city. I mean, look at him. Rottin' aways—been in the waters a long time. Which means he can't come from the city, 'cos he's been a flowing in the current for a while before being snagged here."They all regarded him severely. Clearly, they hadn't seen him open his eyes, which was hardly surprising since his soft pink gaze was crusted with mud and as dark as those staring back at him. Surrounding the speakers was a basic straw and mud village, or possibly a small town. He didn't know. He didn't want to know. Blue hills shimmered in the background. The light of the sun, or suns, on this unknown world formed reddish-yellow hazes around people and things, but that could have been his sight playing tricks. "Well? What do we do? Fetch him to the city or bury him back there?" "Maybe the authorities should be told —the Empire won't like it if he's important and we say naught." "And who's gonna know? We've lived for generations without sticking our necks out, and we won't start now. I say put 'im back in the river and let God decide where he travels. This ain't no accident, I'm telling yous. We don't want involvement in any skullduggery this thing's been up to." They all nodded sagely. Before they could act, Vespasian swung his legs across with an undignified grunt and faced them. He had been in a trough filled with animal feed, some kind of ground maize. They exclaimed as one, followed by a series of gasps and muttering. Others in the settlement stopped and stared. Wordlessly, he got up and stood on unsteady feet. His guts felt mushed, but he didn't know why. Mud and grain shunted off his torso to form a clump on the straw-covered ground. *Why aren't I dead—really dead?* People were cursing but had backed off. Scowling, he started to walk forwards. The townspeople were gawping. He walked past, pretending obliviousness. One of the men addressed him from behind, but he continued regardless. Nearby animals snorted with alarm. Doors were slammed shut. He was in the single high street, jumbled with market stalls, timber shops, and tents full of flickering fires, smoke, and spits of frying meat. Drapes of assorted colours fluttered from linen vendors. A small crowd followed him, whispering excitedly. A few men looked angry, most fearful. He saw a horse drinking and realised with a shock what he needed to have, *had* to have. Stumbling, he passed the lazy looking beast and threw himself in. The muttering rose in crescendo. Dogs barked, and chickens ran and squawked. He drank deeply and longingly. His whole body soaked it in. Water seeped in every pore, bathing his trunk, washing the grunge away. Droplets splattered everywhere; he resembled an animal. He could hear a baby wailing. Rising to his knees, he stepped tentatively over the side as two Imperial soldiers arrived from nowhere, shoving villagers aside like sheep. One approached. It spoke impatiently, with unmistakable menace in its tone. "What are you? Speak quickly—of what troop do you belong? What is your rank, where were you assigned? Tell me your designated number! Why are you out here in the swamplands? There is no log of additional patrol here." Vespasian stared blankly. "Are you blemished, apostate, aberrant, or degenerate?" he continued. "Speak, or I'll summon the marsh guard, and have you dragged back to Caulder-well in irons!" "Mage!" "*What?*" "Mage! I'm a Mage!" "Not possible! You stink too much, even for a Mage." The soldier stepped backwards, as if suddenly unsure of himself. "There was a mission back there: deep, very deep. Got lost, problems ... but sorted. Now get out my way or I'll burn you to straw." Pushing past, Vespasian approached the crowd. They parted in a hurry. He walked in a haze till he saw the swinging sign of a tavern. The skies were dimming. Without a word, he pushed through. Inside, wood-panelled beams were lit by a fire roaring in a central grate. Sawdust, spit, and dirt glued the old oak floor together. The chairs were half full. A large innkeeper stood with his hands on his bar, staring in horror at the bedraggled guest and his odd request. "Water." "*What?*" "Water. A quart." Leaning forwards, the barman put two chunky, tattooed arms on the counter. "Listen bonehead, we don't serve freeloaders. Anyone can see you ain't Imperial approved." Vespasian placed a hand on the wooden bar. A flame licked out, forming a circle of mazarine fire around his fingers. The barman swore and backed up against a row of brown bottles, which made a series of glassy clinks. Vespasian raised the burning hand in front of his face."I've been places you don't want to know. I've lived in hell, and it wasn't even warm. I'd feel more at home in this rathole if I turned it into something similar."The man's eyes goggled.

The Consul's turned his smouldering hand to point at a water jug before aiming at the exact spot between the man's hirsute brows.

"Drink!"

The man's flesh turned cream. He fumbled for a glass and poured one out. Vespasian walked to a heavy table, sat, and rubbed his face. Bits of skin peeled away. He swept them up with the side of his hand and emptied them neatly into a wooden, porcupine-quill ashtray. A nearby table emptied of people.He raised the glass and drank deeply. The Lifeless soldier burst in with his comrade. They stared in disbelief.

"What kind of Mage drinks water? It can be lethal!"

"Lethal is what your brains will be if you don't get of out here and leave me in peace." Vespasian shot a soft orange fire burst at the floor, inadvertently cleaning the targeted area.

The soldiers quickly turned and left. Vespasian carried on drinking.***He woke with a start. He'd been sleeping. The pub regulars had left him a space. No one had dared come near. They crowded in droves round the rest of the tavern, and he scanned them. Their eyes shifted away, none of them meeting his gaze. Except one—a large, balding, middling man stared angrily back. Vespasian ignored him and returned to the bar. Smoke hung over the whole room. A dog ran in for some discarded bones, then darted out the door. There were fits of laughter, but mostly the room was filled with the low drone of talking, like a swarm of drunk and slightly disjointed bees. The Consul looked up. A bar assistant hurried over. "No mead, no wine, no spirits, no poison. Water only!" Vespasian ordered.

The man gulped and got a fresh glass. "And pie. Thick crust. I can't pay, but I'll leave and never bother you again. I always remember a favour."

Where did I get that from?

"And make sure the beast was killed cleanly, or else it taints the flesh with fly larva."

The man's mouth fell open.

"And make sure the thing didn't suffer, as it also contaminates the flesh. Stuffs my guts up; I'm a nightmare when I'm stuffed up!" He thought again. "Actually, make it vegetable only!"

The startled man looked at the barkeeper who, with a face as grave as death, nodded slowly.

Shortly after, he received the steaming pie. Vespasian regarded it in silence, unsure why he was behaving so oddly. The first mouthful made him want to gag, but before he knew it, it was disappearing in great chunks. The inn went quiet. They clearly couldn't believe it either—a Lifeless not only drinking water, a suicide's favourite, but eating organic food: a meatless meat pie. Yet, he felt his body warming. Inexplicable sensations of fullness swarmed within. He scratched his face, his fingernails coming away with imperceptible scraps of dried tissue. A shadow darkened his abstract gaze. He looked up. The large man and two other organic gargoyles stood above him, their tree-trunk arms folded. "What are you doing eating my food and drinking my beer, dead filth?"Vespasian chewed his food carefully before answering. "I'm enjoying it! What else can you do?"

They stared at him blankly. The Consul wiped gruel from his mouth with his sleeve. "Water."

"*What?*"

Couldn't the breathing, husking water bags understand anything?

"I want more water."

"I don't care if you want sulphur. I own this town, and every third groat goes to me. You haven't paid, and that means I don't get paid."

The man was clearly exasperated. His barrel chest and gibbous abdomen squatted over the table like a rubbery incubus. Given his bulk and the high quality of his clothes, it was evident he'd grown wealthy over the years through paying off the local officialdom and ripping his own kind apart. Something told Vespasian that if they didn't pay protection, they went missing. He didn't know why the living preyed on their kind, but he felt a sudden anger, one that went back a lot further than he could suppose.

"Paid? What for? To sit on your spotted ass and tell these udderless oxen what to do?"

"So, it's like that," the man replied icily. "Well, that's not quite *all* I do!" He pulled an iron bar out from his jerkin.

A few short moments later, the bodies of the men were lying in the dirt street like sacks of spuds. Vespasian regarded them darkly from the doorway. Villagers were looking at him clearly terrified. "They're not quite dead," the Consul growled at them. "But they should be. Since I doubt they'll be able to feed off this hole again, I'll be running this town now. If any more thugs try any funny business, I'll have them tried. And that's *after* I string them up by their breeding tools."

"Er, dead man. *Dead man?*"

Vespasian whirled to face a group of people. One of them, a weathered villager, was leaning on a cane next to an old woman.

"Are you talking to me?"

"Errr ... we were wondering ..." stuttered a ginger-haired farmer.

"I'm out of time." That was a lie, but Vespasian didn't want them to realise just how unimportant he really was.

The old woman cut in. "What them guppy's trying to say is what are we gonna do now? There's no protection no more. They won't be back. Perhaps the Empire won't be bovvered, even when the tax goes belly up! In truth, we don't 'ave much coin to pay 'em anyways, so what does we do now?"

"Why *do* anything?" "Well ... we've always had folk who ... manage." "Do it yourself!" "*Us?*" She and the others stared at him, uncomprehending.

Vespasian sighed. He couldn't shake himself of unwanted company, it seemed.

"We want protection, sorcerer. Who's gonna provide it if you don't?"

Vespasian's brow arched. "The thugs are the ones who you need protection *from*. The people who are *providing* the protection!"

"That's not reassuring," cried the woman in a quavering voice. "Who's gonna lead us now!" Vespasian thought briefly. "You will!" The people looked at one another, stunned. "With the authority bestowed on me by the honourable Imperium, in their disinterested absence, I nominate *you*."

People muttered, uncertain, fearful.

He pointed at her. "She's the only one with plums in this town, and she's got brains too. Give her your backing and a handful of thick skulls won't be able to come near you again!"

As he walked away, the old woman somehow managed to hurry after him despite her stick. Waving the others off, she bent close to whisper. "I dunno what kinda trouble you're in fella, but the guards will be back. They ain't got the mettle of the regs, so they'll get help." She shook her head, baffled. "You're not like them. They'll be hunting you down, son—they will want bad words with you!"

"Good. It's been a while since I had a good chat."

Caulderwell was visible before him, situated within a voluminous crater. Vespasian had walked half a day over ridges and swampland. Though paths crisscrossed the tundra like glimmering cobwebs, most appeared to head towards the city. By the time he'd spotted its gates in the distance, the marshlands had dried into roads of dust. Small but spectacular craters filled the final dozen leagues, along with poppy meadows. Vespasian scrutinised a horseshoe crescent of purple-blue waterfalls in the distance. He could just about perceive clouds and stars mirrored in their slowly moving flows.

With the fens and their gnats behind him, the Sythian found he was beginning to relax. Caulderwell sat on a handful of rises within the caress of a white mist. It swept the city walls in a nightgown of silk. A brushstroke of volcanic vents circled the town.

Ominous black smoke was rising from a nearby settlement. Acrid fumes rolled nebulously along the ground. Vespasian walked quietly through, creating rifts of twisters in his wake. As the haze parted, a rubble-strewn tavern surrounded by flaming farmsteads shimmied into sight. Half a dozen charred shapes lay on the ground. Laughter rose and fell, mixed with jeering.

The tattered warlord stopped. Since he'd fallen from the skies above, he'd come to a personal agreement with himself to himself. A pact. He accepted that he was a waste of time, always had been. But there was no remorse, no regrets; he barely felt anything at all. It had its advantages. For one, there were absolutely no obligations. He was free. His compatriots were lost somewhere in the universe, and no doubt were better off. Especially since he was now insane, mimicking the living, and eating their food—though nothing with a face. Typical organics. They would consume anything, even servile fellow organics that slave-tilled their lands. They didn't deserve his help. Whatever was happening here wasn't his fight. He lowered his head and walked past whatever commotion was going on in the blanket of smog.

"Hey ... hey you. Where do ya think you're going?"

Vespasian picked up his pace.

"Oi, I said come back."

A series of shouts broke out, and four Lifeless soldiers stumbled into the clear. Another two looked up at him, startled, by the flaming inn. They were all hopelessly inebriated. A field commander materialised from the swirling smoke.

They were low-grade guards, almost of Pit quality, though not as bad.

He tightened his fists. There was little worse than drunken, badly stitched grunts. To make matters worse, he could see some carrying what probably was the local weed and concentrated spirits in bottles. Like their living counterparts, it seemed the only way they knew they were alive was to resemble non-life by getting blitzed. Thus did the two species come together in the grimmest of parodies.

A scream broke through the night.

He looked up. A female organic, likely in her twenties, twisted on the ground, bound and bruised, at the feet of the soldiers. He stared, dumbfounded.

"You're Lifeless." Vespasian scowled. "What would you want with one of them?"

"Haaaaaaar." Mouldy, sharp, yellow teeth grinned from a sagging chin stubbed with artificial growth. As always, it was bought from a specialised physician for effect, like his skin, though the hollowed cheeks and overdried condition of the purchased epidermis were a consequence of toxic living. "Just a bit of fun ... what's the harm in that?"

"Good thing he's one of us, or I'd drive him through with my shaft," said another.

"Do it anyway, Squawn—he's an apostate. We can do what we like without being flung in the pen."

A peculiar red mist tightened the defective clams that were his lungs. Were they all turning into the living around here?

"What kind of fun could a neuter have with a non-dead? If there was one good thing about our people, it was because we were spared that."

The laughter cut short. The field commander looked at him with scarlet eyes, blotched with yellow scars. "Perhaps the question is what kind of recreant, lost and lonesome, tells his hardworking brethren what to do with their hard-earned coin? We've all heard about you. You lecture us about dallying with breeders while you lord it up in their hamlets, throwing your weight around and feasting on the filth of the meat sack's bovine quadrupeds, freshly quaffed by a warrior's damnation: water. I could barely believe it—I thought my ears had slipped again!"

The Consul rolled his eyes. "It was a leek and tater pie with peas!"

The bony jaws of the others dropped contemptuously. All looked at him with revulsion. "Deviant—gut 'im!"

Someone spat, catching him full on in the forehead, a mixture of synthetic saliva and traces of liquor. Disgusted, he rubbed it off. The skeletal forms were encircling him, faux confidence in numbers.

"I don't know what your mission is, outside abusing people, but it's nothing to do with me," the Consul muttered. "I just want some peace!"

He tried to move, but his route was blocked. Looking around, he tried another path, but the shapes simply obstructed that too. A pilum was shoved into his back. It cracked noisily through his dried skin and ribs, splintering bone and cartilage before thrusting out through his already dilapidated front. Shreds of clothing hung on the point.

"Why did you do that?" He pulled it out of his chest and thrust it away. "Do you have any idea how long it takes to grow skin back when you were actually *born* with it?"

An arrow thwacked into his shoulder, and then a second javelin smacked into his belly. He slumped forwards and crashed to the ground. The soldiers, jeering and laughing, started kicking his prostrate form.

"Some Mage!"

"He's more like a longhorn than a magick man!"

"He's lame, I've seen it a'fore. Nothing worth griping about."

The field commander walked purposefully over and examined the stricken shape. "Nothing but a renegade, a stinking deserter. They always make me heave. Take him back—we might finally get some overdue recognition of worth from the Legate!"

His men cheered. The leader unsheathed a dagger and plunged it into Vespasian's exposed back. "That'll end your aqua-guzzling days my friend—it ain't natural!" He stood again, leaving the knife deep in Vespasian's back. "We'll bring his head back to the barracks in Caulderwell later; I bet there'll be some stout for us!"

They laughed raucously, then ambled over to the woman. Vespasian could just about make out she was still breathing, despite being on the ground. The smoke was clearing now. The buildings were mostly burned, though sporadic flame licked at charred timber. With the emblem of Nethergeist lit clearly on their tunics, the soldiers strode forwards, taking no notice of the intense heat.

"Get up."

She obeyed immediately. A red gash streaked her forehead. "Leave me alone ... I have nothing."

The leader put a thick, bony hand on her head and gripped her hair. "We would prefer to disagree. We've been on patrol too many weeks, and I say we're owed some due, don't you?"

The soldiers whooped. One threw a bottle into the fire.

The woman pushed him away and retreated across the sand, eyes wide. "Please, don't kill me."

"Personally, I think there're too many warm-bloods in this universe. One less is no bad thing, so don't you give it too much thought." His hand shot out and grabbed her neck. "It's nothing personal, it just suits us."

The woman gagged, then pulled away again. Fumbling on the ground, she grappled a rock and struck the Lifeless hard on the face. "Scum."

The others screamed with laughter, but the commander wasn't so impressed. Vespasian watched as he wiped the fluid away from the cut and glowered at her. The jeering died down as anticipation kicked in. No one moved. Rank guaranteed certain privileges. The woman scrabbled for a ragged piece of wood on the ground, but his foot slammed on her hand, while the other shattered the wood. She rose to grab the ripple of tendons barely visible within the neck of his nicked skull and tried to throttle him, but he flung her back to the ground. Seemingly expecting the worst, she squeezed her eyes tightly shut.

Nothing happened.

She flicked them open.

The commander had turned to the others who, for long heartbeats, could only stare in liquefied stupor. A black pustule had opened at the crown of his head. It gave a slight pop and extruded a part of his mind down his dirty face. No one spoke.

The commander slumped ignominiously to the floor; an opprobrious mannequin spread-eagled in soft loam. The troops whirled round. One of them immediately staggered backwards, a burning hole in his torso. He collapsed near the woman's feet, next to the body of his commander. The others dropped their weapons and bolted every which way, two inadvertently smacking into each other. Bolts of plasma hissed through the smog, cutting the soldiers down like flies. Most were eviscerated by Mage Rage, their witless bodies tossed across the scree in fizzling embers and scorched armour. One lucky soldier vanished hurriedly into the smoke, but another, who for some reason looked back, was just in time to see the shot that caved its own head in. Another witnessed its shoulder carbonised into charcoal even as it fled. Disorientated, it tottered off in the direction of the swamps.

The still-defiant woman looked up, a mess of hair and wet cheeks, at the strange Lifeless wizard. Vespasian stared back. She rolled over and picked up a metal bar and cursed him. After brushing the murk off his worn-out garb, he slowly removed the javelin from his body, then the dagger. They came out in a sucking sloop of sickly fluids. Her expression seemed to soften. He sensed within her, a realisation he was different to the other killers. With survival no longer an issue, the woman began to scramble around the rubble until she grasped a grubby amphora. She downed it quickly and cleaned her wound and face as best she could.

Eventually, she stood up and looked long and hard at her gaunt saviour.

"Why?"

He was lost in some far-off otherworld. Finally, he noticed she was waiting for an answer. "You think I saved you?"

"No." She grimaced darkly. "I think you wanted those bastards dead!"

"Then you have the only answer I can give you. This place is safe now. There's only one or two left, and I doubt they'll survive their wounds."

As he walked off, she followed, matching her step to his. "You're going to Caulderwell, aren't you? I am too!"

He arched his brow. "Haven't you had enough of those without souls for one day?"

"You're not like them." She flexed her fingers with a series of loud cracks and massaged her right shoulder, wincing as she did. "You hate them more than us. They must have done bad things to you." He felt her scrutinising him, as she talked. "Listen, this place was just a job, a front for the gangs in the village. The same ones who apparently got toasted by some walk-in derelict! I don't suppose you know anything about that, do you?"

He remained silent.

"Well ... whatever, I was gonna leave for the city anyway. The villagers can rebuild here; the guards killed the rest of the gang before you torched them. You're clearly not from around here. I can show you the safest way if you let me come."

"What's in it for you?"

"Other than protection, nothing! Now, where's my bag?" She stopped searched the rubble. "Imperials don't hassle us; it's the local guards who're the assholes. Many don't care, but the ones who've gone 'native' stagger from one boozer to the next. Occasionally—*rarely*—they go feral, like a wild pig if you get my meaning. Usually the Empire snuffs 'em out, but this lot evaded 'em—no one local dared resist, not even the gang." She heaved a piece of lumber aside with a loud grunt. "But until they lost it today, they kept me fine alright, pulling the pumps, cleaning the latrines, totting up the accounts!" She shot him a piercing gaze. "Why ain't you dead?"

"I am."

"That's not what I meant. They pulverised you with everything they had!"

"Ah, but they didn't take my spirit."

He felt her studying him intently. However, he ignored it, instead concentrating on healing his wounds with his hand. "Well, I'm undead, so what kills you doesn't hurt you."

She shook her head. "I'm not an idiot, dead man, unlike most the dolts round here. I don't need a course in medicine to know what was left of you couldn't build a rabbit hutch!"

The Lifeless' face puckered. "Never heard of them!"

"Whatever." She frowned. "Anyway, I'd appreciate some company. I have no spare coins and I don't offer services, if you get my drift; I'm not a doxy."

He shrugged. "Never heard of that either! Do what you wish, but I have one requirement."

She crossed her arms suspiciously, a subconscious gesture of self-protection. "What?"

"Talk."

"Talk?"

"More importantly, *lack* of talk. The more people talk, the further away my thoughts go, and I'm confused enough as it is. I honestly believe if people stopped the endless gabbing, their lives would be transformed!" Fittingly, he looked confused. "There seem to be a lot of humes here?"

"You mean, humans?"

"I thought only my world was infested."

She looked puzzled. "We live here. It's our world. We're scattered throughout the Imperium on many, many worlds." She straightened her clothes and made an attempt at tying her ruffled hair back with a pin foraged from her pocket. At that moment, she noticed her rucksack lying nearby, partially hidden by ash. "There're helots from other worlds too of course, but I guess we breed the most. We're everywhere!"

He shrugged again.

"Not that I sense you give a crap, but my name is Gala."

"Vespasian," he muttered. He started to walk again in the direction of Caulderwell, carefully stepping over the smouldering bodies of the burned guards.

Gala hurriedly picked up her rucksack. One of the guards wasn't dead, so she put her foot through his cracked skull, nodding with satisfaction at the subsequent mess. "Your name sounds regal!"

"Sounds ridiculous. They gave us asinine names to instil dumb pride, but it only made us look even more stupid."

It was her turn to shrug. Deep down, Vespasian sensed her unease. It didn't take a chartist to realise she believed he was either damaged goods or on the run.

For no reason at all, she muttered, "I'm hungry!"

His answer nearly knocked her to the ground. "I could eat a swamp bison!" He attempted a smile. It looked oddly goofy, despite his otherworldly appearance. It was also something his kind hardly ever did, especially if they were trying to be polite, which was always never.

She resisted the urge to pass out.

"But a leek and tater pie would do just fine!"

CHAPTER SEVEN

ANOTHER PERSPECTIVE

I *want to talk about time—my personal experience of it, anyway.*

Time is an illusion, an empyreal hussy, created by the gyration of suns, atoms, and worlds with a heady dose of gravitation tossed in. It's marred only by the tidal eddies of populations, who squirm like sped-up spore on the atrophying bastions of the worlds they pollute.

Understand?

The living have hijacked time. They abuse it; they mark the futility of their zero-dimensional passage through existence via the compassing of everyday points, such as the days they were spawned, to signify temporal passage. Thus, the illusion that their progress has meaning is created.

I know, I babble like a rill, but I have only myself to talk to—outside that demonic wolf of mine and its addle-pated heads—so it's hardly surprising I blither so. When you live so long, are alone so long, are so lonesome for so long, it becomes second nature to wallow in endless animus, with only your psychosis to feed you. Nevertheless, it's hard to truly appreciate the venal nature of time's deception. The beings that breed like fungus on the ovoid lumps of rock they crawl, rut, and stupefy upon think they understand its vagaries, but they are swiftly snuffed out by a universe heartily sick of the wasted gift of life they have squandered. Drinking, greed, self-obsession, an appetence for flesh, wealth, and status are the eternal counterfeits that define their worth. It's snake oil sold by a perfidious mountebank, cloaking what should be purpose within the magnificence of the universe and beyond

.

In truth, I am painfully miserable and bitter, but my hand is forced, you know. I am the Emperor Goat, and I am the only one who can save creation. You can see that, can't you?

This alone gives me hope and purpose.

Think about the enormity of my task. All the seething infinities of universes fuzzing in superclusters of quantum luxuriance are but a glittering cove on an ebony beach within a boundless pearl of worlds no one will ever visit. I used to tread such places millennia ago, leaving footprints in glass on sandy shores that no one will ever see. All this is at risk by the one thing that ruins its startlingly gorgeous firmament: life. Feel reassured, I only mean the petty intelligences that wriggle out of their primordial grog to dispossess what they find, lollygagging their way to dominance on ultimately defenceless terrenes.

Time is a concept people use to mark the moments they feed and piss, lie and cheat, through what constitutes an existence. Time is the entropy of all things; it takes us on a journey to desolate disorder, but it is the journey itself that is the point, a passage of discovery, union, and awe. Life is the natural by-product of the universe, the waste pipe of its purity. Even the Godhead would appreciate how much I am needed, to prevent the eventual contagion of the pristine by such archesporial ringworm.

It's up to me.

I will save creation for all those not yet conceived, from the toxic destitution of all those that have. I don't expect gratitude, but a spot of worship would more than suffice. There is more to say, but too much time to say it. For now, I am relishing the meeting to come. Arch-pig Mabius himself, receiving his orders from my aforementioned demon Licklespickle. Their mutual disgust brings such hollow pleasure to my antediluvian soul, and to see them together, plotting and scheming but unable to strike because I forbid it, gives me literally ... heartbeats of joy.

The giant entered the Hall of Flame cautiously, seven feet of Lifeless muscle fastened by volcanic theurgy. To an auger, Mabius was thaumaturgically blinding, a being of constrained violence of shocking magnitude. However, the hidden Imperial observer in His faraway place didn't flinch. The Goat's infinite mind was connected to every atomised particle in every square corner of the room via covert theurgy channels, and nothing impressed Him.

The Goat was watching everything.

Mabius entered from a fire-cloaked walkway that winked out the moment his foot touched the hall's rug-covered floors. These also burned, as did the hall itself, but as with the corridor, nothing was actually damaged. A good thing, the Goat mused, for the rugs were of the rarest quality, as was the art. The corridor ran back a good league, panelled by sheets of silver alloy. In between each stood malevolent statues wearing malachite robes. Their white eyes followed everything. They lined either side of the passageway, forming a greeting that sent chills up the most heartless of spines.

Except the giant, of course. He didn't give a damn, despite his caution. At least, that was what he was likely telling himself.

A path ran to a pair of enormous dragon effigies, arranged in a discommoding arch through which lay another chamber. Their tendons were lit by a light that flickered across pendulous tongues and hard eyes. The giant waded through the knee-high flame as though it were nothing more dangerous than a field of rippling buttercups.

Mabius halted before a dais supporting Viceroy Myrian and the bastard's many heads. Though forms danced and pirouetted, courtesy of the rolling flame, none of it reflected off the corneas of the demon's gazes—the eyes were blank. Fire spirals wreathed up the supports of a central throne, perched above the noncorroding heat on legs of gold. The flame poured off the plinth on which the dais rested like molten chocolate. Yet the air was as clean as a morning sunrise, mixed with fragrances from dozens of incense holders.

Mabius shaded his eyes.

He made out jackal faces scrutinising him with glittering irises within the incandescent nova. One of them spoke. It seemed they were nearly identical. The Goat sensed that Mabius could not work out why the Viceroy would choose that particular head to represent them all. Perhaps, in spite all the faces, there was only one mind.

"We welcome you, Mabius."

"The pleasure is mine, Viceroy."

It wasn't. Mabius hated the scum.

"How pleasing!"

The Emperor could tell Mabius knew He was here, laughing at Mabius' discomfort. Yet, Mabius and Myrian had a charade to play. Two beings, both insane, both yearning for the same thing. They were puppets on a bloody cord wielded by a psychopath of multiuniversal dimensions. It must have made Mabius sick with rage. Nevertheless, the warlord patiently waited for Myrian to complete the empty pleasantries before the real nastiness started.

"So, we find you well, General?"

No one unnerved Mabius, ever, but this multiheaded enigma was another thing altogether. He appeared angry and discomforted simultaneously, each emotion feeding off the other until he was mute with arthritic vexation. "I'm as well as anyone impatient enough to take the skulls off the Heretics, yet no longer given the chance. Perhaps, I am not as trusted as other senior officers, in spite of having a hundredfold more theurgy flowing through my significantly superior Geno. Perhaps, it's good, old-fashioned, hayseed politics since I was sired and not manufactured, as were my kin?"

"We see." There was a brief pause. "The war on terror has gone well. The Magi terrorist commanders are all but dead. Only a handful evade capture, but their alliances are crumbling, and their worlds will be ours in little more than one or two Core years. It is all in good hands, be assured."

"Of course, of course. I just want them dead, that's all."

"We all do."

"Of course."

Myrian's many heads observed him with voracity. "We have a ... proposal—a missive from the One Himself, General."

Mabius cocked his head. The demon bastard was getting straight to the point, already. His face displayed a sudden keenness.

"Appreciate what a rare honour this is, Mabius—a very rare honour. Take up the scroll at your feet."

The giant slowly dropped his massive head to see a rolled-up vellum. He fingered the dry material carefully. The roaring flames had left it untouched.

"These are ancient texts, General, older than you could possibly know. They refer to the rebirth of the adversary, the being of which you already know."

The heat was oppressive. Mabius wiped his brow gravely. The renegade demon and its accursed heads clearly brought out the worst in him at the best of times. It was taking an immense effort to not vent his spleen. Even so, he looked intrigued.

"The Al Kimiya?"

"The one and only. We barely credit it ourselves." The faces barely moved.

"The emperor has actually found it?" Mabius' eyes popped. He wondered if those Satanic minds could get inside his own, or at least that's how it looked to the Goat. It was rumoured they had telepathic capabilities. "In truth, I always wondered if it was just a legend, the whispering prattle of the weak-minded, gossip-obsessed flibbertigibbets."

Despite the raging fires, the room suddenly seemed to darken. Mabius visibly steeled himself.

"Listen closely, General; let's drop the niceties. You don't like us, and we barely notice you exist when you're not screaming at someone. Your simplistic thoughts and beliefs count for nothing, but the Eternal Imperator has made Kimiya detection the absolute priority, as you know full well." Myrian leaned forwards darkly. "The Al Kimiya is neither fable, nor is it an insidious messiah charged by the Godhead to deliver the great unwashed from Imperial order. No, that gut-crawling, louse-infested basilisk is merely a mortal privateer, slain in physical form by the

Imperator Goat eons back. This bloodless charlatan somehow deploys necromantic trickery to keep its witless spirit from plunging forever into the depths of oblivion, waiting for the chance to reemerge and take revenge on the Emperor."

Mabius' features clenched, nevertheless he seemed riveted. The Goat could almost read the thug's mind. He was calculating odds, wondering if it was *finally* his chance? The giant believed Myrian had never trusted him, would try anything, do anything, to get someone else for the task. But who else in all the modern Imperium had Mabius' power, his gift for destruction? Who else in the Empire was a Sythian outside his own family, and none of them were worthy of walking in his own shadow?

"What you're saying is, Viceroy, the thing's body can die, but its essence still thrives out there in the void? In other words, the thing is immortal?"

"In 'other words,' it's nothing more than a flimflam stall vendor selling its deceit to the guileless masses, Mabius. It died once, and it doesn't have the theurgy to survive a second time round. It floats between domains, recharging, waiting until the day of its incarnation. That day is now."

"I see." Mabius was regarding the room, likely trying to sense the watching Goat. Despite himself, that natural state of maniacal para-noia was being replaced by a surge of something unfamiliar: hope. "I've had trouble with this whole Kimiya stink pile from the outset with its fairy-tale wings and golden beaks, even if I harbour *some* sympathy with the revenge part." No doubt, he was imagining what he'd do to each and every one of Myrian's necks if he had the chance. "But what the hell can this homesick sparrow do? Talk about bad timing—it's *millennia* late. With the Heretics smashed, there's no one left to lead. Everyone thinks it's all—"

"Who all? The walking testicles that serve us? How many of them were given *minds,* General? They weren't meant to know *anything*. They were meant to invade, take orders, squat their withered rumps over the lands the living toil on as thralls, and not waste their already wasted time talking to factory-drone bitch-bladers. Gossip is for the misbegotten brains of the living, Mabius—it's one of the many advantages Lifeless have over organics. You know what happened when we used organics as warriors ... the sentient beasts? They were just as likely to gormandize our troops as the enemy, so don't encourage them peddling their stitched tongues in blathering wiggle waggle, like the living!"

The thoughts going through the Sythian's skull would probably melt lead. Myrian, however, was waiting for the General's ponderous intellect to crawl to its inevitable conclusions like a snail without a compass. The Goat couldn't help but chuckle quietly at the sight.

"I care not!"

He did, massively.

"Good, as it should be."

"But is the Al Kimiya the Phoenix? When stationed at the Pit, we—"

"Ha!" Myrian's main head laughed. Mabius looked like someone had tipped acid down his ribbed spine. Then all the heads began laughing at the same time, and the effect was magnified. "Just one of many risible titles mutating truth to myth. It lives just like you or me; the only difference being it's worked out how to hold on after the loss of its body after its first death." The head took on a note of menacing seriousness. "As stated, it won't succeed a second time. The task at hand is to find and kill it!"

"As an infant?"

"As an egg!"

"Hardly arduous. Any one of your goons could do it while pissing in an abattoir in the dark."

"The difficulty is not in the destruction of the shell, Mabius. The difficulty is in finding it."

The patronising attitude was clearly grating. "You think I'm stupid?"

"We see you, General. You have overplayed your hand, and your venality is lit up for all to witness. Your naked greed for recognition and power betrays itself, but if there's one thing We understand, it's spite." The voice went quiet. "Pray for the continued and undeserved grace the Emperor gives you. Being of unique seed is not as impressive to the One as you imagine, not when He controls the destiny of half a trillion suns."

Myrian paused for a moment. "However, since we loath each other, let's be swift. If there's one thing we agree on, it is our hatred of the organics."

"You know what I think of them!" Mabius snapped. "They guzzle on fatted oxen and send the flesh on a journey through their gut, resulting in it being gravity-dragged down an open-air drain in some organic's mud village. The *ultimate* irony—all things verdant converted into the contents of a sewer, a faecal paradise created by the act of living itself! *That's* what they do. They turn land into sterility and the trees into death, a death that builds their hovels and fuels their fires! And yet, you want me to sit on my ass and do nothing?"

Myrian chuckled. The Viceroy was thoroughly enjoying himself. "They remind me of my people, the demon, one of the many reasons we joined the Goat long ago. Trust me when we say the Godhead is having a joke, but it's on us, *all* of us." The heads dipped in unison, but the Goat knew Mabius didn't understand if this was an act of regret or part of the act. "However, this is a digression, General. The news is astounding. The

Al Kimiya's reincarnation has already begun, in physical form. Soothsay-ers, including our master Himself, witnessed the coming rebirth in vision quests. We don't know how long we've got but incubation is estimated at only one to two seasons—no time at all before emergence."

Those orbs gleamed in the fog. The fires remained low level, but Mabius glared back, his emotions blindingly obvious to the watcher. Could this be the moment, Mabius was thinking, that the demon mut-tonhead finally acknowledged there could be no one else?

"You!" the demon exclaimed.

Mabius shifted impatiently on the balls of his feet, feigning surprise. "Me?"

"Yes."

"Me what?"

"You are chosen."

"For what?"

"You are chosen out of all the hundreds of generals, thousands of commanders and several hundred thousand crack units to seek and de-stroy this shell!" Myrian's main head curled its lips. "We blocked your ascension to champion some time back, but the truth is there is no one else."

Victory.

Blood flooded the warlord's veins, pumping his head with pulses of Mage Rage. Mabius visibly fought to control it but just as visibly failed. "*About Goddamned time!*"

"Then we are in agreement."

Mabius straightened, eyes shining with malice. "Then, truly, I enjoy a unique presence within all these 'half-trillion' suns?"

Myrian chose to ignore this. "The Imperium will spare you ten thousand legionnaires plus cannon and siege towers for backup. If this is insufficient, this can be raised up to the one million mark. It would be immensely problematic, but there are few battlefields left that could not miss some frontline depletions and redeployment. We sincerely doubt, however, you can take even ten people."

A stabbing pain began shooting up his back. Mabius' brain ached with the heat. The Goat felt it as though it was His own pain. "Fine ... all I'll require is my nailed boot!" The giant wiped his profusely sweating brow, likely sensing the heat was a ruse to undermine any witless sap called to the demon's "office." If so, he would be right. "Why not Generals Yeren Sangui and Golub-Yavan, both superior in rank? Why a rank outsider?"

"You know why," the demon spat back. "Arch General Yeren leads our attack armies and Arch General Golub is a vital provider of logistics across the entire northern and western theatres. They are invaluable Tactical class and not usually for active combat. We need a hunter, a warrior, an emotionally stunted psychopath of low breeding. Remind you of anyone?"

Fortunately, the news was what Mabius had been praying for most his life, or, thought the eternal observer, he'd have surely rammed that head through with his fist. If Myrian noticed, he didn't show it.

"Forgot the war—it's already won, Mabius. If the path to this egg was already known, we'd have already dispatched two mules and a headless thrall! We would not need a Sythian. The only information the prophecies provide is the nature of the incarnation itself. It's potent, General, extremely potent. It reeks with virulent theurgy, a terrifying strength that camouflages the shell from our sight." The head looked thoughtful. Mabius, despite the heat, looked chilled. It went on. "However, there will come a day when the beast will become too powerful to mask its presence. It will light up across the firmament, instantly visible to every accursed Seer, soothsayer, and chartist with half an eyeball and a rusty sextant. But—and this is the thing—there will be only the *shortest* of moments available to us before it actually emerges."

Mabius was interested now. Really interested.

"There will be no time for a squadron, let alone an army, General. We suspect only one champion, one of speed as much as power, can portal jump to wherever this thing is hiding and crush its skull before it crawls free. Fortunately, an intellect is not required, as we have met few brutes who have read a sentence, let alone a book. To get there in time, however, a champion's speed will likely be greater than the capacity of his support to follow."

Mabius huffed indignantly. His voice came out pained and hinted of suspicion and accusation. "If you want speed, pick an antelope!"

The heads did something he'd never seen before and would never forget after. They sighed, again in unison. Mabius appeared doubly uneasy. "You don't trust my kind, General, nor should you, but know this. The hands of those that defied me ended up nailed to the doors of the Forum. I have the Goat's full confidence, or He would not have brought me here. For once in your pitied existence, obey, without attitude.

"It's as clear as a skinned helot, that no one understands the full extent of what is happening, Mabius; suffice to say there is one more piece of the puzzle you should know." Myrian breathed in deeply. The fires seemed to subside. There was an aura of expectation in that inferno. "While the Imperium has a champion, the winged insurgent has a Guardian. The One has had ... foresight, but as with the location of the beast, the protector is an enigma. And that's not all."

Mabius' hands clenched. He'd heard that particular rumour already—everyone had. His demeanour could be read like a book. He simply couldn't tolerate the demon filth and the heat much longer. Even his skin seemed to rage. The Goat rejoiced at the macabre dance of wits and discomfort.

"It's highly likely the breeders will get there first, General. The champion would have to fight on multiple fronts, likely bereft of a backup, such is the portal haste demanded."

"I can handle it!"

"Yes, you can. Your only concern is getting there once the One gives you the go-ahead. Let there be no more concern with semantics for now; just be a loyal soldier, and for once leave it at that!"

He grudgingly acquiesced with a single curt nod.

"Good, finally—accord. Time is ended, as has this *pleasant* conversation."

Mabius turned to go, then paused. "What about the sow? The regent hume I arrested, that Vespasian—my inadequate sibling—let go in the Pit? Still need her?"

"An incongruous person from a preposterous planet! That world is a latrine on the periphery of civilisation. It's infected by vermin, reptile hobgoblins, and a carbonated flotsam of organics. But that was your home, wasn't it, Mabius, where you cut your teeth? Where you screwed up!" He took out a wicked-looking blade from some hidden belt and began to sharpen it on one of his fingernails. "Ayilia of the House of Kiya is still required. If her mind can be extracted and thaumaturgically pickled, the Goat can read it and find the Al Kimiya *well* before the time of emergence. Then, He'd only need a stall vendor and town crier to go to wherever in the cosmos it's gestating and stamp on its neck. Hence, her priceless value." All the heads snapped to stare at him. "We wouldn't need you. Don't ruin things a second time!"

Mabius didn't reply.

"Oh, and one last thing, General. This fire terrorist can't kill us, but the emperor is convinced it can defile the ultimate plan, not that it would be divulged to *you*!"

Mabius swivelled back to face Myrian, sending whorls of flame rolling in the breeze. "Hardly a revelation!"

"Don't forget the Guardian, Mabius!"

The giant nodded mutely.

"When you get the call, kill anything and everything you find at the spawn site. Then scrape the veined yolk of the egg across the width and breadth of the Imperium. Don't be fooled, not for a moment, not ever. It is not a messiah or bloodthirsty prophet. It is a highly dangerous terrorist, a criminal, a killer, and we do not wish the Lord Imperator Goat to have to do our work for us *this* time round. Your brutish skin depends on it."

The giant left, planning the collective hell he'd bring on just about everybody who'd stood in his way for most his life, or so the Goat imagined. It was not hard to imagine, to be fair. Mabius was that easy to predict. He would start with that multiheaded, smarmy bogeyman and his overriding personality disorder. He'd send him back into the clot of demonic sediment he had crawled from, except the heads, of course. They could join the other collections on the door of the Forum.

The Goat chuckled again. It had been far more enjoyable than He had possibly hoped.

Chapter Eight

THE WORK OF A DEVIL OR AN INSANE WAY OF THINKING?

There was a soft tremble. The old gate was shaking. Small rodents with fluffy ears and whiskers longer than their tails looked up, startled. The portal above them had been as still as the rocks for an eternity. The rumbling stopped, and silence returned. Suddenly, there was a violent shudder, as a white-blue flash flared across the darkness. The creatures scurried squealing into holes, just in time to avoid a plume of phosphorescent brilliance and the stumbling figure it deposited against the outcrops.

The portal irised shut, and the plume winked out.

Barrackus straightened, then backed off as the door hissed open into an elongated cloud. Troops pounded clear, running the moment their boots touched earth. A vanguard swiftly formed as others continued to pour into the space. A bristling melee of blades and staves glinted as the force became a lake of neon armour and snorting, undead Prowlers.

There was no resistance. The supply trains and Andromedus and his equipment arrived last.

"No welcoming guard." Barrackus surveyed the blasted moon. "Is our luck finally holding?"

Raiders emptied into the pristine moonscape round him. Beyond lay a haunting ebony land, interspersed with red fern and burgundy brush laced with scarlet fruit.

Sheyna sheathed her weapon. "It's a dream."

"A bad one. Think I preferred the graveyards."

"Could there be hallucinogenic spores in the atmosphere, Barrackus? Look at the colour of that fruit. Doesn't seem real!"

"I can't even see an atmosphere."

"Well, we seem to be breathing okay. I can feel air, but I just don't see it, if you know what I mean."

"Ever since we entered this portal hellhole, nothing's made sense!"

Barrackus looked up at an inky sky spread thickly with stars. Coronal plasmas burned round planetary giants and nebulae.

"That must be our target," Sheyna breathed, looking upwards.

"If Andromedus got his facts right."

"Armerhurst!" Sheyna's eyes widened. Barrackus couldn't help but feel it made her appear childlike. "God, I really thought it myth. I didn't think we'd get so close. We'll reach it on our next jump. Unbelievable!"

He smiled wistfully. "The apex of the Interregnum, its ancient capital and the centre of the resistance of the day. You know, for a time, they actually thought they could lick the Abomination, and unlike us, they didn't even have sortilege."

"Amazing."

Above, a large, white planetary disc with a pale blue tinge hung majestically, like a half-sleeping god. It threw off a dim, spectral light across the terrain. On the far side of the sky, remote suns hugged the darkening horizon with a reddish hue. Barrackus could barely suppress his excitement.

"I think the Interregnum was onto something," Sheyna whispered, clearly awed by the spectacle. "They kept everything hanging together long enough for others to join the fight, no thanks to the Ancients. Had those godlike, supercilious assholes not vanished so completely, the embryonic evil might never have crept in. It might've taken everything with them then, had it not been for the Interregnum. They may have been 'old-world,' but they were deceptively resilient!"

A soldier accidentally dropped a bunch of supplies nearby. Sheyna's reflective moment went the way of the Ancients, as she let off a ream of curses at the hapless Raider. Barrackus marvelled. She never seemed totally happy unless she was shouting at someone.

☠ · ☠ · ☠ · ☠ · ☠

As the commander turned and walked away, Andromedus sidled up to Sheyna. She swirled round, her eyes hot coals. "God's sake man, don't creep up on me like that!"

His gaze appeared transfixed, but to what, she was unsure. Not for the first time, she was under the impression his interest was more than professional.

"Apologies ma'am." He gulped. Emotion rippled across the folds of the Dust Tracker's face.

"Something wrong, Andromedus?"

"No, no. In fact, the reverse."

"Spit it out," she hissed, exasperated. "I haven't finished haranguing people yet!"

He pointed at the heavens. "See that world ... the big one?"

"Course I see it. It's the largest damn object in the sky." She snorted. "It's Armerhurst! Barrackus already told me."

"Ahh." He flexed his ample fingers. To her disgust, they gave off a series of loud clacks. "I'd asked him to keep it quiet until I confirmed it on the gate controls, something that's a hog mess as it's all white static right now."

She inhaled, trying to keep calm. "Don't dwell on it. You did an ... astonishing job. He had to tell me."

"Maybe," came the surly reply. "But it wasn't all on me."

"What the hell does that mean?"

"Oh nothing," he said. She got the sense he was trying desperately to be nonchalant and intriguing at the same time. "It's just that no Raider has ever come this close! It's literally impossible to bypass so much Imperium security. 'Historic' doesn't do it justice."

Her lip curled. Though he was beginning to repulse her, she was hooked on his implications. "What are you trying to say, Andromedus?"

"I suspect he ... helps me. Barrackus looks at the controls, and he senses when there are going to be troops waiting, traps too. He knows stuff that's not possible to know. He's even helping me with the controls."

"So?" She stood over him, hands on her hips. "He's good at his job!"

"No." He looked her straight in the eyes. Sheyna swallowed. "What I'm trying to say is there is no way any Asthen, in all the hells, in all the universes has the ability to sense what's coming in the way *he* does. All

I'm saying is it's not normal. In fact, it's not natural, and everyone knows it."

Sheyna regarded him stonily for long moments before grabbing his collar, blue veins popping along her fists. "And I'm saying, cool it!" She was breathing heavily over him, trying to control her fury. In her periphery, she could see glances being shot in their direction. Embarrassed, she released her grip on the startled man and smothered her hair back from her sweating forehead. "You've done an ... excellent job, Andromedus. You're tired—*we're* tired. You're undermining your own abilities and projecting them on the commander. I'm letting this slide, but by the gods, I will turn anyone who insinuates some demonic link with Barrackus inside out with my fingernails if I hear this crap again. Do I make myself clear?"

A heavy pause followed. He was looking at her strangely. "I never said 'demonic.'"

"Do I make myself clear?"

He nodded.

"Good. Now bugger off before I change my mind!"

He did.

Sheyna mentally kicked herself for being so unprofessional. She may as well have called Barrackus a warlock. However, questions were being asked as to where he was getting his power. People had whispered unthinkable things during the stress of being continuously on the run, fighting, and murdering. A small but undeniable faction of distrust was growing, though so far it remained muted, thanks largely to the enemy dying in impressive numbers. But she, Sheyna, was watching. Watching the troops but also watching Barrackus, convinced that it all led to two separate and inescapable conclusions, at least as far as she could tell.

Either he really *had* discovered something terrifying within, honed by years on multiple battlefields shifting across time and space, or he was going insane.

The melee of sounds died down as the camp began to settle. Sheyna returned to her spot beside the commander, mildly pleased with her rapid organisation of a troop still shell-shocked by the rough trip within what seemed to be a totally disused gate. Barrackus, oblivious to her little spat with their Tracker, was still regarding the disc above with reverence.

"Pretty big news to digest isn't it. Armerhurst, the fable!" He regarded her narrowly. "The others? They're holding up?"

"Nothing a few friendly boots on a passing rump can't cure," she replied guardedly.

"Can't blame 'em for feeling ruffled."

"Don't blame 'em for anything, Commander. Just want to keep the discipline going—someone's got to knock some order into this outfit." A slight smirk betrayed her serious demeanour. "Besides, I think they secretly enjoy it."

"Aye." He grinned. "I suspect you do too."

Sheyna smiled more openly despite herself. The moment felt eternal, their shadows imprinted across the stars like cosmic titans. Their existence seemed fleetingly infinite, triggered by the sight of Armerhurst and, perhaps, the hallucinogenic properties of exhaustion and the thinner atmosphere.

Then her mood abruptly tightened. Andromedus was shambling towards her again. With him, there was always a theory, and often a better time to deliver it depending on the mood of the person receiving it, but at least he looked genuinely chastened.

"I've got it!"

Sheyna and Barrackus exchanged glances. Barrackus turned to face him. "What have you got, old friend?"

"The reason there're no troops here. Considering the historic nature of that world up there, it's the last thing I'd have expected."

"Go on."

"Simple. There never has been!"

"Aha—well, I wish I'd come up with that one."

"It should've come to me sooner—like on Verillion, there's not been a military presence here for quite some time. The Ascendancy's armies never got this far, even in the early days. The only way forwards for us now, and I mean the *only* way anyone can go on, is to go *through* Armerhurst. All paths at this point in this crazy network within a network bisect in one place, one hub—up there." He pointed vaguely at the sky.

All eyes automatically swivelled upwards, even though they'd studied it intently already. It was impossible not to feel it wasn't staring back. "There's no other way to the Core, not through these local portals anyway. Not unless we double back and exit this hidden domain of interstellar gates and circle around for the next six to twelve months or so, assuming the guard hasn't been tripled the way we came."

"Give me the short version," Sheyna prodded. Though the Tracker often grated on her, she was suddenly interested.

"The Ancients built this covert network and used Armerhurst as a portal hub long before the Abomination. A form of protection, perhaps, though against what is anyone's guess—I shudder to imagine. Outside of the fact no one has ever come this far, our target up there is a defence against all defences. I would imagine they, I mean the Imperium, consider there to be no way through!"

"Makes sense." Barrackus nodded thoughtfully. "Though we have the element of surprise going for us. What about good news? Is there any?"

"Apart from my miracle work, that was it!"

"Not that I'm ungrateful, but I had a feeling there wasn't."

"Well, there could've been guards here instead."

In the early days, they had tried the unthinkable. The Asthen had actually tried blocking an interstellar portal.

They had tried to block an obsolete gate on a devastated moon as an experiment. They had tried to keep the Imperium at bay by cutting them off altogether.

It was weird science. They'd tested it within a wild region of space where physics was literally out of control, one that astonishingly still sported a working gate. One moon had collided against another and been knocked into a shallow orbit. The resultant chunks of rock and ice had reformed into a lumpy ball, but the tidal gravities of the moon's towering parent planet would rip them apart again on a regular basis.

Perfectly uninhabited and perfectly ideal for a ridiculously dangerous test, one that put the whole system under acute threat if it was to go awry.

So, they begun work on the tiny, fully operational portal within that melee of orbiting rocks, even if the moonlet it was situated on was somewhat arduous to reach by gate jump. It didn't help that it had one of the quickest spins. There were advantages, such as the spectacular views, but the entire area was alarmingly volatile. Tremors, exacerbated by the ferocious gravity of the mother world, regularly rocked the place with violent seizures. Yet the experiment was launched with much optimism and a sea of patriotic verve. The Asthen blocked this minor portal with the most advanced engineered materials they could create. It took nearly a year, but they managed it.

They were elated. No one, not even the Goat on Nethergeist far off in the dark, had ever achieved such a thing. The celebrations went on for three days, and the chroniclers went far and wide to tell of the accomplishments of this new and vibrant species—new, as the Asthen had only recently declared themselves to a universe already forever at war. It was a statement of intent, a machismo-fuelled demonstration of species virility; theirs was a vibrancy so potent their thaumaturgic testosterone was stamped on a hundred thousand worlds with jingoistic self-regard.

That was day three of the experiment.

On day four, a quasar-style backdraft slammed into the orbiting mother world from the shuddering portal, turning every particle at its centre into atomised mush, the blockading debris shooting across the cosmos like infinite bullets. In less than a rat's heartbeat, a blossoming supernova from the still-intact portal took out the rest of the gas-ringed world along with its solar system and a few dozen red giants nearby and any systems they may have had. When the Asthen scientists eventually returned to the celestial cadaver they had created, it had coalesced into a mini galaxy of rocks, primed and ready to give birth to a miniature stellar nursery of its own come the next few billion years or so. So great had been the pent-up fury, it had obliterated almost everything nearby.

It was hardly surprising.

The gate hadn't just erupted with the blocked venom of its own funnel, but the entire interstellar, interdimensional network behind it. Nothing could stop that power. At that point, they realised the portals weren't part of the visible world but the boundless universe of atomic matter itself. They *were keyed into the quantum matrix, and the two were inseparable. Unlike their creators, the portals were indestructible.*

No one ever attempted that again.

That was the day Asthen nationalism died. That was the day a subliminal realism crept in to haunt every move they made, every plan they formed.

On one of the rocks the silent portal remained, waiting for someone who'd probably never come, to jump through.

The camp was set and rations were cooked. Sentries stood on duty, but no one felt at risk, not that night, or at least as far as Barrackus could tell. Andromedus assured them that he'd laid false tracks several jumps back heading away in a curve towards the allied lines. He again expressed astonishment that it had worked, cheerfully adding how they were the sort of tricks deployed most effectively in the capricious chaos of frontline warfare. However, one serious screw-up and the critical advantage of invisibility would be gone, leading to choleric conflict in fierce firefights across the stars until there was no one left. It would be impossible to hide now, their route was too constricted. Each person intrinsically understood this.

Some were sullen. Barrackus hardly blamed them. If only they knew what he was beginning to know, maybe they'd feel that, perhaps, fate was more a door than an abattoir, not that he expected them to embrace the inevitable any more than he did. Most nights he wanted to scream—too much knowledge always blurred the non-existent schism between genius and thaumaturgic psychopathy. Ever since he'd lost control as a student, it just kept on growing and growing. They called it Ji'naa.

At least Andromedus had done his work. In using the mapping system on their entry portal, they had a working template of what to expect on that imposing world. The major gates on Armerhurst seemed to be facing each other in a massive ring, within the capital city of the same name. He'd also detected a small army unwittingly awaiting their arrival. More correctly, he could *sense* them. It seemed the army was close to the mouth of the exit they had to go through. Their presence created barely enough gravitons to register on the funnel controls, but those tiny fluctuations were enough to confirm that they were there. Was their luck changing? The minute signals degraded into the network almost immediately, but their Tracker had picked them up all the same. Few gates were sensitive enough to even detect such things, and no one else could do it. Not in the Ascendancy, at least. It took a stocky fellow with few graces and appalling sartorial sense to even come close. It helped that there was a refreshing lack of security, but clearly no one was expecting them.

Still, utterly remarkable.

With their Tracker's help and Sheyna's invaluable fidelity, Barrackus had burned a furrow straight towards the Core. The slumbering army ahead was an overdue obstacle in a universe where no one, not even the Goat, had the power to block or destroy gates.

Putting aside all worries, the Raiders broke open the supplies, talked, told jokes. Most had been with one another for years, so food was shared with ritually washed hands and cut with worn but cleaned blades. Many had cut and felled an enemy with as much ease as they diced the dried food now. Afterwards, people started reminiscing, volunteering memories of the hard times and the good. Adira had them laughing, recounting the day Andromedus first turned up during a mission. Assuming the rest of the troop were as obsessed as he was with obsolete incantations and technical schematics, the rookie Tracker had led their first mission straight into a swamp containing millions of tiny larvae that only ate hair. Two Raider taskforces had to be diverted to drag them out. By the time they managed to, every single member was bald ... everywhere. Nevertheless, Barrackus had kept him. Why, Adira couldn't say. Who'd have thought he'd not only turn into the best Dust Tracker in the Ascendancy, but the best in the universe? Barrackus clapped the loudest. Not only was it true, but he knew it was essential as leader to show his support.

Andromedus, however, had gone bright red.

Sheyna jumped in with the story of a training day with Barrackus, this time even further in the past. He caught his breath. She wasn't normally as relaxed as this, and anything could come out. It was something about him accidentally enrolling for a ritualistic dance class, thinking he'd joined astrophysics and psychometric deciphering and physical meditation. After he'd pranced around for what seemed like an age with a vast, obscene-looking candle in one hand and a meditation ball on his head, oblivious to the giggling students pouring in, the amused instructor had to finally tap him on the shoulder. That might have been survivable had it not been for five adjacent classes coming in to laugh too, nearly one hundred people, all told. It sounded tame after so much bloodshed, but the story had done the rounds in the Academy for years. Even as a youth, Barrackus was too intense for his own good.

They talked and laughed, illuminated by the ghostly pearl-blue of the night moons stretched in carcanets across the heavens. Sheyna was, uncharacteristically, talking a lot. Pent-up tension came with each word. He could feel it as if his own. It was impossible for her to stop. Gabbling slightly, she recalled when she met Barrackus for the first time.

"I hated him at first!"

Stunned silence.

"He seemed so vague, so lost. Even then, he was considered one of the finest commanders in Asthen history, so I guess I felt ... disappointed." All eyes watched her with awed muteness. Barrackus sensed how wired she was, as though she were keyed into something. "But then I got to know him. I realised I was judging by appearances—and not for the first time. I'd expected some egotistical lunk with a jellyfish for a brain, but I am so glad he turned out to be a ... considerate man, a reflective man, someone who cares more for those around him than his skin. These years have taught me more than my life combined. If anyone can end a war that has gone on far too long, Barrackus can."

People nodded, smiling quietly to themselves, their growing disquiet temporarily put aside.

She hadn't finished. "Even if we fail this day, I guarantee we'll set off the biggest bonfire this Empire has ever seen, one that will flare across time itself and will have repercussions in ways we'll never know."

Sheyna stood with a drink in one hand, her unsheathed blade in the other. "Let the bastards *know* we're coming!"

She looked godlike in her war amour, flanked by her battle-weathered but striking hair, which lay draped across her shoulders. Around her, her comrades-in-arms erupted in whoops and clapping. When it all eventually died down, she flashed a wry, almost devilish smile. "All I ask is that you keep the commander away from the stove. His cooking is as deadly to us as his stave is to the Imperium!" Spontaneous laughter broke out. People crowded round her and a surprised Barrackus. Rations of diluted wine were uncorked. There was only enough for a mug each, but no one cared. Even their Tracker managed to haul himself away from his deliberations for a hefty snifter.

The fire roared. The second sunset had begun. Lars had already worked the physics out. He told them a "spare" miniature sun was cloaked by a methane cloud in the blackness above and would surface only after dark for a short spell before itself setting, creating a second twilight redder than the first. Everyone was amazed to see him proved right—he was only an amateur sky watcher. Even Andromedus offered a reluctant congratulation despite his chagrin at not being the first to notice.

Stomachs unusually full, the group stretched out in circles round the glowing fire. Jokes, curses, and laughter filled the deathly landscape, bounding off the rocks in a magnified din.

After a while, Sheyna stood up stiffly and walked to the portal to relieve the sentry.

Barrackus watched her stare into the blankness of the gate, waiting to deport them to destruction. Her senses seemed to catch him approaching as cautiously as a wild cat.

"I ought to thank you Sheyna, you know. No one has ever had the guts to tell me my cuisine was so ... lethal."

"Not much worse than mine, Commander," she replied, eyes glinting. "As we probably won't last much longer than dawn on that place"—she pointed up at the bright disc of Armerhurst—"I thought it was time to confess all."

Sheyna scrunched her face cheekily, as though she really had no choice but to tell.

"Well, I still can't believe it. How they always ate my gruel at sup time without even a flicker of disgust on their faces."

She laughed out loud. "That's all you can think about? What harm you've done to their insides via your turn at the pot?"

"The harm's been considerable!"

"So, that's been your secret to success all this time? Our guys'll take on anything after your dinner shift?" She swept her unruly but impressive mane back, grinning as she did. "Honestly, I'd eat your worst casserole rather than go through that funnel and meet whatever's waiting beyond."

"No argument there."

She regarded him pensively for long moments. In that otherworldly light, his austere, Mage-hardened features were ruggedly striking. His silver hair, unintentionally flopped across sharply defined contours, seemed to shine with a power he'd not noticed before.

"Look," she started, "as the second-in-command rat here, I have to say something, something I've been meaning to say for a while. You've saved our lives too many times, and we know it. We'd have never gone this far otherwise; no unit would have. It's been ... staggering, unreal. Also, a little wrong." She cleared her throat, as ever clearly awkward with diplomacy. "But now I truly believe you're going to ..." Sheyna paused uneasily. "It—it doesn't make any sense, Barrackus. It's insane! I sometimes wonder if ..."

"I'm insane?"

She winced. "Don't think we're not grateful. We follow on automation—such is the legend you've become, the damage you've done. That, I think, is the problem."

"Too much influence?"

"Too much power."

His brow rose. "Isn't this a bit late? I mean to be this concerned so far in."

"Maybe it took this far in to realise we really *should* be concerned." She ground her teeth in frustration. Words were definitely not her thing. "Should we be concerned? I mean, all this rampant theurgy you seem to summon that you can't explain. That's the kind of power I'm talking about. Power that in the end ends up running the show rather than being part of it!"

"It's not taking over, Sheyna, that I know." He screwed up his face and shrugged. "It just keeps ... growing. Give me time. I think things are coalescing inside."

Sheyna inhaled, a deep unhappiness obviously growing within. "Well, let's hope you've got some of that for tomorrow. We're going to need it."

He scratched his ear, then wiped dirt from his forehead. "You think we won't make it this time, don't you?"

She shot him a pointed glare. "Will we? "

The portal was dark. It seemed to have been there forever, transcending time and space with undefinable power. It would go on forever too, even if the rock it stood on disintegrated. In such an event, it'd be a silent, unblinking door drifting through the void for all time, waiting for someone to activate it.

"We'll ride towards the centre on Armerhurst where our Tracker's seen those gates clustered together. We can't reuse the gate there on arrival, as it will be wiped out for days by the static caused by our jump. Covert navigation will be therefore impossible, while using Imperial channels instead would bring the Abomination's mutts on us." He paused, thinking. Sheyna was watching his brows furrow. "The same goes for the gate we used here. Fortunately, Andromedus found a second one nearby, so we don't have to wait. Again, it leads only to Armerhurst—it's there or go back." His voice dropped. "We'll smash the army there with all the surprise, weaponry, and sortilege we have and bulldoze a path through to our target funnel. He's convinced it'll have wickedly intricate thaumaturgic locks, but hopefully he'll crack them quickly. To be honest, we think they're pretty old, so he should. Then maybe it's off to the Core with us!"

"Let's hope reinforcements don't jump through before he has a chance to crack it."

"It's a lottery; I've never denied that. Luck, risk, and strategy are interchangeable."

Sheyna stroked her mouth, thoughts racing. For a fleeting moment, she looked strangely vulnerable. Then she fixed him that fabulous glare of hers. "By the gods, Barrackus, this time there's no way back. You know that don't you? We'll be surrounded on all sides before we know it, cut off from behind with no remote chance of retreat."

"It's already happened."

"Meaning?"

"Meaning, they may not be up our collective backs as things stand, but they're not far off."

"You sense it?"

"Andromedus tracks it ... or should I say, them. They're gradually pinpointing us. They still think we're trying to find a way home, but they've most certainly cut off all hope of retreat. It's already too late."

She raised her own brow. "He failed to inform me."

"It's just thoughts."

"Our lives depend on such thoughts; there's no 'just' about it."

"Indeed!"

Sheyna sighed. "Shit."

Barrackus leaned forwards. "We'll run fast, *real fast*, to the target, leaving a plume of flame halfway across the cosmos. They haven't even considered we're this near. We'll have total surprise on our side against a region that hasn't experienced an attack for tens of millennia, maybe never. They'll be stupefied, especially as they know Raiders don't do suicide!"

A prolonged silence followed. He let her think; he knew she'd speak eventually. It wasn't in her nature to conceal things from him. "You know, being here so close to one of the most famous worlds in history, really brings it home."

"Brings what home, Sheyna?"

"Think of it ... the Interregnum knights of Armerhurst and the armed beast-spawn of Nethergeist, arranged in titanic ranks of armoured splendour and fluttering pennants against each other. Perhaps on the very ground we stand on?"

"Must have been something!"

"And all for nothing."

"Never for nothing; always for *everything*."

She whirled on him furiously. "That sounds like more bull, Barrackus."

He smiled. "Not if you look at it from the Interregnum's perspective."

"Hell's toenails, *of course* I'm looking at it from their goddamned perspective, Barrackus, but all I can see is bird crap. They've been dismembered as a state and occupied for all eternity!"

His smile persisted. "Look further, from the point of view of the horizon, not what's in front of our eyes. They lost, sure, but they bogged the early Imperium down for eons. If they hadn't, the rest of charted space wouldn't have had the time to reorganise and resist. The Abomination can't defeat everyone at once! Something or someone will happen to Him one day. Region after region will unite in a long game until the day He screws up, and He will."

"Well, that's all well and good for those who get to stay on the outside of the border."

"Maybe no one gets that privilege."

She bunched her fists exasperated. "Crap! And I'm not talking birds this time. If He takes the whole bloody universe over, Commander, then He takes us too, including species yet to learn of His existence, let alone unite and fight." She was practically spitting. "By your reasoning, we're heading the same way as the Interregnum!"

"Which is why taking the long view is a lot more appetising."

There was such a look of disdain on her face. His mouth clamped shut. A long quiet followed as Sheyna digested the information, venomously chewing it over—and what was left of her lip at the same time. With an impatient flick of her head, she spat out blood.

"I didn't sign up to spill our guts halfway across creation for nothing!" She munched her lip some more, then abruptly looked up. Her chagrin quickly dissipated, however, when she saw his face. "Holy teeth, Barrackus, what's the matter? You know you can always confide in me."

"I'm not so sure."

Maybe he should stop while he could. There was still time. Tomorrow could be too late though. Was she even remotely ready? He'd hit her with enough shocks recently to last a lifetime.

"Barrackus? Is something wrong?"

"It's ... well, I ..."

"Never seen you embarrassed. Don't worry, please tell me. I won't laugh, I promise."

"You won't laugh, I'm sure of that."

She frowned. He picked up the alarm bells tinkling subliminally within her mind, but he couldn't help himself.

"Sheyna ... we've been fighting together for some time. I think we make a—well, a world class team. It's unbelievable how much we've achieved over the years, and how much we've hurt the Imperium." He cleared his throat and took the plunge. "Recently, I've been thinking time is something of a luxury, something impossible to appreciate until the hourglass is closer to empty than it has any right to be. I think we're owed by the Ascendancy—hell, the whole sodding universe. Whatever happens, there's no quick end, whoever wins. If we did get back—and I know that's not looking likely right now—I'd like to take a more ... supporting role. Maybe directing campaigns, planning strategy, not leading them. I'd like to pass on my knowledge to a son or daughter one day. They may have more success."

Bugger, bugger, bugger. He hadn't meant to say that. What a calamitous cock-up. It was more awkward than he had ever imagined, and he'd imagined the worst.

Breathing heavily, Sheyna went rigid, fixing her eyes on the all-seeing planet above, refusing to meet his gaze. If words were difficult before, they were impossible now. He waited, desperately trying to control his own breathing.

"Perhaps you'd better leave this till we navigate Armerhurst tomorrow."

"You said it yourself—there may not be a tomorrow."

She visibly gulped but said nothing.

"Look Sheyna, what I'm trying to say is lately I've grown to ... appreciate your contribution, your skills, your intelligence, that unquenchable spirit. You're more than a right hand, you're a part of all this ... *my* life." *Crap, crap, crap.* No turning back now, despite his fumbling lips. "I would like to be part of your life. We're so close already. Unite ... as a team, you know, for real ... for all."

The blood drained from Sheyna's face. She couldn't speak. He looked at her uncertainly. She clearly wanted to retort—she always wanted to retort, but something indefinable held her, for once.

Standing there for long, long seconds, the great warrior realised she was, against character, now completely out of words. The night was as still as a bone yard, not even the trill of a lone bug to divert attention. Yet, she was struggling to think of a thing to say. Nothing in all their time together seemed to have prepared her for this.

"Listen, don't say anything, Sheyna—think about it."

She was looking at the others, but were too far away, each absorbed by the everyday act of preparing for sleep. Eventually, she raised a shell-shocked face in his direction. "Barrackus, you're easily my greatest friend, family even, but that's it. You're the brother I lost as a child, the father I never knew, the mentor I never once admitted I needed. You're my friend. Crap, you're even my equal—and I never tell people that—but I never once thought of you as ... anything more than that. I'm not sure

I can cross the divide, not sure at all. I need to think." She paused and shook her head. It was his turn to gulp. Knowing her, she'd kill the whole thing off now, rather than prolong hope. He could hardly blame her. "We're better off *not* involved, Barrackus. Decisions would be impaired. That's it. Professional reasons! I ... I don't want to lose what we have, and we will. I just don't see you as anything else as a friend, a comrade, even a wayward, half-nuts god. But that's it."

He gave her an impossible, clenched smile. "I'll ... take that. Friendship as a god, though, if true—and it isn't—that would be the two of us," he mumbled. "Honestly, it's okay, it's okay. The wine and the finality of this push have addled my mind. Sorry ... Not thinking straight. Gets cut off out here so far from home."

"No, Barrackus." He braced himself. She wouldn't stop now. The tap was fully open. "I'm sorry, but I don't see you like that. It's not possible, not at all. You deserve better; I'm a vacuum inside, bent on killing those scum until they're dead or I'm dead. Nothing else matters. There is no future, despite what you say or might be thinking, if we don't kill them. I'm sorry. All I think of is revenge and hate, nonstop."

"It's alright, *really*. I swear it ... It was just a mix up, nothing more."

"Even in peace, no way, not a chance. We're not remotely matched. You and your intense thinking. I like to meet people, visit things, that sort of stuff. You hate all that. We're not for each other in any way; we don't do anything for each other, and I'm sure you agree. I couldn't possibly see you in that way. Not possibly! Just friends. Please say—"

"No, no, *really*, it's all fine, really."

He felt his face turning liquid red. She backed off awkwardly with one final, "I'm sorry."

Barrackus was left standing on his own, watching her walk hurriedly away, trying not to run. His cheeks throbbed like hot coals in the night. An emptiness had consumed everything he mistook for a heart.

❦ · ❦ · ❦ · ❦ · ❦

"We're out!" Seftus was beside himself with emotion. "We finally found our way out that louse-infested, arthropod mausoleum. Give me half a dozen Krayal warriors, Regent, and I'll go back in there and give those bugs a roach fest that would last years! I ain't bragging. They'll do it, mandibles and all, and still have time to take out the rest of beetle city!"

They had exited into a clearing from an exit in a rock cliff. The fact that it was night and streaming with rain was an irrelevance, even to a species that thrived in cripplingly dry environments. The Krayal was practically singing, he was so relieved to be out of the slave camp burning below. Ayilia was close behind. She couldn't resist a smile when he started stabbing the air with his blade.

"We squashed some real big cooties, didn't we, Regent?" he exclaimed. "By the gods, I've got bug guts all over my boots and I ain't finished yet." He raised his fists, eyes shining manically. "There's plenty more room for some more mite meat, rest assured, hume. This is just the beginning."

"Noted." She let out an impulsive laugh. "Come on, before you injure yourself. Hell, you're worse than Aaron."

He snorted. "Don't tell him, but I almost miss the cerebrally challenged bonehead!"

Seftus had given what was left of the attackers the slip back in the labyrinthine matrix of tunnels. Decades of skulking in the Krayal's

144

mountainous hideouts had its uses, as did the inexperience of the guards. The world hadn't been invaded for a long time, if ever. Victims never came out: it was always one-way. A breathless slave had led them from the lower levels, followed by a vast number of captives, faces delirious with freedom. Once free, they ran in all directions, dispersing into a blackness illuminated only by the reflections from the watery rocks. Above, a scattering of stars fleetingly poked through venomous cloud. Lighting crashed and rain pelted, but Ayilia was ecstatic.

The human and Krayal scythed through the torrential downpour, leaving vapour trails in their wake. However, movement on an overhanging rock brought them to a skidding halt. Crouched, dripping figures were nocking some equally dripping arrows. Ayilia and Seftus instinctively ducked as a set whined overhead. Shocked, they looked back to see arthropods emptying out through the exit. The missiles struck them, flinging them backwards over each other with heavy thuds until none were left standing. The stunned escapees looked up, squinting against the drizzle. The hunched, soaked shapes of Stilgen, Soren, and the rebel legionnaires eyed them back, gazes beady. When they saw that it really was Ayilia and Seftus, they lowered their bows, features relaxing.

Nevertheless, both sides starred for long moments in disbelief. They hadn't seen each other since the Pit.

Immense relief swept through Ayilia. She stood to catch her breath, her mouth open to the elements, gratefully letting the liquid run down her parched throat. Grime, dirt, and blood flushed away in the cool shower. Her blade dangled as she stretched both arms out and embraced the wetness.

Seftus, however, true to form, strode over to the ledge and shouted, mouth cupped, up at Stilgen. "Where in hell's hellish hell's hell were you?"

Stilgen carefully slipped down to face the Krayal chief, his expression puzzled. "Here."

Seftus let out an exasperated sigh. "I can see you're *here*!" He pointed back where they'd come from. "But why weren't you *there*?"

"Why?" Stilgen's brow furrowed drily. "It is of prodigious size and operated by an indigenous species of dubious mental virility, employed as allied mercenaries by the Imperium to use slaves to make crap cakes in underground mines. Undead are logical—it is undeniably best to be here!"

Ayilia dropped her arms. No more guards emerged, just collections of darting slaves, each shooting disbelieving glances at their arrowed thrall-masters lying prostrate. A series of muffled *thwumps* issued from inside. Acrid smoke drifted from the mouth. The captives had carried fire torches with them, setting ablaze anything combustible. The place was dry as tinder—it was child's play creating infernos on every level they escaped through.

Despite this, Seftus was still looking decidedly peeved, all dangers forgotten as tiredness and stress came out in a Krayal geyser of blithering ire. "The only reason we were in there was that those things took us there ... otherwise, we would be here, where you were *so* comfortably snuggled. Or maybe, we'd be somewhere else on another dung hole of a world, making 'crap-cakes' for some other Imperium-controlled sodality of inbred aphids!"

This time, Stilgen's whole brow was raised, but in amusement. "So, you *did* make crap cakes?"

"No, I did not make crap cakes you inspissate, stumpy-skulled stiff! We dug up dust and sulphur, and they beat us. And big words don't impress anyone around here, bone bollocks."

"What big words?" Soren frowned.

"'Cakes'," Stilgen replied, clearly taking the piss out of the Krayal.

"You sanctimonious—"

"Seftus!" Ayilia barked.

The Krayal chief's mouth shut. He took a deep breath and shot her a furtive glance. "I can't help it ... he's a bloody know-it-all that—"

"... knows as many big words as you!" Stilgen checked his bow, then carefully slung it over his shoulder. "Not all Lifeless are aberrant lame-brains, though I appreciate that's a common misconception in your race. Howbeit, while I did not expect commendation, some recognition for continuing the conditions that permit the pounding of that organ in your chest would not come amiss."

"See what I've had to put up with." Soren winced. "These mudbricks have been doing my head in."

"Good to see you too, Soren," Ayilia said, wondering if she was going to have to be mother goose again. "However, *all* of you, our eternal thanks for those guards." She inhaled again, still getting her breath back. She was becoming too old for this. "How the hell did you find us?"

"Actually, it was astonishingly simple!" Stilgen replied nonchalantly. "We didn't even need to home in on Seftus' odour." The Krayal's eyes popped, but the Lifeless quickly carried on, gesturing towards the vent as he did. "We captured a drone who, after some gentle persuading, filled us in on what was going on inside. That exit is an auxiliary conduit and essentially unwarded—hardly surprising, as only rodents, lost tumbleweeds, and the criminally insane actually venture here. I sent a scout to covertly fetch you!"

Seftus was not staying quiet. "So, you set up camp at the exact point we exited without being concerned we might have picked another exit?"

"The drone led us to the most unused, desolate entry in the edifice!" Stilgen looked amazed Seftus hadn't worked this out.

"And?"

"Consequentially, it was effortless to send someone incognito inside, guided by the information our captive provided. The scout was in time to see you and your thrall pals heading towards him at the head of a seething riot." He faced Ayilia, eyes flashing. "It did not surprise me, Regent, that you used that bewildering ability you seem to possess to navigate a way through flaming chaos and carnage to emerge unscathed, as in the Pit. It gave us the time to mount an ambush in your favour."

"The people we freed should take the credit by showing us the way," Ayilia replied, before adding in mock indignation: "I'm sure that's a compliment, Stilgen ... the bit about my 'bewildering ability'!"

"I'm sure it wasn't!" Seftus spat almost gleefully. "And it was pure luck they found us."

Disarmingly, Stilgen half nodded. "Partly."

"And if the Regent hadn't led a revolt, dead ears? If you hadn't found a way to rescue us, you'd have left, alliance or no alliance?"

"Something like that."

"You mean totally like that?"

Stilgen cocked his head. "I mean something like that." He shot Ayilia a glance. "We want the Pro Consul back *and* a home, Regent. You are here to contact the Resistance, the only people who can find us one out there in the void. There'd be no point hanging around if you had been turned into insect fodder. You should be reassured that we looked."

She smiled, despite the rainwater bathing her features in liquid marble. "Trust me, I am!" There was a commotion within the interior. "Time's short. We need a portal, and we need it quickly. I assume the static's died off and covert navigation is possible. Do you know where it is? Can you plot a course, Stilgen?"

"It's not far. As for continued travel, we're not a large group and did not cause excessive disorder, so the static would've been relatively minimal." He looked grave. "The lack of preparation meant we arrived here at different times, despite the heartbeats that separated us on exit. I apologise for the disarray."

Ayilia gripped his shoulder. "For God's sake, we'd have been filleted on the spot in the Pit if it wasn't for you. You've *nothing* to be sorry for."

"Gratitude, but I'm also thinking of the Pro Consul."

"Good riddance to badly made rubbish!" Seftus snorted.

Stilgen ignored him. "Fortunately, he was fleetingly detectable streaking through the jump stream towards our intended destination world. He must be recovered."

"Of course!" Her face clouded. "Kemet! Why isn't he with you? And Jarong?"

Stilgen shrugged. "As I said, we all exited at different times."

Subterranean curses were rising from the cavern. Time was running out.

"Okay." She swallowed. "First, we need to get out of here!"

Thunder pounded overhead. Like delinquent ducklings, the motley crew of misfits fell in with Ayilia.

As they bustled away, Stilgen carried on talking. He was back to his usual dispassionate demeanour. "We used the Consul's fire before; we can use it again. We might need it."

"Those bugs need another kicking," Seftus interjected, his verve, if anything, mounting in the intoxicating oxygen rush the open air had brought. "Let's quash some more!"

"We've left their hive on fire." Ayilia grimaced. "No point wasting energy on a declining race of shell heads!"

The dryness of the hive had desiccated her skin, her hair, her pores. She was content to let her soul drink in the rain's melodic pattering and the delicate spray from boulders. Her face and arms were drenched, but the mail and combat gear were resilient. It made campaigning infinitely more manageable. Time seemed to flow like the waters around them. It could have been moments, or it could have been days; she lost track of the universe around her.

The journey was a blur of shiny rocks, black shingle, and the sheer drop they had recently climbed. Lighting whiplashed the skies. Not once did Ayilia complain. The hellish temperatures and the dust of the arthropod city were being washed away. It was a baptism of purity, and she drank it religiously.

"We're here."

She came back to reality. Stilgen had turned to face them. Ayilia blinked. In the dank, inky haze, she couldn't work out if it was the same gate or not.

"Can we go through?"

"It's why we're here." Stilgen growled, amused, before shooting Seftus a glare that spoke of centuries of enmity between the Krayal and Lifeless. "Are you to accompany us, gecko? I refuse to guarantee your safety from my soldiers, but your chance of keeping your neck intact is far higher with us than on your own. This remains our Empire at the close of the day, even if they want to slit us as much as you."

Seftus snorted. "You're welcome to it!"

"I take it that's a yes."

Stilgen began fiddling with a dial. "Again, we're a small unit. Any static from our jump should not hinder us unduly, should we need to jump again relatively swiftly. As you know, tunnel drones monitor all traffic, so it has to be covert. Unregistered movement is a grave felony, but then we are felons anyway, so how much more grave can it get?" He arched a brow.

"We know." Seftus exhaled impatiently. He looked suspicious. "Wait, mud feet—where the hell exactly do you intend to take us? For all we know, you could be planning to land us in a bounty hunter's skin market!"

Stilgen's eyes lit up. "Now there's a thought!" He looked round at the pensive faces. "Humour." No one said anything. "I thought I'd work on my jokes in the spirit of accord."

"Keep trying," Soren said, shooting Ayilia a horrified glance. "We'll be in touch."

"In the heartbeats in which I had to triangulate our way across ten thousand star systems from the Pit, this bleak world crossed our sights like a dark comet across a sun," Stilgen said quietly. "It's an occupational hazard if time is not particularly bountiful, like tossing a javelin through a storm of ballista shot. The chances of it missing each single one are small."

Soren tried not to laugh. "You flubbed it!"

"Yes," came the dissolute reply. "Perhaps, if you had found a way to keep the Pit horde at bay, I might have found you a retirement home to rest your overworked mind cell."

Soren's mouth shut.

"Inexplicably, the Consul is the only one to have bypassed this storm planet and proceeded to the original coordinates. We can follow him, though I cannot tell which gate he exited through."

Seftus had finally calmed. "It pains me to say it, but you did okay, skull balls. However, I've heard rumours that unregulated jumps can dump the unwary into hostile environments like a sea or an erupting volcano, or maybe the belly of a giant stag beetle or the Goat's poop cannikin. Obviously, we'd no choice back in the Pit, but just how adept are you *really* at gate mechanics?"

Stilgen's features darkened. "These machines are so old, sometimes the physical conditions deteriorate around them. Within the Empire, the standard practice is to post advanced warnings inside the tunnel matrices if a surrounding environment has decayed. Alas, only designated users would have this kind of stuff and the latest danger charts."

"'Stuff'?" Ayilia smiled. "A very human term, if you don't mind me saying!"

"Indeed." Stilgen's faded scarlet eyes were twinkling. "I've spent too much time in the wrong company." His face was illuminated as the door to infinity flared into life like a cyan bonfire. Beyond, the universe awaited.

"Underneath that gruff demeanour, you're quite the comedian," she added.

"He's a comedian alright," Seftus muttered gamely, before shooting Ayilia a searching glance. "You look thoughtful, hume. Concerned about landing inside a snail's gut?"

Ayilia was barely listening. Her hands were a halo in the thick wall of rain. Their eardrums resonated with its thudding, like fingers drumming on canvas.

"Problem, Regent?"

She fixed Stilgen an intense stare. "Listen, I can't come."

The silence was so complete, even the pounding of the rain vanished. While Soren's and Seftus' mouths had dropped, Stilgen was glacial. "Without you, there is no Resistance. Without you, we have no home—and consequently, no alliance." His troop shifted into menacing postures in the half light. They'd gone from wayward allies to killers in a heartbeat.

She inadvertently gulped. "It's Kemet and Jarong. They're here somewhere if only the Consul went on. I can't leave them. If you leave the gate on those settings, show me how it's done, I'll follow on—with them!"

"Impossible!" Stilgen bristled. The hands of his troops hovered over their weapons. Seftus backed towards Ayilia, his hand ready for his cutter. Soren hesitantly joined him. The living, like before, were lining up against those who did not. "We join the Consul, and you come with us. He has shown he is integral to our mission, as you well know." Stilgen indicated the other two. "These watermelons can stay here and look for your fellows. We won't miss their gabby gobs."

"'Gabby gobs'!" Soren exclaimed, wide eyed. "I thought we were friends."

"You can't be friends with the soulless, hume," Seftus hissed. "You may as well hook up with a scullery bucket!"

"Think it through, Stilgen," Ayilia said, stepping forward between the opposing sides. "We either stay together, or we die together. One way or the other, we *will* perish if we can't maintain this alliance. Without a home, you'll be hunted down like murmels, roasted on an Imperial spit. Without you, we'll never find the Resistance and we'll die in the Imperium too. Wait, while we look—that way, we stay unified." She faced Stilgen directly. "Think, carefully!"

There was silence aside from the downpour and the clash of the sky. The wind ruffled their garments, their hair. The eyes of her Lifeless allies glittered.

"No need to die on our behalf," came a voice from the darkness. "Though don't get me wrong, it's much appreciated."

All eyes turned to see a soaking Kemet and an extremely bedraggled Krayal step into the clear. Ayilia grinned from cheek to cheek and hurried over to give him a hug. The divided group stared mutely, then slowly began withdrawing arms from swords. The sense of relief was palpable. Even Seftus had to do his best to withhold a smile. He swiftly walked up to Jarong and slapped a warm hand on the other's shoulders.

"Ow!" Jarong blurted.

"I'll give you 'ow,' you scaled birdbrain." Seftus growled, though it was clear he was only pretending to be angry. "Where in all the hells did you get to? And with a hume, too. The gossip bitch-bladers back home would have a field day with you if they heard!"

"We came out at a different time than you," Kemet beamed. "We recognised your tracks and went hunting for you, but the rain washed them away too quickly."

"Er ... that's correct, more or less," Jarong added. "After a long while walking, or well, tottering in this rain in circles, we decided to, you know, keep to the portal in case you came back. We knew you couldn't go anywhere without this."

"Unless there were half a dozen over those bloody mountains, you blockhead."

"A risk for sure, Seftus, but in this desolate bog heap, a worthy one," Kemet interjected. "We used this as a base to search the area and come back, repeatedly. Looks like we were just in time."

"Aye." Soren grunted. "We were about to have a dead man barbie!"

"In your dreams!" Stilgen muttered.

Ayilia held up her hands before matters descended again. It was like managing a lit powder keg. "Okay ... this was a warning shot and a reason to keep our wits *and* our minds!" She gave them a steeled glare. "Or we end up doing the Goat's blood work for Him."

There was no dissent.

Seftus, energised again and eyes blazing, faced Stilgen. "Any chance of using that gate and landing us near a fire, bone bag, so we can get warm at least?"

"Don't tempt me, lizard—the way I feel, you might find I land you *inside* one!"

Trying not to laugh, Ayilia gestured them back to the portal. She was completely bathed in its otherworldly light.

"Okay, Stilgen, ready when you are."

The group turned to face the door, stark but beautifully serene in that stormy light.

﹡ · ﹡ · ﹡ · ﹡ · ﹡

The funnel was an explosion of cyan. Ayilia steeled herself, but instead of darting lights, there was only calm. She was bathed in saffron and the softest of breezes.

She was here again.

A corn field rippled, the husks murmuring like spelt bells in a reed courtyard. She breathed, inhaling the airs.

The skies seemed darker. Every time, they seemed darker.

Ayilia scanned the distance but couldn't see anyone. That included her previous visitor. She wished she'd asked the Consul what he was doing. Wherever this place actually was, it was *her* place, and it was unbelievable he'd found a way in. In different circumstances, before the invasion, she'd have felt violated.

War changed things. Now, she couldn't work out whether it was mildly annoying that he'd parachuted himself in, or whether she should be grateful. Perhaps ex-Consul Vespasian was nothing more than a neural intruder.

You could go crazy thinking like this.

The forests were darkening. The deserted house was on a gently inclining hill, surrounded by flowers on burgundy shrubs. Not only did things seem different this time, but the clouds appeared to drift faster. A tree line was getting darker more quickly than the rest, taking on traces of menace. As a child, she'd always found dark forests spooky.

Ayilia considered the house again, but the Consul's warning kept her back. A ramshackle side track wound through the corn. She took a breath and plunged in. Though the sun had started to sink, there was still heat.

Without breaking the stems, she powered through the crops and lost sight of the white, wooden house.

Caulderwell was boiling, but it had nothing to do with the heat. Fear stalked the cobbled avenues. Around the walled exterior and its heavy gates, terrified people thundered like rolling eyed bovine in an abattoir. Armed troops tried to keep order, whipping townspeople until they fell. But the melee had a collective mindset, and sentries were forced to erect hurried barriers to herd the host towards approved routes. The deceased were few, but fewer cared. After all, what was there to care about, mused the Legate? Fewer boozers, for a start!

Caulderwell wasn't big for a capital, just three million strong. Considering how many urban centres had depopulated before the Imperium's flag was raised, it could be described as sizeable. The Imperium kept its holdings under a steel fist and fleers never came back, preferring rural uncertainty to urban control. The Imperium was everywhere, but they displayed less interest in the network of remote hamlets in the crater—just solitary patrols and bored officials.

Until now.

People were furious; there was no protection. The killings had not stopped, and citizens kept vanishing. The Empire had a vested interest in the minerals mined in the crater, so the sector authorities were keen on cooperation, saving on the costly retraining of thralls. Such a thing was not only unthinkable in the Core—it couldn't even be looked up in a manual. Despite this, despite the city legion being mobilised, a necromantic leviathan was freely pillaging the countryside and shredding the people. Each legion, roughly six to ten thousand, was subdivided into ten cohorts. All of them had been deployed, yet these toughened troops had failed to neutralise the enemy.

The Legate stood on a high vantagepoint. The city was in the largest caldera known, hundreds of leagues in diameter. It harboured a thriving ecosystem around a system of thermal vents running through morasses and bloodsucker-infested bogs. Crystalline falls lined the cauldron's lip, venting gallons of water into the interior. Exits deep within the rock, piped it out in churning tributaries. If Imperial tourism had been widespread in these parts, the city could have been wealthy indeed.

The Legate's heart was a lump of meat bound by artificial capillaries and clotted tissue. It hung like a busted pendulum, a symbol of vanity than a thing of use. In a manner of supreme irony, considering the scorn the Lifeless had for organics, it had been stitched in as a sign of command virility.

Its maroon eyes swept the scene like lasers.

Volcanic mist encircled the city like an alabaster ophidian. Within its see-through nightgown, a latticework of pipes supplied steam to factories, wealthy homes, and even a sphinx-themed public bathhouse. Not that the Legate noticed such fineries. It was another irony that luxuries best suited to breeders were so readily used by drones, soldiers, and centurions. It was also astonishingly shortsighted. Rainfall was manageable, especially if a Lifeless soldier used its crimson cape for protection. However, superheated steam, though not as corrosive to manufactured internals as being stuck in a lake, could haemorrhage the gutting of a Lifeless bather if they stayed in too long. It made him wonder who was doing the colonising, if the ways of the organics were being adopted by their conquerors. He tried to forget his own redundant heart.

A Tribune approached.

"Legate Aurelius, we've dispatched two cohorts this time. They should keep the creature out."

"Unlikely, Probos. Send another to reinforce the gate."

"Liege, the thing failed to enter the perimeter. Only the hinterland's been threatened."

"Yet with every incursion, it draws closer. The slaughter rises inexorably, but the Empire is uninterested in the loss of breeders. I told the Praetor they're an invaluable resource, but he's only concerned with his campaign for the Senate. He forgets his position is loaned from the emperor. Further delay in production threatens the deployment of the DeathHead itself and the execution of *every* official responsible for that delay, plus a decimation of the guard." He fixed his eyes on the Tribune. "I very much doubt we'd survive the process!"

Probos' rheumy gaze was as wide as craters.

"The DeathHead? By the gods, they're the battering ram of the Resistance. Why in all the undergods would they be sent to Caulderwell, when there are plenty of bored regulars available?"

The Legate raised a brow. "Caulderwell is the capital of a highly profitable enterprise with a GDP that's the lynchpin of the sector. It may not be the most valuable Prefecture in the Imperium, but I wonder if the Imperator Goat truly appreciates how our exports touch every corner of His cursed realm."

"Seemingly not," Probos whispered. He bent closer, conspiratorially, in case some wayward cockalorum was listening. "I've heard He has other concerns now that the Heretics are crumbling."

"Be careful, dog-breath," hissed the Legate, looking round for eavesdroppers. "Do not speak of the Kimiya in public." Satisfied no one was sticking their neck into their business, he fixed the Tribune with a fiercer glower. "A war that strode the very eons is nearly over, Probos. The Imperium's armoured glove has smothered all it sees. For the first time since this began, what once was a critical resource is a hindrance. The Empire does not need its thrall subjects anymore!"

Probos looked astonished. "Surely misinformation, Legate?"

"The only thing keeping tens of billions of breeders alive, and those who ward them, *is* the war. Think of the endless factories, workshops, and supply chains. Think of the rapacious killing machine that feasts off these. What will the Imperium do with such a vast enterprise when it ends? There are whispers ..."

"What kind of whispers?" Probos looked genuinely terrified.

"You'll see. One day, we'll all see."

An organic walked up apprehensively. He was a city official, a freedman breeder, useful for admin. The Legate faced him impatiently. "Breeder, ensure the people remember that gathering in large crowds is highly prohibited."

"Sire, the creature—"

"Forget the creature. I *warned* you and the breeder council before, that any unnecessary attention and the Goat will reconsider the lax regime status here. Already, ten cities throughout the central Prefectures are having their stratum reviewed."

"My apologies, sir. The creature—"

"It's an anomaly, a fluke, an unholy accident of nature and delinquent sortilege, from the time of the Ancients. Psychic disturbances and wild theurgy wreak prodigious havoc everywhere, especially within the Core itself, where the phenomenon is centred. We have it easy in comparison!" He towered over the organic official. "I think things have become too lenient of late. Perhaps, I should rethink the abolition of public examples? Circulate my warning before Caulderwell is threatened by someone far, far graver than a wayward conjunction of angry magick and wild science."

The man scurried off. The Tribune swirled on the Legate. "God's teeth, Legate, why wait? These helots enjoy too much leeway. They stink of sweat and rodents and betray each other for the whiff of money or the cheapest whore—they have no values. Little wonder they are the lowest of the low, with—"

"I forget *nothing*, militum! I am Patrician Class and live for the glory of the Imperium, *never* forget that. The bleating of the bitch-bladers and fortune tellers here are insufferable. Never trust someone who wastes time on prattle, as they will turn on their own kith when their tongues have run out of things to say about others."

Probos remained silent. Aurelius leant close. "Sort this out. Coordinate the cohorts. I will see the Praetor."

"Sir."

"Yes?"

He hesitated. "They call for the Stranger. For better or worse, they think he has forbidden knowledge, that he is the only one capable of silencing the aberration. Shall I send him to out fight the creature? He's been doing Mage tricks to earn some coin—it's how the vagabond came to my attention. I confess, I used him once myself for a minor matter, an irksome theurgy infestation. He has no documentation, and had it not been for the current threat, I'd've had him thrown in the slammer. A hume called Gala was helping him blend in."

"That mad Mage? Even *you*!" The Legate shook his head bemused. "You're in good company, then—the Praetor is also a convert, or else I'd have had that pariah run through from his throat to his loins." He turned and shrugged at a world clearly gone insane. "Why not? As if I care."

The Stranger's mystic knowledge wasn't serving him well today. His foot had gotten stuck in a pipe leading to an abandoned brick outhouse, quickly followed by his hand as he bent down to retrieve it. How that had happened was anyone's guess, but it was a good job the Legate wasn't there to see it. As he fought furiously with his stuck appendages, ass waving unceremoniously in the air, cursing loudly the whole time, some squirrel-shaped creatures scampered down a nearby tree and tried to steal the contents of his tattered backpack.

"Piss off!" he shouted, then fired a warning shot over their heads for good measure, but nothing came from his emaciated fingers. Instead, the animals dove further into his belongings.

Furious, he tugged harder, but though there was a cracking of bone within, he only served to get his hand stuck further. The animals gave a shriek of delight and began rummaging through his pack with abandon.

He and his stuck bits were in the district graveyard on a hill outside the city. Though Caulderwell was old, this area seemed older. The trees were withered, and the surrounding shrub was spartan. The headstones were crumbled, their etchings undecipherable. Vaulted crypts with goth-ic doors and decrepit spires were covered with nightshade and white blooms, flanked by gorse. It was almost idyllic. It was a great shame it had to be spoiled by the sight of recently slain breeders and their livestock slaves. A messy boneyard of Lifeless drones also lay nearby in a collection of shattered ribs and still-astonished-looking skulls.

The Stranger cursed again and shooed off an animal, which gave a series of hoots. The damn thing had stolen an ear cleaner and the only mirror he had. Not that he needed it for anything particular—it just made him feel like he belonged. In truth, he'd found it a few days ago, but it was extremely annoying all the same. With a final grunt, he shot free, scattering the animals as he did, but landed so hard on his rump that he was left sprawled on the ground, like a manikin that had fallen off the back of a wagon.

As the Stranger lay gathering his wits, he regarded his surroundings in more detail. It seemed to him, in that lucid moment, that nature and people worked in symbiosis. A series of pagodas ran across grasslands and a scattering of hillocks below. They were empty, their original purpose forgotten, but they appeared to grow out of the rich dirt to blend with the rustling fronds. Horses, with red ribbons streaming from their chestnut manes, wandered serenely among the hillsides. None of them had been hurt, and he found he was secretly glad, although he wasn't sure why.

He thought of slipping away from Caulderwell but knew every cohort on the world would be in pursuit. Some Tribune called Probate—or was it Probe?—had sent some weasel called Gunk to where he was begging for coin and told him to fight something prowling outside the city walls. The Stranger had had no choice. He was a renegade with limited powers, and he couldn't fight them all, so he'd obeyed.

Damn fool! Should've done a runner while the thick-headed dolts were cowering behind their crumbled walls. That would've given him time.

He looked up, startled by something he couldn't put his finger on. Then it struck him.

The thieving squirrels had gone.

In fact, everything around him seemed to have gone. The birds and insects were quiet. Even the grasses were still. Everything was deathly silent. With a growing sense of dread, he realised there was a presence nearby, one with a deeply disconcerting necromantic bent. The Stranger had a reputation as a powerful Mage in the city. In truth, he was so terrified that had he been capable of shitting his britches, he would have.

Slowly, he rose to his feet.

The grass to his far left had changed colour. Wiping his eyes, he peered at it closely. The green was now the hue of straw.

If anything, the grass looked dead.

There was sudden movement. The mighty Stranger whirled round in stark fear. A ribbed tail smacked into him from above, sending him back onto his butt. He hadn't seen it coming, nor the creature at the end of it clinging to a sizeable, ramshackle mausoleum.

Every bone cracked, yet he managed to throw himself through a dilapidated fence in a mess of spinning wood. The tail swished like a scythe and backflipped him onto his head, which crashed through the centre of a broken grave. With a disbelieving groan, he realised he was stuck fast again, his butt pointed helplessly once more at the skies. The ground lurched as the impressive weight of the creature thudded next to him. He was sure it was Lifeless curtains for him, as the thing whacked him so hard that his body and much of the grave's exterior went flying in a smorgasbord of wayward debris.

He tried to stand, but a bone jutted through the parchment-thin skin on his right thigh. His left arm was dangling uselessly at his side. A fork of ribs jutted out at crazy angles, and his right shoulder snapped repeatedly as he moved.

"Hell's—"

He looked up braced for the tail, but it didn't come. This time, a cockerel-shaped, rock-hard claw hit him with such force that an arm immediately detached, leaving him prostrate on the dying grass—a consequence perhaps, he found himself musing for no reason at all, of the thing's necromantic potency. He lay there pitifully splattered in fluid, soil, and livestock dung. The tail followed with another slam. Part of the Stranger's cranium was crushed, along with a good deal of rib cavity in a series of staccato snaps. Something was torn from his back, but he no longer wanted to look, nor could he. There was no point.

Bits of his body seemed to cover a radius of ten to twenty paces in all directions. The part that had gone airborne was a good thirty paces oft. The thing savaging him calmed. Why not? He was dead. Berserk sortilege from his assailant was coursing through its flesh. A large, bristly, very wet snout thrust into his stomach, sniffing vehemently. He sensed disappointment vying with insatiable hunger. There was nothing to devour, as the only meat on him looked like it had spent years on a fishhook.

It paused.

The claw prodded him once more, looking for missed nourishment. Incisors dripped predigestive enzymes on the back of his neck. The concoction sizzled.

Back came the fear of the past. Back came the memories of the Pit, the abuse. Back came that fear he could never forget. It welled up like bubbles of oil threatening to drown him in despair.

He was finally going to die. The coward he'd always been now quailed.

His eyes flicked open.

A series of fleshy nostrils lathered with mucus sniffed, then tried to flip him over.

The thing was going to eat him whole.

"Piss off!" His voice sounded wan, unrecognisable.

It growled, then tossed his body up and down as it tried to flick free any spare meat.

"Stop!"

The head hovered close, a vast eye pressed against his.

"Stop ... *please!*"

The back of its throat trilled softly as it sniffed him again. He could hear stomach juices gargling. It seemed permanently starving. The snout came closer. Horrified, he realised his head was being fitted in between a set of massive jaws. Teeth as sharp as diamond bolo knives began to close around his skull.

He was going to die.

Inside, something clicked.

A surge of old-time anguish enveloped him. He let out a cry as a tidal bore of fury shook the remaining fibres of his body with terrifying vehemence. He screamed, but his jaw was paralysed with theurgy and nothing came out.

A mind-cracking roar followed.

A sequence of detonations ran along his line of sight, convulsing the ground around him. The earth quaked as fire rippled along the graves in thaumaturgic shockwaves. Stone and brick cracked, then shattered. His hands grasped for something, but there was nothing there.

He finally closed his eyes, lost in an implosion of white.

Vespasian felt himself coming to.

Immediately, he knew the danger had gone.

He opened bleary eyes, amazed he could see. His body was covered in cinders. Around him, embers fluttered from a still-rising ash cloud. Deeply startled, the ruined warlord pushed himself upright in a fumble of dirt and found himself at an alarming angle, astride something whale-like. Moving was an art in itself. Flame teased the fingers on the one arm he had left. One of his legs was missing.

He quickly extinguished the light.

Then his bloodshot eyes widened. Horrified, he stared point blank at a mucilaginous tongue. A segmented neck led to a body spined with ridges. Burn wounds at the base of the throat revealed the cause of its demise. Nothing nearby indicated what could have been responsible for such a ballistic impact.

Except, of course …

He swore in self-aware terror.

His body ached and throbbed. It made no sense, yet the dull, repeated gnawing was debilitating. He was Lifeless, so real pain was an impossibility. He and his siblings had once lived, but the Goat had stamped it out at birth until they were as lifeless as a chaise lounge.

What in all the furnaces of all the hells combined was the sensation drilling into the stump of his limb and up and down his shattered vertebrae?

He hand felt his torso carefully before tentatively plunging deep into a revolting crack inside his chest. It was disquieting, probing his own insides, but he had to know if he was going to die. His heart was as lifeless as ever, but the stitched, cloth-like gutting hidden inside to animate him felt intact. It probably was why he was still "alive"—if the leviathan had messed these up, he'd probably be a squashed cootie on the heel of its foot.

For a moment, he went blank, overcome by weariness. When he came to, he found himself automatically hauling himself up to his one remaining foot, incongruously holding a leg in one hand and brushing soil from his body with the other.

"This ain't right."

Movement caught his attention. Vespasian cast a glance downwards at the city. Crowds, attracted by the lightshow, had come forwards to see. They'd witnessed much of the one-sided conflict; one he'd won utterly against the run of play. Cheering, they lined the battlements in a smudge so thin it seemed like a hair had been blown across his eyeball. There was little chance of keeping a low profile now.

An ingrained instinct surfaced from somewhere deep. Though he was still weak and blurring in and out of consciousness, a dim light sizzled at the tips of his fingers. He couldn't imagine what his hand was doing, until it purposefully reinserted the severed leg into the gory stump it had been ripped from. It re-entered within a shower of sparks and smoke, as theurgy bound the ripped tendon within the bone. The bone itself was fused tight, where it was supposed to be. Waves of intensity shot up his shoulders into what was left of his brain, but he still couldn't accept that it was pain. Nevertheless, a pang of nausea curled around his bruised gut in response. So unpleasant was the feeling, it felt it might force his battered innards out of his mouth. Nevertheless, he applied his fiery hand to his crushed skull.

If the leg had been an unsavoury experience, this was hell. Power ignited within the busted part of his cranium and folded it back into shape. What state his tissue was in, he couldn't know, and didn't want to. Those sensations were so crippling, Vespasian turned round and retched blood and mucus across the still-smoking ground.

And yet it wasn't done. More to the point, *he* wasn't done. Aghast and fascinated in equal measure, he saw himself crawl around, looking for bits of himself. Had he remained a breeder, the townsfolk would soon be doing what he was doing now and putting pieces of him in a wooden bucket. But no, he had to be different. He had to put himself back together. So, he crawled around, scooping up what he could and, with thaumaturgic surgery, fixed things back into place. Some kind of physician matrix implanted in his brains, perhaps by Imperial augers as a child, took his hand and swept it over the fractures, using carefully aimed plasma to fix them into something vaguely recognisable. That was a good thing, if true, as he didn't have the first clue himself. Again, had he been a breeder, he'd have scorched his skin to the bone, but he wasn't, and his hide was tough despite its thin veneer. He wasn't looking at what he was doing. So, when another biting wave hit him, he went unceremoniously sprawling.

He must have been quite the sight for the distant onlookers.

Vespasian landed on his shoulder stump in what might have been agony, within grabbing distance of his severed arm. He shook it in a blind rage and tried to comically stick it on again, but only shreds of tissue connected as his healing flame had vanished. He tried again but couldn't get the damned appendage off now. Gasping, he flopped onto his side before peering at the mutilated part of his body.

Time had passed. He didn't know how long, but enough for the pain to subside. To his surprise, he'd actually attached the arm perfectly. Of course it wasn't working, but somehow, he'd Mage-stitched it back, muscle for muscle, tendon for tendon. Could that be why the flame had gone AWOL? The job had been done?

"Why not," he spat through blooded teeth. "Something had to go right eventually, even for me!"

He pushed against the ground. Astonished, Vespasian found his newly reattached hand supported him perfectly.

Out of nowhere, panic exploded. Uncontrollable, horrified panic. "What the shitting hell is this shitting crap?" His hollow cries rang out, but no one answered.

His carcass slumped into a sitting position on the creature's thick neck. It must have looked odd. Unsurprisingly, that Imperial auger thing kicked in again. Vespasian found himself having to watch as his hand pushed ribs back into place with a sickening series of popping cracks and sewed the skin taut afterwards with cobwebs of light between his fingers. Nibs of bone and scraps of hide lay in patches around the turf, but unbelievably, his body felt intact.

The worst was coming.

He couldn't stop himself from putting a hand to his head. The skull was fine now, but not the slush masquerading as a mind. A jolt akin to someone tipping a burning oil lamp inside his brain forced the distraught Sythian against the slain animal. Against the sound of his own groans, something lit inside his head. It felt like acid ants were gnawing at his cerebellum, laying fire eggs in its folds. In between darts of agony, Magi flame remoulded the membrane within the cavity through the skull itself. The crushed part of his mind was welded together before the scalp and its vagrant hair were unceremoniously cemented back over the sealed rent.

He was feverish.

"God damn you all to—"

He blacked out again, and this time he stayed out.

He felt the guards carrying his stricken figure towards the city gates. They would realise he, the Stranger, had lost an undisclosed amount of body weight, much of it left lying around the corpse of his assailant. Flailing everyone away, Vespsian attempted to stand in an undignified fashion on one leg. The other leg felt healthy but didn't seem to function properly.

"Why don't you one-eyed yo-yos leave me *alone*—I did your dirty work. Exorcise your own bloody basilisks!"

No one replied. He was supported by one of the guards as they ushered him towards the city. Dead citizens speckled the area everywhere, along with their slaughtered longhorns. It was a final, if somewhat macabre, equality between master and subservient thrall via a shared if brutal death, though for the animal perhaps a swifter demise than the slaughterhouse. Wooden shacks burned quietly. An assortment of snow-clad peaks towered in the background. The crater was fleetingly magnified by an optical illusion created by volcanic light refracting with a passing ecosystem of wayward sortilege. That happened a lot in Caulderwell. The townspeople were granted, via nature and a thaumaturgic pollution from the depths of antiquity, a close-up glimpse of something so distant it was normally a blur. During these moments, the city, elevated as it was above the caldera, met the distant crater walls practically eye-to-eye for several heartbeats.

The phenomenon passed swiftly. A series of doors opened, and an Imperial official approached, flanked by guards. It was the asshole he'd seen before—Tribune Proboscis or something with a massive sentry. Vespasian saw, with a start, the Tribune was with the hume female he'd saved earlier, Lala or something (he was really shit at names these days).

Vespasian shifted uneasily. If he went back in, he'd never come out. The Imperium's reps had thought him a homeless eccentric, a street gut-terpup, and the Praetor had only recently gotten word the Stranger even existed. When they realised Vespasian was a Mage, the hard-pressed Tri-bune had, reluctantly, enrolled him to purge a wayward manifestation. That involved some drifting, aimless theurgy which somehow become imprinted on some dying man's consciousness. Combined, the necro-mantic bedlam had achieved basic instinctual awareness and promptly manifested inside a sorbet wagon. An exorcism was urgently needed. A clergyman would have once been summoned, but the main religions had been banned, leaving only the Imperial temple system dedicated to the Goat to deal with such inconveniences. Unsurprisingly, the clerics appeared to possess no spiritual powers of any kind.

At the time, Vespasian had been passing the "Soothsayer Quarter," essentially a drained alleyway behind the bazaar next to a fedora store, when some local witch had suggested he have a go at fortune telling. She was a charlatan with, paradoxically, some very basic levels of gift, and she had inadvertently used this to "out" him to a local official, desperate to find a way to destroy the necromantic aberration. Tribune Probos had agreed.

The thing had proved impervious to spears and had, inadvertently, developed a highly concerning degree of public flatulence. Whole sections of the city centre had become a no-go zone. Anyone who tried to move the sorbet wagon had spontaneously vaporized. Vespasian had been dragged there, and much to their astonishment as well as his, had somehow driven it off with a burst of low-level ... something. He didn't know what. It wasn't genuine possession, just chaotic magick, yet the effect was instant celebrity and a queue of people wanting balms for warts, finger stumps, hairy elbows, and even, in one case, oversized genitalia. For the cost of a little attention, he'd gotten coins to buy some new rags and pay for the dirty hovel he'd started renting. Wisely Vespasian, the fallen ruler of a forgotten world, had kept his identity secret, so someone had called him the Stranger and it'd stuck, fast. Recognising some use in a world blighted by alarming manifestations of thaumaturgic powers, many inadvertently sentient, the Tribune had resisted the urge to throw him in the clink. But he had the Stranger watched, closely. The Imperium never changed, no matter where you were.

"Undead hobo, you will accompany us." Probos' eyes seemed to shine with a sharp intellect.

Gala regarded him sternly. "He just saved your city, Tribune. Once from the fart wagon and now from that snout-cockerel hobgoblin. I told you he was useful."

"And I told you that you risk much with that piehole of yours. If it continues to master your mind the way it does, you may find the Praetor nails the head it is attached to upon the Forum's outhouse."

"It comes with the territory, boss," she replied, her head cocked. "You used me to manage the Stranger. The piehole comes with the deal!"

Probos glowered, then fixed that stare back on Vespasian. "Follow!"

"If there's going to be a celebratory banquet, I'll pass."

"The Legate demands audience—and likely the Praetor too."

Gala visibly flinched. "The Praetor's demon. He probably works for Myrian, the demon head honcho. They'll kill him."

Vespasian's eyes widened. "She's right, Prober. Demons are demonic. I don't stand a chance." He leaned closer to the Tribune. "Who's gonna waste the fart fiends if I'm gone? The priests can't even exorcise a water closet!"

"Demon or not, the Praetor is overlord. If he says he is to see you now, then now is when he'll see you."

Vespasian shot the Tribune a filthy glare, but Probos looked unmoved. "We checked your background, Stranger. There is no record of your role as an Imperial exorcist in the Eastern Command. In fact, there is no record of you at all. It is unheard of for Magi to have no official documentation. Your continued existence is a mixture of bored expediency on local officialdom's part and the belief that you are a malfunctioned mendicant on ours."

"Check again!"

The Tribune ignored him. "Furthermore, I find it disturbing you've been with us for over three months and, until I became aware of your existence, you did not once present yourself to us." His tone hardened. "And now the population has become ... animated by your presence. We like things quiet here in Caulderwell."

"Tell that to the dead bogeyman in the cemetery."

To Probos' visible astonishment, Gala grabbed him by the shoulder. "That's two dead bogeymen, Tribune, *and* he saved me. Saved you a lot of shit, not to mention the stink from high up if these things weren't stopped. Gives our demon overlord a lot more time to do, you know, demon things."

The guard next to them had heard enough. "Shall we put the hume in a clink, Tribune? She could talk the arse off a horse!"

"No." Probos sighed wearily. "She's been ... useful. Escort her to somewhere in the city and let her loose, may the gods help us." He tuned back to Gala. "Remember what I said about that gob!"

She smiled coquettishly. "I love it when you talk dirty." She turned to Vespasian. "I won't forget you. Thank you, and please—stay safe."

Probos shook his head as the guard dragged her off, then indicated for Vespasian to follow, before heading towards the city. Vespasian did so reluctantly, flanked by a small phalanx of guards.

They strode through gates decorated with dragon wings and spears and pushed through a growing crowd. The guards dipped through the winding back streets of the residential quarters provided for the non-industrial workers and low-ranking living officials, to give the throng the slip. The sewage running on open roads was unpleasant, but they succeeded in evading the onlookers. Here, figures slumped smoking or toyed with their snouts between thumb and lemon-stained fingers, while washing fluttered across rickety balustrades.

Presently, they came upon Market Crawl, the central street of the city. Most of the region's traders and vendors congregated here to sell and buy. It was easier to control, easier to tax, easier to bribe, and easier to be bribed. The Legate began to change some of this. He had tried to bring some degree of transparency, something unheard of from the higher orders. His motivation was unknown.

The market was a smorgasbord of colours. Vespasian followed his line of sight down to admin centres bathed in vapours from the grilled meat stalls and a metal foundry. Odoriferous smells mixed with the scent of perfumed leaves stuffed with rice, exotic vegetables, spices, and chromatic fruits. Carts arrived at warehouses flanked by horses, Prowlers, and an assortment of mules. He was awed by the sheer variety of produce available: lentils, oranges, alien-looking roots, pistachios, aromatic herbs, black hunks of sugars, thick tubers, sacks of seeds, and slabs and slabs of cured fish. The cobbles were layered with discarded food and coarse cloths that diametrically contrasted the quality silks flapping from the tops of stall racks. These looked more like grand pavilions than market tables.

Rectangular squares with tables and open stoves surrounded it with more upmarket delicacies. Shrimp and rare swamp lurkers, tree canopy livestock, bush meat, turquoise snakes, and giant beetles fried under clouds of sweet-smelling smoke. Workers ate greedily at the tables, stuffing in flesh with their hands or using odd-looking instruments or slurping noisily from bowls. To Vespasian's surprise, Lifeless officials shared the tables with organics, clearly enjoying some of the more disgusting flesh. The marquee classes of undead did not suffer the indignities of an animalistic digestive system like a drone but were gifted rudimentary taste enzymes triggered by poignant food. It was still shocking to see them share a table. Vespasian caught a glimpse of the public latrine and rows of men, both living and dead, squatting happily together over a collective trough that took the combined waste away courtesy of gravity—which meant it took forever, as the incline wasn't inclined enough. That was the trouble of eating the living's food: it had to come out again. A sickening concept to the rest of the Imperial classes, but here they clearly liked to do things differently.

Vespasian's thoughts drifted. He should have been a hundred unsightly chunks of debris on the cemetery hill, lying in the graveyard breeze. Not even a Lifeless could take that punishment— the fact he had once lived should have made no difference. Ultimately, they were just another form of existence, one based on chemicals and artificial, neuron-fired tissue. Without that little spark milked from the Goat's Ichor, it was doubtful they could ever animate. Yet life was what they had, or perhaps unlife. Who said you needed a heart to be defined as conscious? To have a mind was to have existence, and that was life.

As for the healing, he hadn't been able to quite finish that off. Flakes of skin peeled free, while scars crisscrossed his emaciated frame. Astonishingly, he was walking almost normally now. But it remained an uneven gait, and one arm hung semi-immobile at his side.

Was this a Sythian thing? Perhaps the species had self-healing abilities? He couldn't exactly ask his brothers. The whole escape from the Pit, his Pit, was a disaster. Perhaps, it was time he gave up the proverbial ghost and slit his gizzard before some Lifeless cretin did it for him. Loneliness had been a burden he'd longed for all his life, and now that he had it, he found he hated it with a passion.

They left Market Crawl behind and entered a central piazza of fountains and mosaics. An imposing, Gothic stair rose on either side. It led to a triumphal arch at the top, flanked by tall fountains with watery plumes shaped like trees. A sulphur-yellow palace with ivory balustrades dominated everything. Spiralling figures bent towards each other above the entry, interlocking in fantastical shapes. For many, the artworks would've appeared sinister, but to Vespasian they were beautiful, surreal sculptures, reaching for power in a futile grasp for glory. His inner eye sensed tones of subliminal mockery at those who hungered for influence inside a machine that despised them as much as they parasitically fed off it. Surprisingly, the guards were all breeders, in green-yellow tunics, with no talking corpses in sight. His fists clenched when he noticed a grubby platform on one side. A dozen bodies hung feet-up in neat rows, slit from naval to neck, innards fluttering almost serenely in the wind. Dark clumps lay beneath each on the fly-infested ground.

Bile rose in Vespasian's throat.

The pain in his head worsened. For the hundredth time, he staggered. No one took notice, outside the odd curse and tap from a spear. Already he felt like a condemned man, and he hadn't even seen the Praetor. In his madness, he smiled. His brother would love this, in his bittersweet fashion. He, Mabius' runted elder, actually *did* possess some Sythian traits after all: an inexplicable power of self-healing and bogeyman slaying.

He urgently needed medical attention, not to be frogmarched to someone who mistakenly thought he mattered.

The deranged smile still haunted his lips. A guard took offence.

"Something amuses you, dead man?"

"Plenty of things amuse me, breeder."

"Perhaps you wouldn't find it so amusing if you were to join the Praetor's guests over there. There's plenty of spaces left to swing from."

"A bit optimistic, considering the Praetor hasn't seen me yet." His smile was acidic. "He might be persuaded to let you join the fun. After all, I *might* be useful!"

The guard swore.

Probos interjected firmly. "Have a care, Stranger; you have no friends here." He leaned closer. "Our master suspects you are renegade. That's a crime that *always* invokes death!"

Vaults, corridors, and tunnels passed in a whir. To Vespasian's surprise, they descended to the grimmer lower levels and a series of gothic catacombs. At the end of a dank passageway, heavy doors swung open to reveal crypts with dark arches and the smells of tombs. A spartan throne sat in the centre with a jade jewel embedded on the top. Thrust firmly into its hard seat sat a grotesque, pot-bellied creature. Three arms hung on either side of the dormant body, layered with rolls of flesh and a menagerie of curling teats. An elongated head was monopolised by a set of cobalt eyes that studied him with rapacious intelligence.

Vespasian faced the creature along with the Tribune. He was prepared to die, maybe wanted to die, but life wasn't going to make it easy. The guards remained by the door. Others glowered from archways that ran like spliced herring bones to the central space.

The silence was overpowering. Vespasian stared back, unblinking.

Finally, it spoke in low mutterings causing vibrations within the fabric of the stone.

"Artifice and duplicity!"

Silence.

The ex-Consul shot Probos an uncertain glance, but the official stared ahead. The being spoke again. "Do not mistake us for the dulse that live here and what they pretend they think they know!"

Vespasian caught the sudden movement of small animals in the dimness. There seemed to be rats hovering near the throne.

"We are presentiment, we are multitude, and we are not fooled, Stranger. You are a gilded thief come to rob this fiefdom in the night at a time of flux."

Vespasian's eyes squinted. Another look at Probos' stern face provided no help. The thing he assumed was the Praetor continued to glower. Obviously, it was up to him to reply.

"Pardon?"

The thing leaned forwards. It seemed a part of that solid seat.

"We are Shaitan brood, pulled from domains so terrible only the Imperator Himself dared to intercalate. Now, we serve Him and Him alone, not the bedevilled Demon Monarch of yesteryear. So many hellion brothers and sisters captured; so many slit from gut to neck or, if insidiously unfortunate, recruited. Demon Imperial do *not* hesitate to do whatever is asked. And they are loyal—the Goat ensures this. He *makes* them loyal." It fixed the fallen warlord with a malevolently studious gaze. "And they are powerful. Their theurgy is not hewn or sewn." The thing spat across the floor. By either some miraculous aiming, or even more miraculous timing, it hit a rat on the head, which immediately began devouring the treat. "Now here you are, a soulless servant with theurgy. A soulless servant that neither came off an assembly line nor was grown in a vat."

The rat was joined by the others. Some were black, some were brown, and some glowed like multicoloured candy overloaded on witchery. Vespasian realised, with a jolt, that they were stuffed on sorcery courtesy of the demon's spit. As if on cue, it let out another disgustingly large white-green bout that splattered across the floor. The rodents squealed with delight and began feeding once more. They were its pets.

"Our Legate checked on what you claim to be. No viable connection with the Imperium was established; you have no rights. You are an apostate, an iconoclast!"

Probos shifted uneasily on his feet. "Liege, he dispatched two necromantic infestations. The economic dislocation they caused was significant!"

"Ahh yes, the leviathan on the tomb yard and the ... what did they call the flatulence fiend again?" The Praetor bulged its head at the subcommander.

"The Canker, sir!"

"We heard it might not have perished."

"If that's the case, I can track it," Vespasian butted in glibly. "Shouldn't be hard. It leaves an odour impossible to miss."

The Praetor waved a dismissive hand. "Tribune!"

"Liege?"

The demon's eyes dimmed. The room chilled. On cue, the rodents bolted, and the Consul tensed. If there was one thing worse than his brother Mabius, it was a demon, even though this was his first time actually meeting one.

"Core orders were passed to us only as the sun marked the light's third quarter of the day."

"Orders?" Probos looked lost. "From the Core itself? We didn't hear anything!"

"You think the One would talk to you?"

He hurriedly bowed. "Of course not, Liege, I—"

"We have been granted exclusive pre-eminence of Caulderwell and its world, recognition of the inestimable work we provided against the Resistance in this sector during the wars. We can do what we want;

we have been liberated. We can finally give vent to repressed hellion ... impulses."

It smiled wolfishly. The shadows lengthened. The air grew fustier. Probos' face was a picture of discomfort; Vespasian almost felt sorry for him.

"Scribes estimate four months and six. On that mark, a new Legate will confine all breeders into formations of one and one thousand, to be ..." It rolled its head, looking for the words, then seemed to think better of it, even though demons did not savour diplomacy. "Needless-to-say, any spare thew will be recycled—those that we don't *personally* need, that is."

"What does that mean?" Probos' growled. Anger furrows creviced a brow worn by austerity and service. "You are to dispose of them like refuse?" His mouth was working like a grit digger on speed. "These people have served us well. They have served the Imperium well. Aurelian has cultivated *true* cooperation. We need fewer guards to maintain order and—"

"There must be secrecy, naturally. No one must hear."

"Why weren't we informed?"

"You *are* being informed."

"But—"

"Have a care—every flagstone, every brick has an eye here, Tribune. Do not be concerned with Aurelian. He comes from lowly lines, not officer models. He worked his way through probity. He also shares an affinity to thralls, something expressly prohibited. We assume full Imperial functions, this sand-fall on. You will function as Legate."

"*Me?*"

"You keep your counsel. But you are also tedious, unimaginative, underwhelmingly obedient; it is why you will keep ownership of your gullet."

"I don't—"

Those eyes bored into the Tribune's. "All demon, *all* Shaitan, regard the living as contamination ... that's what the likes of us think about the likes of them. The living are poison, toxic, much like this wolf before me."

Probos looked at Vespasian, who was nodding grimly. "That's what you get when you serve demons, Tribune. Without your Emperor's intervention, this demonic bilge would be dead within half a dawn. It can't survive in our realm. When I was a child, I thought those things were mythical."

"So, we are a myth?" The voice was seductive, a torturer's murmur.

"Apparently not!"

"I don't understand ... I don't understand any of this," Probos hissed.

"Vespasian does! Is that not right, Pro Consul ... Pro Consul of *squat*!"

"A Pro Consul?" Probos looked at them both sharply. "*Again*, I wasn't informed."

"*Informed*! We only learned it now by inhaling the stink of his thoughts linearly. For a being who should play dice with moons for fun, pathetic cannot describe the absence of any mind shield." It shot a penetrating, spiteful glare. "But he is nothing save the black-hog sibling of Mabius."

"*Mabius*?" Probos stared at the undead with wild horror. "General Mabius is one of the most venerated generals in the Imperium. He serves Myrian directly. By the gods Praetor, they are also Sythian!"

"He is no Mabius, Tribune. He is neuter, the laughingstock of the Empire. He'll die like a dog. Calm yourself, Probos—a new destiny dawns."

"You mean a new genocide," the "neuter" broke in. "The occupation thing is problematic enough, but if you try killing your subjects, you'll unleash shockwaves that will shake this whole world apart."

Probos looked traumatised, but the Praetor leaned closer. "Oh? How so, Sythian?"

"Isn't it obvious, even for a punk-skull like you?"

"Tell us!" The voice was caustic.

"Purify this place to the bone, and you're left with empty factories and depravity. Any organisation who tries it dies. Exclusion equals catastrophe."

Probos broke in, flustered. "Heresy. Maybe the Legate got too close to the breeders, but you can't rule without a population!"

The thing's mouth was a moist, venomous pit. "Perhaps our faith in the soulless is ... flawed?" A row of guards entered the room. "We will... repopulate."

"With what?"

The response was bloodless. "This is on a need-to-know basis, Probos and you don't need to know. Not now, anyway."

Vespasian put a hand on the Lifeless' shoulder. "Think," he murmured. "It's not going to be the likes of us, so who's left?" The other's mouth had gone full goldfish, so he continued. "*Them*! All the Imperial demons the Goat converted—they need a home. A whole world of them, serving the One—maybe the first of many. It's kind of poetic, really. If you're insane."

The demon seemed unable to resist breaking his own rule of keeping it all secret. "Fret not, Legate elect. The Imperium is vast and will not miss one Protectorate, one island in a galactic archipelago that touches itself ass to claw, one end to the other. This is a gift *to* us, not a theft."

It flexed and unflexed its gnarled fingers, hocking across the ground. "The Goat is powerful, but so very old. Older than you can dream. It suits Him to find a way to replace the bovine sub-breeds infesting this city and the armoured excreta warding them. Imperial demon will be the new blood of the One. The Lifeless replaced the beasts, and now the demon will replace the Lifeless. No more will He have to dissipate His life force to stimulate another ossified cadaver into nonbeing. There is little Ichor left!

"Go now, Tribune-past ... *leave*!"

Probos, disturbed and pallid, even for his type, hurried out. Vespasian scrutinised the Praetor silently.

"Have we crushed your spirit already, Sythian?"

"I'm soulless, remember?" The demon cocked its head. "I've just one question for you, 'Excellency.'"

Ever so slowly, the thing nodded assent.

"Who's next?"

The demon raised its head. "Explain."

"Breeders gone, soldiers gone, undead dead—not that I care." He leaned in, making sure their eyes locked, one set lifeless, one set damned. "When the Goat has no one left to ward and no one left to fight ... who do you think will be next?"

Seared plasma pierced the warlord's chest. Vespasian collapsed, paralysed. Spitting black fluid, he muttered: "Won't change anything, Praetor. You'll still be next!"

The Praetor regarded him darkly, then beckoned to the guards. "Remove him. By nightfall, the guts of a Sythian will decorate the amphitheatre, the last show Caulderwell will ever see."

Chapter Nine

TROUBLE AT THE INN

"I told you already, we don't serve your type this side of the divide, gecko. If you can't produce a permit *clearly* showing your designated times, you'd better scutter off right back to the breeder zones or I'll summon the night watch!"

The bad-tempered bartender folded his arms defiantly. Lifeless soldiers were gathering at the bar, slamming chunky tankards down in slopping thumps, laughing broken-toothed in each other's faces and slapping powerful, skeletal hands on every available set of shoulders. In the background, a squabble had just finished. A round of hoops went up, as a soldier floored a drone to the sawdust in a scattering of jaw enamel.

"You what? *You what*?" The "gecko" leaned menacingly close. "You dare to deny us drinks, even while you're whoring slop for the bone-breaths around us? You're *one* of us!"

The innkeeper, immersed in pumping kegs and foaming suds, a glass seemingly balanced on every finger, crashed everything to one side and thrust two ham-sized fists on the stained panel. His heavy set, blood-shot, lobster face propelled into the Krayal's.

"I ain't paid to take verbal meadow muffin from a badly dressed *snake*!"

Before Seftus could reply—and he had a killer response—something pushed him aside.

"Breeder, bring us our mead; our throats parch with thirst." A Lifeless leviathan slapped a strong, boney grip on the fleshy, puckered arms of the barman. Another lurched inebriated against the bar and, via a motley collection of spittle-flecked, carmine teeth, screamed something to the effect of, "Gut the scaled slopsucker and serve us our Goddamned stout!"

They were surrounded by a timber-lined series of long, drinking rooms, swollen to the brim with casks of ale and overfilled, hump-backed amphoras of wine on the brink of rupturing. Crisscrossed scythes decorated, and perhaps held together, plastered walls overlooking ranks of oak benches, overwhelmed with undead clientele of all classes. The only ones who could mix with the soulless, the living Patrician classes, cussed, ate packets of expensive, dried rodent livers (the highest delicacy imaginable), and slurped and burped from jugs brimming with arrays of vicious-looking liquors from a separate space of their own, at least that's how it looked to Seftus. It was rich in scarlet pennants and roaring hearths each with carved grotesqueries on the mantels, though the curtains were stained with blood. Outside this surreal sanctuary, there was unbridled chaos in the communal area, with the shapes of the living slumped on the dust within their own spit amid handsomely carved struts or under tables. Eventually, the hired help dragged the worst for wear to a special "soak pit" outside, or more accurately, the back courtyard, where dregs were tipped over them when a cask was emptied. The kitchen drains did the rest.

Most woke before dawn, usually.

The rest were packed with streams and counter streams of milling soldiers, drones and workers shouting and shoving. To Seftus, the elongated bar seemed vast. It stretched from the far end and cut through six rooms. Adorning all this, in pride of place, hung an alabaster-white basilisk skeleton of titanic proportions. What kind was anyone's guess, but it had a series of serrated horns in a bone tiara at the crown of the thick forehead, which ran down the massive vertebrae to the forked tail at the back. In another section, poorly separated by tatty curtains, a subdued collection of people gathered. Full of "breeders" of many species, including an unexplained scattering of humans, they sat sullenly, not daring to attract attention. They looked surprisingly similar to one another, as though an eon of liquor and duty had merged them into a homogenous coagulum of limbs and teeth. Occasionally, one would stagger through the archway and vomit loudly in the privy.

Seftus rolled his eyes at it all and focused back on the barman. "Let me get this straight. A breeder barman is threatening to call the watch, because another breeder is interfering with his living ass, as it slaves for a pissed hash of boned-brain larrikins so they can feel some kind of life, by getting mind-numbingly, gut-twistingly lifeless!" Seftus jammed an accusatory finger at a stunned drone. "Insane—it makes *no* sense!"

"Where's the bloody drink, breeder? What are these stinking meat-sacks doing here?" The barrage of abuse rose from other Lifeless around them.

The barman's hand grasped a scuffed warning bell hanging by a nearby beam, additionally decorated with weaponry, farm tools, dead bats and a giant, curved-horned earwig.

"Wait."

The hand involuntarily halted. Something in Seftus' carried unexpected authority. "Hire extra help if this rabble of stiffs are too much for your sweating mitts but serve me first—and not because I want your wares, because I don't, but because I am *next*!"

"There are side rooms for your kind, terrapin-bowels," the barman puffed, glancing anxiously at the baying mob. "For God's sake, piss off or you'll incite a riot!"

"I'll *start* the goddamned riot," Seftus growled, instinctively reaching for his blade. "There's no service there, other than a stable boy who can't reach the pulleys and a dolt who thinks a gin is a card game!"

"He's had too much mead. He's coming with me," a voice suddenly piped in.

"I'm *not* being demoted to the wino's corner by some maroon-hued cuttlefish who—"

"You're coming with me," Ayilia repeated firmly, her head covered in a thin shawl bought in Market Crawl hours earlier. Kemet was beside her. She had been watching the Krayal's attempts to purchase a pitcher for quite some time. "Outside, they mix, but in this inn, they don't like it."

"I don't care if they want me to drink in the city's aviary; I'm staying put."

Kemet sniggered. Ayilia frowned impatiently. "Seftus, if you don't stop acting like a petty bar thug, the constabulary is going to put us in a sop house. Come on. Now."

He followed, still fully bloated—Ayilia couldn't help noticing—with his own sense of self-importance, in the manner too many fermented hops can create. Instantly, a swelling of arms and legs swarmed forwards to fill their space at the counter, further overwhelming the barman.

"I can't help thinking our lizard friend reminds me of Aaron when he's on the lash," Kemet said, eyes twinkling.

"You mean the sheer amount of brain he kills off in one session?" Ayilia added.

"Bloody goo-sh fun too!" the Krayal gushed, tottering. With his anger now subsiding, he seemed to be losing control of his vowels. "Krayal don'tsh drink, but I thought it'sh was important to merge surrepti'sh-iously with the sh'ocals."

"Oh, you merged alright," Ayilia muttered darkly. "Anymore 'merging' like that and we'd be picking your guts out of the buckets they keep behind the bar!"

Seftus stared at her uncomprehendingly. "Shisssh, you really are no fun."

Before she could reply, Stilgen strode up, openly agitated, accompanied by Soren. "We draw attention, Regent. That's not a good idea right now—the place is getting increasingly volatile. Soulless drinkers are migrating into breeder zones. The tavern is so packed, things could boil over. We must calm before they, how do you humes put it? Kick off!"

"*What*? They allow stinking cada'shers into *our* area." Seftus was appalled. "I s'hee *that's* allowed. It's un'gienic and *damned* insulting. Our coinage'sh just as good, but we get the rap. I'm not going anywhere."

Stilgen didn't look happy. "Reptile, I would point out you've lived with me and my Lifeless 'cadavers' for quite some while now and accepted our guidance through the portals, without complaint."

"Here we go, the imperioush lecture again—you *knooow* what I mean."

Ayilia inhaled impatiently, but Soren, for once, was the voice of reason. "Seftus, don't spoil our cover. Some of 'em aren't too plastered to make life difficult. There's lots of armour outside, so let's just melt into the lowlife over there, out of sight!"

"Agreed," Kemet said, still looking highly amused. His normal battle-hardened eyes were twinkling in the chaos. He began to forcibly guide the frustrated Krayal to the breeder section.

Soren turned to Ayilia, eyeing the furious stares around them. "What's he been up to this time? Don't he care about us? Actually, he reminds me of Aaron."

"I have good hearing, hume!" Seftus glared back at Soren, but Kemet, openly smiling now, thrust him through the melee to the enclave. "To be compared to that sh'trawberry haired thug is'sh bad enough," he wheezed. "But *twice* in one breath leaves'sh me ..."

He couldn't seem to think what it left him. Ayilia, concerned Kemet might not be able to cope, sent a reluctant Soren after them. Kemet, suddenly pulling rank, decided he'd had enough and unceremoniously left the flustered man with the drunken Krayal, and promptly rejoined the group. Ayilia, shaking her head at it all, led them towards free benches at the back in an area that somehow had both soulless and organics mixing freely together, a deeply pensive look on her face.

"Despite his undeniable prowess with a blade, I'm worried he's a dangerous liability."

Stilgen's brows were sky high. "There is little doubt about it, Regent."

Kemet inhaled thoughtfully. "Our dead pal's right. We'll have to dump him along the way."

"Dump him? I intend to kill him!" Stilgen exclaimed. "That Krayal tongue is far too ill-disciplined in the presence of any kind of liquor."

Ayilia stared at him, mortified. "Commander, we don't execute people just because they can't handle their booze. Remember, we agreed to stick together until we made contact with the Resistance."

"That is proving more difficult than anything we faced in the Pit." He paused as an awkward silence took over. "Maybe you should reconsider my proposal ... about the gecko. The only way he knows he exists outside his skull is if he's annoying someone."

"Just like Aaron, but *he* does it even without the booze." Kemet laughed, looking surprised at Ayilia's resulting glare. "Though I think Aaron is better bred ... Actually, I'm not sure."

"I seriously doubt killing Seftus will help matters!" she added, as if trying to inject some sanity into proceedings.

"You'd feel better!"

She fought a sudden impulsive urge to smile, not quite knowing why. Fortunately, Soren suddenly appeared with a wooden tray of sopping drinks. Seftus was close behind, clearly bored with the designated "living" sectors of the bar.

"Not too arduous after all, folk," Soren said, looking highly pleased with himself. "We lifted them from some blitzed legionnaires. We didn't rob anyone living, though I'd have liked a pop at those Patricians!"

Seftus was nodding. "Night's still young."

Ayilia resisted the temptation to burrow her head in her hands. "Okay, great. Hopefully no one saw that, Soren. Stilgen, didn't you say you heard something in some emporium about the Consul? That he might in fact, be here?"

"Indeed. He is to be executed tonight at the Apogee of the Three Moons."

Everyone spluttered in astonishment. Somehow, the news was exacerbated by Stilgen's usual deadpan delivery. Ayilia's mouth was practically touching her lap. "Say *what*? The Apogee of the *what*? Executed for *what*?"

"When their three moons directly trisect, they radiate a beam of disc-light at Caulderwell at the exact point where the Imperium has constructed a gladiatorial ring. A midnight execution ritual, their most popular sport. It might involve a chained beast!"

Seftus slumped into a chair. "With the putrid muck they drink here, I hardly blame them. Never had worse, not even in the bleakest wasteland of the Ranges'sh, even though, of course, I don't drink."

"I advise you to keep your voice lower, reptile. We are too outnumbered to risk offence."

"Can't be worse than the Pit," Soren cut in. "The killers there jarred the very marrow out our bones!"

"A ground murmel could jar the marrow out of your bones, hume, and just about everything else," Stilgen cracked.

"Hold up," Ayilia said, trying to steer the conversation back to what really mattered. "Even if the Consul is there, the person you talked to is likely exaggerating, Stilgen. I bet there's no chained beast, just the usual gossip mongers unable to chain their bored tongues."

Soren's eyes were pits of bottomless despair. "Ma'am, you're not thinking of rescuing that dead pile of dead death? *Please* tell me you're not thinking of doing that?"

"If we don't, he's *really* dead!" She shot him a not-so-reassuring grin. "I heard them talking about executing a 'Stranger' today. Didn't even occur to me that might be him. We don't have the time to haul him out of whatever highly guarded clink they've thrown him in, so either we forget the whole thing, or we drag him out directly from this circus as it's going on. It's just some small provincial show, so a great deal easier than escaping the Pit."

"We forget the whole thing!" Soren said firmly.

Kemet shook his head. "He may not be a good Sythian, but at least he's a Sythian."

"That'sh more like it—fighting talk. We'll show those planks of wood who really deserves to be served first!" Seftus blared loudly.

Soren wasn't having it. "They'll massacre us, then hang us out to dry, then force us to dance in front of some chained beast before killing us again. There's no portal to jump through this time!"

Ayilia put a comforting hand on his. "Soren, I guarantee there's no chained beast, and no one will make us dance. And I happen to have a plan."

At that moment, Jarong bustled up. "Regent, they are going to, um, execute the Consul tonight in some ... fair I think—no, circus." He was beside himself with anxiety. "I was talking to some scullery drones making um, blue pancakes, or was it Imperial doughnuts. Actually, I can't remember, but if I had to bet on it, it was pancakes ..." He looked at their glowering faces. "Okay, doesn't matter, but what does is that there is some kind of chained beast." He was visibly trembling. "The Consul is going to be consumed alive, or dead-live, if you see what I mean!"

Seftus looked deliriously happy. "Hell, let's do this. God, I feel good. Let's take them all out. They're ssshhhhhhoooo pissed, I bet we could cut a swathe all the way to this shhhcccircus and back.... Hell's nobblers, I looove you guys. We're in thissshhh ... together..." Flecks of warm beer splattered them in minute drops. Looking momentarily thoughtful, he added, "What about that... hume vagrant you endlessly talk about? Arrow-head? Aaron-head? Kill him too, I say."

Grimacing against the ebb and flow of undead danger, Stilgen answered sotto voce, "He's still on Etherwolde, dolt, our home world. I told you earlier, I left a man in the Pit to give him and the X Gemina our rendezvous details. We regularly liaise in case we move, which we seem to be permanently doing from one rundown rathskeller to another, keeping cover." He gave a Lifeless version of a shrug. "In all truth, it's a non-living nightmare, logistically."

Seftus shot him a skewered glance. "I didn't undersh'tand."

"Nor did I," muttered Soren.

The Lifeless commander was looking visibly pained. "We know where Aaron is. He will know where we are—that's all you need to bear in mind, hume."

Soren shrugged. "Frankly, I don't give a damn if the blonde one is mounting tree cones, but what about the chained beast? That would be highly typical of our luck."

"Aye," Stilgen said. "Your paranoia, for once, is accurate."

"As I said, it's just usual shrunken-brained, macho talk from the drones in this city," Ayilia snapped, the din in the bar getting to be too much, let alone the company. "Forget it!"

"Perhaps, but I got the impression my source was level-headed."

Ayilia sighed loudly, her patience fraying. She held one finger up, making direct eye contact with each and every one of them, pausing longer on Soren. "Listen, all of you. I won't say this again. There ... is ... no ... chained ... beast!"

᠅ · ☠ · ☠ · ☠ · ᠅

The chained beast roared. It happened the moment the circus drones pulled a billowing hood from its head. Squatting on all fours, it lunged at the bound man in a cloud of sand, violently shaking the pillar it was tethered to. Giant leather girdles groaned loudly with the strain. Ayilia jumped out her skin, as a crescendo of approval rocked the largely Lifeless crowd, many of whom were happily inhaling brain-rotting toxins. No one questioned how they huffed the acrid vapours into Lifeless chests, but any good undead physician would gladly confirm it risked turning their defunct tissues into carcinomic time bombs.

The beast lunged again in a series of pyrite teeth and lathery phlegm.

"I told you; I told you!"

"Shut up, Soren."

"Well, look at it. It's a bloody beast, *and* it's chained."

Stilgen muttered urgently into Ayilia's ear from behind, "Do your men always repeat the obvious?"

"No," Kemet said, leaning towards him from Ayilia's left side. "Only that one!"

Soren tried to look indignant. He sat to her right in the stands.

Seftus, next to Stilgen, had cheered up, though the others did their best to mask their concern at the lopsided manner in which he handled his seat. Fortunately, the spectators were less discerning than those in the tavern. The fresh air was also proving to be a tonic. They sat amongst a mix of peoples: the allied Imperial citizenry or Socii, the Peregrini (those who lived outside the capital), the Provinciales (the ex-slaves), and the general plebs and patricians who made up the city. If there was segregation here, it wasn't obvious.

"Are we sh'ready?" the Krayal hummed, wavering. "It's 'bout time we put an end to this! How do you humes say it? Kick some grass! Yes, let's kick some grass in!"

Ayilia put a gentle but restraining arm on his shoulder. "Not quite what I had in mind."

"Phew." Soren slumped in his chair.

"We wait until our Sythian pal wounds the thing," Ayilia continued conspiratorially. "Knowing the Pro Consul, which I don't, he'll drive the maddened beast at the crowd, creating mayhem, at which point we strike."

"Why don't we do it for him? That'sssh what we did in the Rangessshhes back in the mountains if a comrade's innards were hanging out."

"You probably did that with a thousand more people on your side and twenty thousand less on theirs."

Seftus' gaze was still glossy-eyed with alcohol. She wondered just how quickly this testosterone-overfilled lizard had succumbed to the "grain juice." It would be more than prudent to remember these things in the future, if they were to stick together for much longer. Jarong, on the other hand, was unusually calm. He seemed content to let her handle his friend.

"Ma'am?"

"Yes, Soren."

"Can we go?"

"No, Soren!"

"Okay, but I'm not sure if our favourite dead man is in any state to create any kind of confusion. In fact, I'd say he's more confused than confusion-creating, if you see what I mean ..."

All eyes fell on the figure menaced by a now not-so-tethered beast. As the thing mauled with ferocity at its restraints, making alarming, high-pitched, mewling noises, the "Stranger" had somehow cut his own tethers and was wandering aimlessly around the sand, looking more at the spectators than at his fate. Because of the robes he'd been forced to wear, which covered his face and most of his body, his identity was masked.

"Well," she wavered, "I'd say he's weighing up his moves as we speak. He's planning something pretty big this very moment."

Stilgen shook his head. "He's planning his death!"

"Well, that's that then," a relieved Soren muttered, slumping back in his chair. The alcohol was visibly making him sleepy. Everyone else just starred at Stilgen, slack jawed.

Eventually, Kemet leaned over to whisper conspiratorially in Ayilia's ear. "You had no plan at all, did you?"

She looked furtive. "The plan was to have a plan ... once I'd seen what his plan was."

Kemet smiled. "I stand corrected."

"To be honest, I don't have a clue. Our Lifeless friends won't come without him, and we can't sneak through the Imperium without them." She shrugged haplessly. "Their constant bickering plus the booze does my skull in. Besides, he *is* meant to be a Sythian, after all."

"Indeed."

"But?"

"But ...?"

"Yes Kemet, *but*?"

"Not much of a but! More an umm."

"Umm? And what does that mean?"

"I wonder whether he risks us in other ways."

"Other ways?" She threw up her hands. The scene in the arena was getting increasingly tense. The beast would be free imminently, and she still didn't have a plan. "Hell, I've turned into a minor parrot. What other ways?"

Kemet's eyes darted suspiciously. "Maybe he possesses links to the enemy, maybe even his brother Mabius—or perhaps that demon bastard, Myrian, the Goat's number one gut-hog?"

She shot him an anxious glance. Old scars danced around his neck as he chewed on honey-bark soaked in moonshine, purchased from a disheveled vendor. He'd been guarding her a long time, yet never let it obstruct his family life. He hardly mentioned them, but he'd once spent every moment he could with his two daughters and his quiet but steely wife. Not being with her had to be killing him. His wife would understand there was no choice, but it made Ayilia ever more desperate to find the Resistance, so they might go back.

There was another burst of noise.

They looked up. The crowd surged forwards to see better. The ring was a five-pronged pentacle with alarmingly low barriers. Pink shreds of breeder and undead flesh mixed liberally with animal fur and the corpses of things completely new to Ayilia. They'd missed a multi-armed Gladiatorial Class of drone responsible for the carnage. She gave silent thanks that the famed moons were hidden by black clouds, delaying the release of the creature. However, it was pulling free. A handful of clowns, all breeders, bolted for the exit.

"If he's really a ... spy, Kemet, they'd better act quick. He's not doing anything to keep his unbeating ticker even slightly unbeating."

"It could be an act?"

"An incredibly convincing act,"

"They often are ..."

Ayilia's hands were getting clammy. She'd banked on the Consul doing something chaotic but dramatic. Instead, it seemed like he had only moments left.

"Or perhaps he's bait ... for you?" Kemet added.

"*Me?*"

"He's the best shot they have of finding you, again."

There was a splitting crack. Everyone sat upright. The creature had jerked free of its tether. The Pro Consul, or whoever he was, stared blankly at the thing, making no move to defend himself. The creature was much larger than when chained.

The Stranger threw back his hood. It was Vespasian after all. Dark eyes irised into obsidian dots. A line of fire circled them like gold vultures. The thing reared, dwarfing him. It paused briefly, perhaps stunned that its prey was so cooperative, before crashing down. He was sent sprawling across the dirt, like a child's doll. Fleshy, wet nostrils sniffed him, searching for the best meat. Hairy jaws opened and three thick, salmon-coloured tongues closed carefully round Vespasian's legs. After another pause, it tossed the Consul up before flipping him effortlessly into the fuchsia chasm of its mouth, wolfing the entire meal down in a gulp.

Horrified, Ayilia's group rose as one as the crowd whooped in delight. Suddenly rowdy, they began shoving and pushing against each other. The arena's wooden seats were ripped up in cracking wrenches and tossed in all directions. Ayilia grabbed Stilgen's arm as he went for his sword, furiously shaking her head.

"Stilgen, there's nothing we can do."

Eyes black with fury, the normally impassive Stilgen shook her hand free and shoved his face close to hers.

"You let us down!"

She recoiled, stung. "He was meant to fight! What can we do against thousands of people?"

"I trusted you."

"We would've pulled him out once he started flaming them to bits. He always does that. Well, once or twice at the least!"

"Bullshit! You could've entered his head, like before."

Ayilia grabbed him again by the shoulders, her voice nearly breaking. "I tried, the *moment* I saw him, but I can't ... I don't know how it happened before. I'm not some kind of Mage, Stilgen, you *know* that!"

"Forget undead help—track the rebels on your own. You'll thank me anyway, as they're likely slain by now."

"Let's talk this over, for God's sake." She shot furtive glances at nearby soldiers who had noticed the unusual sight of an organic arguing with an undead captain.

Stilgen turned to go. Kemet immediately blocked him. "That man had a death wish, you said it yourself. He surrendered to the thing. There was nothing to be achieved going in after that, except our deaths."

"Kemet's right," Ayilia hissed. "The Consul thought he was alone out there. He's given up. Half an extra day's notice and we might have pulled him from jail."

Stilgen shook his head. "Our deal was unnatural, a curse on the gods. With him truly dead now, it's over."

"We can cut it open!" Kemet suggested, as though he'd just mentioned something as banal as not forgetting the herb sauce for the annual bar-beque.

"What?" Stilgen looked aghast.

"Say *what*?" Ayilia knew her face carried the same look.

"Why not? He wasn't .... chewed. He doesn't breathe, after all, and I doubt any stomach juice is going to have much effect on his Sythian hide—not yet anyway."

"Cut it open?" both replied simultaneously.

"Like I just said, he's probably alive."

"Forget him," Soren said matter-of-factly. "I doubt that creature's going to live long with his whiney ass inside it, anyway."

Kemet took a step closer to Stilgen. "That thing didn't chew, it *swallowed*. And as undead are exactly that, undead, he doesn't breathe, eat, drink, fart, or crack jokes, so he should find it remarkably comfortable inside for at least half a night. He'll sit in that stomach, grumbling, fed up it's taking so long."

Ayilia was shaking her head. "Are you saying we should drag him out before he dies of boredom?"

"He has a point," Stilgen rasped.

"I do?" Kemet seemed genuinely surprised.

"Who would need to guard the creature in its pen tonight, once the show has ended and the prisoner is ingested?"

A still squiffy Seftus was delighted. "We're going to kick some grass after all?"

"Sounds like it." Kemet was grinning. "We pay the creature a visit, gut it open neck to groin, and release the warlord before he becomes poop!"

"You're all insane." Soren sighed. "He'll be thing-shit before you know it!"

Stilgen wasn't listening. "I would lay a wager, stomach juices of beasts like that are harmless to our toughened flesh ... for a while. We were designed to fight and survive most things—for a while!"

"Soren's right, you're all mad!" Ayilia said.

They looked at her with raised brows.

"However, what the hell do we have to lose? But he'd better help. We don't need a fallen, undead god with a personality disorder and no pulse trying to kill himself while we're trying to save his life hauling him out of the steaming gut of a bad-tempered circus troll."

The first guard didn't know he was dead until his bloodied head thudded on the soft dirt and found itself staring at his own feet. By this time, Stilgen and his man, a scarred, older Pit warhorse called Smerk, were already on the second. Mouth open, only slightly less surprised than the first, she crashed backwards into a set of wooden barrels. Her guts mixed liberally with the goo of what looked like beast feed. There was a quick jostling, and Smerk jangled some rusty keys into the entry lock. Stilgen nodded at a group of undead led by Kofi and backed up by another, Morack, to join them. There hadn't been enough last-minute tickets to get all the Lifeless that had come through the Pit into the arena, so the group of seven waited outside. Ayilia was glad they were back, even though she, Soren, and Seftus had nearly come to blows with them outside the portal on the raining bug world.

However, it was taking a while to crack the lock, despite Smerk's best efforts.

Stilgen, giving in to unusual cursing, shoved his man aside and tried the lock himself with little success. If anything, the language only got more colourful. Even Soren winced. Ayilia found herself wondering if he was perhaps a little too delicate for Gemina duties.

"Here," muttered Stilgen's man after retrieving another set of keys from the dead guards.

"What?" Stilgen huffed impatiently.

"Here. Those were the wrong keys."

He snapped them out Smerk's grasp. The crusty doors opened with a massive creak.

"Gods, we'll bring the city cavalry on us."

They piled into the inner sanctum. The keep had been startling easy to infiltrate once the show had ended. Separate from the catacombs of the Prelate, it housed only prisoners, gladiators, ring performers, and giant harnesses for the creatures. Apart from the bored night watch, no one was in. Open prisons below revealed a plethora of cells, many with shapes stirring uneasily. As they ran along iron catwalks to open more sets of doors, they came across more guards. These were quickly dispatched in splatters of fluids. One was already slumped inebriated against a wall, so they left him unharmed, on Ayilia's insistence.

"No unnecessary killing," she said.

Perplexed, Stilgen replied, "They're dead already."

"I know, but I don't want to get used to it."

"Fine, but you'd be doing this one a favour. He's so poisoned on illicit narcotics he could join the Pit as moral officer!"

They descended into enclosed areas that stank of dung and straw. A menagerie of mottled creatures regarded them with a variety of different-shaped eyes—some were angled slits and others pointed stalks that looked directly at them. Going forwards, they came across cages containing members of the same species as the one that wolfed up the Pro Consul. They stopped to stare.

"Hell's udders," Kemet muttered. "Which one, Stilgen?"

"And I would know? Did you not take account of its markings?"

"I didn't 'take account' of anything, other than that it was large and had a smelly butt. I also didn't think there would be so many of the bastards."

"It's that one," Ayilia said quietly.

One of the huge beasts lay in a dark corner, apparently sleeping.

"How do you know?"

"Because it's cut navel to neck and its guts are all over the floor ... outside that, no idea."

"She's right, Stilgen, old friend."

The voice came from nowhere. They spun around, weapons drawn in the dimness.

"Those bloody things talk as well." Soren's saucer eyes filled his face.

"If they did, they certainly didn't say much to me!"

A figure stepped out the dark. It morphed into the form of the Sythian warlord. In the background, Ayilia noticed a smorgasbord of pink-white entrails running to the slit belly of the creature. Its rib cage was partly visible, containing a sausage-shaped twine of intestines from a ripped-open stomach. The partially digested remains of sacrificed breeders formed a glop of limbs, jaws, and flesh within.

"*Consul*!" Stilgen's face widened into a jubilant grin. Kofi clenched his fists triumphantly and whacked Smerk on the back with joy. A winded Smerk almost knocked his block off in return but just about contained himself. Morack immediately began to laugh and seemed to consider slapping Smerk on the back too, but wisely decided not to. Stilgen immediately regained enough composure to add, "We thought you killed yourself."

"Not for the first time, I couldn't find my fire." Vespasian smiled grimly. "So, I got swallowed to get out. Admittedly, the thought of ending it surfaced a few times in that pink hellhole, but the thought of tearing out the Praetor's gizzard proved more persuasive."

"Impressive." Stilgen looked close to tears. Ayilia studied him closely, really closely. Despite a lifetime of distrust, she felt strangely moved.

"It's okay—the thing had no teeth, Stilgen. I was told that before they threw me in the circus. Someone called Gala told me; she knows Caulderwell inside out and has many friends, which is how she got in. The creatures swallow whole—keeps the meat fresher or something." He rubbed a forehead wet with mucus and digestive enzymes. "I had enough theurgy in me to stop its heart, then cut free ... just. To be honest, I felt bad killing it, but it wouldn't vomit me up."

"Lovely." Ayilia walked up to the bars of the enclosure. "I kind of loathe saying this, but it's good to see you, almost. However, we need to find the Heretics. It's suicidal to go sniffing round the Praetor's quarters, looking for his *gizzard*."

"We have time." Vespasian put both hands on the grill of his cage. With a bright fizz, the locks snapped away. He pushed the gate open.

"I intend to free the other creatures first. I feel ... guilty slaying their comrade. Probably something to do with the fact the Imperium's kept us all prisoners one way or another over the years. Besides, he was elderly—and apparently a mentor to them."

"This just gets barmier," Soren muttered.

"If we let them loose, those things will create a diversion," Kemet said, eyes gleaming. "We can slip away quietly."

"I know a covert way to the Praetor's inner sanctum," Vespasian replied, still dripping intestinal gunge. "A dilapidated network of sewers runs through everything, including the catacombs. Some prisoners told me that before they ended up as beast meat, and Gala actually gave me a map. It got digested inside the thing's gut, but I remember every nook and cranny. It's funny, but the thought of slicing that pig inside out does wonders for the memory!"

"What are we waiting for?" Soren growled with evident sarcasm. "With him covered in troll crap, we can stink them to death."

Vespasian turned to go. Stilgen, Kofi, Smerk, Morack, and the others followed.

Kemet shot Soren an amused glance. "Will you at least try and pretend we're not a rabble?"

Soren looked pained. "Hey, this whole universe is a rabble!"

Ayilia was left standing there shaking her head again, practically abandoned on her own mission.

Chapter Ten

ARMERHURST

The dark skies were grey and heavy. Within the whitened city, a hoary portal juddered. Its iris ground open, flooding the snow-shrouded surroundings with creamy light.

It was as quiet as a mortuary.

Abruptly, the iris bulged, attenuating into an elongated cone that radiated ferric oxide hues a quarter league into the horizon. Accumulated ice vibrated off the surface in streams, silhouetting the gate in ivory mists. Disbelieving Imperial guards jerked awake from positions of inertia, each imagining the visitors to be official yet finding no flight plan.

The billowing cloud immolated the nearest to carbon.

A bayonet of Raiders came through in a bristle of weaponry, shields, and theurgy. They were swiftly followed by the hand-held artillery with their sloshing phials of tannan juice strapped to their backs, then the main body, which spilled out in a riptide of people, staves, and equipment, everyone steaming from the jump.

"Now!" came a shout.

Sheyna's stomach clenched. She was in the centre. It was highly irregular, the loss of all senior commanders in one go would have been catastrophic. The fact Barrackus was nearby made scant difference. The man chosen to replace them at the front was Skyron, normally in charge of the shooters. He'd be the one cut down if the resistance was overwhelming.

The Raiders had been subdued, expecting the worst. Barrackus, however, felt surprise would get them halfway to the next set of portals before the defenses could blink. As no one had come this far since, arguably, the fall of the Interregnum, he swore the enemy had developed a sense of lax invulnerability. He even swore the Emperor Himself would be caught kipping across His vast checkerboard of death as they made their final approach.

Yet, all the while she hoped, prayed, he would forget about last night.

He'd flicked Sheyna an anxious glance before the jump, but her face was as grim as a tombstone. It was astonishing that they were attacking the historic citadel of Armerhurst, the once-indomitable capital of the Interregnum. Once inside the portal, the target world had rushed to greet them before erupting into cloudbanks the hue of milky amethyst atop squalls of sleet. Who would remember a conversation in the face of that?

Barrackus didn't look like he did. But she knew better.

They'd arrived at the cusp of a winter storm growing alarmingly darker. A pale city of plinths, pillars, pointed temples, coliseums, arched roofs, and opulent piazzas lay softly shawled in flurries and ghostly mists. Within, the grand central square was ringed by granite statues of warriors and around seventy portals arranged in a boundless semicircle, shimmering in the winter light.

Sheyna was spellbound. She'd never seen so many in one place.

She marveled at how space and time had failed to rupture the city under the pressure of the immense gravimetric, tidal forces of so many portals, condensed into just one geographical hub. She gaped at how the tectonic plate dynamics of so much invisible sheer should have torn the entire continent off its hinges, sundered the planet from Arctic to Antarctic. It was an impossible feat of scientific architecture. It proclaimed what everyone already knew—the Ancients were crafters of unparalleled skill.

But there was no time to stare. The cries, threats, and screams of dumbstruck beast-soldiers split the airs. The vanguard rammed through them, even as they emerged from barracks and guard houses; the power of a fully armed Raider unit at its height. Ultimately, they didn't stand a chance, but they'd light the Imperial heavens with a fire it'd take ten hundred millennia to put out. Sheyna found herself propelling through the past even as she charged.

Images of her weapon's lecturer at the Academy scrolled across the back of Sheyna's mind in super-speed. She recalled his seminars, how they always seemed to follow the particle physics classes, the thermodynamics lectures and the dreaded, even soul-destroying, afternoon-long electromagnetic harmony and chromodynamic reasoning sessions.

What a mouthful.

She could never handle them the same days as the marvellous stave lessons. There, she'd throw mind, body, and soul into a whole new level of existential study. It piggy-backed on an endless stream of preparation involving neural "cleansing," crystal meditational techniques, and thaumaturgic "fire" disciplines. Not real flame, of course, but the purest plasma direct from the lecturer's mind. It bathed the initiate in a descending canopy of vibration and light, a veritable baptismal shower.

It was all utterly gorgeous. But to combine it with practical theory classes was frustrating.

You simply didn't do it.

QuainGall, her tutor, had insisted they were in a war that specialised in appalling timing and said that such restricted thinking would get you killed all the sooner. After all, he mused, successful ambushes weren't always the forte of the allies; sometimes even the enemy could pull them off.

"Get used to it," he once whispered with a mischievous wink. "Life can't always be bent to your will. Stay humble, Sheyna, mask that temper ... be flexible and focused. Arrogance is the enemy's problem. Given enough time, it can bury him!"

QuainGall clearly relished the stave seminars. He sincerely believed a mace wielded by a disciplined mind was an extension of the soul and incalculably powerful.

"Live modestly," he thundered, knocking his palimpsests off his podium. "No need for excess piety, but personal extremities are nonstarters! Practice self-restraint. Respect people, even if not reciprocated. Doesn't mean you can't defend yourself—integrity lets you do anything, but it averts soul-sapping pettiness. Let the toxic's deeds poison his existence, not yours!"

She was twitching impatiently. The old fool was particularly full of shit that day.

"The universe watches us ... every step. Ego dwells on our wants rather than our needs. It blocks the voice that lovingly guides us if we choose to listen and, unlike ego, is there forever." His voice went quiet. "If there is no meaning, there is no joy—something status and self-regard cannot provide. At the point the individual has truly excised the emotive, the well-rehearsed construction of the personality, anything is possible. At such a moment, no matter how fleeting, an Asthen master connects; she is part of, every rock,

every blade of grass ... everything! At that moment, an Asthen master, po-tentially each and every one of you, rises above the petty, three-dimensional cravings enslaving the lesser species of our alliances, to encompass oneness. You will be immeasurably—"

"Bored and fed up! Pet food for the Imperium's armed animal-shag-gers." *Sheyna had stood, ignoring the shocked gasps of her fellow students. "My ego got me through, not-so-learned one; it most certainly didn't hinder me. Without it, I'd be still be violator meat. Without it, I wouldn't have cracked the skull of that head warden against the wall and beat him with the stick he was going to..."*

She trailed off and looked around at the cold eyes and the even colder hearts. What she saw staring back was the product of a privilege that didn't give a damn about cold orphanages and mentors with tastes that didn't match their roles. The rage never strayed far. And to listen to some gas-sack pretend people like her, who breathed in and shat out hurt every day of her Goddamned life, could be bathed in zombified stupidity by the love of a cosmos that sat by and did sweet FA—it made her want to vomit blood.

"Sit down!" *yelled another student, the entitled son of a city money man. She kicked his desk. It flipped over, its lid unintentionally whacking him across the forehead. Blood spirted down his face. Despite the gasps, QuainGall remained calm.*

"Glinthorn, take Heth-San to the physician swiftly."

A student helped the stunned man out the room. Flecks of blood spattered after them. Fierce hatred surrounded Sheyna on all sides. She'd seen that look many times, but she knew she was no sociopath, even if some called her that.

"Sheyna" *QuianGall was almost whispering now, forcing everyone to strain to hear.* "You will face judgement for that."

"I expect nothing less."

He regarded her through rheumy eyes. For the first time, she noticed a blister of fine, white scars down the left side of his cheek. People said he'd done things in the war that the enemy would never forget. "Let hate be the mausoleum your detractors bury their self-loathing souls in; don't let it bury you."

"Crap," she hissed back. "Far better to bury them with my dirk!"

He shook his head sadly. "This isn't the first time we've had issues, is it? You are this year's most promising student, but bitterness claws at you. Given time, it will claim ownership of you." He paused and rubbed his hands over a riot of knuckles bent and twisted by time and the Wirral he had killed. "You know Sheyna, some of our most practiced adepts even thank their detractors for the lessons learned on the thorny path to enlightenment. Challenges define us; they don't have to destroy us!"

A number of students rose and applauded him with such vigour that the windows shook in their gold-licked frames. Sheyna felt so much venom, she wanted to go over and cut his patronizing throat out as it bobbed like a goblin's testicle in a wet stocking.

She'd already served before they sent her here. They'd wanted her to become a master, but a calmer one if possible. Fighting had only made her anger worse. She'd left a path of bloody footprints everywhere she'd gone. Sometimes, the things had died screaming. Sometimes, she'd wondered if they'd die at all, lying there with their innards open to the predators on some alien world, the rest in black-red slabs on her blade.

"Swords have thaumaturgic agency, but nothing conducts theurgy like the mace." The fool was rambling again, like nothing had happened. Everyone had taken a seat again, so she did too. "Not only does it harness plasma effectively into a living extension of one's thought, it is also

214

mind-bendingly efficient at gathering that plasma from everything that surrounds us in the first place. With this instrument, the wielder brazenly harvests the very earth of its fathomless ocean of atomic charge and re-arranges the elements into something ... godlike."

His eyes gleamed with messianic danger. Would she always rub shoulders with powerful Magi who might be sociopaths in disguise? They were the danger, not her, but no one could see it. Deep down, they scared her.

"Once built for peaceful purposes, the stave has simply become a quantum battering ram, coalesced into physical puissance via the duality of the bearer's mind and discipline."

He was the one who was insane, yet people talked about her. The injustice made her almost back out with rage.

"That is, for me, the greatest tragedy of this war—outside the bloodshed. Using it to butcher has violated every principle we hold dear and the principles of existence itself. It is the reason why we will eventually succumb, because we could not find a way to destroy the Abomination without becoming Him first!"

Honesty? From a famed Magi like him? The authorities would loathe it.

The fury stopped in its tracks. Her jaw slacked wide at the searing openness, an openness no politician, pamphlet writer, or authoritarian had ever admitted.

Strangely grateful, Sheyna looked down in shame at the bloodstains on her tunic then up again, only to see him staring at her. In that fleeting moment, she felt understood. He saw everything in that piercing, theurgy-filled glance. In that instant, she felt ... joy. Someone actually cared who *she* was, not *what*.

She was valued.

She had never forgotten.

Reality returned. It hardly mattered, Sheyna was on automatic. Joined by her comrades, she rained shot into scattering Wirral. Those still standing were hacked to the ground as the unit forged through the torrent. Survivors were quickly left behind.

A dark flow of bristling weaponry appeared from the recesses of the city, beast troops unsheathing blades and buckling on battle gear. Taking advanced positions, the Raiders emptied stave shot into the approaching ranks. Hundreds of Wirral were carbonized, teeth and skulls fusing into the metal of their armour. A phalanx of Magi, wielding Imperial maces, erupted from a nearby basilica in a blur of ritual, saffron robes. Gossips swore their garb was to defile the once holy buildings of defeated foes in blood sacrifices to the Goat, but no one really knew. Whatever the case, they were swiftly immolated by Skyron's heavy mobile guns, fuelled by the volatile tannan fuel on the backs of the gunners. A second swarm were similarly engulfed within fire, leading to a macabre rainstorm of jackal heads tossed pitter-pattering down the cobbles, in a clacking cacophony of bones and body parts.

Other cohorts were similarly eradicated, along with anything even vaguely military that surfaced from the streets and spaces facing them. Old buildings were haloed in fire as the defence forces were openly torched, most in disbelief. Despite their superior numbers, it was nothing more than a turkey shoot.

As the Asthen swept forwards, Barrackus rode towards the front. Skyron was shouting, telling the troops to mind the city and to concentrate on the resistance within. "God's teeth, this is Armerhurst, people—don't destroy it! And conserve the ammo; we've already gutted the defence here."

Sheyna joined Barrackus, watching everything he did, wondering if this was the day they would die. On one hand, his death meant the Ascendancy would never get another chance to annihilate the top brass in a surprise strike with the best they had to offer. On the other, they might have gotten rid of a maniac in the nick of time, one on the brink of insanity as he evolved into something staggeringly lethal. One that might do the Ascendancy more damage than good, if he went mad or bad.

He clearly noticed her Prowler straying close. He didn't need to shout above the battle din.

"What's up? Normally, I'd be pulling you back right now."

She forced a smile. "Gotta keep an eye on you, Commander. No one else is pulling this shit off if we fall."

"Sheyna, we're both too far forward. We have to spread, dilute the target we present, look after the others."

She scoffed. "That's bull, and you know it. The targeting's all one way." She was panting slightly, no longer a sprightly youth.

Keeping his voice sotto voce, he added, "I don't need a bodyguard."

"And the troops don't need one either," she hissed. "Skyron has it sorted. Lose you now and we'll never reach the Great Ass's inner sanctum, if that doesn't sound too obscene!"

Darts twanged off the group's plasma field. Created on collective instinct, it shot up the moment incoming was sensed. Like a shimmering umbrella, their shields merged into one giant canopy.

Lars was passing nearby on the left with his company, their staffs a blue/white brilliance fed by minute traces of magewolde. The priceless powder boosted the intensity of their theurgy whenever intense firepower was required.

The commander pointed. "Lars, take out that cohort, then meet us before the grand piazza beyond."

"Aye!"

Sheyna, eyes now wild with desperation, pulled up mount to mount and grasped Barrackus' shoulder. "Are you mad? We'll be split and weakened!"

He shook his head vigorously, his bright eyes taking in the efficient eradication of the cohort facing them. After days of unmitigated tension, it felt to Sheyna like they were a sun igniting across that fabled society once centred at this porcelain ghost of a city. The Interregnum had once spread its light across much of known space. Although the Ascendancy had never encountered them, they'd been fascinated by the legendary culture. Even the Imperium had absorbed much of it, including the architecture. Buildings like the ones in this glorious citadel were now standard across half the universe. Though the One had stamped Armerhurst's light firmly out of existence, the memory persisted in the subconscious pulse of ten thousand species.

"They're disintegrating. Don't let them congregate—keep shooting, stay mobile!" Barrackus was almost ranting, his eyes ablaze with fanaticism. "See over there? We scattered that mass on the right; they've split to block Lars and take us out too, thinning themselves in the process. We'll take 'em in a two-pronged thrust and meet dead centre of the formation!"

She didn't answer. No time. Volleys of shot fizzed off shields in cartwheels. The enemy ahead divided further, as they poured down streets like water filling up a dried riverbed.

"Just down that street, that company there ... and that one too." He pointed. "Leave the others—they're trying to separate us. Fight to the centre. They won't swamp us if we keep moving and firing!"

They picked up speed towards the freshly emerging lines. Their shields were being struck by heavy objects as well as incoming shots. She was uncertain what they were but soon recognized rocks, spear heads, and axe blades. They ricocheted in all directions off the shields as the sound of the enemy chanting rose in crescendo.

The cry went out, but Sheyna wasn't sure which leader said it.

"Starburst!"

The Asthen began to generate an energy sphere of intense brightness. The enemy formations hesitated, ranks piling up on each other. Skyron barked something, and the burning ball was flung into the ululating melee.

The detonation flattened every legionnaire like steel hay. It was as though a blue nova had erupted across the faces of thousands of Imperial soldiers. The Raiders had to rein up violently in a swirl of hooves and grit as they covered their faces. The screams turned Sheyna's stomach. Seemingly unmoved, Barrackus raised his stave and fired into the moving shapes. She shot him a dark glance. Though the forces facing them had been eviscerated, she could see yet another Wirral darkness collecting further back. Thankfully, she also saw a great many fleeing in the opposite direction.

Barrackus and Skyron led the unit at the gathering horde, sending furrows fanning through the lines with electrifying accuracy. Blood and heat surrounded her, yet she butchered as hard as any of them. Wirral entrails splattered down her mount's legs. Countless thousands had already been slain. Despite their sharp teeth, heavy weapons, and bulbous armour, the Asthen battlehead tore them apart, creating a passage towards the enemy's rear.

A Wirral commander leapt at her, cutter raised, but she fired a charge that imploded its skull, covering her feet in white mind-meat. It took everything not to retch on the spot.

The Asthen had regrouped again. Imperial ranks looked dangerously thin now that the center had vanished. Barrackus' face was teal, the look of a hatchet-faced killer. She felt it all, the synergies of unparalleled power coursing through his bloodstream, a necromantic slaughterman in his prime. She accepted the combat, the half-cleaved heads and gutting in the cold light. What she objected to was the shared bloodlust, the joy in the destruction, and the fact he seemed to have the biggest rush of all.

"Ha, we're the best of the lot."

Another wave of revulsion overcame her at the sight of that pulled-back grin. He was unrecognisable.

Overwhelmed with years of pent-up emotion, she rode straight over to where he sat proud and arrogant on his Prowler and slapped him hard in the face.

"Fuck you!"

Barrackus recoiled, eyes wide with astonishment. Shooting her a black stare, he gripped his Prowler's reigns and rode off. Deeply embarrassed, she abruptly terminated her thaumaturge's inner eye. No one would say it, but her comrades must have sensed the rising power inside him. She looked at them, but everyone had been too busy to see the confrontation. The agonized cries of the dying reverberated round the ancient streets, distorted by the closeness of the ancient stones.

"Regroup ... *Regroup!*" Skyron was still at the front, bellowing at the top of his lungs.

Barrackus rode up to take the front, his voice grating dryly. "Things are going to get worse!"

Sheyna prompted her Prowler to catch up, gesticulating at stragglers to follow. As she drew near, he vaulted off his saddle onto an iron veranda amid a series of white terraces. With lightning dexterity, he sprang towards the roof past a well-preserved belvedere. Not to be outdone, she unhooked somewhat stiffened legs to balance precariously on the heavy saddle. The city, people, and smoke swirled as she reached for the rapidly approaching balcony.

Gripping the cold metal with white knuckles, Sheyna swung over the railings in one go, skidding on the ice upon landing. Feeling stupid, she glared down at anyone who might be smirking, but they were too busy regathering round Skyron. Such was the crushing nature of the victory: the enemy flanks had disintegrated, leaving burning corpses fused macabrely together as far as she could see. Nevertheless, something was wrong. She knew Barrackus had sensed it also.

Sheyna pounded furiously up worn stone steps to an esoteric yet bewitching rotunda at the pinnacle of a terrace of roofs. Barrackus was staring through a window there, out at the cityscape. Everyday details registered at the back of her mind: ornate paintings, a silver vase frozen to a shelf and, incongruously, Imperial curtains wafting chimerically in the breeze. Dark flurries descended from growing cloud mountains in the sky, while snow-devils twisted down streets. Minarets, cupolas, and steeples flanked the host of Raider staves, twinkling within the fading cyan light against the oncoming storm.

It was poignant, timeless.

"I killed a lot of people back there, Sheyna, probably three times what was necessary." He continued to stare out, his back to her. "I know most back home wouldn't give a damn, but I also know our tutors would feel it's important to maintain the division between us and them, because there's no point fighting otherwise."

"No argument there."

"Wirral are fierce, but once their spirit is broken, they fall apart. In fact, I *encourage* that, to save their lives as well as our own. Scant wonder the Abomination's giving up on them!"

"I know, Barrackus—the manuals contain numerous examples of Raiders funnelling Wirral as weapons against other Wirral, as well as Wolverine, Proto Goblins, and Skinners."

"That's not what you want to hear, is it?"

"Why? Why so much carnage?" She approached the window. "We butchered so many. Raider units are terrible things when wielded properly, and this one is the most lethal, ever! We could've scattered them with a fraction of the kill rate. I ... fear the consequences."

"Because I lost control!" he snapped. He closed his eyes and breathed heavily. "The only reason Skyron's regrouping is because he has the time. We don't have the luxury of playing it safe, not all the way out here."

"I understand. Believe me, I do ..." She was struggling for the words, trying to make him see he how dangerous it felt standing next to him. Something wild was growing inside him, something that defied thaumaturgic physics. "Don't you think you should be telling me how the hell you came to wield such catastrophic sortilege?"

His brow shot up questioningly. "Shouldn't you be asking the Abomination that?"

"Concerning the sheer lust involved in the killing of sentient soldier-beasts, actually, yes, I *should* be asking you! But that's not the whole point, is it? I know the Ascendancy's backed you on this suicide run, one that's signed our collective death warrants, but do they know what you're becoming? Because I sure as hell don't, and I loathe the fact that my life no longer depends on *you*, the person I once knew, but on the person you're becoming." She struggled to get the last of it out. "I'm losing faith, Commander."

He looked ahead gravely. The sounds of the continued route of the Wirral were all round them. Though it was nearly done, their faces were lit by the disjointed flashes of sporadic Magi butchery. Sheyna flexed her fingers anxiously and studied the ramshackle formations forming at the end of the grand piazza.

"We've hit a ... snag," he finally let out, along with a pent-up breath. "Ahead."

The fire in her went out. "Snag?"

"There're more than we feared." He'd taken out a spyglass. "Look at them swarming."

"What's new." She tried to muffle a surge of irritation. "We've cleared a path halfway across the universe, further than I could ever have thought possible. They can't block gates or the portal macrocosm would back-flare this solar system out of existence. We have a clear run if we go now."

He didn't reply.

"There's something's you're not telling me." She whispered. "I've never experienced devastation like we've wielded, yet you look like someone's crapped in your oats. Perhaps, we should ... reconsider our options, while we can?" She was clutching at straws now.

"The Ascendancy really *is* as desperate as you think, or they'd never have used me otherwise." His eyes were coal. "They've known for a while something's wrong, but they felt there was no choice."

"Okay then, we *definitely* go back," she hissed, trying to mask something new: fear. "It makes sense on many levels when you think about it. The Ancients made this snow-world a portal bottleneck, which is probably why the Interregnum made it their capital later. No other way in, no other way out, apart from small entry points. A sea of gates ass-to-cheek, controlling whole sectors from here. Must have taken godlike spatial engineering and the resources of a galaxy to build. There's nothing like it anywhere, as far as I know, and it's likely the only way to the Core! Maybe we've come to a dead-end, Barrackus, right there in front of our faces."

Sheyna swore and impatiently wiped a knot of Wirral blood and snot from her tunic. Unsurprisingly, the fabric remained stained. Visibly disgusted, she rubbed at it furiously but without success. "I want to go home," she snapped, still brushing vigorously. "That's what I want, Barrackus. I want to go home and relax by a roaring fire in my simple dwelling, doing nothing. If we go ahead, that's it in this life and the next! Let's hang on, wait for the static to clear, then jump, jump, and jump again, with you and Andromedus using all your specialist skills until we're out of their collective asses. It's a long shot by anyone's standards, but at least it's a shot. And, if we get back, our intelligence might change everything."

Time felt stretched so much to her, the moment became psychologically non-ending. Somewhere along the line, she had become convinced that the lives of ten thousand generations would depend on what they did. Despite there being two or three choices, only one was actually possible. When it really mattered, there was no such thing as freedom, no matter how much free will was available. Her dreams of returning home were dissipating like sand through outstretched fingers.

"Sheyna, you don't understand."

"I understand that I understand absolutely nothing!"

He gave her a painted, muted look. "Pharsalus is there."

She turned to face him, her grief and anger one and the same. "Impossible!"

"We can't turn back. We have to take him out."

"He's the most lethal war dog the Empire's ever had. No one's beaten him. He's pushed back Ascendancy lines far more than eons of unremitting war have." She wanted to scream. "For the love of the gods, Barrackus, you've gone insane!"

"He's just one person."

"So is the Abomination!"

"If we take him out, there'll be a collapse in the entire sector, he's so influential. We can go onwards, unopposed, buy time for the allies while we're at it." He seemed to be towering over her. "We'll confront him on our side of that square Sheyna, full visibility on approach. We're in his comfort zone. Paradoxically, it'll be his weakness."

"How?" She sounded like a one-syllable, yapping dog.

"Arrogance equals complacency. He's never lost in our territories—let's see what happens when we're in his!"

"That's your strategy?" She shrugged and looked away. "Of course it is."

He held her gaze for a few long seconds, then walked out. Sheyna was left staring at the snow. As she followed, she wondered if having no control over her life was either predetermination, something in their DNA chaining them to their decisions or if, in fact, they'd replayed this drama a million times already in time and space, until time itself ended. Whatever the truth, she was sure of one thing: she didn't have a choice.

"Skinners!"

The anxious Raiders looked up a set of stone steps flanked by gaunt sculptures towards a massive piazza of classical urns and pyramidal superstructures beyond. Immense statues of beast warriors, griffins with feathered talons and curling serpents lined the peripheries, while a pair of cyclopean horns formed an imposing entrance. At the geometric center, a fountain churned out purple waters two hundred hands in the air before chundering back into an ivory gaggle of clams.

"Where?" Sheyna grabbed the startled scout, veins blue tendrils in her neck. "Where are they?"

He was stammering. "You ... need to follow me."

He led Sheyna, closely followed by Barrackus and the others, up the steps and thrust his finger towards a host milling around their target, a crescent of towering portals lining the circumference of the vast quadrate like brooding, silver deities. She wanted to marvel, but the ripple of enemy weaponry held her rigid.

Barrackus held up his hand. "Halt."

The troop pulled to an undignified stop. A roar of derision rose from the swelling horde facing them. Sheyna could hear individual threats floating across the divide.

"Goblin Skinners." She faced them. "Just what we need!"

Skyron's mouth dropped in horror. His face was bone white. It was as though a ghost had walked across his soul. "God's teeth, no one's seen those shitheads for decades."

"Maybe it's their thuggish cousins, the Protos?" Lars grumbled, straining to see. "This lot are meant to have died out!"

Adira's eyes shone murderously. "They will have by the time we're done."

The Asthen took formation, ignoring the profanity echoing off the ghostly buildings and grandiose courtyard. Phalanxes of malachite, brawny torsos in clunky, belt-tight armour, were framed by concrete-hard heads beneath racks of horns and shorn hair. Grotesquely shaped biceps strained within leathered straps as coriaceous hands grappled axes and nicked cutters. Sour, ornery eyes, four of which were studded deeply into the hanging folds of each bruised face, glared at them.

Masking her exhaustion, Sheyna kicked her mount towards the one man who had a chance of saving their hides for the second time that day.

"Sheyna, listen," Barrackus said before she had a chance to speak. "You told me you would trust my final decision, no matter how much you objected. Well, this is one of those times."

"Lately, it *always* seems to be one of those times."

"You know the rule: *never* attack on their terms. Pharsalus is most assuredly waiting. He's treated our false trails with disdain, choosing the one place to welcome us if we proved mad enough to try— here. He's trying to bog us down before cutting our throats himself."

"Then why hand the most successful Raider unit in history over to a bunch of armed animals, Barrackus? God's teeth, they're gonna kill us the moment they're done laughing."

The enemy were banging weapons on shields, goading them to act. Wirral reinforcements streamed in continuously from all corners of the city and hidden vaults underneath the snow. The Imperium should have been unprepared. It was the only attack they'd faced since the fall of the Interregnum. It had the stench of entrapment; Sheyna didn't need Barrackus' senses to realize that.

"You're the acting commander, Sheyna. You're more than qualified to get our lot out and cause some mayhem on the way."

"You're getting worse, Barrackus. How do you think we could manage that? A little friendly chinwag with Pharsalus?"

"Something like that." He smiled. "Remember, the choices are making us. Besides, I like the idea of that 'chinwag.'"

She was gobsmacked. "You're going solo?"

"I'm going in. There's no going back, not now."

"Glad you cleared that up, then," Sheyna replied icily.

"I sense him ..."

Barrackus turned on his mount and addressed the others. "When I'm not here, do what Sheyna says. In fact, *always* do what Sheyna says. Prep your maces and your weaponry. There's no force like us when we get going—the Abomination doesn't stand a chance. And perhaps, if the gods are gracious, you can snatch some rest in between butchering their filth!"

There were some dark smiles and one or two wry comments. Even Sheyna smirked. It was like the old days when they did colossal things to hurt the Goat. Barrackus turned back to his side arm.

"There's something we've forgotten in all this bloodshed, Sheyna. Who we are and what we stand for. The Ascendancy only sees with its eyes these days; it doesn't use its soul. When you narrow your options, you narrow your life." He gestured towards the now-howling Skinners. "The foe think numbers are the key, but that's arrogance. Such complacency begs to be punished."

His Prowler turned and bolted forwards.

"Barrackus? Are you insane?" Sheyna called after him.

"They're blind without Pharsalus—I'll give you time ..."

He was gone. She cursed furiously, then whispered to herself, "Be careful, old friend."

"Aid me."

Ayilia watched Vespasian's gnarled hands claw at the grimy grill, his eyes staring rabidly from the small, wet tunnel they were holed in. His dried fingers closed around the bars before sprouting Mage flame. As Stilgen, Smerk, Kofi, and Morack reached out to help, red sparks sizzled briefly, and the grill came away in his hands.

The Consul grunted with satisfaction. "Everything's coming apart here."

Before anyone could move, he put both hands on the ledge and vaulted from the stinking sewers.

The living contingent of humans and lizards, Ayilia, Soren, Kemet, Jarong and Seftus, watched mutely.

Vespasian stood on a pile of brick slabs on either side of a channel full of languidly moving, very smelly shit. The sewers stretched like a network of capillaries under the city, transporting the waste and assorted detritus down into the volcanic lakes and the swamps beyond. Rodents and unfeasibly long, horned millipedes scurried among their feet and up the dense walls. Olive mould carpeted everything. Their clothes quickly picked it all up.

"Follow him," Ayilia mumbled with resignation.

Soren winced and made to move, but he was shoved brusquely aside by Seftus, who seemed to be tormented by an inner reckoning. Jarong mumbled an apology for him, then quickly followed. Ayilia was going to go next, but Kemet held her back.

"Ma'am, I'm concerned."

"Because the Pro Consul's an undead, Sythian, *and* the brother of Mabius himself?" She smiled wryly. "What's there to be concerned about?"

He hesitated.

"Kemet?"

"Why are we here, in a stiff-guarded sewer and not the official chambers?"

"Apparently, the Praetor retires near here when the hour's late." She shrugged. "And there are far fewer guards, which kind of makes sense."

"Figures." Nevertheless, Kemet's brow furrowed. "I don't think I like the Consul much."

"I like the Praetor even less," Ayilia said, flashing him a watery look. "And I haven't even met him. Plus, he's demon!" She placed a hand on his arm. "If the Heretics are still alive, we'll find them. Then, they can take this Kimiya crap out my brains and maybe give us back our world. We're each other's only hope."

It sounded good, but she had to set her face against the depressive hound inside. A hardness had begun to set in during their exile, cauterising some of that self-doubt and life-long malaise.

Under her watch, the last vestiges of free humanity had been annexed. She and her group were on the longest paper chase in history, searching for a Kimiyan shadow in a location only she allegedly knew. Yet she could do nothing until they contacted a miasmic Resistance who'd melted into the ground, hoping some protector no one had ever seen would prevent the soulless from cracking the egg of a mythical reincarnation who'd probably never existed. And all the while, the hourglass was emptying rapidly on their strand of humanity. The fact there seemed to be humans throughout the Imperium was both reassuring and dispiriting, as her group might be the only hope for all of them.

Kemet spat in rare fury. "Sod these cadavers; they don't eat, sleep, puke, or piss. I know I sound like Aaron, but God help me, I think I miss him."

"Now I know you're troubled." She grinned. "Come on, let's get out of this poop hole!"

With a grunt, Ayilia heaved herself through onto a rug of grime before levering up the wall with a kick jump that ended up with one knee on the rim. She squinted against the dankness. A disparate array of iron torches, bolted to the walls, created wavering swirls across her retinas. A handful were extinguished, creating black gaps. They could burn for a considerable time before maintenance, a gift from the Imperium. The group were nearly gone, their silhouettes forming dancing blurs against the walls. Beside her, Kemet frowned.

Soren came back out the gloom and hissed, "This way, quick."

They hurried past the cordite kiss of the torches, then entered a labyrinthine mesh of tunnels tapering into oblivion. Oaken doors leading to nowhere, with chunky handles used by no one, angled at irregular intervals. Rooms bristling with bones and teeth vied with cobwebbed darkness, antiquated portraits, and gormless gargoyles. Metal chests, discarded on all sides, were tipped open and eroded, their rusted struts like ribcages on old kills.

Ayilia quickened her pace. Nearby, Soren swore in obvious panic while Kemet cussed furiously at him to mask his own unease. Seftus, however, strode on, seemingly oblivious, with Jarong barely able to keep up. To Ayilia, he seemed psychotically desperate, his mind struggling to make sense of his crumbling view of the universe and the certainties he thought he held. Unhelpfully, he swore at a large, purple earwig, startling them more than the unfazed creature.

A cumbersome spider with what looked like twenty legs sprang with unexpected alacrity at Ayilia's neck. She yelped, brushing it off in a fury. To her absolute disgust, several of its legs remained on her scalp, twitching frenetically.

Kemet, ever at her side, pulled at them with expert fingers. She successfully muffled an unprofessional scream.

"God damnit, I hate these places! Are they gone?"

"Probably."

"What's happened?" Stilgen huffed, looking uncharacteristically ruffled. He'd run back, sword in hand. "Are you telling me you're scared of cooties?"

"Cooties the size of a giant hog!" she snapped, somewhat embarrassed.

"It's a hume thing," Seftus muttered nonchalantly, again being spectacularly unhelpful.

"It truly amazes me the map to the Al Kimiya itself is entombed in a head unable to cope with vermin."

"Entombed in a head almost *consumed* by vermin," she mumbled angrily.

"Dead man, the regent's head is the only thing standing between your people and that array of skulls back there," Kemet growled.

"I saw the cootie." Soren grimaced, his eyes wide. "It was bigger than a hog, far bigger."

"You saw your arse disappearing into the distance," Seftus cut in, then laughed, sounding immensely pleased at his attempt at humour. Jarong eyed him uncertainly.

A shape loomed into view. They all looked up, startled.

"Enough. We may yet wake the dead," Vespasian said.

Ayilia, now composed, faced the slim yet ominously powerful figure of their de facto ex-ruler.

"It's a matter of conjecture who exactly is dead around here," she said levelly. "More to the point, this is not the road trip you outlined."

"Academic, considering we're here," he stated without emotion.

"Could you be a little bit more specific? What, or where, is 'here'?"

"At the Praetor's inner sanctum, adjacent to this underground disposal system. You can stay here if you wish; from here on, we shall likely encounter resistance."

"About time!" Seftus exclaimed. "I hope they're better armed than the cooties."

Stilgen shot him a withering look.

Ayilia put a restraining hand on the Consul's arm. He flinched as though stung by a wasp. Glaring fiercely, he seemed to tower in the gloom. Determined not to be intimidated, she returned the glower and did not let go. "We're a team now, like it or not, and that means everyone goes. It means the Lifeless and those with hearts that actually work are equal. I trust you don't have a problem with that."

She could sense Kemet readying himself behind her.

Stilgen answered first. "We take care of our own, female; it's the way it's always been. You, in the short term, will need us far more than we you, as you will struggle to exit this place safely, let alone travel the volatile climes of an undead universe that's been in existence infinitely longer than you've been crawling within its boundaries. Nethergeist does not quiver at your presence!"

She flashed a sardonic grin. "I'll remember those words when we reach the mid and long term, then."

Vespasian scrutinised her. "Your 'Phoenix' is no friend of ours," he whispered. "Should it hatch, it will consider *all* Lifeless its foe, including us."

"Not if you stand with us, it won't. The Heretics will guide it. And if it isn't a figment of some chronicler's over-furtive imagination this ... Guardian will too."

Stilgen had clearly had enough. "Pah. Make-believe; the dying wet dream of a living cosmos considerably past its sell-by date."

"At least we had one," Kemet shot back.

The two faced off. Ayilia repressed a weird impulse to laugh. Both men looked like flea-bitten mutts after their spell in the sewers. Ridiculous, and hyped up like armoured cockatoos. It was hot and hard to breathe. She rubbed her face, blinking hard. Her eyelids drooped with heaviness. Then she realised someone was talking to her.

She turned to Vespasian. "What?"

The Consul repeated the unheard question. "Do you sense now where it resides?"

"Who?"

There she went again. Doing her parrot impression.

"Al Kimiya, your mythical Phoenix!"

Everyone looked at her expectantly, civil war seemingly postponed. Undead irises glittered in harsh judgement, occupying the same space as human outcasts, lizard renegades, and a Sythian warlord. It really didn't help that the air was as fetid as an abattoir.

"No, Consul. Unfortunately, that's the Heretics' job, and they won't get that done until they extract this... chart to its birthplace out of my head." Ayilia fumbled for her water pouch and took a deep swig. "So, we better find them soon. The day is rapidly coming when it's going to be too powerful to evade the Goat. Then it'll be a rat race between His forces and who or whatever the Resistance can muster to get there first." She wiped the sewer's fust from her face. "The better the head start, the better the chance they have of saving its egg and our collective butts."

Vespasian regarded her a little longer, then turned and strode back down the corridor. "Then you'd better follow."

Kemet shot her a questioning look. She shrugged.

"Let's go!"

After climbing up a particularly vile brick funnel, the group scrambled out through a rusted hatchway and took positions on a peeling balcony. Vaulted ceilings and classical arches faced them. Dim tunnels led away from once-resplendent doorways, guarded by massive skeletal forms in crimson robes. Fluttering fires crackled from lanterns scattered like saffron gems at the bottom of a dark millpond. A breeze ruffled white feathers above crossed rapiers, yet the heat remained cloying, and it was getting to her.

Vespasian stared intently. Ayilia found herself wondering what drove him.

He was in the flesh—every dried, desiccated sinew of it—a walking, talking Sythian. God's teeth, those things were hard to come by, even she knew that. A mutated seed of power hopping from species to species like a galactic magpie, capable of lying dormant for a millennium before erupting onto an unsuspecting populace. The tissue, such as it was, appeared manufactured, but he was spared the kiss of the Emperor's blood, the Ichor used to impregnate life into the soldiers, drones, workers, and machine serfs on the assembly lines.

"Female, I demand you step back, lest they spy you and ruin the mission," the captain's voice hissed, interrupting her thoughts.

Ayilia swivelled round in a burst of red mist, a brew of stress, weariness, and heat, triggered by a charisma-challenged corpse kicking her like a child's mannequin.

"And I demand you use my name rather than 'female,' Stilgen, before I cut your dead gullet open, plug hole to plug hole. She growled. "Don't forget, you need our allies."

"The same allies who lie crucified across seven hundred star systems?" the Consul interjected.

"The same allies who can still find your people a home within seven hundred star systems!" she asserted, jabbing a finger at his chest.

"Remind me Regent, are these are same allies that you have no idea where they are? Are these the same allies you hope your half-sentient Kimiya mind-intruder will track and locate?"

His acidic reply hit too close to home. "You cadaverous wrym," Ayilia raged, losing all semblance of control. Sweat caked her dirty, exhausted face. "Try finding them on your own. Try getting their help without us, even if you do. Without them, your dreams, whatever they are, don't stand a murmel's chance in shit of succeeding!"

"My dream is to provide my kith with a homeland. I did not seek your aid, or the aid of organics, to escape the Pit." His stare was corrosive. "I hate breeders and always have. They ransack lands of goodness, slaughter lesser beings for succour, destroy their brother and sister for material or political gain, are obsessed with the bubbleheaded fickleness of appearance and status and foul everything they touch. Stilgen thought you useful, but I was in a stupor, otherwise I would *not* have sullied Lifeless purity with the unctuous hypocrisy of the living."

"Bubbleheaded," Seftus chuckled. "I *have* to write that down."

Ayilia thrust her face hard against Vespasian's, their mouths practically touching. "You mean the stupor when you were as helpless as a preemie? How did that go? Who the hell got you out when Mabius, your psychotic sibling, was about to exenterate you with his spare toothbrush?"

"It couldn't be a toothbrush!" All eyes swivelled to Seftus again. He regarded them, nonplussed, then added, "It was his stave." Realising they were staring at him oddly, he added, "His laniary looked particularly unkempt."

"Someone take him out," Kemet growled in disbelief.

"Now you understand why I hate Krayal," Stilgen said, obviously pleased a point he'd forgotten he'd made was made.

Soren started sniggering.

Jarong was practically shaking. "Please ... we're all, er, in this together aren't we? Who cares who has a beating heart and who doesn't? I know I don't." He smiled haplessly. Everyone ignored him.

Ayilia could barely breathe. Something about the Consul gnawed at her. And the heat was getting increasingly oppressive, making her increasingly tired. "Listen, you dysfunctional slab of deceased cock meat, you can stuff your homeland up the place the three suns don't warm because when this is over, I might ram my sword through that rotted capitulum you call a head." She slapped her sweating forehead against his noticeably dry one. "Then, and *only* then, will I consider talking to you!"

Neither blinked. It occurred to her it was yet another unintentionally comical moment. Nevertheless, blood would finally be shed among them, whether red, transparent, or faded yellow.

Stilgen darted for his blade, but the Consul put his arm out. His eyes twinkled darkly.

"The Goat doesn't have a chance!"

Without warning, he turned and vaulted over the side. Everyone could only stare except Stilgen, who landed deftly on the ground next to him. Ayilia rushed over to look. Both the Sythian's hands were suns, firing at the guards in all corners of the chamber, then at the far door. The wood splintered into embers, as a score of disbelieving sentries were hurled into the walls in a firestorm of sparks and bone.

"Oh god!" Soren exclaimed. Ayilia wondered if he'd wet himself in shock.

Seftus roared approval before somersaulting over and crashing in an undignified mash of legs and weapons. Somehow, he sprang up, charging towards the melee with a Krayal battle cry. A burning soldier staggered up to him, but Seftus swept his sword through its head, cutting it neatly in two. Flaming blood spotted his armour; nevertheless, he attacked another two guards, thrusting his blade through the eye socket of the nearest. Its companion, brutalised by Sythian Mage Rage, saw its skull cap swiped off next by the Krayal, taking the contents with it in a spew of gunk that splattered everywhere.

"What's that, dead man?" Seftus exclaimed triumphantly at the partially beheaded guard as it began to topple. "Murmel got your tongue, boy?" Despite only possessing a fraction of his wits, the Lifeless still managed to mouth something unpleasant before falling face first into his own brain.

Kemet had heaved free both sword and battle axe, but Ayilia stopped him.

"Regent?" he gasped.

"It's over—those things were too stunned to pass wind." She smiled and patted him on the shoulder. "Come, let's find this demon. Apparently, there's a surprise waiting for us, or at least that's what our Consul whispered to me on our way out of that zoo back there."

"Ahh yes, the mini portal! The one a guard told him about."

"He told you too?"

"He does a lot of talking for someone who doesn't enjoy talking."

Chapter Eleven

THE PRAETOR'S SANCTUM

Ayilia stepped tentatively over the remnants of the oak door, etched with gold leaf and precious jewels. The group was right behind. The smoking forms of dead guards lay beyond. A shadowy passageway, decked in ox skulls and antlers slashed with white wytch paint, ran into darkness at the far end. A stone expanse encompassed them, dotted with iron grates and sputtering fires. Tripods of sulphur encircled the perimeter. On the ceiling, a voluptuous, ruby sun studded with thousands of mosaic pieces overlooked a golden pentacle beneath on the floor. Jackal skulls, jaws prised open in rictus displeasure, were placed at each point. Every skullcap was cut off at the crown with a veiny wax candle thrust pointedly into the gaps.

"Nice place," Soren wheezed.

Vespasian, the Pro Consul of nothing but a broken bunch of degenerates, stepped into the space. Ayilia regarded him grimly. Who knew how long his strength would hold? He probably didn't. However, some of his degenerates, led by Kofi and Smerk, were left warding a number of halls leading up to the room. Guards had been a problem, and the last thing anyone needed was to be ambushed while they tried to make a gate work.

The others began to circle the voluminous room. Saturnine statues grimaced from dark alcoves underneath stubby horns. Each figurine was different, each a frozen representation of a demon race stolen from domains only the Goat knew. Stilgen and Morack followed, flanking the underlord several paces behind.

Ayilia, gripping her faithful broadsword tightly, beckoned the humans and Jarong and Seftus over to a doorway to their left. Stilgen, looking both curious and suspicious after the recent row, elected to join them. A tangerine, bittersweet odor rose softly from what sounded like distant, clanking foundries far below.

"Arsenic?"

Kemet shook his head. "Not sure, Regent."

"Not dangerous anyway, not in these quantities," Stilgen muttered. "Of course, I mean to your kind."

Seftus looked unimpressed. "I won't ask how you became so expert in the frailties of 'our kind.'"

Stilgen's forehead creased. "You might be disappointed ... it was not via violence."

"I'm not disappointed at all," Soren said, looking pained that it might even be considered.

"Please, enlighten us anyway." Seftus rolled his eyes.

"I learned about the living and their myriad frailties by watching them at pigskin matches and gaming in taverns in the Occupied Territories." He snorted disdainfully. "I found the experience so coarse I never went back."

"And this was worse than the Pit?" Soren gaped.

"I must admit, it doesn't sound exactly ... appetising." Jarong grimaced, inadvertently siding with Stilgen. "I mean, watching humes getting inebriated. Krayal are, er, different."

"You don't play pigskin," Stilgen said dispassionately. "But honestly, I couldn't hold a flea's fart between humes and Krayal—you're both so similar to us!"

Before anyone could reply, Ayilia cut them off. "Look at that." She pointed ahead.

A twisted clock hung freely from a vault, and it seemed to slow the harder anyone looked. With a jolt, she realised it had started going backwards. The dense atmosphere felt like thick mould.

"As promised," the Consul said, gesturing ahead. Something suddenly lit up in the darkness triggered by their presence, something they had not noticed in the dim light. Their eyes adjusted to the gently oscillating surface of a mini portal splashing its surroundings in sapphiric waves. The closer they got, the more its watery shine flickered along their bodies, rippling in riptides across walls and the miens of the statues.

"So, you weren't lying," Kemet said softly.

There was no time for further comment on the bizarreness of having a hidden gate in the Praetor's sanctum. Deep within, Ayilia knew something had changed. Their breath clouded despite the warmth. It dawned on her mind's eye that a gelid intellect was watching. Instinctively, Kemet faced her. She knew he respected the "witch" insights she had, though he'd never felt comfortable with it.

Eyes narrowing, he hissed in her ear. "What?"

"Can't say!"

"Where?"

"Beneath ... somewhere."

He gestured to Soren, nodding downwards. Soren, also familiar with her curse, looked with alarm at his feet. Kemet shook his head and pointed impatiently at the ground. Soren still looked down cluelessly. Kemet, angry now, gestured repeatedly at the floor, but the dark shape of the underlord suddenly appeared next to them, head raised in concern. The Consul was sensing the very airs.

Soren was trying not to freak out. "For the love of God, he's gone bananas again. Let's get out of here!"

"Bananas?" Seftus queried, genuinely perplexed. "What has—"

Ayilia held up her hand. "*Quiet!*"

All went rigid, regarding her intently. They waited as patiently as possible, which wasn't patiently at all.

"We really shouldn't be here," she whispered venomously.

"That's it?"

Kemet shushed Soren up, then faced her, eyes burning. "For once Soren's right, Regent. Let's just use the gate. Let the Phoenix that isn't a Phoenix have the Praetor."

"It's complicated!"

"The bird or the portal?" Seftus looked at her, utterly lost. Jarong joined him, eyes darting feverishly.

She gesticulated towards the gate. "Doesn't it strike you as odd?"

Their gazes remained blank.

She sighed. "It's open."

They looked blanker than ever. It was like asking a kindergartener to divide.

"It's open ... it's already open."

Kemet remained confused. "And this is a problem?"

"It is when something might have crossed this way."

Soren's orbs couldn't be rounder. "Some ... *thing*?"

Jarong was aghast. "It *always* has to be, er, a thing. Can't it just be a cat or something? I've heard they often travel via left-open gates."

"You never heard anything of the kind," Seftus said tartly. "Everyone knows it's really the souls of the unburied, who use them to find their lost corpses before they rot into stink and mildew."

"It's a *thing* though, isn't it?" Soren said transfixed on the word.

"Depends," Vespasian muttered. "Who has access to a high chamber of the undead, one controlled by a renegade demon Praetor? It's not going to be the local periwig maker!"

Seftus was becoming worked up again. "If they're a friend, we greet them; if they're Imperium, we skewer them. What's the issue?"

"The issue is we don't know what the issue *is*," Stilgen growled.

Kemet's eyes were almost as wide as Soren's. "Then something *is* here?"

"I want to go." No guessing where the whine came from. Jarong was happily adding to Soren's whine.

Ayilia froze suddenly. "It's all around us now."

Dread encompassed them. It seeped into their armour, their flesh, their minds. She joined the Consul at the cavernous centre, sword raised.

"We must leave, *immediately*!" Vespasian made towards the gate. "Once you're through, I'll fetch the others. There's only a few of you, so there'll be barely any static to stop us following, as we can't use open official channels." The others rapidly beelined for the portal, fear chiselled into every face. At the mouth, Kemet, Jarong, and Soren paused, transfixed by the pulsating, cyan glow of infinity. Seftus tried to scowl menacingly but only succeeded in looking absurd. Vespasian, deeply troubled, examined the gate, hands a blur on the controls.

"Unfortunate!"

"How unfortunate?" Soren asked terrified.

"Seriously unfortunate." He regarded them sternly. "The Regent's correct—we are not alone!"

"Who's here?" Kemet asked in a guarded voice. "I see nothing!"

"Someone unbelievably powerful is using this device." Vespasian was almost whispering. "It's off the scale—we cannot gain entry!"

Ayilia shook her head in abject denial at what both he and her Kimiya instinct were telling her. The room was blurring in and out of vision. She felt giddy at the sheer power emanating around them.

"Bullshit!" She wiped the grime from stinging eyes with her equally grimy sleeve. "I don't believe it. Are you claiming that all-seeing Bastard is here *now*, around and under us, as we speak?"

"I'm telling you He is in open communion with the Praetor."

An odd squelching sound followed his words. Ayilia swore either Soren or Jarong had lost control of his insides, but it might simply have been a gust from the hellish regions below.

Seftus looked like he was in worse trouble. He shot Ayilia a disbelieving stare. "How can the most tyrannical Arch Mage in existence be in open communion with the Praetor?"

The sound repeated. The list of suspects was growing by the heartbeat.

"Wait," a panic-stricken Soren blurted. "Who the hell are we talking about? Who's in contact with demon green-nuts here?"

Vespasian's regarded Ayilia with a hunted stare. He looked like he was floundering, courtesy of a lifetime of hapless floundering.

"The Goat talks but does not travel," he husked. "He has interstellar reach but does not move! He sees us, but no one sees Him. Only the scum-dog demon, the Viceroy Myrian, is permitted audience, but for the rest the One will find a way to reach out, *if* it suits Him." Vespasian cleared his throat. "They say the allies of old, the Asthen and the Interregnum, hunted Him throughout the stars in futile attempts at assassination, but the Great Ass never even left the homeworld ... not once!"

"Let Him rot," Seftus exclaimed. Ayilia swore he was trying to mask the sound of his gut bubbling. "What do we care."

Vespasian looked like a wayward boy who'd robbed a stall trader of fly-infested fudge and instantly regretted it. He stammered for a moment. Ayilia was oddly astonished, despite herself. "It ... it ... was once whispered to me as a sapling in the Pit, how the One wanders around in the silence as a disembodied spirit in the hours of night. While the body slumbers in eternal contemplation, His consciousness soars via ten million gates, each serving as His sight, His touch. Unwittingly, perhaps, we have walked across the icy mind of the Emperor Himself." He hesitated. "If He really is here, it is already too late."

An animal like lowering vibrated through the room. It came from the portal. It tightened her throat and reverberated amongst the molecules of stone and wood in every part of the space.

In the centre of the chamber, a form bulged and flexed, fed by the open gate. A doll-like figure rose at the end of an umbilical cord of sibilating current, jutting from the mouth. The group stared, transfixed. In the horror of the waking nightmare, they felt their deepest inadequacies ripped open like gangrenous cuts. The power of the thing left them denuded.

Cursing, Stilgen bolted towards the shape, his blade a grim light, joined by Kemet wielding a double-headed battle axe. The thing drooped, then fell to the floor, making way for the electrifying appearance of the Praetor squatting on a dark throne, holding an elongated, ebony stave. The far wall had become a recess, revealing the ruler in the centre.

The two warriors continued, seamlessly changing direction towards the many-limbed lord. Morack tried to join but was sent flying by a stray charge. Stilgen landed squarely in front of the demon, sword descending at the point between the eyes. A flick of a hand sent him skidding across the floor in a trail of vapoury wisps. Kemet sent his axe spinning, deeply slashing the side of one of the Praetor's arms. The weapon ricocheted off the seat, blade clotted with gobby sinew. The Praetor let out a cry, followed by a wave of Mage Rage. Everyone scrabbled for cover as the demon lit up like a sable sun. The blast sent them sliding along the flagstones, ending in a huddle next to where Stilgen lay spreadeagled.

The Praetor collapsed against the chair, blinded by pain. Deep-set, beady orbs looked up as Morack's sword angled at its head. Demon theurgy immediately blew the weapon skywards. Undeterred, Morack smacked it in the face repeatedly with his leathered fist at bullet speed, raining punches at its bleeding eyes before yanking free a dirk and thrusting it into the bobbing throat.

The blade shattered.

Morack retched as a glut of squirming entozoan, scarlet millipedes and chitinous scarab beetles poured down his front. Only his armour kept his flesh from burning, but the smell was fetid.

"By the gods!" Morack roared in pain.

Diabolist fury sent the Pit fighter tumbling against the others in a macabre comedy of disjointed limbs. The Praetor thrust forwards, upsetting the grubs that emptied down his neck in writhing clods. Teats pierced with razors and feathers overhung a naval of churning larvae.

The demon's anger seemed to have turned to excitement. "An under-estimation on our part? We think not ... just the comical efforts of some renegade exanimates and their rubber-skulled imbeciles!"

Flame licked the caecilian skin of its fingers as they held his staff.

Stubbornly refusing to die, Morack stuffed grey guts spilling out like carbonized sausages back into a bloody cavity. Grimacing, he strapped strips of tunic round his side to contain the precious packaging before clamping his battered breastplate across the impromptu suture. Finished, he sat up to glower, face splattered with milky fluids and residues of rancid Ichor.

Ayilia lurched forwards, but Vespasian grappled her back. She whirled on him. "If you don't let go, I'll drag your dried arm out your socket!"

His eyes were black with betrayal. "Your sword will fail."

"You think I'll let that inbred wart throw us around and do nothing?"

"No one said anything about nothing."

He turned and approached the Praetor, much to the demon's amusement.

"The godless mongrel! Look at you now. Does anyone other than the human call you Pro Consul anymore?" Burgundy lips pursed. A tongue several hands long licked the louse that resembled blood.

"I know you," Vespasian spat. "I've known sorcerer narcissists like you all my life, bleating with artificial superiority, bloated with unjustified self-regard, inflated with thaumaturgic testosterone. Guess what, no one gives a fuck!"

The demon flinched. It had been for the most fleeting moment, but the hands tightly gripped the throne. Seftus let out a whoop. Everyone started, but he didn't care. Clearly, the demon wasn't used to dissention. The thing leaned slowly back.

The Praetor fixed the fallen warlord with a canted smile, cracking knuckles on a hand with hollow popping sounds. The fallen warriors were too winded to rise. Ayilia and Vespasian watched him without blinking.

"What you call sickness, Sythian, I call realism. What you condemn as evil, I term strength; what you label pointless bloodshed, I call ... purity!"

Ayilia gripped her blade but couldn't move. Something was holding her back. The others seemed to be in a similar state of difficulty.

There was a murmuring, a barely audible rasping. The elegant wickedness of an intruding voice evoked the same dread Ayilia felt as a child when she unintentionally "dream-visited" every terrain imaginable, from deserted moonscapes to black shorelines at the edge of space itself.

It was one of the worst sounds she'd ever heard.

"Did they like my mannequin, Praetor?"

The voice was impossible to locate, but the demon seemed all too familiar with it.

"Artistic to the end, our lord and master!"

"Do not forget, the female is mine."

Though her mind was swimming, probably doing some neural breaststroke, Ayilia could make out a feral disappointment in the demon's reply.

"By all the suns, my liege, the woman was the one we wished for the most. The Consul is as dry as his exanimate chattel, all of which are in plentiful supply any time it pleases us, while the human mercenaries are no more than low-grade carrion. We—"

"You will accept what I decree, or our arrangement, and much else that is important to you, is annulled with the most extreme of prejudices."

It was coming from the gate. Ayilia struggled to raise her weapon, but she could barely move. Her eyes flitted to Vespasian. Caught in the same trap, his face was a mix of emotions alien and terrifying to her.

"Of course, of course, Liege ... All and sundry know the respect I have for—"

"My generals have mobilised six of my best legions in your prefecture to retrieve the female receptacle of our adversaries' battleplans. You understand what this means to me, don't you, Praetor?"

The demon nodded frenetically. "Yes, Lord, we understand that this human is the crux of everything."

"I sincerely doubt you understand anything beyond your rash-infested genitalia! However, failure to detain the breeder in mint condition would force me to depend entirely on my ingenuity in detecting the Al Kimiya's camouflaged carapace, and there would be little time left to slay the flagitious miscreant once this was accomplished. Damage, then, to this helot would be ... unacceptable, when so much is at stake."

"You have our undivided fidelity in this, we assure you."

"A judicious choice."

Ayilia clenched her fists. The voice was scrolling *through* her mind. Next to her, the Consul's entire body was trembling. Flame licked his fingers and dripped to the floor like black lava.

"However," the demon piped up, possibly taking its life in its hands. "Can I not be trusted enough to deliver one pitiful—"

"Trust, Praetor? Can you imagine the wonders of a multitudinous universe being tamed through such a concept?"

"Well—"

"Do you think I deployed such weaponry to pacify the Heretics?"

"Our liege!"

"Paradoxically, be assured that you are regarded with greater tolerance than my armies of officials who continue to strain my patience with their asinine, sophomoric blithering."

At that point, the Consul snapped.

It was like a crystal chandelier had fallen from a great height before detonating inside their skulls. The Praetor's eyes shot to him, white ovals in an imbroglio of spidery vessels. A blast of Sythian power smacked him in the chest, boiling the skin, leaving scarlet cobwebs of exposed capillaries. Despite its pain, the Praetor laughed, relishing the excitation it brought.

"Curses of a lapsed swine—time to sleep, Sythian, eternally!"

Networks of hexagonal lines flowed across the floor from its stave towards the transfixed warlord, latticing his legs, torso, arms, and neck, encasing his face in a vice. It pulsed, then constricted. Vespasian resisted, before keeling over.

Ayilia's Kimiya-enhanced mind finally shattered the grip on her body. Teeth gritted, she swept over her stricken ally and pushed her dirk against her throat.

"Look at me, green-nuts!" She had Soren to thank for that. "You think you've won, but not without the map!"

The atmosphere tightened. Her hand clasped the dagger tighter, though it was slippery with sweat.

"Oops!" She smiled. "Might have nicked myself a bit." She let the demon see the red bruise swell against her skin. "Oops again. I get the impression your admirably grubby gullet is as dependent on my neck as I am."

She took a couple of steps forwards. The thing stared belligerently, something predatory cornered in a nighttime scrub.

"I'll cut a deal, Praetor. My neck and, critically, the Al Kimiya's map in my skull for the necks of all my companions."

It snarled bloodlessly. "A hollow threat."

"You sure?" She grimaced. "I'll slice my carotid artery just about ... here. I mean, what do I have to lose?"

The thing made to speak, but she was quicker.

"Hard to believe members of your dilapidated species are now the thralls of the Unholy Ass. What did it take to buy you?"

Tendons tautened under its flexuous skin, like gamey cables beneath a tarpaulin. She was ready to die and take the map with her. If there was a way to get the others out first though, she'd take it.

Something struck her with a bolt of sorcery, and it wasn't the demon.

Life fleetingly left her body as the dagger skittled across the floor. The hard ground nearly cracked the back of her head open.

Shit!

Ayilia found herself theurgy-winded and lying in a spectacular heap next to the wretched Consul. Their bad luck rubbed off on each other like a shared scab.

The mannequin, the thing that had just struck her, rose back up. It was an Imperial avatar, the calling card of only the very powerful, and as rare as a happy serf. She knew this because the Kimiya magpie in her head downloaded the data in a split heartbeat.

"*The demon is my underworld gimcrack, Regent, a dangling gewgaw on a stick of shit. Other than the fact it has no choice, it enjoys both being in power and tyrannized.*"

The Goat laughed, more vibration within the microscopic particles of the stone than sound. The avatar abruptly vanished, replaced by the horrific form of the demon itself leering over her. Seemingly lost in venereal bloodlust, it thrust a bone dagger through her left shoulder. Though Ayilia stifled a cry, her body, paralyzed by underworld sortilege, twitched violently on the ground.

"This just started," it said in an unnervingly soft voice. "We can't use you, but with a lick of discretion, we can abuse you."

As it crouched, its grotesque belly flopped onto her legs. His tongue licked her wound, then slimed across her face before pausing almost tenderly over her eyelids. Yellow saliva bubbled in the pits of her eyes, stank in her nostrils. Disgusted, she could do nothing as she watched his horned head lower towards her own, invading her space with its musk. Her muscles refused to budge, held fast by its will. Insects wiggled within the wounds on its body. Some pattered onto her shoulder before scuttling into her garb or slipping down her neck.

"Hellion physics lies in the realms of the alchemist, female. Agony and pleasure are one in the real."

It was gibberish. Her mind was frantic. "The Emperor will string your warthog throat up for this and empty your guts across the Forum! You are meant to *preserve* me!"

"The Master?" Snickering. "Departed! Busy, bored, one cares not—only that He is gone. The sorcerer mannequin expired; a distance too expansive even for Him to maintain. Do not concern yourself. The demons have methods that leave their recipients *almost* undamaged." The voice was as soothing as a rattlesnake's tail. One of its hands began rubbing her thigh. "There are solutions to the complication you present."

"I'm thaumaturgically trussed up like a pig ... what complications?"

"You are treacherously dangerous. You reek of it." It coughed messily. Ayilia turned in disgust from the slabber from that ophidian hole and it covered her hair in mucus. "We can deliver your thoughts to him perfectly preserved but shorn of the casing that goes with it. All He wants is the information, not the stink it's encased within."

The thing paused, looking unexpectedly pensive. "The hourglass is nearly up, human. A cosmos-ending war is coming ... an edacious inferno that involves our kith, Regent of nowhere. When it starts, one does not wish to discover the ... wrong side has been chosen. This winged insurrectionist you serve *might* just tip the weighting scales in an unpropitious direction. It must be purged from this universe—and time itself!"

It descended closer, its spiny, pointed teeth scratching shavings off her cheek. To her revulsion, the hand was rubbing her leg. She saw her face refracted back within the saffron enamel. "It is possible, human, to take the clods of silage out your risibly thin cranium and feed it the juice it needs to churn. This grey mind-lump of sagged tissue will still function, in a fashion. The Kimiya's squalid secrets will be perfectly pickled."

Its tongue teased her lips, then forced them apart, exploring the pinkness of her gums as it tried to force itself through her closed teeth. As it pushed further, she abruptly opened and slammed shut her jaw, severing a gloop of tongue between her teeth. It shot back in a spray of dark blood, but there was no sound. If anything, its eyes shone bright with a carnal glow.

"Try it, fuck-face," she spat defiantly, feeling ridiculous that she couldn't move. "I'll still ..."

Her voice stuck in her throat.

The Praetor's eyes were widened, unseeing. They bulged within fleshy sockets. White liquid began dripping from its cracked lips and nostrils as its heavy head slumped slowly downwards. Jutting from its thorax, sticking between its ribs, was one of the pointed legs of a large tripod.

The demon twitched, then fell forwards.

All around, the alabaster miens of the statues stared, death masks within alcove coffins. Vespasian appeared behind the Praetor, his weapon more accustomed to supporting expensive, incense candles than butchering demon. His body was still smoking. Ashen crisscross patterns, like the burnt furrows of a field, were welded into his frame, though they appeared to be healing. An empty space nearby, free of cobwebs and dust, was the home of the unlikely weapon.

"It's iron," he said. It seemed meant as an explanation. He was panting slightly via redundant lungs.

The Praetor was still breathing. Hugging his frizzled sides, Vespasian addressed the creature in a hoarse whisper. "Despite all that yakety-yak, you can still die, just like us!"

Ayilia's Kimiya senses finally broke her free. She rose from the floor, kicked the demon's cranium hard, then raised her blade and hacked the head off. Inky fluids splattered her legs as the meaty object cracked against the tiles in a trail of ligament. It lay there, googling her, the malachite tongue lying across the floor at least a dozen hands long.

"About Goddamned time," Seftus said venomously, now also free of the power that held the group. "I thought green-balls would never shut up." He lifted his foot hurriedly as bloody head-ooze spread towards him.

Stilgen stood stiffly and made his way over to Morack. Soren staggered upright, wincing as he did, and shot Ayilia a wry glance. "Pity you couldn't have taken out the smell while you're at it!"

She flashed a wink before wincing at her shoulder. Kemet's face creased with concern. "That needs attention, Regent."

"Just a jab."

"A deep jab." He regarded it closely. "We'll have to get that fixed. Thank the gods, you're still in one piece."

Ayilia tried to smirk. "More like three."

"The thing nearly killed us," Stilgen growled.

"Let it try," Seftus growled, seemingly unaware of just how belated the sentiment was.

The Consul coughed. It wasn't loud, but everyone looked at him, even Morack, who by rights should have been dead. Fortunately, his entrails were more or less back inside where they belonged. "The demon is a predator that enjoys the slow demise of its prey. That's why you're still talking." Vespasian shrugged. "I guess it doesn't get out much down here, despite its wealth and cheap parties."

"It has cheap parties?" Soren quizzed.

Vespasian snorted. "I made that up."

While Kemet was cleaning her wounds and doing his best to remove the gunk from her hair, Ayilia examined his injuries in turn. Like the others, apart from the unfortunate Morack, they were mercifully super-ficial. Their chainmail, padding, and armour had kept the theurgy at bay, though there'd been little doubt the Praetor had been toying with them. Vespasian shot the humans a glance, then joined Morack. After quiet contemplation, he mustered some faint power and channelled it into his palms. Carefully, he placed them over the exposed rip in Morack's torso and brought them down the fissure. Like drying mud, the rents fused together.

"Gratitude, boss."

"Don't thank me—you've got broken eggs for guts."

Morack smiled thinly. "Fortunate, then, that they were superfluous from the start."

"Umm ... not quite all of them."

"All the same, gratitude."

"When you're feeling better, can you fetch Kofi, Smerk, and the others? They missed this little shit show, and I get the feeling they'll be miffed we left them behind."

An icy sensation ran down Ayilia's spine. She looked round but saw nothing. She caught Vespasian's eye.

"Time to go!"

His eyes narrowed. "You sense something?"

"Something senses me ... we have to go."

He looked unsure. Everyone looked unsure.

Kemet butted in, "When the Regent says it's time to go, rest assured, dead one, it is time to go."

Stilgen wasn't convinced. "And the Regent is normally accurate?"

"Always!"

Vespasian turned to Stilgen. "Prepare to leave."

Stilgen's features hardened. Morack was walking towards the gate.

"Morack, what are you doing?"

"I thought I'd check the destination."

Stilgen was unimpressed. "That's my job."

Morack wasn't listening or was choosing not to. "Sir, it's *still* open! It's got top-level Imperial clearance too, and it goes *all* the way in. We won't be piggybacking illegally if we jump now. No static backlash, no concerns over Imperial authorisation, and no fuzz to overwhelm navigation. We don't have to hang around ridiculously dangerous areas until the fuzz clears on the other side. We won't be fugging our way ahead using stealth jumps, like murmels in a quantum pipe."

Stilgen gently pushed him aside. "I said, *I* will do this. The fact that it is an open, official channel available for use is indisputable, as is the certainty there will be no static degradation. However, portal security is intense this deep in, and it will be a one-time jump only, even with the Praetor's personal codes. This requires experience." He pointed at the gate. "Besides, you are required elsewhere."

"I'm going somewhere?"

"Yes, back to our allies on the home world, assuming they're alive. You are without life, you're alone, you have portal experience, and you will pass Imperial lines with considerably more ease than our living … friends here." He retrieved a slate and examined the gate controls for many seconds before inscribing numerals on it. "Find them, collect them, then meet us at these coordinates—*that's* where we're heading. On the Praetor's charts, it registers as an exotic world with an impressively large hub of gates."

"Not bad," Ayilia muttered, joining them. "Gives us lots of routes to lots of places."

Kemet nodded. He'd decided to join the fun as well. "Such as the Resistance."

Morack wasn't listening. "Sir, I am—"

"Damaged, and I need a messenger. The door is now set. Go!"

"All the way back?"

"The Praetor's high-level codes allow you to bypass flight control. They will think you are the underworld toad itself. I have cleared a path home, via a continuous succession of gates, *only* possible due to those priceless codes." He fixed Morack with a hard look. "For us, it will be difficult. It seems the Praetor's retinue have high-level codes too, which are not here, so we can't pretend to be them. That means we have only one jump before security is alerted."

Morack winced. Ayilia, concerned, observed him holding his guts tightly, clearly still in discomfort. "Makes sense. A world with lots of gates is a world with lots of choices."

Stilgen offered a grave nod. "You will be alone and can be 'him' on more than one jump! We, however, will be spotted. The Praetor's codes will be immediately rescinded, but it gives us one invaluable super-jump to this hub. With all portals open, you will reach your destination swiftly. We will depart the *moment* I see you've arrived. They will question how the 'Praetor' can jump to two different locations from one gate, but it won't matter, as you will be there and we'll have blown our cover anyway." Stilgen flexed his hands impatiently. "Got it?"

"Yes ... no!" Morack sounded despondent. He looked up. "Boss?"

"What?"

"The portal's back home in the Pit. I'll be diced like a dead turnip!"

Stilgen released a dry smile. Ayilia found it reassuring somehow. He did that more and more. Was her humanity rubbing off on him? "Dead turnip or not, I'm not sending you there," he said softly. "I am sending you to the remotest of deserts, the Widow Maker, where, hopefully, some of the few loyal people I had left took the Regent's people. It should be safe—no one sane ever visits." The smile got drier. "There's at least one more gate in that desert, Morack; we didn't know precisely where. Using the Praetor's highly classified charts, I found it immediately. Clearly, it's on a need-to-know basis and us goons in the Pit didn't need to know. It's a long shot, but it's the only shot they have. All the gates are now waiting; all are conditioned to take you." The smile had turned so dry, cacti could have grown there. "Gates opened in unison are as rare as a Lifeless boner, so it won't take long. Remember, the Praetor's codes don't have clearance for large groups, so in the unlikely event you find them, they will have to join us at those coordinates ... *one* jump at a time. And we will not wait—they could take weeks, maybe months."

"A remote desert? I'm going to a remote desert?"

"You are Lifeless, designed to withstand the worst of them."

"Boss?"

"Leave before they shut the damned codes down." Stilgen's hand was pointing at the waiting mouth. "*Go!*"

With that, Morack turned without a backward glance and stepped into a ripple of plasma. His body was a dark silhouette against a cyan pond of light. It split into ten thousand miniature stars that shot away to a far point.

Ayilia smiled darkly. "I'm glad you think we're friends."

He looked sheepish. "I was being unusually ... exuberant. Breeders and non-life are not welcome bedfellows!"

She smiled caustically. "Well, isn't it a good thing we're only travelling!"

"This whole alliance doesn't feel natural," Seftus added unhelpfully.

Looking irked, Stilgen turned to face him. "Who in this upside-down universe can specify what is natural? Who has the authority and by whose authority do they pledge it?"

The Krayal looked genuinely bemused. "Welcome to my world, deadhead!"

Ayilia wanted to laugh but couldn't. Something was still horrifically wrong. She turned to face Vespasian. "I take it you're in favour of keeping the show on the road?"

He shrugged, a wry smile attempting to crease the dry parchment that purported to be skin. "Why not keep this circus going a little longer."

"Not too long, I trust," Kemet said wearily. He was spent; they all were.

"I thought you liked the dead, Kemet," Soren chided. "It's gratifying you're really on my side!"

Kemet let out an amused snort. "Kill me now!"

Footsteps sounded. All looked up to see Smerk's worn face next to Kofi's more hapless one. They were joined by the handful of other Lifeless guarding the halls. Kofi took one look at the demon mess still seeping across the floor.

"Looks like you slit a hog."

"And we missed the fun," Smerk added, brow crestfallen.

They went to join Stilgen. Ayilia's hands, however, were fidgeting wildly, always a bad sign. They longed for her weapon, but she couldn't see anything to fight. The air was thick with threat, but no one seemed to notice. Yet again, she was forced to go inwards, deploy those loathed Kimiya-impregnated senses. Not only was she increasingly dependent on them, she was actively fusing into them. The absence of permission was still a living violation, and that made her hate the Al Kimiya with a vengeance.

But something *was* here.

Ayilia could hardly breathe. Something was blocking her gift with spite.

"Shit. He's still here!"

They regarded her, completely nonplussed.

"Morack?"

"No, Kemet, the bloody Goat. He never left. Oh God! Why can't you feel—"

Ribbons of light blazed out of the portal, encasing the room. They caressed every statue, bathing everything in a moonlit glow. Stunned and blinded, Vespasian went over to the wall and pulled a sword from a display, his eyes darting in all directions. He also recovered the sable stave from the headless Praetor, which he held tightly in his right grip.

Soren turned to her. "Can't we leave? *Please.*"

She was trembling, but no one seemed to notice. It probably had something to do with the fact everyone was doing the same. The non-light was profoundly unnerving, like being electrified without pain.

"He's blocking the exit. We can't jump through," she murmured. "Not off world anyway."

Vespasian eyed her keenly, with a look that could have been respect. "How do you know? You've no sortilege!"

"That makes two of us, Sythian. We need a way out!"

"Why doesn't the Scum just take us now," Seftus growled, clearly hoping he sounded dangerous. He was rubbing the sore parts on his body that had been tossed round the room like tumbleweed in a prairie gale.

"As the Praetor said, too far away," she replied.

"You can tell that too?" Vespasian whispered, almost to himself. "Impressive!"

A sharp crack. The "moonlight" switched off. The candles dimmed. However, they still gave out enough light to reveal shapes moving in the gloom.

"Ideas, please!" Ayilia barked.

The tension hit meltdown. Excess occultism screamed at her senses, bled seemingly from the walls. The world felt upside down, visually mutated. In the dark, shapes blurred. Twisted horns, curved spears, and a brood of red eyes glinted within the murk. She glimpsed thick pelts, spiked clubs, and armour.

Something like an ox bellowed. Everyone jolted.

"By the gods," Stilgen cursed.

It was an animalistic cry of pain.

"What the f—" Soren muttered.

"Shell!" Kemet barked.

They instinctively formed a protective cordon around the only avenue of escape available, though the portal was still blocked by the Goat's distant theurgy. The shapes shuffled towards them. They seemed to be in no hurry.

Ayilia felt her blood freeze. It seemed everyone felt the same.

Ayilia shot Stilgen a distressed glare.

"Only the undergods know," he hissed back, looking for all the world like a being who'd lost his religion and much more than that.

Soren turned to go, but Kemet hauled him back. "I need every man ... you'll have to do!"

Ayilia shot an anxious look at Vespasian, hoping he might try one of his tricks. But she could only sense fear and a desperate attempt to stay calm. "A thaumaturgic defence trap. All top officials and Senators have one," he muttered grimly.

A pot clanged on the floor. The smog parted almost biblically.

A disfigured statue with an anuran skull lumbered out the murk, followed by another with a black goat's head. A third, a bulging-eyed steer with a lipless mouth and kicked-in teeth, joined them. Others lurched forwards, dread faces in the dark.

On cue, the rebels were battered by a wall of growls, spits, grunts, shrieks, chants, bleats, and howls. Their unwitting circus had become a zoo. The orchestral cacophony of the spiritually anathematised filled the room, hallways, and keep. Sepulchral pictorials were tattooed onto every feature, into each knotted tendon. Designed to terrorise, it worked well in the stone coffin of a space.

Ayilia sent a dirk spinning between the eyes of a toad, but it twanged off the forehead. The creature raised a multibladed axe beautified with feathers and shrunken pygmy heads dangling on the end. The goat attacked simultaneously, but Stilgen deftly sidestepped a spear to fling his dagger at the throat. The weapon flicked off with a reverberating clack. The thing turned and flailed repeated strikes at the Lifeless commander.

Vespasian, belatedly recovering his wits, raised the demon stave and fired a charge that struck the toad in the chest, immolating it in liquified flame. It refused to succumb, aimlessly slashing in all directions, a walking torch. In the confusion, Kemet and Soren rushed it, swiping at its impervious surfaces, sending burning hide airwards. Giving out a series of unsettling croaks, it swung at them, forcing them back, step by step. Jarong, recovering his wits, joined them. Smerk and Kofi let out a battle cry and led the Lifeless against the lifeless, swiping vehemently at everything with everything they had.

As Ayilia's eye swept across the melee, desperately searching for weakness, she noticed the lack of movement from the Underlord aside her.

"Fire, Goddammit, why don't you?" she spat out.

He looked lost, childlike.

"What's the matter? You're *still* Sythian!"

"I can't ..."

"What do you mean, you can't? You just did!"

"I'm out ... out of—"

"Well, that figures!"

A wolverine rammed her with a javelin emblazoned with flesh-tearing pincers and fluttering ribbons. Instinctively sidestepping, Ayilia dropped a double blow on its wrists, partially severing a hand in a frenzy of chips. Arching her blade back with a mighty grunt, Ayilia used the momentum to slash across its brow, forcing it backwards. It retreated into the maelstrom under a flurry of blows from her broadsword, leaving fluttering particles in its wake. Kemet, Jarong, and Soren were embroiled in similar darting strikes and retreats, while Stilgen was pushed to the far periphery. One of the Lifeless allies fell, their throat a gash of fluid. Smerk cursed furiously and battered a chunk out a statue's cranium. It screeched and staggered into some others. The group battled furiously, dancing manically among the rabble.

The animated gargoyles swept forwards, unkillable and relentless. Ayilia ducked between several of the figures before turning and parrying spear blows. With a fierce cry, she returned what should have been a deadly thrust, but it only juddered off a weasel's head. Backing frantically under assaults, she dug the blade furiously at the face, gouging an eye free, before coming to a standstill in an uncertain combat stance. Her lungs were burning, and her back muscles ached but she barely noticed.

Ayilia glanced Vespasian by the gate, staring mutely at the goat and toad. They looked like something out a chronicler's horror fantasy. Behind them rose a tide of ragged pelts, clusters of feathers and assortments of blood-coloured amulets studded into armour. He tried to fight but was too slow. Both figures lunged their spears violently into his midriff, pulling out grey, shale-like tissue with each retraction. He stood there stupefied as grotesque rents opened across his stomach, milky-dark tissue mazing haphazardly in the swirling vortexes of the wounds.

"Consul!" Ayilia screamed, but she couldn't close the gap. Stilgen was also shouting but was unable to free himself from a mob close to over-whelming him. Soren and Jarong were backing off into a corner, while Kemet swung his weapon manically, axe heads filling the room with deafening crashes and storms of sparks. The Lifeless soldiers were doing their best, but they too had been surrounded. Heavily outnumbered, they were cut down one by one, leaving just Smerk and Kofi.

Vespasian came to, eyes fixing momentarily onto his assailants before igniting them in an eldritch blaze. They stumbled backwards, blos-soming furnaces on legs. The exertion of sortilege was too much, and Vespasian sank to his knees as both statues exploded into shards of clay. There was no respite. Another pounded directly in his direction. Stilgen was fighting frantically to reach him while the others were forced further back. There were only moments left. Ayilia's mind raced. Outnumbered against an enemy that could not fall to steel, the group began to buckle and disintegrate.

An idea forced itself to the surface, assaulting its way into a disbeliev-ing mind.

Surely it's not that easy? Surely I'm not that dense?

Her breathing quickened. She plunged into a whirlpool of calculation even as her body fought on automatically. Her group was now living, and Lifeless, meat. There was no question as to what had to be done. Whether it was her own instinct or an insight from the ethereal violator in her head, she saw their foe were no more than lethal puppets on invisible strings, wielded by a distant mind.

No power, no life.

The static fuzzed in the air over and around them.

She could feel it. It had a source.

The Goat.

She threw herself against the wall before sprinting round the seething brawl. Throwing a glance at a gate separated from her by four creatures, she made out the controls. Breathing heavily, Ayilia flung a dirk as hard as she could, but it thunked to one side of the clunky dial, leaving a silver scrape in the stone.

Kemet shot Ayilia a perplexed look.

She gestured manically. Without question, he tossed over another dirk. Catching it midair, she tossed it at the controls again, but it also missed. Cursing vehemently, she bolted towards Soren and wrenched the dagger from his belt while sending her mailed foot into the back joint of a creature's leg. It buckled inwards with a heavy crash, allowing the wide-eyed soldier to regain his balance only to wilt from another flurry of powerful blows on his battered shield.

A third closed on her, but she turned and flung Soren's weapon directly at the controls. With a hollow and highly satisfying clunk, it clicked the dial.

The gate's iris shut with a grinding hiss. She felt the unseen mind-waves of the being snap. The oscillating circle of light fanning out from the funnel in space abruptly vanished as the aperture sealed.

The statues froze, poised in the middle of the air like gargoyle ballerinas, cracks networking across their faces and bodies.

It was Seftus' cue. He was born for this moment.

He strode up to the petrified figures, weapon firmly gripped in both hands, and gave each a whack, one by one. They splintered like glass monoliths before atomising across the flagstones.

The rest watched in silence.

Kemet, battle axes suspended, was staring wildly. Soren was cowering under his beaten shield. Jarong's knees were shaking. Stilgen stood at the far edge, disbelief clouding his normally expressionless face. Vespasian was staring at his hands, now lit up like cathedral candles. Clearly, a vestige of power had returned. Wordlessly, he placed them over his injuries, quietly cauterising them together, before gesturing towards Ayilia's bloody, demon-inflicted wound.

She found herself nodding. He placed gentle hands over the affected area. The rented flesh fused as he flame-cleansed it. She sighed with relief at the sudden absence of pain.

Smerk and Kofi were standing over the bodies of the few Lifeless who had accompanied them. The cost had been high. Stilgen went over and kneeled at their corpses. One by one, he kissed the forehead of each, his eyes moist and bitter, a moment shared by his two remaining men. The air was silent as he wept. Ayilia stared, staggered, her eyes wet. Even Kemet bowed his head, the folds of his forehead creased with weariness and pain. No one said anything as Stilgen paid tribute. Vespasian bent down and put a gentle hand on his shoulder. For those long moments, the room was united in silent respect, differences forgotten, blood irrelevant.

Eventually, Stilgen looked up. His face was lined and bloodless, even by the standards of his kind. "The Imperium's acolytes no longer function. You cut off the Seer's mind!"

"Can He reopen the door, at least remotely?"

"An impossible act considering He is countless jumps from us. He would need physical help here from the Praetor, due to the sheer number of gates in between. It astounds me nevertheless, how He can control things with His thought alone, since the curse that is Nethergeist lies so distant."

"Let's do it again," Seftus snarled, eyes gleaming like daggers. "That was fun!"

"For the love of the deserts, Seftus, if I, er, have any more fun like that, I think my gut pipes will expire."

"I think I soiled something," Soren whispered a bit too loudly.

Stilgen wiped his eyes and faced Ayilia. "Immediate departure is critical. We may have scant time before the Goat notifies security."

"But where?" Kemet breathed hard, as if trying to suck some life back into his depleted body. "Think about it—the Unholy Ass heard everything!"

"No, He didn't," Vespasian growled, grey blood flecking his already ruined tunic. He seemed to be panting heavily, which made no sense. "The Great Ass *did* leave—I sensed it. When the Praetor got a gutful, it was a significant thaumaturgic event—after all, that green-eyed bastard was powerful. The portal was open. The Emperor sensed it and returned. All we had to do was close the connection to sever the link." He looked around at them sheepishly. "And no, I didn't think of it at the time."

"Our hume leader did." Stilgen scowled, but with a genuine respect in his eyes.

Inexplicably, Ayilia felt self-conscious. "It was that shit the Kimiya dumped in my head." No one said anything. "It could've happened *a lot* sooner!"

"The 'shit' the Kimiya 'dumped' *in* your mind is one and the same *with* your mind," Vespasian whispered almost reverently. "Your consciousnesses have melded—it feeds off your thoughts as much as you do. You are, and have been for some time now, the same being ... whatever that is."

"Great." Seftus sniffed. "Part hume, part feather."

Soren giggled before extracting his foot from the mouth of a severed head that had somehow evaded Seftus' blade.

Weary, Kemet stretched himself to the full. "Time to go, before the Goat activates the candelabras next!"

"Wait," Ayilia said hurriedly. "We've lost that priceless Imperial connection. The gate's shut now."

Stilgen turned and walked over to the portal. "Not quite." He thumbed the dials. "See here?" They bent close to look. "Those are the Praetor's personal codes. And see these here?" He pointed at a set of pictorials in a golden frame. "Those are the coordinates the Goat used. They go all the way in!"

"All the way in," Soren repeated wanly.

"*All* the way in." Stilgen was flashing that dry smile again. "Of course, we won't go all the way in, but the hub world I spotted is on the way. We can use the vast choices it gives us to find the last vestiges of the Resistance, because I have no idea how to find them otherwise. We'd better be swift, before they realise our dead demon's dead, of course, and rescind the codes. Or before the Goat has time to tell them, which will be soon. Otherwise, we have clearance ... for one very sizeable jump." He flashed a wry glance in Ayilia's direction. "Impressive work, Regent."

Despite the distrust, she sensed something different in his demeanour. Not only had a hume saved them, but an enemy hume. In undead terms, that surely was akin to heresy.

Good. They could choke on it.

Chapter Twelve

PHARSALUS

B arrackus was a silhouette against a line of outrage. The hind of his Prowler thundered grit in its wake as he unsheathed his sorcerer mace. Shouting and cajoling, Sheyna herded the bewildered Raiders into formation, readying them for their third assault of the day.

There was a soundless detonation. They froze.

Barrackus' mace beaconed across the square, throwing shadows across the stone, penetrating the lids of those who'd closed their eyes. The Wirral reinforcements were transfixed, taunts strangulated. Barrackus was on them, torching ranks until the metal-plated tides parted, leaving a sluice of corpses fused to the flagstones.

As the Wirral fled, the Goblin Skinners rushed him in a mesh of slaver and cockeyed incisors. Barrackus' mount skidded to a stop. Inhaling deeply, he flung charge through his sword, shredding them in throngs. Dumbstruck, Sheyna watched them implode into pink clouds where they stood. It was impossible to believe his blade didn't shatter under the excessive theurgy. Barrackus turned, firing cannonades of shot through sword and mace, ripping chasms through the fragmenting ranks. Those that fled were conspicuously unharmed.

The screaming was overwhelming. Carbonized bone clacked across the tiles like dice. A counteroffensive of attack Goblins swept up from the back, passing Wirral running the other way. Without pausing, the Asthen fighter fired. Power surged through the ground in paroxysms, Barrackus at the epicentre. Superheated theurgy danced in arcs over the enemy, silencing hearts in waves. They went down like bamboo reeds in a hurricane.

Sheyna and Adira didn't need prompting.

With everyone marshaled, they drove into the dazed ranks, scattering them with ease. Even so, battle Goblin reinforcements began swelling at the peripheries. Barrackus, scoping the devastation, kicked his Lifeless mount on. Adira shouted after him, but he was too far away to hear.

Sheyna's inner eye caught a searing anxiety, an Asthen's anxiety. It was an individual's pain, one that rose above the emotions of the others.

Adira.

The woman's eyes were dark. She was scrutinising the commander with an intensity unmatched by any in the group. Sheyna shot her a sharp look, but before she could process what it meant, an unearthly din took her attention.

Something insane was happening.

The Goblins, the remaining Wirral, and the freshly arrived Imperial Wolverine Carnivore troops were chanting but, for once, not in derision. With a shocking jolt, Sheyna realised they were singing *to* him, not at him. It was absolutely unmistakable. The Raiders stared in astonishment. The beast troops believed the Raider captain was some kind of god.

The Skinners, Wirral, and Wolverine—a lighter version of the Wirral but infinitely more vicious—milled forwards with a respect Sheyna found staggering. Their Imperial commanders, clearly surprised, issued a furious welter of barking grunts. Hefty ogre henchmen began whipping the troop back into formation, but the animal soldiers immediately retaliated, and every one of them was submerged within a flurry of weapons. The violence was ugly but short lived, and the singing began again.

The large, silver-white sentinel portals faced the Raiders in a mighty semicircle. They were austere but beautiful. A wind tousled the snowflakes into alabaster shrouds around their bases. The blood and gutting of the fallen were transformed into frozen, cyan artworks of glittering ice.

Andromedus pushed himself to the fore and shot a dumbstruck look at the singing masses.

"Side Arm, we *must* exit this world. Maybe they love him, but they still hate us!"

"Patently." Sheyna nodded towards the portals. "Find us a route. I don't have a clue which gate to try first."

"The third from the big one in the centre, on the right."

She faced the pallid Tracker. "How can you tell?"

"It's open!"

She smiled despite herself. "You always get too technical for me."

His dour heart seemed to be lifted by her demeanour. Animated, he gestured repeatedly at the door. "It's still gonna take a while to set the coordinates as I don't know what's ahead, but —"

"I get it, Andromedus."

"Obviously, we can't jump on official channels, but if we can piggyback on that already open signal, we could go really deep."

"I got that too," she replied, amused. She faced Adira, who had just joined them. "You're the third. Take our Tracker, rig up a cordon of staves, swords, and thaumaturgic shields, and cocoon him like a bug in a rug while he works. Enlist Skyron's firepower to soften any assault, just in case the Imperial mutts get bored worshipping the boss."

"What about you?"

"I'm going to get our glorious leader in case they hug him to death."

She kicked the Prowler and sped towards Barrackus while Adira ushered the taskforce towards the gate.

As Sheyna approached, she heard the drone of a million insects moil towards the square's edge. Barrackus looked up, almost in slow motion, as the brimming mass dove at him. The Raider released burst after burst of Mage Rage deep into the horde, scattering swathes in all directions, but it closed in undeterred.

She rode towards him, screaming his name as she did. Merging theurgy, they forced the flux back, but only by paces. He seemed unhurt, but the stormfront, now enraged, surged against their combined shield with renewed vigour. The ferocity appalled her.

"Hell's ass, Sheyna, I told you to stay. This isn't a game; I can't keep you safe!"

"I'm not a farmyard hound, Barrackus. Don't you think I understand, you dumb idiot? You think we're better off watching you hacked down by Vensa, of all things. They're not semi-trained animals—these things are demon! Lower-class, domesticated demons, but demons all the same!"

Both mounts were dangerously jittery. They were Lifeless machines of stitched sinew, but somehow the longer they spent time in Barrackus' company the more alive they seemed to become. The hissing sibilation of the Vensa ground into their minds like a million metallic wings grating together.

"Back off, Sheyna—I'm not in the mood for one of your stubborn fits. Without you, the troop is just as screwed." Their combined firepower was forming a neon umbrella against the swarm. "Save yourself! I can keep them off our collective asses while Andromedus finds a way in."

"I've got news for you, *Commander*—if we get through, there'll be many, many more surprises like this. We're out of space and we're out of time, so either you come, or we all get butchered like one big happy family."

The mounts were backing away so rapidly, they were tripping. A stench of rot, the calling card of demon, was overpowering. She almost retched as Barrackus' mace drove blinding suns into the squall.

Sheyna wiped her mouth and eyed the threat. Closing her eyes, she furiously muttered rituals, magnifying her strength.

Such thaumaturgic concentration couldn't be maintained. Ideal for skirmishes, drawn-out combat could kill off reserves in moments, not to mention her. Nevertheless, her sortilege-enhanced mind soaked up the untapped quantities of free-flowing energies on the quantum scale in every flagstone, every edifice, and every piece of grit and shit in the vicinity, before twining it around the mace. Sheyna fired at the hovering malignancy with such force it sucked the life out of her lungs.

A vast cloud of Vensa vapourised before her eyes.

Panting but delighted, she flashed the commander a sweaty grin. "Told you, you needed me!"

He wiped the grime from his face, eyes twinkling. "I believe you did!"

"You *do* know you're putting the indulgence of hate above the safety of the others?"

Unfair perhaps, but in her book, they did things as a team.

"It's not hate!"

"Maybe, but what does it matter if we're dead?" Sheyna turned to go. As she did, she nearly blacked out.

Melanoid darts pierced her aura, ripping her witless Prowler into clusters of meat. Barely enough of her shield remained, or she'd have joined her luckless beast, but her spine was a byzantine maze of sorcery. Instinctively, her theurgy gloved her in an amnionic caress, healing the wounds, stopping the necromantic poison from infecting her bloodstream.

Barrackus swore.

Brimming with potency, the Asthen chief dragged out perilous quantities of electrified current from the infinite sea of particles embedded in a radius of a league in all directions. Engorged with power close to consuming him, a soundless annihilation from within blew him to his knees, eviscerating the Vensa on sight. The Raider lay there prostrate, head pumping with blood. He was as vulnerable as a baby but as powerful as a mountain, the demon awakening something that had been brooding for longer than he knew.

Bloodshot eyes opened slowly.

Fluid trickled copiously from cracked lips. His head still pounded with the force of a thousand Prowlers. Anyone could have finished him off. Slowly, his lungs gathered air.

Blinking hard, he focused on a descending curtain of demon cinders falling across the snow.

He staggered to his feet in a series of undignified movements, scooping Sheyna in his left arm as though she was made of papyrus. He looked for his Prowler, only to see it mindlessly galloping towards his troop by the gate. Somehow, he caught the eye of Adira. Her eyes were creased with concern. She made towards him, but he gestured her back.

The detonation had confirmed something. Using the right discipline, it was theoretically possible to plunge into what was—by rights—an unending supply of energy. Asthen did such things in their sleep, but it was the unfiltered, perdurable scope of it that was terrifying.

An adept could do literally anything, be anyone.

In such a state, knowledge grazed the horizon of universal consciousness. At this point, the Asthen chroniclers hissed reverently, an adept attained the soul-mind of a deity. The duality of existence and spirit, fused within the neurological forge of a master practitioner, becoming one.

The adept attained the Ji'naa.

Get it wrong, and he would burn like the greatest candle in this part of the sky. Get it right, and he could become a god.

The Goat knew this. The Abomination was probably the greater sorcerer existence had ever known, at least since the Ancients had passed.

And He was getting stronger.

Sheyna groaned. She was coming to. She'd taken out much of the Vensa without his help. With a bit of patience, something as likely as Andromedus getting an engaging personality, she might join Barrackus' godhood insanity. But a deep-seated bitterness made her angry. Anger came from distrust, and that came from dread. Anger blocked everything. It was only an energy, an energy that could be harnessed, but she refused to do it. Keeping it was too comfortable, too easy. It was her default over doubt, and she did it well. But the pain, loneliness, and spite that feasted inside were poor bedfellows in life. Ultimately, it was no life at all.

"Barrackus?"

He was looking down at her. She swiftly regained a composure of sorts.

"Gone?"

"The Vensa?" He put a supporting hand on her shoulders. "From this life, yes!"

A handful were flying away. He let them go. She was unimpressed with this belated leniency.

"They might come back."

"In a few centuries, perhaps."

The Imperial troops were watching them with beady eyes. The singing had been replaced by a low-level hum. It was more unnerving than the fighting.

"It's not about them," she said, still weak. "I keep telling you over and over—it's about you and what you feel when you kill and why you feel you need to kill so many! I don't mean the Vensa, I mean their entire damned army here. You may think you're doing good wiping them out instead of giving them a bloody face, but you just degrade your soul, and believe me, it will count. It always counts, no matter the time, place, or situation."

She spluttered, giving in to hacking coughs. Acrid vapours clung to her throat, and tears of frustration quickly followed. She loathed him, felt in this moment that she always had. He'd betrayed everything they stood for—their team, their beliefs, everything they fought for—to indulge in messianic godhood and the butchery required to prove it.

"You should've left me to die. I'd rather die than become like you, Barrackus. There's nothing separating us from them now."

"Why? Because I defended us?"

"Because you love it, the killing."

"I do it because I have to."

"You do it because you want to play God. That's also why we're here, isn't it?"

He was panting hard. His irises were engorged on theurgy. They had turned the colour of hell.

"Have you any idea what Wirral, Skinners, Wolverine, Vensa, Proto Goblins, attack Goblins, and demon do to people like us? Do you think they give a rat's ass about your grand theories when the cutters violate *everything* you hold dear? Have you any idea how long it will take them to do it!"

"Of course I do, and I don't really give a waking shit how many demon you kill while you're doing it," she spat back, before taking a great gulp of air. Pains were shooting up from places that she'd forgotten existed. She lowered her voice. "But you forget we're all empathic—I sensed your mind as you became a narcistic demi-god, pissing on all our scriptures and all that's decent in this crazy universe. I know you loved it, and I know in those moments you're subconsciously linked with the

Abomination—you're one and the same! I could feel it, Barrackus. It's happened ten million times in history, and every time it leads to worse!"

A fleeting look of sadness crossed his face. He looked away, but Sheyna barely cared. She suddenly felt something was terribly, terribly wrong. She wiped speckles of blood and spit from the sides of her mouth and pulled herself to her feet.

"Barrackus ..."

"I ... didn't love it. I was ..." He shook his head. "I couldn't control it."

Her anger melted. "I'm scared, Barrackus. I'm so scared you're becoming—"

"One of them? Hell's guts, Sheyna, I'm not a serial slayer, a coldblooded pig butcher. I'll never work for the Abomination!"

She shook her head and wiped her grim tears away. "Not work for Him ... *become* Him!"

The hurt in those dark eyes pulled at her heart. He was suddenly a ten-year-old boy.

"If I was destined to become Him, you'd already know. Trust me on that if nothing else!" His hand gently brushed the hair off her stern face. "Do you believe me?"

She refused to acknowledge someone who had the power to start a thaumaturgic genocide, should that thin membrane in his mind keeping the vandal from the sophisticate rupture. However, it didn't matter. Barrackus' face had atrophied into something else. She'd seen it before.

It came when something bad was coming.

"Barrackus, what—"

"Shhhhhhh." He held up a grimy finger.

What was left of the cold sunlight was fading. Twilight angled across the grandiose buildings, the arches, and the squares, severing them from the light as efficiently as a Goblin's sickle. Even the Imperial troop stopped their humming. She remained rooted to the spot, though her fingers trailed towards her weapon, the tips nuzzling the belt. The stave was nearby, on the ground. Almost absentmindedly, her mind summoned it to her hand in powders of ice.

"I knew it!" Barrackus scowled. "Sheyna, move. Now."

"What's there?" Her hand gripped the hilt of the thaumaturgic weapon.

Another voice permeated the graveyard quiet. Her blood solidified. "I think you really mean: who."

She turned slowly to meet the speaker. A figure grinned back.

Even though their features were distorted by the smoke and demon ash, she could make out the silhouette of the traitor Asthen general and the dull gleam of his teeth.

"He ..." Barrackus breathed. "He is exactly what I rode out to meet."

There was a pause before the figure whisked out a mace and fired so quickly there was no time to blink. Standing still, frozen to the spot, Sheyna looked down to the smoking hole on her left. She sank to her knees, curls of vapour drifting from her lips.

Visibly horrified, Barrackus tried but failed to grab her. He scrabbled across the snow and debris to where she lay gasping like freshly landed prey. Gently, he turned her over. Blood trickled openly from the corners of her mouth, forming bubbles that popped delicately as they ran down her neck.

"*Sheyna!*"

She could not focus.

"I'm ... I'm sorry, Barrackus. I couldn't be what you wanted. Honestly, it's only quickened the inevitable ... If only ..."

"Don't move. I'll take care of the rest."

"I'm so ..."

"Shh. I'll sort this, even if it kills me."

But there was no honour that day. A bolt split his ribs, catapulting him across the debris dozens of times until his smoking body came to a halt against a shattered urn. The Raiders froze, watching the proceedings with despair from the artificial safely of the gate. The Carnivore Legions regarded the Asthen death duel without flinching, a duel between gods. The stakes were enormous. It was clear from their expressions every feral mind knew it. Even Andromedus could be seen gawping.

Pharsalus dismounted and strode purposely towards the felled commanders, an Imperial crack team of hefty Proto Goblins stomping behind him. They moved like living tree trunks, war armour as thick as tanks, flesh bulging like captured bison in bice sacks. Their teeth were thick, each stubby eye leaked purulence.

Pharsalus' irises flashed livid-blue intellect. They raked their surroundings, taking every detail in. Though well preserved, his skin was bleached by neon suns and measureless battlefields. A network of thin white scars capered around his neck.

There was a sudden commotion.

Sheyna caught a glimpse of an Asthen fighter thundering towards them on his Prowler, discharging thermogenic bolts, but Pharsalus deflected them with an abstract flick of a hand, returning a solitary shot. The man's hair-matted head went spinning to where Sheyna lay. A groan went up from the others. She watched a distraught Skyron barking commands at them to maintain formation and to keep monitoring the Carnivore Legions. The Raiders fanned out, crouching low like armed panthers, concentrating all their firepower on the renegade general, but he seemed unfazed, never once taking his eyes off the prone figures.

Pharsalus spoke in a whispered rasp. Sheyna barely caught his words; she felt rather than heard them. The vibrations were reverberating through the ground, up through her body and directly into her ear. His lips were already on the next line before she'd heard the last. The intent was to disturb, and it was successful.

"You spent years carving out furrows of flame and blood inside Imperial lands, sowing unfettered mobocracy across the welkin vaults and yet you die so ... whimsically!"

Skyron nodded at Lars, who in turn nodded at the shooters. The general raised a withering brow in their direction.

"Tell them not to bother," he whispered with a calm but menacing inflection. "My gift, admittedly a rather gawkish term, is enhanced by Myrian, a bonus for unswerving fidelity to both Imperium and purity. I would advise your coffin-dodging vulgus over there to give some thought to how best they can deprive the indignant grave of their debatable nourishment. Because if they continue to approach, that, for certain, will be the last act they perpetrate under your sallow wardship."

Barrackus shook his head at an indignant Skyron. Reluctantly, he gestured them to back down. They grudgingly complied but did not retreat. Baring one or two wardens, Andromedus was suddenly exposed. He didn't seem to care. There must have been some particularly up-to-date security-elemental within the open gate, which was hardly surprising considering where they were.

Pharsalus ignored Sheyna. He was only interested in the commander.

"The gains to be had if I'd succeeded in Tracking you face-to-face, instead of rotting in campaigns against the Asthen herders and their witless allies. Think of all the Imperial armies I would have saved from that wicked stave of yours!" Pharsalus' calm demeanour suggested he didn't give a damn about those Imperial armies. "You know, they said I was mad waiting in a place no foe has ever been able to reach, but I knew you'd try—the big one, a state assassination. I imagine what you feel, Barrackus. I've crawled under your skin to the dreams that haunt you every single, battle-scarred night."

Barrackus raised his eyes to the nihilistic irises of his counterpart. As far as she could sense, there was no insight within; the way was blocked. Instead, his thoughts skimmed her consciousness, begging her to flee for the questionable sanctuary of the others. Somehow his spirit drew strength from her, despite the condition she was in. He had to draw attention, give her time. So, he fixed everything he had on the malevolence in front.

"Aren't there better things to do with your time?" He grimaced, teeth black with blood. "Does Imperial gold compensate for the fellowship of a kith you can never reclaim?"

The general's eyes shone like permafrost, perfectly matching the streaked white of his hair.

"I sensed you on that moon last night, Commander. I left it untouched, gave you a good night's sleep. It's a favour that includes forgetting to inform the portal guard they only had till sunrise to live." He flexed his fingers. "Let's not forget, you're the only rat I know who can reverse back when his army's still halfway through a gate, before the static closes in. I would have loathed to lose you before we had the chance to chat." He took a step closer. "To catch you is a thousand times harder than jumping your own shadow before it has a chance to move."

Barrackus was clearly in pain. "I must have really gotten under your skin."

"You have no idea."

He pushed himself slowly up. A shoal of debris rained off his garb. "I'd guessed, to be honest, by the dubious pleasure of this extended discourse."

Pharsalus smiled. For Sheyna, it was like being gently skinned alive.

"It's over, Commander. No matter what you think you can do, you and your august troop are now no more than dated stock for the market flesh-monger. Be pleased you have the opportunity to die with dignity, like a true Asthen. I prevail on you, therefore, not to judge me as a person without manners."

"Tell him to stick that shit up—"

"Sheyna!" Barrackus snapped.

Pharsalus regarded her levelly, taking his time. "The things I shall do to that mouth of filth will make your past seem like a Sunday school clambake. It won't be the first time either, will it Side Arm? What was it again ... an orphanage?" He slowly tapped the side of his head. "I'm no mind reader, but yours is an open book, comrade."

The general was bathed in falling snow. The contours of his hair were frosted, giving him the appearance of an impious seraph. "You don't understand just how much I enjoy my achievements and the look in your necromantically mutilated mind as you squirm for options. The way ahead is stark, Barrackus."

"I know!"

The general shook his finger. "Not sure you do."

"Stay and fight or run. I get it!" Despite the pain on his face, Barrackus was managing the blood back into his right shoulder.

"Stay and *die,* Commander. Run and die, also. The only choice is where that death is to take place and the manner of it, but you can be guaranteed it will be—"

. "Pitiful!" Barrackus smiled, finishing the sentence for him.

Sheyna, despite her injuries, was surprised. He didn't look like a man about to die. The diversion seemed to have given him strength.

"People like you always say stuff like that," Barrackus added levelly. "Can't you be a little more inventive?"

Pharsalus' grin was rictus, like that found on something long dead.

"Before we do this," Barrackus continued, now in his stride, "can you enlighten me on one thing?"

"That might be possible."

"You were the best the Ascendancy ever produced. You've taken everything you learned from them, merged it with everything Myrian, the demon viceroy, gave you, and turned it on your people." He leaned forwards. "Is this an identity thing?"

Traces of argon flickered round the pupils. "*Identity*? You mean the crumbling Ascendancy?"

"*Our* crumbling Ascendancy," Barrackus replied caustically, his strength seemingly returning.

Pharsalus' half-smile thinned. "You insult me, begrimed in your own spit and blood, representing the best the Ascendancy has left." He breathed, milking the moment as much as possible. "You *are* aware, Commander, that you have thaumaturgic schizophrenia?"

Sheyna visibly flinched.

Paranoia swirled inside, but she swallowed it back. She wanted to get up and fight, but her wound was grievous. Barrackus however, was openly goading the all-powerful general. She swore she saw his eyes twinkling, like they used to. Somewhat unnervingly, he looked more like a predator than victim.

"One day, Pharsalus, when you're toothless and spent, regarding your cruel face in some gilt-edged, Imperial mirror at the nadir of a life of greed, narcissism, and soul-corroding power ... what then?" Barrackus' stare was black. "You will be entombed in a palace vast and shiny, staffed by obsequious servants with spite in their souls and death in their hearts, courted by mannequins stinking of sweet-smelling powders and stale sex but with no warmth in their eyes. The place will be as sterile as your epicurean existence, devoid of kinship and love and incapable of grieving when the day belatedly comes when your oily shell finally passes away, alone and despised."

Sheyna made to rise but failed. Her head was spinning, her mouth as dry as a corpse's hairpiece. As she was about to pass out, a pair of hands thrust a pouch of water to her lips. She drank greedily. The same hands placed a cloth against the wound. It was immediately saturated red. Looking up, she saw Adira's bright, anxious eyes staring down as she staunched the blood with healing Mage fire. While she worked, Sheyna caught her shooting Barrackus concerned looks.

"The Ascendancy considered me a helot just for the crime of being orphaned," Pharsalus spat. "Ultimately driven into the crystalline mines of Shanti as a twelve-year-old wretch, just because I had no home. It was comfortable and the education adequate, but their famed compassion is sporadic when it comes to those who have no voice and no wealth. Strangely, they appear to exert a little more care more now, as I burn their lines with the breath from my lungs and the fire from my mace, than they did when I was being beaten for hiding. It's not *because* of that I hate our people. I hate our people for claiming they didn't do that, even when they did." He glowered darkly at his prone adversary, lost in thought. "Don't fret too much, Commander. The places I went during those times, the things I learned in those dark corridors of grief … well, I learned it was possible to reach halfway to Ji'ann by the time I was fourteen. Myrian only cemented what was already inside."

Pharsalus spat across the glittering carapace of ice surrounding him. "I wanted *you* to understand, Commander, that even the most enlightened in the most splendid of halls still sweep the shit under the rug when it suits them."

There was silence apart from Adira's efforts to patch Sheyna's wound, the padding of flakes, and the breaths of the demi-gods. The dimming light was only broken by the cobalt outlines of the sentinel gates and the shapes of the square's grand architecture on the peripheries.

Both men stood, embedded in wild theurgy, eyes blazing with a violence that threatened to strip every atom around them of energy.

"Honestly, Pharsalus, that's got nothing to do with it. You like hurting people because you're a psychopath."

Barrackus blatantly didn't see it coming. He was on his shoulders again in a spume of smoke, his retinas whited-out by a blinding glare. Pharsalus, a dark, brooding silhouette, was framed by twilight snowfall. He seemed ten times taller.

"Reconfigured your shield, Commander? You think oscillating its vibrations keeps me out?"

Two shapes rolled over suddenly, staves firing. Arcs pirouetted across Pharsalus' face, distorting it into a Mephistophelian effigy. Genuinely shocked, Pharsalus flung full-throttled Mage Rage at Sheyna and Adira, crushing their fields, tossing them further across the ground.

But it was enough.

Barrackus discharged a bolt so concentrated, it barely registered on the thaumaturgic spectrum. Pharsalus, distracted, attempted a stave block, but the charge drove directly into his heart. Conceit became disbelief, smugness, mortification. Vapours curled from his open mouth. Wisps of smoke rose from his flared nostrils, ears, and eyes. The mighty general, the all-powerful necromancer who single-handedly threatened to bring the Ascendancy to ruin, thumped to his knees before keeling forwards.

With a triumphant holler, the Raiders let rip with a barrage so murderous the still-astonished crack unit of Proto Goblins were practically eradicated on the spot. Bolt after bolt penetrated armoured chests, sending gutting steaming across comrades like red tripe. Some began to run, but their legs were tied within the intestinal track of their colleagues, wrapping around ankles, forcing them down. For once, the Raiders fired without mercy, and the heavy infantry platoon fell like blooded lumber: meaty heads cracked, viscera streaked across the floor in maroon smears.

Barrackus scrambled towards Sheyna among the blood and the slain, until he hunched over the stricken side arm. With a thought, he quickly summoned their remaining Prowler back. Suturing her wound with a flaming palm, he carefully placed her over the mount's saddle and sent it across the bodies towards friendly territory at pace. Adira joined him at his side. She had been winded, but her shield had saved her. For a fleeting moment, their eyes locked, but a rising sound from across the square disturbed them.

Wounded and dizzy, the commander glanced towards the squall. Reams of Imperial beast troop took to their knees, rank after rank. They were singing to him again, chanting his name. Despite the hoarseness of their throats, the pitch was deafening. It was also coarsely beautiful. He looked at his company. There was awe in their eyes—and something else.

Fear.

Fear of the armies, fear of how far they'd come—or, maybe, fear of him. He couldn't tell. Some were smiling, some had tears down their faces. They were overcome, pushed to the edge. Others were hugging each other. Whatever happened, they had reached and survived one of the most iconic places in the universe.

Armerhurst, ancient capital of the Interregnum.

It's a shame, Barrackus thought. It was a shame they couldn't take this army with them, but there wouldn't be remotely enough to take on the Emperor and He would see them coming a million leagues off. You couldn't travel covertly with so many soldiers.

No, he would do the next best thing.

He would set them free.

If the Goat was to be slit open, it would be through stealth and surprise. This was one tyrant who wouldn't be brought low by revolution knocking at the door.

This Emperor, this Imperator, would be brought down by assassination. He, Barrackus, had decided for sure now.

Forget the High Command.

He, the killer of Pharsalus, would Track all the way to the Goat's lair, and he would sever the throat from the rest of the Emperor's body. He would butcher him like swamp swine, then toss the body to the seat of His throne—and he, Barrackus, would sit there instead.

Chapter Thirteen

Another Gate, Another Universe

T he lake lapped peacefully at the desert shore. Grasses rustled like silver streamers around their legs, playing out a scene that hadn't changed in millennia. Despite the paucity of plants, feathered seeds drifted across the waters and over the watching group. Flanked by dusty hillocks, it was hard not to deny the Widow Maker could be startlingly beautiful when it wanted to be.

Aaron actually felt relaxed, a feat in itself considering his time was spent with a bunch of Lifeless renegades with maroon death for eyes, like the hell-bound that had haunted his sleep for as long as he could remember. Of course, he still didn't trust them. He doubted he ever would. His hatred of their kind superseded anything felt by most humans. So, it was doubly bizarre he was the one standing between the sneaky-looking Breasel and the sharp sword of the Pit group leader, Youssif.

And that leader was doing his head in. Aaron could barely credit his own thinking, under the blazing suns of a home world he might never return to, but Youssif actually seemed … noble.

Unbelievable!

He'd learned that he had more in common with Youssif than most humans he'd ever known, at least outside the familial doctrine of the X Gemina. He was controlled, thoughtful, reserved. Aaron himself had rarely been accredited with such things, but nevertheless an unexpected mutual respect had grown from somewhere. Each understood how anxious the other was to reach their respective commanders; that they repeatedly saw eye-to-eye on most matters.

Surreal.

Yet again, another long-cherished misconception had gone out the window. If this kept up for much longer, he'd end up some willowy peace activist with herbs in his hair and slogans seared into his rump. Not that he'd seen anyone like this, which made him realise this might be another piss-pot of unverified bias he'd lovingly nurtured all his life, but he was damned if he was going to let go of another dubious opinion without at least some fight.

Youssif carefully sat on the patch of sand Aaron had contentedly made his own. For what the Krayal called "the soulless," the warrior seemed unexpectedly at ease. Neither spoke for a while as they contemplated their surroundings and the fairy fluffs wafting in the air. Not far off, a group of renegade drones were in animated conversation with the upstart Breasal. Occasionally, they shot glances in Aaron's direction.

"What do you think he's doing now?" Aaron asked finally.

Youssif cast a wary eye over the group, and Breasal in particular. "He's telling everyone how useful he is, again."

"I suppose he did find what we were looking for: the gate."

The other nodded guardedly. "Aye, something my people failed to do in all the time we were here, once Stilgen ordered us to look. I guess the old Krayal charts he and Breasal somehow found in the decomposing hole that was the Pit library were more ancient than realised. I had begun to think the thing was a myth."

Across the lake, standing serenely as the day it was first made, was the unmistakable shape of a mini portal. Though hewed from old stone, it glinted like burned mercury across the waters in front. Close up, the contours were callused as though crafted from the heel of an old giant, but from a distance it was a seraphic lens.

Aaron scratched his head furiously.

The lake was home to a retinue of savage, flying bloodsuckers. And these things seemed to home in on him more than anyone else.

"Curse these cursed curses of Goddamned bluebottles. They've got it in for me, every single one of them. I'd blame Soren, but he's not here."

His lifeless companion shot him a quizzical glance. Aaron swore he looked amused. "Agreed."

"Agreed?"

"Agreed." Youssif's eyes twinkled. "I noticed the moment we arrived that the parasites appear to avoid the others in your company and go directly for your head. They must sense something appetising in your blood."

"At times like this I wish I had your Ichor for blood, trust me."

"Pit Ichor is old and mottled. Any bug feasting on that would be dead in heartbeats." He looked thoughtful. "Shame, in a sense... they might have rid us of Breasal!"

"A-bloody-men to that." Aaron snorted. "I'll find something else to suck his desiccated guts out if he doesn't honour his promise and work that portal out."

"You mean, the promise you forced him to make?"

"There'll be plenty more if I have my way. It's the only way to shut him up." Aaron swore again as he flattened a particularly whiny bug: "Should've let you skin his lying throat. He's clearly good for nothing but the creation of hot air, the last thing we need in a Goddamned desert." Aaron shook his head and sighed at himself. "Yet, he found the gate. He's already delivered. It's just these bugs are making me unreasonable. Normally, I'm as calm as a—"

There was a sudden whoop. Breasal had raised his fists triumphantly. Astonishingly, he'd managed to switch the gate controls on, something none of the others had managed. He'd even sent a covert message and claimed there had been a response, that someone was actually coming. At least, that was what it sounded like.

Aaron looked oddly abashed. "Hell's balls, I really did speak too soon!"

"Perhaps it was a good thing you stayed my blade after all." Youssif regarded his weapon thoughtfully. "You surprise me, hume. You risk your hide for that recently worthless pile of dung, and now that you have done so, you are not afraid to admit fallibility. Not what we were taught about your kind."

Fleeting images of cracked incisors poking through rotten soil under orbs of psychotic fire flashed through his mind. Aaron brushed the nightmares back into the troubled recesses of his mind. "Guess we all laboured in the dark, if truth be told."

The Lifeless scrutinised him quietly but said nothing.

"Incidentally, changing the subject, you found this location in the middle of nowhere in the worst desert I've ever been in, slipping those deep field patrols with some ease," Aaron said.

"It's hard to forget that."

Youssif snorted, but not in derision. Aaron cursed himself again. For a moment, he'd felt happier being in the company of this thing to some of his own people, especially Soren. The dreams were always there: fields of hands grasping for him, skulls glowing dully in the moonlights. Here was a companion made of the same death, yet a companion who'd nevertheless fight at his side to defy death and, if necessary, die with him. It could drive him mad.

There was a long silence. Eventually the Lifeless broke it.

"Forgive me for inquiring, hume. I understand it's not my business ..."

"Go on."

"It was something Breasal reckoned."

"Uh-oh."

"He's been telling my people you are mated with the female who leads your command. It is an ... anomaly to me. Does this not affect decision-making?"

"What, that slimy, skin-challenged, sneaky, toad wretch of a passing wart on sticks has been gossiping about me? After all I've done for him too!"

Youssif stared at him, perplexed.

Aaron's hands slapped the midges repeatedly in frustration. "I *had* a ... thing with the regent when we were young. Didn't work out. Frankly, it might have had something to do with me." It was his turn to snort. "Actually, it did have something to do with me. Well, that's what she told me. She's ... intense. Maybe she thought it was going somewhere. I dunno. I was a dick. Isn't that youth's prerogative: being selfish?"

"No!"

"Honest to the core," Aaron grumbled. "Got to appreciate that, I suppose."

His companion's brow was deeply furrowed. "Hume courtship rituals seem a waste of energy to me. Could you not reclaim her?"

"*Ha*. You do not reclaim Ayilia."

"But you harbour intentions still?"

"My only intention is to find that gibbering Heretic she worships, get him and what's left of his pals to extradite that garbage the feathered freak of a Kimiya dumped in her head and pray it kicks the stiffs off this world, no offence intended. Then, I intend to go back to the Prancing Cock and get every part of my body as pissed as a lost pustule." He hawked across the ground. "In the end, Ayilia devoted her entire existence to helping the spittle-eating gnashgabs of our city and those in the Occupied Territories, to the exclusion of everything else. Eventually, intimacy of any kind of went out the window. I think Lorelai and Jacob were the last straw, and if you ask me, she's better off without that shit too. Nothing like human relationships to ruin things for a good soul, especially when you could be doing some mead time."

"I see." It was clear he didn't.

"Take my word for it, that's one thing the undead are better off without."

Youssif grunted, perhaps in amusement. "In the Imperium, the closest experience we have to procreation is being glued up in some birth vat. A machine stuffs our prestitched guts in, then hammers our pelt together while a tiny drop of viscous blood from the Emperor gives us being." His voice lowered. "And yet, some drones have allegedly found ways to gain intimacy, if their souls should connect. Trust me, that is not common."

Aaron tried to keep a straight face. "Sounds like some of you hanker for some kind of life, on the quiet."

Youssif shook his head. "Believe me, almost every soldier or drone you encounter off-world is as dead as a rock. Their only meaning is slaughter, illicit herbs, slumber, or ale." He looked up. "Having said that, such things were on the rise in the Pit."

Aaron whistled. "I blame your old Consul."

Before Youssif could reply, the heavens split and the ground shook in front of them. The gate shone like a green sun, blinding the watchers with malachite light. The brightness gyrated, then flared into the shape of a figure before winking out as abruptly as it begun.

The fighters shot up and joined the melee gathering round the temporarily rippling waters. The shape exited the vicinity of the portal and sploshed towards them. As it drew near, there was a soft murmuring and a sound of resheathed swords. The figure looked around, spied Youssif, and made a beeline in their direction. Youssif put a firm hand on Aaron's sword wrist, gesturing him to put his weapon away.

"Do not concern yourself over this one. He's with us!"

Aaron squinted at the nearing figure, clearly another Lifeless, then slowly rehoused his weapon. "Looks it, too." He grimaced.

The figure stepped out of the lake and faced them. Vapours misted off his arms and shoulders from the rapid series of jumps he'd been forced to take. He looked dazed, phased out by the massive, quantum synergies of the network. The Lifeless regarded each other for long moments. Eventually, Youssif spoke first.

"Morack! You're early."

"I am?"

He eyed him darkly. "Do we have clearance all the way back to Stilgen?"

"No." The newcomer was almost panting with exertion. "But we have a destination." He handed Youssif the coordinates of the hub and turned to look at Breasal, who had just joined them. "And *he* can take us there. On the way to the Praetor's portal—it's a long story—Stilgen mentioned Breasal a number of times. He has the charms of a devil, but the skill of a murmel hunting for fossilised meadow muffins. Stilgen believes he is the finest operator and schemer on this world, providing you never turn your back on him!"

"Reassuring," Aaron chirped.

Youssif's face was carved disappointment. He gestured towards an inexplicably sweaty Breasal. "This schemer is still needed?"

"Hard to believe, but it's true." Morack looked away as if embarrassed. "You should know, the chain of gates I came through was severed at the final hurdle. Probably a local administrator cutting the—admittedly—highly unorthodox link Stilgen sent me through. I thought I was lost but detected Breasal's signal searching for us. I wouldn't have made it without him."

"That's what I do. I do things like that," Breasal said, his tone both satisfied and hugely surprised. "What exactly did I do?"

Youssif straightened. His people and the X Gemina had crowded around. Aaron breathed in slowly, eyes darting from face-to-face with suspicion. "What now?"

The Lifeless commander turned to face him. "We have coordinates and apparently a portal genius at our disposal." He smiled like a viper about to strike. "We go in. Before, it's too late. Before that administrator triangulates attention towards the unexpected reactivation of this disused and forgotten gate. Then I and Breasal will do as the others did: take one jump at a time until we find this nodal point marked on Stilgen's diagrams. Stilgen seems to have accessed high-level information that will make our journey infinitely more palatable than his must have been." He looked at Morack. "I guess that belonged to the Praetor mentioned on this information you handed me?"

Morack nodded gravely. "Indeed, but the codes I used will be useless anytime now."

"Unimportant. Stilgen has included invaluable numerical charts stolen from this clearly high-ranking official that will still allow us to bypass a lot of" he looked at Aaron "how do you humes say it ... shit?"

Aaron's eyes creased with amusement. "That'll do!"

"Good." The commander looked at the assembled group, both living and Lifeless watching with bated breath, or whatever would suffice for those without lungs. "Prepare yourself. Gather the supplies and mounts. We're going in. Time is already too late!"

With that, he turned and headed across the waters to the awaiting portal. Breasal flashed a toothy grin and joined him. Aaron and the X Gemina were left standing there, jaws open. But not for long. As the gate blinked into life again, they hurried towards the otherworldly light and their collective date with eternity.

Burning light farmed outwards in concentric circles across the lens of the gate. Something undefined glistened within, then fell as snow, seemingly formed of crystalline alloy. It sparkled as it fell, an incongruous sight of serenity within the current of infinity beyond.

Barrackus was visibly awed. Despite himself, Andromedus was almost grateful. Even someone with the powers of a god could feel humble. That was strangely reassuring. Each door was different, but the beauty of this one was staggering.

"Almost there, Commander." Andromedus was paying unusual attention to Barrackus as he hunched over the controls, eyes studying the commander with dark concern. He was more wary of his superior than the route ahead. "Perhaps you're right, boss, to do this thing you're doing, destroying the High Command. Sand jar's emptying for the Ascendancy, I guess." The Dust Tracker kept looking at him. "Incidentally …"

"Yes?"

"How'd you do that?"

"Do what?"

"Heal yourself. Your ribs were spliced end to end—never seen anyone recover from that."

Barrackus smiled. "I see the gate's ready."

Andromedus carried on working, but his frame visibly sagged. "So, no chance of a return when all is said and done?"

He put a hand on the man's burly shoulder. "I can't fight all their armies, Andromedus. They'll have closed off our entire route home after this. Probably more behind than ahead anyway. Core's our best chance, our only chance!"

The Tracker inhaled deeply. He was flat, resigned. "It's done. The gate might've been on, but there was an elemental lock all the same. Not as intricate or as ancient as the first back on that rain world at the start of all this, but a nightmare all the same. On the positive, I've picked up *significant* surprise at our impact—they really, really did not expect a unit to penetrate Armerhurst itself, let alone break through beyond. The centre won't know we're even here yet, but I'd love to be a bug on the wall when they find out."

There was warmth on Barrackus' face. "You've no idea how proud I am at what you've achieved. No one has, or ever will, match your skill with the portals. Of that, I'm as sure as I've been about anything, ever."

The Tracker was taken aback; his eyes almost misted. "As it can take decades to manufacture a good necromantic lock, we'll be long since done by the time they put another one on, assuming they even bother. They have rudimentary minds, you know, these locks. I managed to link to all their tiny, ethereal brains at once. Some kind of theurgy neural net exists here—guess it makes things easier in an emergency."

The Tracker heaved himself up and dusted the snow from his clothes. He caught a glimpse of himself in the icy reflection of one of his navigational tools. Grey furrows ran down his face. His skin was courser. Age marks drifted along his cheeks like puckered clouds. The strain was taking a toll on all of them.

"By breaking into the limited mind of one lock, I found I could link in with them all, effectively ruining the lot, Commander," he added wearily. "I won't bore you with the details, but every door is open ahead now: months, weeks, maybe only moments, I dunno. I'm still talking in terms of covert travel. When that changes ... well, depends on portal security. They're so complacent this far in, I'd suspect it'd take them a while to figure out they're even open, let alone being used. If I had to be honest, and I may as well be as no one's going to hear about it anyway, the devices were as tight as a mudflapper's gut, but their mechanics were obsolete. Portals were never designed to be locked anyway, so they'll get no sympathy from me." He cleared his throat. "You should know this utter complacency's left them far more depleted in sentry numbers than I'd have believed possible ... for now."

"So, we're actually going through?"

"Now we get to die on another world instead of this one."

"It's not the dying that matters, Andromedus. It's what we might do with the time left to us before we die."

"Please don't tell me that's the plan?"

"I'm speaking of logic, not intent; I don't do suicide!"

"Relieved to hear it." Andromedus sighed, sounding anything but. "Actually, no, I'm not."

Barrackus didn't reply. If he'd known the man better, maybe the words would've sprung to mind, but there was a lot about his people he hadn't taken the time to find out or at least that was what Andromedus believed anyway. The commander's obsessions made him an unqualified success, yet he didn't know with any kind of genuine depth the owners of the bodies they'd permanently leave behind. A wave of intense regret flooded the Tracker.

"Is there a path for us?"

"Several, Commander—typically all lead through the ravenous jaws of spite."

"Show me!"

Andromedus whisked out a reed drawing he'd scribbled on. "Can you follow these?"

Barrackus scanned the etchings. He knew instinctively what to do.

"We'll try Terrakain!"

Andromedus's jowls almost hit the ground. His haunted eyes scrutinised the commander as though he'd lost what remained of his wits.

"Boss, that is the *one* path that is completely out of bounds. To even cast your eyes down that route brings worse than death! It's swarming with enemy, probably more savage than even the Wolverine, not to mention God knows what type of domesticated demon."

"Which is why we have to go. They'll expect those far less arduous paths, not the 'no-hope' way. I'll wager reinforcements will *still* swarm those routes, even from Terrakain itself. No regional general or Praetor will expect that. We'll throw them entirely off kilter."

"And I thought we didn't do suicide."

Barrackus pulled him gently up and faced him, his expression hard in the dim light. "I said the Elders hated what I told them, but what I really should have said is that they *feared* what I told them, the things I was speaking of, what I think an adept can do. In that moment, they feared me more than the enemy, but they gave me the authentication to do exactly how I felt, because whatever happens, I will give the Goat hell."

He took a breath. "Andromedus, we've been here before, and doubtless some part of us will be here again." He patted the Tracker's shoulder. "Don't worry—we've a few tricks yet to play."

Andromedus felt like he was doing nothing but worrying.

The commander strode towards the troops, cajoling them into formation. The iris was now a tempest. As the troops poured through, Barrackus turned. It was then Andromedus saw in his eyes what the Elders had so feared. The gleam was there, but it was piercing, and it glittered like ten thousand steel suns. Within his mind's eye, Andromedus swore he saw the mindless beast of eternity gestating within that empyreal gaze. Within, he swore he saw the Ji'aan, the purest stage of being for any Magi, though one that sold a soul in exchange for power. A walking Ji'ann was the living personification of every single element in every single object for a hundred thousand leagues, maybe more. The super Magi would take on the powers of a sun by sucking up the atomic swarm that held every single grain of sand together. Andromedus swore it was somehow burning inside their chief, and no one could handle that for long.

His commander was going insane.

"Come on Andromedus. Time to face eternity, again!"

The thaumaturgic beast beneath the face smiled. The Tracker felt the suns implode as temporal fate twisted to serve that countenance.

"You know what," Andromedus whispered under his breath, "I think I prefer the Goblins."

ABOUT THE AUTHOR

After graduating from university in history, social science, and politics, Nick Stevenson began work as a magazine editor. After putting in his time at a desk, adventure called, and Nick became an extensive traveller. After years spent in south-east Asia, China, Australia, New Zealand, and Australia, Nick returned to the UK and took up a career as an editor and writer of various e-zines. Fifteen years ago, Nick left the online world to run an English Language School and focus on crafting the *Nethergeist* books.

www.ingramcontent.com/pod-product-compliance
Lightning Source LLC
Chambersburg PA
CBHW020429030726
47495CB00006B/1727